"PLEASE," I CRIED,

"NO MAN EVER TOUCHED ME THERE . . ."

I wept. I protested. I begged. But it was all to no avail. I, Willa Starch, was helpless, completely at the mercy of the red-eyed, lecherous McTare.

I felt myself being rolled over, the blanket drawn up above my hips. I began to yield, to resign myself to the inevitable.

McTare patted my bottom. "That be the fairest behind I ever laid eyes on."

"Ease it in," I heard McTare say. "gently . . . gently . . . ah, that's right. All right lass, hold on tight."

I moaned, and then felt myself swept away in a powerful, overwhelming flood . . .

THAT GIRL
FROM BOSTON

ROBERT H. RIMMER

A SIGNET BOOK from
NEW AMERICAN LIBRARY
TIMES MIRROR

SIGNET TRADEMARK REG. U.S. PAT. OFF. AND FOREIGN COUNTRIES
REGISTERED TRADEMARK—MARCA REGISTRADA
HECHO EN CHICAGO, U.S.A.

SIGNET, SIGNET CLASSICS, SIGNETTE, MENTOR AND PLUME BOOKS
are published by The New American Library, Inc.,
1301 Avenue of the Americas, New York, New York 10019

FIRST PRINTING, OCTOBER, 1969

10 11 12 13 14 15 16 17 18

PRINTED IN THE UNITED STATES OF AMERICA

For those who occasionally let their hair down and just laugh because life is not that serious, but love is.

1

"I was born twenty-two years ago on Trotter Island in Boston Harbor of good parents. . . ."

Does that sound familiar? It should. That's the way Robinson Crusoe starts the story of his missing years.

My first twenty-two years aren't exactly missing and Trotter Island isn't a tropical island with swaying palm trees, either. But I do have something in common with Robinson Crusoe. I'm looking for a man Friday.

The Princess, my mother, thinks that there must be some basic flaw in my personality. Why haven't I discovered *the man* already? She may be right. But if I ever do find the right Friday he'll have more fun with me than Crusoe's had with him.

I can see him now. Tall, dark . . . sort of piratical (clean shaven and washed, of course), spending most of each day kissing me . . . from the top of my fluffy brown hair . . . slowly, oh so slowly . . . enjoying the trip . . . grazing and nibbling here and there . . . all the way down to my number ten feet.

Yes, number ten. Not that I'm too tall. Or too big, either. I probably inherited my feet from my father, who is a professional wrestler, but the rest of me came from my mother, and men from the front row all the way up to the balcony have ogled her in the best burlesque houses in the country. No, it's not my feet, nor the rest of me. I guess what I've got is as good as most girls have got; it's the damnable fact that despite the Sexual Revolution, my only revolt thus far is talking a good game. Attached to the lure is a Puritan brain that says "no" when the rest of me is yelling "yes" . . . and *that* so far as men is concerned is downright calamitous.

So I've tried to improve. Taking this job as a secretary to

Sawyer Priestly may be a way off this toboggan that is swooping me toward middle age and what the Princess would disparagingly refer to as an untouched hymen. Of course when I started work here three weeks ago I did have somewhat higher hopes.

Here it is eleven-thirty in the morning, and the only difference between this day and yesterday is that it's hotter and stickier. A warm June rain is splattering on the opened windowsill and trickling down the broken wainscotted walls. The varnished woodwork beneath the window is stained grey and streaked from rains long forgotten. So far I have dreamed away at least three mornings trying to reconstruct life in this building since the Revolutionary War. Maybe that's an exaggeration. This murky pile of granite may not be that old, but, so far—despite eager New Bostonians, busy erecting towers of cement and glass, feeling badly because *their* city doesn't look like every other city in the country—Sawyer Priestly's headquarters clings grimly to a more stolid, dull and stodgy world.

Sawyer Priestly hasn't arrived. I have to open the office at nine o'clock. Something to do with "being sure the telephone is covered." I still haven't figured what Sawyer does for a living. His most important daily task revolves around opening his office door, staring at me for a moment, clearing his throat, and asking some such world-shaking question as:

"Will you be taking your lunch at noon today, Miss Starch?"

When I, instead of being sarcastic, very politely answer "yes," Sawyer mumbles the usual something about the office being "covered." He goes through variations of this ritual three or four times a day.

I'm not so naïve as to think that it is the telephone or the office that is worrying him. It's getting so that when I hear the chair in his office squeak I squeeze my legs together a little tighter and give my skirt a careful tug. It's not modesty. Though when I wear it (and carefully hoist my stocking panties as a last line of defense), I still can't help but feel my mini-dress is advertising what I'm not too certain I may be ready to deliver. With that tense look in Sawyer's eyes, I have the nervous feeling that one of these days he is going to dare all. (What Sawyer's all may be so far as I am concerned, is interesting and a little scary to contemplate.)

I really should have known better. Less than four weeks ago I took a job-for-the-night as a waitress at a bachelor's dinner at the Harvard Club. Tony Mills, a girl I knew at Radcliffe, convinced me that among the hundred or so guests there

10

might be some prospective slave Friday who would notice me. You can see that I'm somewhat gullible. One look at the thinning hair, bald heads, and extended tummies of this group, and I knew that I was on the wrong program.

But suddenly, as I was walking through the swinging door that led into the kitchen, I could actually *feel* strange eyes nudging my behind. When I came back with a loaded tray I was blushingly certain that the man with glazed eyes and lean Harvard jaw who was staring at me had discovered that under my black skirt and demure white apron I wasn't wearing panties.

Placing his shrimp cocktail in front of him, I made the mistake of looking sideways at the firm line of his Back Bay profile and got the eery sensation that if I stayed a second longer he would have inhaled me. By the time I deposited his soup he had me so jittery that I shifted locations with one of the other waitresses, who agreed to serve this character out of Marquand for the rest of the dinner.

But it was no use. He must have mesmerized me. After the dinner, when the other men had gone downstairs, he was alone in the Athenaeum Room waiting for me. Very formally, he handed me his engraved business card which read: *Sawyer Priestly, Investments.* In the corner was his State Street office address.

"Can you manage a typewriter?" he asked, his accent very much Harvard, his eyes engulfing me.

Lacking the poise of that superior kohl-eyed type you see in Vogue magazine, I nodded a weak yes.

"Come to my office, tomorrow," he said. "You don't have to wait on tables. I have a much better job for you, Miss. . ? ." He looked at me expectantly, and I, a frightened goose, said: "Starch. Willa Starch."

If it is possible to stay on the verge of anything for more than a minute or two, then I guess that Sawyer has been on the verge of propositioning me ever since he told me to come to work. I wonder when, if,—and how—he'll take the plunge. Will he invite me to one of those dusty men's clubs on Commonwealth Avenue? Or maybe he is the romantic type and knows some quaint cellar restaurant on Newbury Street. Anyway, I'll probably go. Sawyer owes me a lunch. If only to repay me for practically solitary confinement in this little four-walled prison he calls an office in a building that gives sanctuary only to men way past forty.

The truth is that Sawyer's telephone seldom rings. When it does, I have to remind myself not to jump straight out of my seat. It rings as if announcing a five-alarm fire.

Every morning at ten the five-alarm fire is Sawyer's wife, Abigail.

I won't say that I wouldn't be here had I known about Abigail. After all the pay *is* good. But I was a little chagrined that first day when she announced herself with a real cheery veneer voice acquired at Wellesley to impress Garden Clubs. Sawyer could have warned me!

"Miss Starch . . . you do sound so wide awake this morning. Sawyer told me about you. I'm Abigail Priestly, Sawyer's wife. I'm really going to break away from all these activities and get in Boston one of these days and meet you. Sawyer says you are such a bright young thing."

After the preliminaries Abigail usually gets around to asking for Sawyer. Mostly he hasn't arrived or has just gone out. Purposely, I'd guess. Why does it give me so much pleasure to say: "I'm sorry, Mrs. Priestly, Sawyer isn't here," with my most crisp and efficient sounding Radcliffe voice?

"Bright young thing." That gets me. Sawyer has probably told her that I'm cross-eyed and wear my hair in a pug. Abigail does sound more subdued when I finish with her. Four years at Radcliffe taught me one thing: how to take the bounce out of dimply Wellesley creeps.

There is another call that Sawyer gets regularly. What is attached to the languid female voice that says huskily "you tell him that I called, darling . . . I'm expecting Sawyer, today, to go over my portfolio . . ." would make interesting speculation.

I've been tempted to ask Sawyer when he comes in with a harried look whether he has been examining Miss Smoky's portfolio. Smoky is not her name, but she has the voice to remind me of Grandma's favorite expression about smoke and that fire slush.

However, I purposely don't ask Sawyer leading questions. While he looks perfectly trustworthy—somewhat like a reincarnation of the late George Apley (especially when he is wearing his black rubbers and carrying a tremendous black bumbershoot)—nevertheless, there is something in Sawyer's eye and in his lean Phi-Beta-Kappa manner that indicates a certain restlessness. It's that on-the-verge manner of his that makes me certain that, if I were his wife, I'd stop puttering around my garden in Marblehead and occasionally pop in on the old boy.

The truth is that I don't know—at least I'm not positive yet—why Sawyer hired me. If he knew about my mother's occupation that could be a reason. Sawyer may never have been in the first row when Princess Tassle was on the Old

Harvard Circuit, but, unless he led a very protected adolescence, he must have heard about the famous ecdysiast who could spin five tassles at once as she rotated various parts of her anatomy. It's unlikely that he would have known that this "sex-pot," as the Princess was advertised, also had a daughter.

In her business my mother had to be singularly careful about revealing details of her family life. The vision of a mewling brat hanging onto a stripper's G string could dissipate any sex appeal she might have had for her bald-headed and pimply-faced audiences.

I'm sure that Sawyer isn't aware that his secretary is living on Trotter Island. How could he be? He was so eager to take me on that he never even asked me to fill out one of those cradle-to-now employment forms. I just sat down and went to work—doing nothing.

No, whatever Sawyer's reasons may be for employing me, I am certainly not going to do him the favor of asking him. My slightest curiosity could push Sawyer over the verge and start him chasing me around this battered oak desk.

Maybe that's not being fair to Sawyer. He is fortyish and growing on fifty. As he pointed out to me the very first day that I came to work, I could be his daughter. But Sawyer has never fertilized Abigail. They haven't any daughter . . . or any son either. It's too bad, really. If they had a son, I'm sure that I would have enjoyed Sawyer as a father-in-law. I mean in a figurative way. About Abigail I don't know. Over the telephone she sounds like the type who would have kept her umbilical cord firmly attached to the male progeny she fortunately hadn't had.

There you are, that's the kind of mind I have. I don't even know why Sawyer hired me or how he makes a living (maybe he married Abigail for her money), but give me a second more and I'll have myself pregnant by a son Sawyer hasn't got!

I suppose I shouldn't look a gift horse in the mouth. Sawyer does have all his teeth, and come pay day he will hand me an envelope containing ten new ten dollar bills. I wonder if he is taking out my social security and income tax? Maybe he thinks I'm going to become tax deductible . . . an entertainment fund of some kind.

While the salary is good, flopping around this musty little reception office all day, staring at its brown wainscotting and dreary yellow walls, not only gets a little boring, but worse, it's keeping me out of circulation. When Sawyer isn't here I read, knit, or lean out the window and wave at a couple of

13

boys who work across the street. Sawyer's office looks down on State Street. If I balance on my stomach and lean far enough out, I can see the wharves on Atlantic Avenue or, by looking the other way, see the Old State House sitting tranquilly in the middle of Boston traffic—while coolly ignoring the naked glass and stone of the forty-story Merchant's Bank Building trying to seduce her into the present.

I was hanging out one morning last week when Sawyer walked in unexpectedly. How long he stood there watching I don't know, but he looked a little flushed when I—finally sensing that he was there—screamed, and probably would have fallen out if he hadn't grabbed me. He didn't say anything, but I realized afterwards that the window is quite high. My legs were spread parallel to his vision. Sawyer obviously had enjoyed a contemplative view of me usually reserved for husbands and doctors. It made me decide that no matter what the Princess says . . . in the future I would wear panties.

2

Today when I went to lunch I made up my mind. Being a wee bit on the introspective side, I told myself: "Willa, it's time you sized up the situation and decided what you are going to do with life."

To my mother, this would mean: "Willa, when are you going to get a boyfriend and get married?"

This is a subject I'm not averse to pondering. I ponder it several times a day. Sometimes I even consider marriage with Bucky Bonnelli, and it seems like a logical though prosaic business. Not that Bucky is dull. Occasionally he has flights of fancy that are quite startling.

But Bucky is at a disadvantage. I've known him since I was six. Gosh, I can even remember playing doctor with Bucky and discovering the useful appurtenance boys have attached to their middles. How can you get romantic about someone you've *known* that long?

And then there's Converse Cabot. This spring Converse graduated from Harvard Law School. Since I met him nearly a year ago we have had six dates. Converse is a gentleman. On five of the dates he took me to Symphony Hall. We discussed music avidly all evening. On the way back to Cambridge we agreed that we really had something in common. We loved music.

Usually when Converse said good night, he would squeeze my hand, look at me with a man-to-man look, and say "Willa, it was great. We'll do it again sometime." He'd then climb back into his red Jaguar and, like a "Chevalier sans raproche," roar toward Harvard.

The sixth date, three weeks ago, we went to the opening Pop Concert. Afterwards, when I told him that instead of leaving me at Radcliffe he could drop me off in South Boston at Grandma Starch's, Converse for the first time became a little curious about my geneaology. I gaily told him about my mother's occupation and finished with a rabbit punch by explaining to him that Henry, my father, was better known as Mad Man Starch, famous for his hammerlock. Converse didn't squeeze my hand. He looked at the shabby three story house—with its flat roof that belongs to Grandpa Starch and has taken him a lifetime to earn—and said: "It was fun Willa. Have a nice summer."

I didn't cry. I just lay in bed. "Okay, chum . . . go get yourself a nice fluffy Wellesley girl whose mother is head of the local chapter of the D.A.R. See if I care." . . . Then I cried.

I often wanted to ask Converse what his father's name is. Maybe it's Increase . . . that's a good old New England name . . . or Cotton. No, Increase is better! Maybe his mother's name is Purity, or Goody. Or maybe Pleasantly. That's a good combination, Increase Pleasantly, with Converse as the male offspring to refute the whole notion. To hell with Converse.

Too bad I forgot to tell him how I happened to be named Willa. My father liked a comic strip called Buck Rogers— and particularly his half-clothed girl friend, Wilma. The Princess compromised. Her father's name was William. It's a good thing I was born before Barbarella was popular. In his old age, my father seems even more entranced with erotic females.

Imagining marriage to Converse is like eating warmed up beans on Sunday morning. Despite Grandpa Starch, who approves of this savage bean indulgence, I don't think Converse's flavor would improve with age.

The only other man I have to consider at the moment is Sawyer. So it is apparent that my future does need analyzing.

I've often tried to keep a diary or journal, but, feeling that I as yet have had nothing of any great shakes to say to posterity, these abortive attempts have never gotten much further than: "I was born fifteen . . . sixteen . . . seventeen years ago on Trotter Island"—depending on how old I was when the inspiration seized me.

I suppose I have a tendency to be a little flighty, but when you are born in New England, no matter where you emerge from the womb—Beacon Street, South Boston, Roxbury, or Trotter Island—you unconsciously develop a Benjamin Franklin-H. M. Pulham mentality. The kind of conscience that says, for instance: "Willa . . . this morning instead of wearing high heels with pointed toes, you should have worn your low heels and rubbers; particularly since an utter stranger (he didn't look back) had to help you across the mud puddle at the corner of Atlantic Avenue and State Street.

Or maybe that kind of needly Cotton-Mather feeling gets brainwashed into you when you're in the third or fourth grade and you write your first autobiography. I remember mine—with colored paper covers, tied with a shoelace, and filled with snapshots and details of my summer vacation painstakingly scrawled over ten lined pages.

Probably the reason that all my autobiographies have gone awry stems from the first one. Unknown to Grandma, I pasted on the inside of the back cover a glossy picture the Princess had left around the house of herself wearing her famous tassles, and nothing much else.

"Well she *is* my mother," I protested to the school principal when Miss Pill Box ushered me into his office. "Even if she is only wearing a string around where she pee-pees."

Well, heck, I was only in the third grade. Grandma Starch made me go to bed after supper for a week when the episode reached her, and she said innumerable "Hail Marys" for me. I'm still a little puzzled at all the fuss. Maybe the Princess has a point. "If ladies weren't so careful to hide their little treasure," she says, "men wouldn't make so much fuss over it."

I could point out to my mother that her career as Princess Tassle would never have got twirling if her intrigued audience could have seen this piece of female scenery at will. The

16

Princess would tell me that it's not the scenery that counts, it's what you do with it that makes the difference.

3

I remember two summers ago, when my nomadic father and mother were once again installed for the summer on Trotter Island and I had bid farewell to Grandma and Grandpa until fall. The Princess watched me arriving from South Boston on Bucky Bonnelli's weather-beaten lobster boat. While Bucky was tying up to the pier, the Princess said, "Well, sugar, I see you are still not getting anywhere. After two years at Radcliffe, I should think you could have found something besides muscle-brains."

"Muscle-brains" isn't fair to Bucky. He is very handsome. But I knew what the Princess meant. There are two kinds of men in her world: wrestlers, like my father, Henry (Mad Man) Starch, who even a few years ago could still toss a two-hundred-pound opponent into the laps of his audience; and some ethereal other kind of man, the genteel hero type, who would kiss the Princess's hand (she would have considered Converse) instead of crunching it the way Henry does. The reason I had been sent to college was to grab off one of this other kind.

"A man who thinks going to bed with a woman is something more than two falls out of three . . . with the winner snoring his brains out ten minutes later," the Princess told me. "You know sugar, I keep away from your father when I'm on the road. If I didn't, there wouldn't be enough left of me to shake a feather, let alone a tassle. Honey, this Bonnelli boy has your future all spelled out. A few years after you are married you'll be cooking spaghetti and ravioli for him. You —fat and placid, and him, expecting you to adore his rancid smelling hair oil. And his breath: a garbage-can mixture of garlic and stogies. It ain't that I'm perjudiced, honey . . . but I sure hate Eyetalians."

Of course, Bucky isn't at all like the Princess's description.

He doesn't wear any hair oil, and when he plays Italian folk songs on his guitar his hair falls in a curl over his forehead, and his jaw is lean and hard—and almost blue-black—though he has just shaved. . . . Well, believe me, Bucky can set any female heart fluttering.

"I don't know," I told my mother, "with the exception of Bucky, who has known me forever, I guess I just repel boys. They don't like female eggheads." If I am an egghead! It gets confusing sometimes. I'll have a date with a boy, and he asks me what I *really* would like to do. If I say I'd like to go to Symphony Hall, or a new foreign movie . . . or, God forbid, walk around one of the museums . . . then I'm immediately talked out of it. "You're among friends," one boy said to me last winter, "you can save that jazz for when you're old and a mother." So we went to the Top of the Pru, and he spent forty dollars trying to seduce me with lobsters and manhattans. How could I have told him that a sandwich at Hayes Bickford and the balcony at Symphony Hall would have earned a more feverish good night kiss?

That same night, when I was undressing for bed, the Princess came into my room for her annual inspection. She had been on tour, and I hadn't seen her for a year except that Christmas week at Grandma Starch's when all the family gathers to admire the hatchets they've been sticking into each other all year.

The Princess lifted my breasts, weighing them appreciatively as if she were buying cantaloupes. I wanted to tell her that she didn't have to shake them—there were no seeds inside. But with the Princess you learn to develop patience. Cantaloupes and breasts were meant to be shaken.

"You've got good tits, honey. They feel better than mine did at your age. I know. I've seen em all. But the first thing you've got to do is learn to display what you've got. I'm going to take you to a shop where they make my bras. You've been tying them in too tight. The Good Lord didn't give them to you to hide. They've got to have a little freedom to live a life of their own." She patted me on the rump. "Don't you worry, Honey, you've got the merchandise. Just because your father and I could agree on only one thing in our marriage—that you should have an education—doesn't need to stop you. Only immediate trouble with you is that you need a repackaging job."

That summer the Princess taught me how to walk. It was an interesting experience. I discovered that, given a little encouragement, parts of my anatomy went into business for themselves. When I went back for my junior year at Radcliffe

I had developed two personalities . . . one, the little old maid who had lived upstairs and had carefully guided me for twenty years (she looked like Grandma Starch)—the other, who lived downstairs and warned me. "Willa, the bloom is on the rose. Live it up a little."

The Princess was blunter: "Travel through life with your pussy proudly thrust out and your ass teasing those behind you," my mother told me, "and you can sneer at the cabbages and have all the kings begging for it."

I didn't ask the Princess whether she had developed this homespun philosophy before or after she had met my father, but that fall, when the Princess and Henry had gone on the road again, I discovered that female cabbages, at least, don't appreciate the Princess's theories.

"You've been weaving around the kitchen like Salome carrying the head of John the Baptist," Grandma said indignantly. "Even though your grandfather is seventy-six and shouldn't be thinking about such things, I don't like the glitter in his eye. No respectable woman walks that way. While you live in this house you can stop trying to copy your ma!"

When I made the mistake of quoting to Grandma Starch the Princess's "travel through life" advice, Grandma crossed herself: "Holy Mother, forgive this child. She knows not what she says." And then, angrily, "I'm going to write your father young lady. No young woman should be allowed near a brazen hussy who undresses in front of men. The Lord should take pity on you with such a mother. It was a good day when the Cardinal closed those dens of iniquity in Scollay Square." Grandma's Irish accent was becoming stronger. "No daicent man would want to look at a Jezebel like your maw without her clothes on!"

Grampy Starch roused himself out of the sporting page and winked at me. His pale blue eyes were watery with some past memory. I guessed his little chuckle was a prelude to a reminiscence about my mother's career, but he withered under Grandma's glance and held his tongue.

Later, he knocked hesitantly on my door. Sheepishly looking around at the scattered mess of clothing and books, he asked how school was going.

"Grandma says you're not to visit in my room," I teased him, knowing that he wanted to talk.

"She's gone down to Mahoney's Market." He grinned furtively at me, and sighed. "You and I understand each other. Your grandmother doesn't appreciate sex. It ain't like it used to be, Willa. Those dives down in the Combat Zone have no

19

class. Ugly-looking girls shaking their behinds and titties. Like African bushwackers in heat . . . the music just noise. You can't even think. Scollay Square, the Crawford House, may not have been so much, but Anne Corio, Sally Keith, and your ma . . . they were real sexy women." He patted my head and chuckled, his face a hundred timeworn grins. "Don't tell your grandma I told you, but you have the same style. I remember your ma back in forty-four . . . before you were born. Sweet as a picture, comin' out on the stage of the Old Howard while the orchestra was playing 'A Pretty Girl is Like a Melody'. . . . There she was, wearing a big picture hat, dressed as modest as you please, carrying a pink parasol. She looked just like a girl on her way to Sunday School."

Grampy explained that was before Henry and the Princess were married. She got a bang out of getting free tickets for them "so that the old geezer (Grampy) and his firehouse buddies could have a little fun." Once she tried to get free tickets for all of the Odd Fellows. Grampy was chief factotum at the time. Anything to spite Henry's old lady. When Grampy was in the audience the Princess really outdid herself. It was at one of those performances that the Watch and Ward Society closed down the place until a certain stripper mended her ways.

"A danged shame," Grampy confided to me. "All your ma did was give a few extra bumps without her G-string."

Burlesque in Boston was a memory of Grampy's by the time I was fully aware of my mother's profession. During the season, the Princess lived in cities where shabby theaters mixed movies with burlesque but still couldn't survive television.

When the Princess did come to Boston she always stayed at the Statler. "No use trying to bunk in the same house with that old bitch," she'd say, referring to Grandma. "I don't know how you stand her. You don't have to live there, Sugar. Henry just bought a yellow El Dorado Cadillac. He can afford it, if you want to live at school."

But I hadn't wanted to. I knew that Grandma and Grampy, having brought me up most of my life, would be lonesome without me. "Besides," I told her, "Henry said that you and he are saving up and plan to retire on Trotter Island in a couple of years. There's no need to have the additional expense of rooms at Radcliffe."

I didn't tell her the truth . . . that when I started Radcliffe I was so shy it seemed the path of least resistance just to keep right on living in South Boston. It actually got so that I enjoyed the subway ride to Harvard Square. I could finally equal Thomas Wolfe's record and hold my breath from all the way across the Charles River to the Central stop in Cambridge. It just goes to show the rationalizations a shy person can make.

4

By noon, Sawyer still hadn't put in an appearance. After a typically busy morning which I might just as well have spent contemplating my navel, I hiked up to Filene's to see if I could find any bargains.

When I go up town I walk through Washington Street, trying not to look in Lauriat's book store as I pass. Too many times the siren call of all those books and all the things I don't know in this world has bewitched me. Not today, Willa, I cautioned myself. Knowing more things in books absolutely will not get you a man. Keep your mind on something like a bright orange dress which goes well with your coloring. A gay print, maybe, with a daring neckline.

I heeded my own advice . . . though to what dance, or on what special evening I was going to wear this dress was still an unknown quantity. Filene's basement was crowded. I tried one of the fancy shops upstairs. I know it's silly, but the snotty saleswomen seem to be waiting for me when I get off the elevator and, with their cool where-do-you-think-you're-going stares, somehow know that I am Willa Starch from South Boston. In a couple of minutes I am completely bewildered, mumbling and blushing like a jackass, telling the woman with the phony Back Bay accent (who is probably from South Boston, too) that the three-hundred-dollar dress she is showing me is a little out of my range . . . as is the two-hundred-and-twenty-five dollar one . . . and the hundred-and-ten-dollar one. What I want is something for maybe twenty-nine-ninety-five.

With a sneer for my ignorance, I get this advice: "Oh, you

21

are on the wrong floor, Miss. Why don't you try the basement? I understand they are having some lovely sales down there."

Yes, I told myself on my defeated way back to Sawyer's office, there are some things, Willa Starch, that you *do not* learn in books . . . or from a Bachelor's Degree from Radcliffe. I wondered if I would ever learn. Maybe I wouldn't have to. Maybe somewhere in the world there was a boy who wasn't looking for a bitchy female, or one with green eyelids, but would prefer a soap-washed face snuggling in his neck and nibbling his ears. Believe me, I have even better daydreams than that when I let myself go.

The office door was unlocked, which meant that Sawyer finally had arrived. When I sat at my desk I really blushed and cursed myself for my carelessness. The paper on which I had started my typically abortive attempt at a diary was still rolled in the typewriter. "I was born twenty-two years ago on Trotter Island in Boston Harbor of good parents." Beneath this were words I *had* not typed: ". . . and now I work for Sawyer Priestly who thinks I'm adorable."

Oh-oh, I thought, now you've done it, Willa Starch. I wondered whether I could sneak out without Sawyer hearing me. If I stayed in the office I had a premonition that today I was going to discover the missing link in Sawyer Priestly's character . . . something new and not quite so tidy. If I didn't show up this afternoon, Sawyer might revert to type by tomorrow.

I had my hand on the worn brass door knob of the outer office door. Why couldn't I just go without looking back? I couldn't. When I looked back, there was Sawyer leaning against the jamb of his office staring at me with a quizzical expression.

"Are you back from lunch, Miss Starch?" he asked.

That's a help, I thought. At least I'm still Miss Starch. I told him that I was just closing the door. There was a draft.

"It's a warm enough day to appreciate a draft," he said still staring.

Impasse.

Okay. "Maybe, you're right," I said opening the door. If I had to scream, someone in the building might hear me.

"Miss Starch, I have to dictate a letter. My dictating machine isn't working. I've called for a service man. Can you take shorthand?"

I shook my head. "I told you I didn't have a business education, Mr. Priestly." I'd have bet a week's pay that there was nothing wrong with his dictating machine.

"Well, get a pencil and some paper and come in my office. I'll dictate slowly, and you can write it in longhand and then type it. It must go today."

By the time I had fumbled in my desk, found a piece of paper, sharpened a pencil, repaired my lipstick, checked my stockings to see if they were straight, and fluffed out my hair —it really only took a few minutes—Sawyer was sitting behind his desk with a smile that I knew was a little grim.

I sat in the leather armchair next to his desk and took a quick look around the office. It was the second time that I had been in the inner sanctum in three weeks. Glass-doored bookcases hiding dusty law books and real estate abstracts covered most of one wall. Yellowed photographs of Boston streets in the time of the Civil War, drawings of historic buildings, and maps of Boston the way it used to be in the days of John Adams and the later Clipper Ship era crowded every available space on the remaining walls. The floor was covered with a shabby Oriental rug that Abigail had probably discarded from her house in Marblehead. When you walked on it puffs of dust gathered on your instep.

The entire front of Sawyer's desk was littered with primitive African wood carvings, largely droopy-breasted or vastly pregnant women who couldn't possibly have sat on their inflated buttocks. They seemed to stare at me stiff-legged and disdainful.

"The African appreciates fertile women," Sawyer said noticing my reluctant fascination.

"Kind of ugly," I said, unable to take my eyes off one who had a bursting belly. "What's that she is holding?" I asked. Darn it, why do I have to be so conversational? I no sooner said the words than I knew.

Nothing jars a proper Bostonian. "It's a phallus," Sawyer said without a smile. "You know what a phallus is, I presume?"

I nodded hastily, feeling the blood surging to my face.

"You are a very attractive woman, Miss Starch," Sawyer said coolly.

I didn't answer. I know, you think I'm adorable—I thought it. I wasn't saying a word aloud. I was afraid that the trembly feeling in my stomach would show in my voice. Darn it all, why couldn't I be sophisticated and toss him back as good as he sent?

Sawyer was continuing: "I'll never forget the first night I saw you at the Harvard Club. You gave me mixed emotions, my dear. You have such a fresh virginal look . . . disarming . . . a simplicity that most women lose, or never achieve. I

23

confess, Miss Starch, I feel very fatherly and protective toward you. A strange feeling . . . sometimes it is difficult to refrain from taking you in my arms." Sawyer was not the least embarrassed as he spoke. Not even *my* obvious embarrassment deterred him. "All very paternal, I thought at the time," he continued. "You know I have no children." He stopped and stared at me.

For a second I wondered if he wanted to adopt me or something sentimental like that. I knew better, but I always have the naïve reaction first. "You don't feel that way, now," I said. I broke the silence of his penetrating look mainly to get rid of the tension, but also working on the Clausewitz theory about the best defense. I might just as well attack. The tinder was struck the minute Sawyer left his message in my typewriter.

"Yes, I still feel that way," Sawyer said. He was still quite at ease. He tapped a pencil on his desk ruminatively. "Perhaps it is out of place talking to you this way, Miss Starch. But you are more than just a college graduate. I understand that you are Phi Beta Kappa. Very commendable for a woman with your appearance. . . ."

I looked at him, startled, wondering when, where, and how far he had been sleuthing into my life. I listened fascinated in spite of myself.

"With your learning, Miss Starch, you must be aware of many things even though you may not have actually lived them. A man—any individual, man or woman—may experience emotions which in the eyes of polite society are somewhat contradictory."

Oh, brother, I thought, I was really going to get the greased-wolf treatment. Could I dissuade him? "I know," I said eagerly, "whenever I look at you, I am reminded of a former Governor of Massachusetts. Then I realize you aren't *quite* that old."

Would you believe it? Sawyer missed the point. He chuckled, "Heaven's no, Miss Starch, age means nothing for some men. I'm in my prime." He paused, reconsidering his approach. Now was the time to tell him that he was embarrassing me or to retaliate with some wise remark that would cut him dead in his tracks, but I hesitated. I couldn't help it; I was curious as to what was coming next.

"As a matter of fact, Miss Starch, I always try to be quite honest with myself. Somehow you made me feel that I can be quite frank with you. Last Thursday I was forty-two years old. It occurred to me that I am now what is commonly referred to as the older generation and that, for me, the experience of ever knowing a younger woman is probably past. For many men this might be a minor problem, but to me, Miss Starch, enjoying women as I do, it seemed particularly unfortunate. I believe that any man truly grows old when he closes the door on any corridor in his life. A life without possibilities is not a life. It is simply a living death. You, no doubt, have studied philosophy. The act of creation is a powerful life force. Am I making myself clear?"

Too clear, I thought . . . intellectual approach and all . . . but, darn it, all this time I was wondering if I shouldn't say yes. I knew that Sawyer was going to ask me, by some roundabout route or other, to go to bed with him, and the thought occurred to me: why not? I'm going to have to do it sometime. When I thought about it, it really wasn't that I was waiting for marriage—it was just that I am a little fastidious, and the several promising boys who had proposed the idea had given me the impression that it wasn't love of Willa that interested them so much as a desire to prove their gymnastic powers on a blanket, or worse, in the back seat of a car.

The danger for me was that I remembered once reading a novel (probably written by an old gentleman of forty or fifty) with the thesis that older, more experienced men might be gentler, more tender, and hence better able to initiate a young woman. Shows you that even reading book club selections can lead to juvenile delinquency. I had sense enough, however, to hold my tongue. I just shrugged my shoulders, trying to leave Sawyer in doubt as to whether I understood him.

"Possibly," Sawyer continued, "some people might consider it an indulgence, but I am convinced that some men are made differently than others . . . have different corpuscles flowing in their blood. For example, I was rereading some of Casanova in the original French recently. Can you read French, Miss Starch? You can't possibly understand Casanova in translation."

I nodded, but I was silent. It wasn't sensible to tell Sawyer that his whole novel egghead approach was leading me onto very thin ice.

Sawyer chuckled, "Of course, I don't equate myself with Casanova, mind you. But under this forbidding Boston Brahmin exterior lurks a man who does appreciate femininity. I have tried to analyze this desire to share a few moments with you. Am I attracted to your youth? Your vigor? Your beauty? Yes . . . but this is not all. I'm gambling in a way. You might, by the very shallowness of your short life, prove not only boring but actually repulsive to me." He paused, looking a little disappointed when I didn't challenge this thought.

"No, I don't think that is possible. After all there is the inescapable fact that you are Phi Beta Kappa. . . . this, plus the protective feeling that you inspire in me makes me believe, Miss Starch," Sawyer said, finally coming nearly to the point, "that a mutually shared experience might not only be pleasant for you but, in your later life, could become a treasured memory. I say this from the wisdom given by the great distance in age that separates us. The woman you will be at forty, for example, far from being affronted at my proposal as you well might be, now . . . this Willa Starch, matron, mother of children, with her flowering past, will, I assure you, treasure the moments of discovery shared in her youth with a man who believes that he is—how do they say it?—sympatico toward her?"

Wow! This was more interesting than any conversation I had ever read in a novel. It made me wish that I could use my pencil and jot down the gist of it so that I could review it later. Sawyer had tossed the ball in my lap. I had to throw it back indignantly, acquiesce, or temporize. I temporized, deciding that, if Sawyer wanted to keep things on an intellectual basis, far be it for me to make an emotional scene.

I said: "I read a book about a man once who liked only young girls, nymphets, he called them. He was a professor, I believe, and educated along other lines." I blushed. "How do you know, Mr. Priestly, that you don't have the same kind of . . . problem?"

"I suppose that you look in the mirror occasionally," Sawyer said smiling.

I nodded.

"Well, really, Miss Starch, from all outward appearances, at least, you have passed your puberty."

Touché. I tried a different tack. "There's Abigail. It might be shocking to a Wellesley girl . . . not experienced in such things . . . to discover that her husband had such devious ideas."

Golly, that did it. Sawyer turned a dull red.

"Damn it all, Miss Starch . . . there's nothing deviant about asking a woman to share an . . . ah . . ." Sawyer groped for a harmless word ". . . an experience. I appreciate that the approach may be a little unusual, but I knew from the moment I saw you I could never resist the compulsion to ask. Nothing ventured, nothing gained—they say. If I have learned little else in life, it is to play the game straight . . . so few people do, that I have discovered they are often either

26

confused or confounded by me." Sawyer grinned. "I'm pleased to see that you are neither. I'll admit that it has taken a certain amount of courage to ask you. All I could guarantee is that our blithe affair would be a tender and happy experience for you, with an aura of magic that I'm sure you would recall pleasantly all your life."

Sawyer picked up my clutch purse where I had left it on the corner of his desk. He opened it, held up a small key, and swiftly dropped it in. "That key unlocks the elevator to my apartment on Beacon Street. Before you answer yes or no, I would like to have you think it over for a few days. . . . Now," Sawyer said crisply, "there's that letter I must get out. Are you ready, Miss Starch?"

This *was* a practical man, I thought. No chance for rebuttal. A flavor of Sawyer's English inheritance, perhaps. Something like: "Well, Willa old girl, now that's off the docket, let's get on with it, what say?"

I tried to collect my fluttering thoughts, wondering whether I should snatch my purse off his desk, remove his key and fling it disdainfully at him, or maybe just sneer at him and say: "Mr. Priestly, don't you think you'd better join an athletic club and sublimate your emotions?"

The trouble is that all you have to do is see Sawyer Priestly with his firm Roman nose, his hard angular jaw, his black hair greying at the temples, and make the mistake of looking directly back at those slightly quizzical eyes of his, and, if you are female, you might have wondered, at least momentarily, whether you weren't being honored instead of insulted. In essence, Saywer is the kind of man you see in the advertisements wearing a homburg hat, a white muffler, and holding the door of a Cadillac while his escort climbs aboard. All being accomplished with a certain flair, of course. I'm surprised that the President hasn't discovered him as a possible ambassador to England.

I was so lost in my thoughts that I missed completely what Sawyer was saying. Patiently, he repeated it for me. "I was saying, Miss Starch, that we have the Billings correspondence in our files. You can look up the address. It's down in the Wall Street area of New York City, I believe. This letter is to Thomas L. Billings. Are you ready?" Sawyer smiled gently at me.

I wasn't ready . . . probably never would be . . . but I nodded yes.

"Dear Tom: Reliance and I met with the City Council two weeks ago . . . a frowsy lot. . . ."

"Do you want me to write that?" I interrupted. "Or was it an aside?"

"You'll find frowsy in Webster's, Miss Starch. I see no reason for deleting the word, since it describes the participants exceedingly well. To continue: I don't think you know this city too well, Tom. From a tax standpoint it should be a suburb of Boston. Perhaps, wisely, however, the city fathers feverishly hang onto their identity. As you know, title to the property we have been seeking passed to this city several years ago, but, considering the general poverty of the residents, the lack of sewerage and the primitive electrical facilities, the area is no great asset. Many of the residents live on social security or are on the unemployment rolls. The houses are substandard, and there are no proper roads or streets except in the area of the abandoned Army installation."

"Hey," I said finally interrupting him. I had been scribbling crazily, trying to keep up with him. "I told you, Mr. Priestly, that I don't know shorthand. You'll have to slow down."

Sawyer apologized and continued at a slower pace. "To sum up, the area is really a tax drain on the city. Most of the residents are no more than squatters. While they have built homes on the land, the land has never been deeded to them and, historically, has only been leased on an annual basis. We should have little or no trouble in that area. Our proposition to buy fell on happy, but typically greedy political ears. I told Reliance that our initial bid was just a feeler—that this would give the council the opportunity to promote the deal. This morning, I am glad to report to you, it was voted favorably. The sale was consummated at our offer of forty thousand dollars, including all the Civil War buildings on the Army post. Since we purchased for twenty-thousand under the original figure set by you and Reliance, I know that you will be pleased. Up to this point, your name and Reliance's have been kept out of the negotiations, but the Boston papers are showing interest. You can expect a howl of thievery when the story breaks. I'm send you aerial photographs under separate cover. You already have harbor maps, so you can understand how excellently the area will serve the North and South Shore. I look forward to seeing you again when you are settled in Cohasset for the summer. Very truly yours, Sawyer Priestly."

I read the letter back to him. As I did, a cold shiver tickled my spine. The horrible thought occurred to me that Sawyer was writing about Trotter Island. It had been sold—and he

28

was admitting that the residents might be forced off the island. I questioned him point blank.

"It will be no secret in a couple of days," Sawyer said, confirming my fears. "An investment group that I represent has bought Trotter Island. We plan to develop a million-dollar marina at the Eastern Head and connect it to Hough's Neck with a bridge." Sawyer smiled warmly at me. "I didn't know until I read it on the paper in your typewriter, Miss Starch. You were born on Trotter Island, weren't you?" He shook his head with great understanding. "You *have* come a long way, Miss Starch." I realized that Sawyer assumed that, having graduated from Radcliffe, my sorry origins had somehow terminated. I didn't disillusion him. "What will this mean for the people who live on Trotter Island?" I asked.

Sawyer shrugged. "Probably nothing. They'll pay their rents to a corporation instead of the city. All development will be on the eastern end. . . . When you type that letter you can sign it for me, Miss Starch. I have to go up to City Hall, and I won't be back. The photographs will be delivered this afternoon. Be sure and get them mailed with my letter to Mr. Billings."

As Sawyer was leaving, he looked at me quietly for a moment. "I hope you won't forget our earlier conversation, Miss Starch."

I smiled at him and said sweetly: "I'm awfully pleased that you like me and all that, Mr. Priestly . . . but I'll be as honest with you as you have been with me. . . . I just wouldn't plan on a favorable decision, if I were you." I paused and looked at him sincerely. "Perhaps, everything considered, Mr. Priestly, I should give you my notice."

Sawyer looked at me with a good-humored expression. It was frustratingly impossible to shake his aplomb. "Miss Starch," he said, "if I never put a finger on you in my entire life, I shouldn't want to sacrifice the joy I get out of seeing your face, listening to your voice, and breathing the joyous femininity of you even at a distance." He put on his Homburg. "See you tomorrow, Miss Starch."

Brother . . . what should I do now?

5

It took me most of the afternoon to complete the letter to Mr. Thomas Billings—not because I am a slow typist. Actually, typing is the one mechanical thing that I do efficiently. It was just that I couldn't keep my mind on the letter. One minute I would think of at least ten smart retorts I could have made when Sawyer was propositioning me, such as: "Don't you think that a young woman would be too much for you, Mr. Sawyer?" or "I've heard that men past forty regress into second childhood. Are you trying to return to the womb, Mr. Priestly?" . . . Then the next minute I would be angry with myself for not having risen up and, with maidenly indignation, squelched the Lothario forever. I blushed when I remembered the casual way that I had countered his discussion with asides on nymphets and his wife Abigail. It was tantamount to acceptance, and Sawyer knew it! By not being properly shocked, amazed, horrified. Why, I bet in the nineteenth century some women would have been so terrified at the prospect of sharing a stranger's bed they would have screamed or said tremblingly: "My dear Mr. Priestly, I am chagrined by your innuendos"—and then fainted dead away.

But not me . . . not Willa Starch. Bodily virgin, but not a mental one. No sir, not Willa. She just sat there watching the kettle on the fire, enjoying the agitation and the clouds of steam as it came to a boil.

No, I wasn't shocked, but I *was* scared! First, because by being so incredibly naïve as to stay and type the old goat's letter, I was tacitly agreeing to consider the idea, and, second and probably worse, I was developing an unhealthy curiosity about this Sawyer Priestly whose demeanor suggested a reincarnation of Increase Mather . . . yet who could continue to call me Miss Starch while proffering a key to his apartment . . . a place that was obviously designed for seduction of innocents like me. I giggled and wondered if I ever did get in

30

bed with Sawyer if he would call me Miss Starch as he made love to me.

Somehow, by four o'clock, between dark thoughts of walking out of Sawyer's office and never coming back and brighter thoughts of my sophisticated self, dressed in a sheath gown, a sparkling conversationalist, holding a Dry Martini in one hand and airily fending an importunate Sawyer with the other—somehow, I reached the last sentence of the letter to Mr. Billings. As I was finishing I had an eery feeling that someone was standing in back of my chair watching me.

I looked up into the astonished face of Converse Cabot. It was difficult to tell which one was the more disconcerted. Converse's mouth was a turned-down "u" of dismay, and his eyes had a distinctly guilty look as he finally muttered, "Good Heavens, Willa Starch! Are you working for Sawyer Priestly?"

It was obvious enough, since I was in Sawyer's office, but I nodded, hoping grimly that Mr. Converse Cabot was really good and embarrassed. When a fellow dates a girl four or five times and then never shows up again, it is only poetic justice that someday he finds himself trapped with her.

"I've been meaning to call you," Converse said limply.

"Oh?" I was real cool. "Well, telephone service to the wilds of City Point is quite erratic. I have heard it said that connections between Beacon Street and South Boston sometimes are scarcely audible."

Converse looked puzzled for a moment. He didn't get it. It's a Harvard education. It makes one ponderous and not given to flippancy.

"I brought some photographs for Sawyer," Converse said, depositing the envelope on my desk. "Is he in?"

"No. He's gone for the day, and I'm leaving, myself, in a second." Maybe permanently, I thought, as I angrily banged Sawyer's name at the close of the letter. I yanked it out of the typewriter, folded it into an envelope, and handed it to Converse. "Maybe, considering our past friendship, you'll do me a favor."

Converse smiled brightly for the first time.

"Mail this letter to Mr. Billings in New York along with your photographs, and the next time you see Sawyer you tell him that a daily workout on one of those cycling machines or cutting down his calorie intake will solve his problems." I smiled, tossed a few odds and ends in my pocketbook. "You can also tell him that he doesn't owe me anything. I've been overpaid for three weeks."

Converse followed me to the rickety self-service elevator

and pushed the button without comment. When we reached the street it occurred to him to ask: "Willa, why are you quitting your job?"

"It's boring," I said and then decided to shock him. "Besides, I'm looking for an eligible man. Here I am, free, white and twenty-two . . . available Willa. Are you interested, Converse?"

It wasn't playing the game, I know, but, until Converse had arrived looking for all the world like a younger, even more Ivy League version of Sawyer, I hadn't really thought about quitting. Converse looked at me reprovingly. Like medicine and the law, in the profession of husband seeking it's unethical to advertise.

Then, surprisingly, he grinned. "You know, Willa, I like you. You are the only undevious woman I know. Your manner is breathtaking, but it does make life simpler." He squeezed my arm affectionately. "Let me drive you home."

"Has your car got pontoons?" I asked and laughed at his bewilderment. "Sorry, Converse. In the summer I don't live with my Grandmother in South Boston. My summer home is with the displaced elite on Trotter Island.

"Trotter Island?" Converse asked, astonished. "But there are only shacks out there."

"I know," I said, "no marble and tile bathrooms for this girl. When I perform my functions, I toss a coin to see which side of our two-hole Chic Sale I'll sit on." It wasn't true. Our house has a flush toilet. But I was pleased to see Converse blush.

"My car is across the street," he said lamely. "I'll give you a lift to wherever you are going."

"I'm just going about two blocks to Commerical Wharf, where my daddy, the wrestler Mad Man Starch, is waiting for me with his garbage scow." I was so mad at Converse by this time I decided to really lay it on. "In the summer Daddy is chief garbage collector for the harbor." That's me . . . sometimes I can't distinguish the thin line between truth and poetry.

I was glad that I had said it, though, because there we were standing beside Converse's red Jaguar, and, looking up at us impatiently, was a tanned blonde with pale platinum hair, icy blue eyes, and lids to match.

"Converse, where have you been?" she demanded in a peeved but carefully husky voice. "I told you that I had to be home by five. I'm a windblown mess. It's going to take me just hours to get ready for the dance tonight. I told you I shouldn't have spent the whole afternoon with you." She looked at me expectantly . . . not a hair out of place.

"This is Willa Starch, Steve," Converse said. "Stephanie Billings is my fiancée, Willa."

I suppose that there were tears in my eyes as I acknowledged Stephanie's disinterested nod. I'm not very subtle. "I'll see you, Converse," I said. "It's only a block."

Converse insisted that it was too hot to walk. A Jaguar has two bucket seats. The rich buy them to prove they can afford to travel two-at-a-time. I stared at Stephanie . . . Steve . . . ugh. . . . "Which one of us do you want to sit on the hood and be your radiator ornament?" I asked sarcastically.

Stephanie opened the door and pushed sideways as close as possible to Converse, practically sitting in his seat. "There's room," she said curtly.

There wasn't, but we were all cornered, so I got in. Converse wouldn't let me off at the entrance to Commercial Wharf. He insisted on driving out on the long pier, ignoring the envious stares of the dock workers and fishermen. I figured that he was probably hoping to catch a glimpse of Mad Man Starch collecting garbage. But Henry wasn't waiting for me. Bucky Bonnelli was.

I groaned silently as I saw the long grin on Bucky's face. He strode over to the car, six feet of chunky muscle, wearing a half-opened shirt that exposed his hairy chest and blue jeans so faded, tight, and wash-worn that they looked as if they might burst at any moment. Looking down at the three of us squashed together, he guffawed.

"Hey, you," he said, pointing at Converse, "You should get in the middle. Then you'd be a thorn between two roses . . . or a bag of bones packed between two succulent sardines."

As I limped out of the car, Bucky's eye caught Stephanie's. Her white skirt was hiked nearly to her crotch, revealing her smoothly tanned thighs. They stared at each other, primitive antagonists, unable to conceal some atavistic sexual response. While Converse and I watched, they measured each other. I wondered if they had discovered some elemental telepathic form of communication lost to man when he started to use his brains. It only lasted a couple of seconds. Converse obviously didn't like it. It didn't surprise me. I knew Bucky . . . but I was embarrassed because on the surface, at least, he seemed to lose the battle. I introduced them.

"It smells so fishy out here, Converse." Stephanie nodded disdainfully at Bucky. "Please, Converse, let's go."

Converse whipped the Jag in a narrow circle and headed

33

off the pier. "Nice to see you again, Willa." He waved at me. Neither of them looked back.

"Check and mate!" I said to Bucky. "Pull your tongue in . . . you're panting so hard you'll bite it off."

Bucky chuckled. He helped me down the ladder onto his trawler. "It wasn't the fish smell that bothered her," he said. "She just caught her first glimpse of a man. Who's that creep she was with, anyway?"

6

We were well past Castle Island before Bucky spoke again. He had a sour expression on his face as he steered his boat into President Roads, and we caught the first impact of the unobstructed waves and an easterly wind blowing directly off the Atlantic. He was thinking about Converse and was not at all pleased that I knew someone rich enough to own a Jaguar.

After the shock of finding that Converse was engaged—it must have happened since his last date with me—I decided that today was one of those days. Between my encounter with Sawyer and the obvious permanent loss of Converse as a prospective husband, I might just as well have stayed in bed. Fortunately, there is something about the ocean that, for me at least, makes the prospects of ending up an old maid temporarily insignificant. I couldn't help but enjoy the warm afternoon sun in a cloudless sky and the pungent smells of the harbor, fresh and salty. Even the cool east wind could not quite overpower the ripe smell of decaying fish, garbage, and unsewered slop that had been recently jettisoned from boats of all descriptions.

There's nothing placid and tropical about Boston Harbor. It's old and dirty and ugly, and its shores and islands are encrusted with broken bottles and oil slick and debris and the shambles that man makes out of his environment. But I love it. As with all of Boston, the present and the past walk together holding hands, and, if I wish, I can look around me and visualize these uninviting shores when they were deep forests, and here and there actually see Indians paddling in a canoe or Miles Standish coming up to Merry Mount from Plymouth—being a spoil-sport because Thomas Morton had been getting the Indian maids tipsy with his own home brew and dancing with them around the most ancient of phallic symbols, the Maypole.

Somehow the thought of Miles Standish reminded me of Converse and Sawyer, but the wind was in my face, my hair was whipping against my cheeks, and my behind was vibrating pleasantly from the throb of the engines, and I decided that I simply wasn't going to let the austere vision of Converse or the exotic one of Stephanie disturb me. I hadn't really wanted to push my fist in her self-assured face or trip her and send her sprawling on the wharf. No, I could do better than that. It would have been much more fun to have pushed her off the pier into the offal floating by, to watch her surface with oil and garbage streaming out of the hair plastered against her head. I would have listened happily while she screamed for help, and, of course, Converse would have to dive into the slimy mess to rescue her.

I should have told Bucky my thoughts. He still had a grim look. "Hey, sourpuss," I yelled from my seat on the gunnel. He could scarcely hear me above the noise of the engine. "Smile a little. Be like me! I love everybody."

I did, too! It was good, wonderful, glorious, heavenly . . . to be alive . . . to feel your heart beating and the sun glistening on the waves and to return the smile from passing boats . . . people who couldn't help but smile back and share for a moment the fleeting wonder of strangers happy with each other's existence. It was an intoxicating, dizzy feeling to be me and, through my body, maybe, someday, communicate with eternity. I didn't know exactly what I meant, but I was singing and obviously too much at one with the world. Bucky couldn't stand it.

"That dame, Steve . . . Stephanie Billings . . . she must be loaded with dough."

"What makes you think so?" I asked. I knew that Bucky was right. The letter I had written was obviously to Stephanie's father who must be the Billings of Billings and Cabot Development Corporation. But I thought I'd make Bucky happy. "Maybe she works for the telephone company . . . maybe she's an actress. There are a lot of summer stock companies around."

Bucky shook his head. "No. You can tell. She has that inherited breeding. A nose-in-the-air, Newton, Wellesley, Beacon-Street feeling those dames exude. . . ."

"You mean they don't sing when they are happy . . . they don't bubble . . . or say crazy things . . . they just emanate breeding and culture and charm?" It sounded slimy to me, but Bucky didn't think so.

"Yeah, some of those people don't even have armpits like you or me, Willa. In fact, I'll bet they don't even sweat or take a crap or anything. They are born with an advanced kind of osmosis. . . ." Bucky's voice trailed off. Maybe he was deeply considering what Stephanie would look like sitting on the toilet. *I* was.

"Would you like to find out?" I asked.

"What do you mean?"

"Oh," I said airily, "I think Stephanie could be had. She was staring at your tight jeans as if she was about to hand you the second apple."

"Hey," Bucky said delighted. "You're jealous!"

"Oh sure," I said, "if you go for women like Stephanie you can have them. They all look alike to me . . . as if they had plastic heads . . . interchangeable from one model to another."

Bucky's only comment was that Converse looked like a dull turd to him. Bucky's language when he talks to me is convincing proof that I've known him too long.

We turned into Nantasket Roads, a deep channel between Rainsford and George's Island. The tiny excursion boat which plies between Boston and Nantasket Beach was just ahead of us, overflowing with hundreds of steamy looking city people. I waved at their hot, tired faces and wondered if it was going to make them cooler to fill themselves with grapeade, and plunge in a sweat down the roller coaster at Paragon Park. Americans are funny. Very few of them know enough to spread a newspaper under a tree and just lie down and daydream on a hot day.

Bucky wasn't enjoying my happiness. He reminded me that the tide was dead low. Low tide meant that the only pier on Trotter Island would now be standing majestically in a sea of mud and clam shells, its pilings covered with slippery green sea life. Since few of the islands have natural channels, island dwellers in their diurnal movements around Boston Harbor have a built in tide-consciousness and eventually develop an oceanic patience that makes it possible for them to come and go on high tides with a minimum of inconvenience.

At high tide Bucky could have pulled into the pier, let me off, and, after tying up at his mooring, would have rowed back to shore in his pram. Now, however, his mooring would be in a few feet of water, and a thousand or so feet of soft slimy mud and very low water would separate us from the shore. We had two choices: wait until the tide was high, or walk in.

For the third time since I had started working in Boston this summer I reminded myself that I would have to plan better. The two other times I had been caught like this on a low tide, I had been with Henry, which gave him an opportunity to recall for me every wrestler he had fought in the past ten years. This was somewhat boring, but, at least, safe. Just as soon as I caught up with my father I was going to remind him in no uncertain terms of his promise to meet me. I wasn't going to be out in the harbor with just any stray character Henry might find hanging around Trotter Island and send to meet me because he was busy with other projects.

"What are you going to do?" Bucky asked as we approached the island. He had cut down the speed of his motor and was steering with one hand, hanging over the side, watching the water grow shallower.

"I don't have the least idea what *you* are going to," I said, trying to keep an angry sharpness out of my voice, "but *I'm* not sitting around out here for two hours waiting for the tide to come in."

"Why not?" Bucky demanded. "What's the matter? Why can't you ever sit and talk with me? I haven't got a Jaguar . . . but I'm clean, and I used a deodorant this morning, just to please you."

I scowled at him. "I don't feel like being chased around this boat by you for the next two hours. There's not enough room to get a head start."

"If you walk in you'll get your dress all muck."

"I'll take it off."

"You'll sink in goop up to your tits," Bucky smiled lecherously at me.

"I can always wash them."

"I thought you loved everybody today," Bucky said, trying a different approach. He grinned at me in that irritating way of his.

I didn't answer. The whole of Trotter Island was now clearly ahead of us. It is easily identified by its two high hills connected by a crescent-shaped strip which is nearly a mile long and about a thousand feet across. As we approached the island on the inside of Crescent Cove I could see from our port side my mother's little white house nestled in the lee of East Head. At high tide Bucky could have stopped at this end of the beach, I would have yelled or Bucky could have blown his fog horn, and either the Princess or Henry would have come down to the beach, shoved our little rowboat with its two-and-a-half-horsepower outboard into the water and brought me ashore. With the flat tide this, of course, was impossible.

Bucky had steered his boat toward his mooring off West Head, where most of the island's inhabitants lived.

"Too bad your house isn't in civilization with the rest of us," Bucky said. He cut the engine. Using a boat hook, I caught his mooring can and hauled it aboard.

Bucky was referring to the fact that the Starch house was the only private house on the eastern end of Trotter Island. On the East Head of the island, during the Civil War, the Army built a permanent installation composed of forty-five brick buildings called Fort Harrison. Sometime during the First World War, after being abandoned for a quarter of a century, the fort was reactivated, and the Princess's father, William Homulka, a master tailor from the Old Country, was given half an acre just outside the fort as recompense for his service to the U.S. Army. In what is now my bedroom had once hung dress uniforms, custom made for the top brass of the Fort by the best uniform maker in Boston. So I can say men's clothes have hung in my bedroom . . . but the men are mouldering in their graves, and they never heard of Willa Starch.

I never knew Grandpa Homulka. When I was younger the Princess often made sandwiches, and on a Sunday afternoon we would walk around the abandoned fort and have a picnic near Grandpa's grave. Grandpa had been buried beside a general and a colonel who died while on duty at the Fort and probably been interred wearing dress uniforms made by master tailor Homulka.

I suddenly remembered Sawyer's letter. If a marina were constructed on this end of the island, the Princess's property which backed up to the deserted fort would no longer be a peaceful haven. If I knew my mother, she wouldn't take this lying down . . . nor would Henry, who often claimed that he married my mother to get her old man's land as a dowry. It wasn't that the land, or the whole island for that matter, was worth much, but it was there . . . certain and permanent, and, for entertainers like Henry and the Princess who travelled from one honky-tonk to another and lived most of their lives in hotel rooms, I suppose it represented stability in their changing world. I liked it, too, but for different reasons.

Mainly, I suppose, because it was lonely and uncrowded and conducive to daydreaming—of which I am fond.

Bucky had finished tying up his boat and was looking at me with his smoochy look.

"I guess I might as well face the inevitable," I said, and making the only decision possible—undid the zipper on my dress and pulled it over my head.

Bucky whistled. "I didn't know you wore panties."

"Do me a favor, and keep your comments to yourself." I handed him my shoes and pocketbook and slipped off the side of the boat into water up to my belly button. Immediately, I sank a little further into soft, ucky mud. I tried to shake the scary sensation that I was in quicksand and well on my way to hell. Bucky jumped in beside me without taking off either his sneakers or levis.

I held my dress in the air to keep it from getting wet and started the long trip to shore. With each footstep my feet sucked up at least a ton of sickening, odiferous mud. The glucking sound it made was both frightening and disgusting. Of course, Bucky didn't help things by mentioning that the mud was full of bloodsuckers and sea worms. I had already considered that nauseating idea. It turned me into a hundred and twenty pounds of goose pimples. As we struggled toward shore, Bucky regaled me with a detailed discussion of the merits of sea worms as bait.

When we reached firmer bottom, covered with only a few inches of water, I noticed that Bucky was examining me with more than usual interest. "A few more minutes in the water, Willa, and your panties would have dissolved," he said, enjoying my embarrassment. "You have a pretty bush, brown and curly. Needs to be trimmed a little though. It's growing toward your belly button. I'll lend you my razor . . . or maybe you'd like to have me shave it for you."

"I can borrow Henry's razor, thanks," I said stiffly, trying not to blush and knowing that I wasn't succeeding.

"Who shaves your ma's pussy?" Bucky asked, not fazed a bit.

The shaving of her pubic hairs being strictly a business affair for the Princess—and now, since she had retired, a matter of habit—I didn't see that it concerned Bucky. Besides, the conversation was rapidly passing the bounds of propriety. Whenever this happened, Bucky would become amorous. In my present state of undress, I knew this was asking for trouble.

We finally reached shore. Bucky handed me my shoes and,

before I could say no, he grabbed me and was kissing me and feeling me with several hundred hands at once.

I pulled away. "Careful, chum, you'll blow your stack!"

"Willa," Bucky groaned, "what makes you such a frigid dish?"

I ignored him. "Henry promised if I took the job that he would meet me every night without fail. What's so important about today that he had to send you?"

Bucky chuckled. "You'd better come back later and spend the night in my house. There's going to be big doings on East Head tonight. Henry has sent out the word that the summer's first 'gasser' will be at your house. Everyone's going. The city has sold the island to some speculators. And . . . it's been a long dry winter. The Trotter Island Association has problems. My guess is that they won't solve them tonight, but it'll be a donnybrook." Bucky was edging closer to me again. "I'll probably be the only one sober enough on the island to get you to Boston tomorrow."

"Henry will take me, don't you worry," I said, retreating. "Thanks, anyway, for the ride, Bucky." It occurred to me that I hadn't made up mind whether to go back to work. It was Thursday. And theoretically, at least, tomorrow Sawyer owed me a hundred dollars.

Bucky grinned. "Okay, I'll take up where we left off a little later, Willa. But I'll bet you a dollar the only way you'll get to Boston tomorrow is with me . . . or by swimming."

As I walked along the beach to the East Head I knew that he was watching me. I was glad that there was no one else around. I must have looked funny from the rear, my behind clearly visible as it wobbled in my panties, and my legs caked with black mud up to my knees. But I didn't give a damn, because I did love everybody, and I had to admit that the meetings of the Trotter Island Association, fondly renamed "gassers" and "pows", were fun to observe—even if the inhabitants did occasionally run amok.

The sun, sinking slowly toward the skyline of Boston, felt warm and sensuous as it reached over the water and mud and caressed my body. I walked along the rocky beach examining the debris washed in by the winter tides: broken bottles worn smooth, sun-bleached driftwood, rusty pieces of iron, half-visible wrecks of old scows protruding from the mud, abandoned boats held together by disintegrating ribs, billions of shells of razorback clams whose occupants had vanished years before, and, here and there, a fugitive contraceptive that had passed through the sewerage system unscathed—lingering evidence of a forgotten copulation. As I looked at this

40

lonely shore with its water-cleansed, sunburnt remnants of civilization, I felt a surge of joy at just being alive and being me, Willa Starch—hungry, sensuous, with an electric sense of communion with whatever or whoever was running the universe. I knew, of course, that I needed a man. A love. Not only for the depth of intercourse, and penetration and the intimate perusal of our amazing selves, but, just as much, a love, a man, to share this wonder of the earth and the sky, and the two of us beholding it, silent and aware and woven together by the depth and breadth of our happiness.

I wondered if other girls felt the way I did. If their skin was sensitive and charged as mine was; if their breasts felt eager and erect like mine did, wanting a masculine touch too long denied them. I wondered, too, if I would ever meet a man who had retained his childhood sense of awe. A man with an ecstasy and joy for life that was so much a part of him that it surged and bubbled in his eyes and words and made the man-created narrowness of living disappear when he was present.

It was early . . . only about six o'clock. The sun was searing my face, producing unwanted freckles. Supper was an erratic affair in our island house, and Henry and the Princess would be busy with their plans for the "gasser." I decided to let the earth and sun and the breeze have its way with me for a while. I took off my bra and lay down on the rocky beach, enjoying the bite of the pebbles and shells marking my skin with tiny welts. The breeze tiptoed on my knees, whispered over my stomach and breasts, and nestled for a moment in my armpits, blowing the faint odor of myself in my nostrils —reminding me before it frolicked away, that I needed to bathe.

Watching, through my eyelashes, tiny bubbles floating and skimming through the sky, I tried again to evaluate my life. Today, I had gained a new perspective on Sawyer. For him, I was youth and endless possibilities. I wasn't exactly laughing at his desire to be young again, either. Being brought up the way I have been, I can't think of man and woman and the act of love as anything bad. From what I've seen on this island, anyway, men who are even older than Sawyer and still have retained a vigorous interest in women are a lot more fun to be with than some of the dried up commuters I have watched making their daily obeisance to boredom, as they come and go between the suburbs and Boston—men who have dissipated their sexual urges in the sterile pursuit of money. But not Sawyer. He had proved to himself that he was one of the alive and virile ones.

41

But I couldn't oblige him. Not because I felt virginal about it either. I'm not kidding myself on that score. My virginity at the ripe old age of twenty-two is strictly an accident. No, it was just that I was beginning to discover that the man I wanted to roll in the hay with would be a quietly laughing man. A man who wouldn't think it odd to lie on a rocky beach and smell the sad smell of the uncovered ocean depths waiting for the tide to return. A man with warm good humor who would watch these clouds, spattered with the red and yellow glow of approaching sunset, and find, after the surfeit of our lovemaking, an even stronger bond as he held my hand and looked in my eyes and said nothing . . . and everything.

Was Bucky that kind of man? Somehow I didn't think so. Bucky's love was a time-and-place love carefully wrapped and kept in a small compartment which he would open on schedule so many times a week. If I married Bucky, we would eventually be like the Princess and Henry who regularly on Wednesday and Saturday evening in the summer, as soon as it was dark, took a blanket and walked down the beach so that I wouldn't hear them when they made love. They would return in about an hour, looking a little sheepish, making me feel that now that that was out of the way they were ready for more important pursuits such as watching television or having a beer and sandwiches with anyone who might drop in.

I followed them once last summer, and, from the top of the cliff about fifteen feet above them, watched their moon-lighted bodies on the beach. It wasn't beautiful, and it wasn't ugly, either. It was just sad and mechanical and necessary, and their motions seemed dulled to me, and enervated, as they silently brought their work to its gasping conclusion.

Marriage to Bucky, after a little while, would be like that. Neither bad nor good . . . just average . . . without wonder, because it takes two people to wonder and evoke for each other the everlasting mystery of man and woman. If I tried, for example, to grasp the moonlight, to hold it in my hand and offer it as a gift to Bucky, I am afraid that he would be not expectant—only bewildered.

What would marriage to Converse be like? I tried to day-dream on this for a while, but the irritating presence of Stephanie Billings kept getting in the way. Any man who could want to marry her, I thought grimly, had no imagination at all!

Besides, it was all speculation . . . like a bachelor or old-maid marriage counsellor giving advice. What did I know about love or the act of love anyway? Nothing but a few trillion or so descriptions that I had read in books—novels by the millions that were probably written by men who conned the whole business from one of those how-to-do-it marriage manuals or, worse, copied their love scenes from a psychiatric case book of abnormal psychology. Writers who tried to make you believe that the epitome of love was being enjoyed by their newly created world of mechanical monsters who scratch, kick, knife, whip, embugger, disembowel, rape, practice necrophilia, or cacophagia, or spit through their teeth at one another, but who would rather be dead than admit to a deep-down, sissy thing like love and affection for another person. . . .

7

I must have dozed, because, suddenly, instead of looking at blue sky and clouds, I was staring into beady blue eyes, a grey whiskered face, and bobbing Adam's apple that all belonged to Abner Thurston.

"She ain't dead, Prin," he cackled, staring down at me. "Darned if your daughter ain't stacked better than you are."

Hastily, I scrambled to my feet, clutching my brassiere around me.

"She should be," the Princess said, helping me fasten my bra. "Willa's only twenty-two, and two kids newer than I am." My mother smiled at me with the little grin that was always flickering about the corners of her mouth. "I don't see why you are so modest about your tits, baby. The rest of you is on better display than the Boston police allow."

"I guess it is too late to worry about him," I said, ignoring Abner's interested appraisal of my body. "After all, he tells everyone on Trotter Island that he practically pulled me out of you twenty-two years ago."

Abner beamed at me. Abner Thurston, at eighty-two, has the honor of being Trotter Island's oldest citizen. Long ago his skin shrank tight against his bones, making him appear

43

almost translucent. Abner attributes his good health and longevity to the fact that over the years he has slowly pickled himself in alcohol.

"Like those things you see in bottles," he tells everyone. "Don't worry about me. I'm going to last forever."

With his name and his predilection for liquor, he is known on every island in the harbor simply as Thirsty. Thirsty has been caretaker of Fort Harrison for the past twenty-five years. Long ago the Army forgot that he was there, and, when the island was finally sold, the city council was completely unaware that Thirsty went with it. They have missed an excellent source of income. So that he would never have to spend too many hours sober, Thirsty put together, from debris he collected on the island shores, a very efficient distilling plant. I have often walked up the dirt road, past the rusty gate and fence that girts the fort, to visit him. Within two hundred feet of the barracks and half-open roof with rotting shingles that Thirsty calls home, you can smell various batches of his garbage fermenting. He calls the stuff he makes "grappa," a recipe that one of the Bonnellis gave him. It is made from the skin of grapes which Thirsty grows as methodically as the farmers of Provence. I sipped a glass once. Going down it paved a new path in my esophagus, and I was seriously dizzy within minutes. Thirsty sells his product in clear pint bottles for one dollar to bona fide residents of Trotter Island. While the Internal Revenue Service is deprived of income by these untaxed activities, Thirsty craftily points out that he has never drawn Social Security. Since his distillery supports him, Thirsty considers that he is roughly even with the government.

Walking along the beach toward our house, I noticed that Prin was wearing very tight white shorts cut high on her tapered calves, and a very brief halter. A white ribbon encircling her hair was tied in a tiny bow on top of her head. There is no denying that my mother, with her firm shape and undyed blonde hair, looks a lot younger than her forty-three years.

Thirsty, now that the subject had been unearthed from the debris piled high in his long memory, persisted in recounting details of the gory night that I was born. He had been the only available midwife, while Henry was over in Quincy trying to persuade a doctor to take a sea voyage and superintend my arrival.

"You were a squaller, Willa. I used to be an old hand in those days . . . had done it a dozen times or more. A couple of the brats were mine, I guess. Yup, I cut your cord and

44

slapped your little behind, and, all the while, your ma was whimpering at me, afraid I didn't know which end was up!" Thirsty patted my behind now in a friendly way. What could I say? After all, he had proprietary rights of a sort.

I asked the Princess what she had been doing all day.

"Your ma has been posing for Mendes East," Thirsty grinned. "He's painting a picture of her without any clothes on. Your pa ain't too pleased about it. But you can't tell what Mendes' paintings are when they are done anyway. Henry agreed to let your ma do it, so long as I went along to stop any funny business and watch out generally for your ma's morals."

I could see Henry's point. I've long since come to the conclusion that the Princess has no sexual moral sense whatsoever. Not that she's bad. In some ways she is very prim. I don't believe she would ever tell even a white lie or cheat anyone or steal a penny. She just happens to believe that sex is fun . . . and no one has been able to convince her differently.

Mendes East is somewhat of a mystery on Trotter Island. Along with Thirsty and the da Rosas, he is the only resident that lives on the island year around. I think he fancies himself on an island in the West Indies. According to Bucky, he has a wife somewhere in a suburb of Boston. There's also a rumor that he is pretty wealthy and came to live on Trotter Island to escape the boredom of Boston society. His one-room shack has a north skylight that leaks. Mendes eats, paints, and sleeps in this room and occasionally has parties that last all night.

Two years ago Mendes took up Calypso. He taught Mama Bonnelli to play steel drums, which he carefully tuned by pounding the rims of some old Esso gasoline cans. Mama weighs close to two hundred pounds, but she's got rhythm. It's a delight to watch her and Mendes pound out resonant music on these pans hung around their necks. And it's impossible to sit still . . . you just have to get up and move your hips. When he isn't playing the drums, Mendes dances the limbo, a native Caribbean dance he tries to teach any who show the slightest interest. Passing beneath a pole raised less than two feet off the ground, with Mama Bonnelli pounding on the oil cans, Mendes' back is nearly parallel to the ground before he finally springs to his feet on the other side. He is constantly challenging the Princess to dance the limbo without clothes on. I think Henry's prudish presence keeps her from trying.

There is something lithe and exciting about Mendes that awakens primitive feelings in me. I know that he has probably had hundreds of women. No man as sharply handsome as he is with his lean, tanned almost Arabic face and wiry body could escape women. If Mendes ever made any overtures to me, I might hesitate . . . but not for long. The trouble is that Mendes likes older women. To him I'm just a nice kid.

"Want to argue philosophy, Willa?" Mendes will say to me.

I don't, but we do, and I try to keep my mind off his flashing brown eyes. Mendes surprises me with how much he knows. There's not a book in his shack. "I read a million of them," he told me. "I tried for twenty years to know everything. Then it got to be a pain in the ass. I finally didn't have anyone I could talk with. So I followed Walt Whitman's advice and threw them all away. Now, at forty-six, I know that the ultimate for a human being is to share life with someone else."

Since Mendes lives alone and is not too communicative until he has drunk at least a pint of Thirsty's liquor, I guess that he isn't achieving the ultimate. I hoped for his sake that he wasn't seeking some kind of rapport with my mother. I don't think Prin is the intellectual type. I do know one thing about Mendes East, though . . . that Mendes East isn't his right name. Sometime when I'm alone with him, I'm going to startle the devil out of him . . . I'll tell him that I know what the name Mendes really means.

8

On the rocky beach about two hundred yards in front of our house, just below the cliff which is about twelve feet high and protects the land from tidal washouts, Henry and King Rose were gathering driftwood in a huge pile. They were obviously getting ready for the "gasser."

"It isn't the Fourth of July, yet. Why the bonfire?" I asked, forgetting that I was still carrying my dress, and somewhat visible to the world.

Henry, who is about five-foot-seven and almost as wide,

stared at the Princess with the fierce expression that he uses in the ring to scare his opponents half to death. Because he is shorter than the Princess and has to look up at her this, demonstration lacks force. The Princess is not easily frightened, anyway.

"For God's sakes, Henry, what's the matter?" she asked. "You look as if you swallowed a clam . . . shell and all!"

"Look at the way King Rose is looking at Willa," Henry hissed at her. "A fine mother you are to permit your daughter to walk around half naked, enticing all the men on the island."

My mother shrugged. I couldn't help but laugh. How, I wondered for the umpteenth time, could anyone with such Victorian ideas about ladies' morals have ever got hooked up with a stripper named Princess Tassle? It was like self-flagellation. Maybe Henry thought that he could reform her . . . but in the twenty-two years that I had known them he hadn't seemed to accomplish much. My mother observed the expression on King Rose's face. He seemed to be entertaining the idea of lapping me up.

"Da Rosa, you wipe that silly look off your face," she said. "And you, Henry, stop being so modest. Willa's only a little girl."

King Rose smirked, showing strong white teeth below his black moustache.

"Willa's a little girl that very damn good to look at it. Nice-a boobies, hair on her belly. Don't worry," he said, noticing my mother's exasperation, "King Rose, not touch . . . got plenty women touch . . . just look. Like to look at alla woman, big ones, little ones, skinny ones, fat ones . . . all nice." He dropped some driftwood into the pile that he and Henry had accumulated. "Where you go all day?" he asked my mother suspiciously. "Little BoBo yell for you like mad. Granny Starch can't shut him up." King Rose shook his head disgustedly. "BoBo needs milk from tits . . . not from damned old bottle. What you got boobies for anyhow . . . not just to wiggle, I betcha."

"My God!" the Princess cried, ignoring him. "Get your dress on quick, Willa. Henry," she wailed, "why did you have to go to South Boston and get your old lady today? It's only the first of June. I told you not to have her around when we are having a gasser. The old witch will flip her lid. How long is the old bag staying, anyway?"

"The old bag is staying three weeks!" We all looked up, startled to see Grandma Starch and, a little behind her, Grandpa Starch staring down at us from the top of the cliff.

It was too late for me to put on my dress. I resisted the temptation to close my eyes and put my fingers in my ears. It wouldn't have worked, anyway. Grandma has a pretty shrill voice.

"Willa! Willa Starch! I can't believe my eyes! Whatever has got into you? A floosie, you are . . . parading around in front of men without any clothes on. It's a sin, you dirty men!" she screamed at Henry and Thirsty and King Rose. "Turn away. Don't look at her." Grandma, in her excitement, forgot to include Grandpa in her tirade. I guess Grampy felt that he was an innocent bystander. Standing behind Grandma, he was grinning at me and his eyes were dancing with delight at the excitement.

"Granny, I've a bra and panties on," I said, trying to pacify her. It was no use. She was bawling Henry out. Long experience had taught her it did no good to argue with my mother, so she chomped on Henry, ignoring the Princess completely. "I warned you, Henry . . . I told you years ago when you first brought that woman to my house. It's a bad woman will show her private parts to any man. Now look at your daughter . . . the sins of the father, I tell you, are visited on his children."

Henry listened to her without comment. He probably agreed with her, but neither Henry nor Grandma together were a match for the Princess if they got her started. Although I tended to agree with the Princess, I knew that there was nothing so wicked in Grandma Starch's world as being undressed. I am of the firm opinion that once she was old enough to be in complete possession of her own body Grandma has never been seen naked by anyone including God, if he happened to be looking. Not only that. If she could help it, she never looked at anyone who wasn't decently covered. Grandma took the story of Adam and Eve seriously. For her it must have been the ultimate ignominy to have had a creature worse than Eve living in her garden for twenty-three years, constantly tempting her innocent son.

Walking toward her house, Grandma led the procession followed by Henry, me, and Grandpa. Thirsty, King Rose, and the Princess came along behind at a discreet distance.

"You listen to me, Willa Starch," Grandma said in a voice loud enough to be heard by any stragglers. "I don't care how disgracefully your mother behaves. I raised you most of your first twenty-two years, and I tried to make a daicent woman out of you. I've told you over and over again how a lady should act. Just look what happens when you get out of my sight. I'm ashamed of you, Willa Starch!"

48

"Gram," I said cheerfully, "you can stop worrying. I put my dress on five minutes ago. You are absolutely right. I've been very sinful today, and I'm sorry."

Grandma wiped the tears from her pale blue eyes and patted my shoulder. "You are a good girl, Willa, I know it, but you have one fault. You enjoy bad company too much." She sighed. "I know that none of you want me here. If your mother had her way, I'd never get to visit my only child. She's glad enough to have me take care of her children though. Imagine a woman as old as your ma having a six-month-old baby. It's downright sinful!"

"Maybe Prin thought she didn't need her pills anymore." I grinned, guessing that this would precipitate an explosion, but hoping it might indirectly take the heat off my state of undress.

"Willa! I hope you don't mean what I think you mean!" Grandma said, peering at me horrified. "Father Duffy was right. I should have insisted that you receive proper instruction." Grandma Starch looked at me sternly. "When people get as far along in life as your mother and father, it's high time they thought about other things . . . or, if that is impossible, at least they can use better judgment."

I wanted to ask Grandma what she meant by "judgment." If she meant what I guessed she meant, Grandpa must have had a pretty dull life.

"As I was saying," Grandma said to my father, "your wife is not only too old to have a baby, but I have been looking at BoBo pretty carefully this afternoon. Grandpa and I agree. There is something very strange going on. . . ."

"Hey, Ma!" the Princess yelled, interrupting her, "are you still yacking at Henry?"

"Yes I am!" Grandma said stiffly. "You heard me all right, Prin. I'm not talking behind your back. Where have you been all day, that's what I'd like to know!"

"I've been having my picture painted," my mother said, grinning.

Oh, brother, I thought. Wait until Grandma explores this further. But Grandma Starch had something else on her mind. "Henry," she said, "this afternoon is the first time I got a good look at your son." Her pale eyes searched my father's face for a moment. "I'm sure of it! BoBo looks more like a Portugee fisherman than a son of Ireland. He doesn't look like you at all, Henry!"

I'm afraid I gasped. The truth is that I was of the same opinion. My baby brother is much darker than my father. Henry has sandy hair and blue eyes. The Princess has dark

49

brown eyes. I have brown eyes and so has BoBo . . . so I guess that doesn't prove anything. But my hair is light brown . . . almost blonde, like the Princess's. BoBo has very black curly hair and big dimples on his cheek that remind you of King Rose. I took a quick look at King Rose, who had caught up with us. He followed the conversation with interest. If it weren't for his darned bushy moustache, King Rose, with his snapping brown eyes and swarthy devil-may-care look, would be really handsome.

"It's a fonny thing, Grandmaw," he chuckled and put his arm around her. "My liddle woman, Dathra, got me a liddle girl most same time as Prin got BoBo. . . . You seen my Bridget yet?" he demanded. "By God, she looked just like she came from the old country. Okay . . . no care. Already got four boys . . . now King Rose got liddle girl."

"Sure," my mother said laughing. "Dathra Rose and I swapped babies." She looked at me affectionately. I couldn't tell whether she was kidding or not. "Bringing up one girl, and trying to get her married is problem enough. Henry and I traded for a boy."

"Sure what'sa difference?" King Rose guffawed. "Alla kids . . . good. I like a whole island full. Halfa boys, halfa girls!"

Grandma snorted but didn't pursue the discussion. One thing was apparent. King Rose was not worried about the population problem. In fact it looked to me as if he should be shut off. I decided, however, that some rainy Sunday afternoon when I had nothing else to do this conversation deserved a little reviewing.

Before I took a shower I sat at the big kitchen table with Henry and the Princess. Henry opened a quart of beer and poured us both a glass. Grampy, Thirsty, and King Rose had gone over to Thirsty's shack with Henry's wheelbarrow to bring back a keg of grappa. When they returned, Henry would help them dig a hole on the beach, fill it with seaweed, and be ready to cook clams and lobsters for the gasser tonight.

"It's good to sit down," Henry said, burping the beer appreciatively. "I've been workin' my ass off all day. This is the last year I'm gonna be President of the Trotter Island Association."

The Princess didn't comment. She was watching Grandma, who was warming a bottle for BoBo and basting a pot roast that was in the oven.

"What's she cookin' that for? Ain't lobsters and clams good enough for the harpy. I leave my only house in this whole damned world for a few hours, and what happens . . . your old lady is here flippin' her butt around, cooking a roast . . . because her poor Henry ain't eatin' properly with that hussy of a wife he's got." The Princess's voice, starting low, had increased in intensity. It was a good thing that Grandma Starch had been having difficulty with her hearing lately. She went blithely along testing BoBo's bottle on her wrist and cooing at him when she put it into his mouth.

"I'm telling you, Henry Starch," the Princess said, not coming up for air, "I'm not having that old lady of yours spying on me all summer. Jesus and Mary, you must have been off your noggin' to bring her and Grampa here tonight of all nights."

"Aw, Prin, shut your trap," Henry said amiably. "The old lady will hear you. I was in town to see that guy Joseph who is on the city council. Then I got to thinkin', my old man's probably sitting around in those big fireman's suspenders of his, boiling in his sweaty long underwear. Here we are nice and cool, and he and the old lady are hot as hell in that firetrap of theirs. I was with Pierre Grass. We were out all day pickin' his lobster traps for the gasser tonight. A couple of his traps are near the Boston Yacht Club, so I asked Pierre if he'd wait a couple of minutes while I called them up from the club. Ma and Pa were pleased as crap."

"Well, it's your red wagon," the Princess said ominously. "The old girl will probably pop her eyeballs when she starts spying on us tonight. Just keep her out of my hair."

"What's so special about tonight?" I asked.

"It's this letter!" Henry said excitedly. Taking a crumpled paper from his pocket, he smoothed it out. "Every family on Trotter Island got this damned letter. We'll fight 'em. Stinkin' Back Bay Bostonians, that's what they are. They think they can screw us out of our island. Listen to this, Willa." Angrily, Henry read the letter. "This is to notify you that the island in Boston Harbor, known as Trotter Island, has been purchased by the Billings & Cabot Development Corporation. Families occupying certain dwellings on the island are reminded that title to the land has never been deeded to any individual and that buildings which have been erected at the risk of the owners are subject to renewal of the annual leasing fee. This is to notify you that the annual leasing fee of two hundred dollars for an eighth of an acre, due on August 1st of each year, is hereby increased to four hundred dollars for an eighth of an acre, effective August 1st for the coming fiscal year. Arrears in payments due the former owner are payable immediately to the Billings & Cabot Development Corporation. Default in any leasing fees due or payable in the future will subject the tenants to immediate eviction."

Henry tossed the letter on the table. "It's a stinking trick to get us all off the island. Frank Otto hasn't paid his lease for three years . . . neither has Pierre Grass. None of us can afford that kind of money to live on this pile of rocks. By God, we're gonna fight," he said grimly. "Ain't we, Prin?"

"No Boston blue blood is kickin' me outa my home! The United States Army gave this land to my Daddy." The Princess burped. "Honestly, Henry, I don't know how you can drink so much beer. It makes me feel pregnant." She picked BoBo out of his crib. "At forty-two I get a charge out of havin' this one. But no more! The thought of ever again carting a bloated belly around for nine months gives me the hee-bee-jeebees. This chicken ain't bringing any more Starches into the world . . . and don't you forget it, Henry Starch!"

"It ain't Starches that I'm worried about," Henry said good naturedly. "Just see that there aren't any more Roses."

The letter made me good and mad at Sawyer. Trusting soul that I am, I believed him when he said that the sale of Trotter Island wouldn't affect the residents. Worse, it was now apparent that Converse was involved, and, of course Stephanie Billings. I should have suspected when Converse arrived at Sawyer's office with the air photos of the island. The Reliance whom Sawyer kept referring to was obviously Converse's father. Sawyer Priestly, like the villain in oldtime melodramas, was not only plying me with immoral suggestions but was foreclosing the mortgage and forcing my family out into the freezing blizzard. I decided right then and there I *wouldn't* give up my job. Somehow I would find a way to put a spoke in the wheel of the Billings & Cabot Development Corporation.

I told Henry and Prin about Sawyer's letter. "Why do they want to build a marina here?" I asked Henry.

"Because every damn fool in the country with a few bucks in his pocket is buyin' anything that floats and calling himself a sailor," Henry said. "The way it's going, in a couple of years you won't be able to see the water in the harbor. Every inch will be covered with some stinking put-put or hydroplane or water skier or souped-up Chris Craft and this island will be invested with Sunday captains strolling up and down, high and mighty in their yachting caps, while their damned families are eatin cruddy picnics and their brats are running all over the place." Henry looked mournful. "Your Boston friends don't give a crap. They just figger it's a fast way to make a buck . . . pullin' and haulin' and servicing boats for the clucks who only use them about ten weekends a year."

Henry patted me on the shoulder. "Anyway, it's a break that you are working for this Priestly. You gotta help us, Willa! I spent most of my life chucking pugs around a ring to give you an education. Every time I was on the canvas with some sweating pig, I'd think about this place and the day when I'd retire here with your ma. Now when I finally retire, look what happens. . . ."

"Don't worry, Pops," I said feeling sad for him. "We'll think of something."

"We won't pay them a damned cent," the Princess said. She pounded the table. "We'll make them evict us. We'll write the President of the United States, and if he sends the National Guard we'll fight 'em with pitchforks and broken bottles." My mother waved her glass, and I noticed that she had switched from beer to a mixture of grapefruit juice and Thirsty's grappa. "Henry, where is that old shotgun of yours? A picture of me defending Trotter Island, taking a potshot at Mr. Billings and Mr. Cabot will make every newspaper in the country!"

"Not without clothes," Henry said uneasily. "I'm not going to have any more pictures of you in the *Daily Record* wearing just a G string. Every time it happens, Ma yacks at me for a week, and every friend I got tells me how lucky I am and asks me when I'm gonna share the wealth."

The Princess stood up and surveyed herself in a full-length mirror that hung on the bedroom door. She sucked in her belly and stuck out her chest. "You know, Henry—considering that you look like a cross between a caveman and a gorilla—your friends are right—you are. . . ."

The Princess didn't get a chance to say "lucky," because Henry calmly picked her up and held her wiggling and screaming over his head. Paying no attention to Grandma Starch, who watched horror stricken, Henry turned around and around in a circle until my mother screamed that she was getting dizzy . . . to please let her down . . . that she was sorry . . . that Henry Starch was the most handsome man she had ever known. . . .

9

At eight-thirty, Henry and King Rose lighted the bonfire on the beach. Easily seen by the residents on the West Head, it was the signal that the gasser could begin anytime.

Meetings of the Trotter Island Association are usually held two or three times during the summer. Over the years the difference between a gasser and a pow have been pretty well defined. The real difference is degree. A pow is just a friendly gathering of families sharing a few bottles of beer on the beach. Some of the beer might be laced with Thirsty's grappa, but, since children were usually invited and played in the shadows cast by the firelight or went swimming when the tide was high, the tone of the evening was generally genteel and circumspect. Occasionally a few residents like Herman Snole, business representative of the International Brotherhood of Electronic Workers of America, and a bachelor, together with Thirsty and Mendes East, might stay on past eleven-thirty—especially if Mendes had brought his guitar. Then, with bellies full of grappa, they would sing folk songs in a surprisingly good drunken harmony.

When that happened I used to sit on my bedroom windowsill before I went to bed and dangle my legs on the roof of the porch below. I would listen to the sibilant whispers of Henry and the Princess as they talked with some friends who had come over to sit on the porch and be summer-lazy for a few more pleasant hours, reluctant to go to bed. As I watched the stars and the remote lights on boats occasionally passing in the harbor, as I smelt the faint aroma of tobacco on the damp air and the restlessness of field mice bustling through the tall grass on the island, I would sometimes cry, because the songs that were being sung seemed sad and fragile and because the softness of summer and the stars so remote and cool, were filled with wonder and so impossible to possess.

A gasser started later. Children under sixteen were put to

bed. Older and more curious teenagers spied on the proceedings from a distance or took one of the boats and went to Boston or Quincy to the movies

As I grew older I recognized a resemblance between gassers and ancient Saturnalias. Perhaps there is some kind of therapy in a gasser, a human need to blow the lid off and let loose the energies that boil up in the day-to-day business of living.

Observation of a gasser was a simple way to acquire a precocious sexual knowledge. Often, when I heard some of my roommates at Radcliffe talk about Sex and Life, I was tempted to invite them to Trotter Island, making sure they arrived for a gasser. I'm sure that life and sexual manners of the lower lower class would have come as a revelation to them. Somehow I never did invite anyone—not because I was ever ashamed of Henry and the Princess—rather, I think, because I would have been good and angry if they thought the way we lived during the summer was terrible or shocking. I liked it. All my education has done for me, in the last analysis, is to make me bashful about letting my hair down—necessary physiologically and psychologically if you want to be a true Trotter Islander.

I remember the morning following a gasser last summer. Hardon Pine was found snoring on the bare chest of Susan Otto, who lay beneath him in a drunken stupor on the pebble-covered beach. Knotty Pine, his wife, was watching them, giggling.

"Her tits are so big," she said hilariously, "that everytime she exhales it sounds like Hardon is breathing in a paper bag. The old fool. He's lucky he hasn't smothered." Knotty Pine, who is flat-chested, wasn't mad, either. "He's always lookin' at Susan's boobies. Poor dear is frustrated, that's all." She yanked him to his feet and kicked Susan's behind. "I got better hips," she said, punching Hardon in the stomach in a friendly way. "I can swivel you better, papa! You better stay home."

Susan Otto (who lives with Frank Otto, together with Penelope Otto and Jessica Otto) didn't know how she got there or how her blouse or brassiere got removed. She grinned a sickly grin at Knotty Pine, who, tall, skinny . . . with a mop of yellow hair, towered over her. "Your old man is a raunchy hound-dog," she said. "You better let me borrow him a week. Take the strain off yourself."

Frank Otto, who is a bartender at the Half Crown Bar in the Combat Zone wasn't angry either. Actually, I haven't figured out whether he has any right to be angry. Four years ago he was a bachelor. Then three summers ago he appeared on Trotter Island with a housekeeper. Frank never described her status, but she introduced herself as Jessica Otto, his sister. The next summer Penelope Otto, another sister, moved in. Last summer he acquired a third sister, Susan Otto.

Frank's house has only four rooms—kitchen, living room and two small bedrooms; he doesn't need three housekeepers.

"He's a slob," Henry said. "My guess is those snatches ain't his sisters at all. They're just worn-out whores who drifted into the Half Crown without a dime to their name, and he felt sorry for them. They're probably so used to humpin for their meals . . . they don't give it a thought."

"You mean you think he's servicing three women?" The Princess looked incredulous. "Ye gods, what a man!" Henry frowned at the interested tone in her voice.

Whatever the relationship of the Ottos may be, I like them all. Brown-eyed Jessica, who let her platinum hair grow in white and black, has developed a firm rosy-cheeked look. Jessica loves to cook, and she is constantly delivering samples of her latest pie or cake to the Princess. Jessica is about the same age as the Princess, but Susan is only thirty. She has big blue eyes, freckles, and reddish hair. Fascinated by the Princess's career, she listens in awe when my mother describes details of her life on the burlesque circuit. The Princess has taught her to twirl a pretty fair tassle. But Susan's breasts are quite large. When the Princess tells her that it isn't physically possible to get so much lard in motion and keep the tassles twirling properly, Susan looks sad.

My mother advised her against trying a burlesque career at her age.

"Count yourself lucky that they still stand up pretty good," she said, examining Susan's breasts like some female Lysistrata ready to give advise to her female cohorts . . . and then, airily, "If Frank Otto ain't your brother, I'd hook him fast before they slip down on your belly."

"Not me," Susan said darkly, "not this chicken. I'm not lovin' or honorin' any man . . . ever again. There ain't a good one anywhere, not even Frank, who isn't a bad old crock. But no man is gettin' life, liberty and pursuit of happiness out of this carcass. Not at his beck and call, leastways."

Penny Otto, who is thirty-two, is a skinny pixie with dark blue eyes and an Italian haircut. All last summer she shadowed Mendes East who doesn't seem to know she exists. Penny, according to Susan, has been married twice. Both husbands unaccountably disappeared. Poor Penny. Mendes painted an abstract portrait of her . . . a horrible thing in which Penny has a green face and pink tears on her cheeks. Mendes calls it "South Boston Madonna." Last summer it won third prize at the Boston Arts Festival, although no one has bought it yet.

Tonight, the first meeting of the year, was quite definitely going to be a gasser. Henry asked me if I'd like to take Grandma Starch over to Nantasket to play bingo. I politely declined, telling him that any problems relating to the defense of Trotter Island were my problems too since I was working for one of the enemy.

"All right, but I don't want you drinking any of Thirsty's grappa," Henry said, "and since you are still pretty young I think you should be in bed not later than eleven o'clock." Awkwardly, he put his arm around me. "We've had a strange life Willa, and I haven't been the best father in the world, but I know Grandma has done a good job and you have good morals."

"Too good," I said and left it at that. I was wearing my real tight faded blue jeans and a sweater I knitted last winter. Sitting on a driftwood log, hugging my knees, I watched the last vestige of day as it hovered in the west, silhouetting the skyline of Boston. The tide was nearly high, and the water, rippled by a light easterly breeze, was phosphorescent and sparkly. It was going to be a cool, star-lighted night. The first flare of the bonfire had died down, and now the fire was burning comfortably hot. I could feel the early evening dampness in my hair and on my clothes. I knew that by morning the temperature would drop to fifty.

Thirsty's huge keg of grappa, securely held by two large rocks, was perched near the forward deck of the hull of an old schooner that had broken up in a northeaster, last fall, to come, in bits and pieces, to its final resting place on Trotter Island. The deck, about four feet higher than the rest of the beach, was flat enough to make a twelve-foot stage. Shuffling around on it, Henry, who had consumed at least two glasses of grappa already, beamed happily at Grandma, King Rose, Dathra Rose, Thirsty, and me, all of whom were the only arrivals so far. The Princess hadn't come down to the beach yet . . . probably waiting to make sure Grandma had gone to bed.

"This will make a fine stage for dancing." Henry smiled at Dathra, who agreed with a happy nod of her head. "I think it might be a good idea to have anyone who has anything to say tonight come up here where everyone can see him." Henry peered into the darkness. "I guess they are finally coming. I can see Pierre Grass' lantern!"

Along the shore from the far end of the island, a procession of bobbing flashing lights and lanterns slowly weaved toward our fire. It took about ten minutes for the lights to reveal the dark shadows of those who held them. Finally, by ones and twos, the fifty or so residents of Trotter Island arrived in the circle of firelight, complaining about the letter they had received from Billings and Cabot and demanding a can of beer or a drink of Thirsty's grappa to revive them after the arduous walk across the stony beach. Some of the people I knew well, others by sight, and a few I guessed were new to the island. Continued residency on Trotter Island was claimed by only about ten families. A continual trading and subleasing of the remaining accommodations went on all winter. To become a permanent enthusiastic resident of Trotter Island requires a special outlook on life and an intestinal fortitude that is, I guess, no longer a characteristic of Bostonians.

Mendes East grabbed me around the waist and gave me an affectionate hug. "You get prettier every year, Willa. Wish I weren't such an old man!"

"Don't let age stop you," Bucky Bonnelli said sarcastically. "Willa has a yen for the cultured type."

Penelope Otto, giggling in a confused way, tried to pull Mendes down on the beach beside her.

Jesse Otto handed me a huge box, sighing, "I hope the frosting ain't shook off. It's a cake. It'll taste good later." After kissing me, she warned Frank Otto, who had just drained off a glass of grappa, to please use a little sense and not get as drunk as he did last Saturday. "He was so potted," she confided in me, "that he woke up with a big head. I was feeling kind of crocked myself . . . so he puttered around the medicine cabinet and got us some aspirins. . . ." Jessie laughed hysterically. "Next day we were both pissing blue, and I thought, sure enough, our time had come. Susan called Dr. Daniels over in Quincy. He finally came on Harry Able's boat. At first he couldn't figure out what was happening to us. 'What did you feed him, Jessie?' he asks me. "Looks as if he swallowed a bottle of bluing.' Finally, Dr. Daniels, who always makes himself at home, pokes around in our medicine cabinet and finds a bottle of medicine Frank has for the dog. Sure enough we had both eaten a half dozen of Fritzie's worm pills, thinking they were aspirins. Damn things got something in them called methylene . . . makes you piss blue."

Henry was listening to the conversation. "Doc Daniels may come over tonight. He's a card. Told me that he was thinking of calling himself the Hough's Neck Hoodlum and challenging me to a wrestling match."

"I love the Doc," Susan said approvingly. "He told me he wrestled his way through medical school. Showed me a headlock right in his office. I said let go Doc or I'll tumble you right on your 'tochas.' It's a Jewish word meaning ass. Doc nearly split a gut laughing."

I accepted a glass of grappa and grapefruit juice from Thirsty warning myself to sip it and make it last all evening. Everyone had arrived. Papa Bonnelli had rowed over. Mama Bonnelli was so fat it chafed her legs to walk; besides, Papa admitted it was easier to carry Mendes' steel drums in the rowboat.

"He say," Papa said, pointing at Mendes, "if I get the drums over here, your ma has promised to dance the limbo and twirl her tassles all at the same time."

"You keep your fat eyes offa da Princess," Mama said. "I dance the limbo for you. Go unda sticks only two feet offa da ground. You wait and see." All two hundred pounds of Mama shook happily at the thought.

I watched the line of people at Thirsty's keg. Cackling happily, he was turning the spigot, filling each glass at least half full and letting the imbibers pour in grapefruit juice from punctured cans to suit their own taste.

Herman Snole had just received his first ration of grog. Harry Able was tasting his appreciatively, informing Thirsty that this was the best batch ever.

Hardon Pine, Knotty Pine, Morris Shapiro, and his wife, Betty, were drinking with Pierre Grass.

"Figure it out for yourself," Morris said. "They don't want to kick us off Trotter Island. I heard they paid forty thousand dollars for this heap of sand and stone. There's fifty houses on this island right now, and they can build more. They get four hundred dollars a year lease. That's twenty thousand bucks. The taxes are peanuts . . . so they make 50% interest on their money, and they don't have to do a damn thing. Pretty neat, I call it. So . . . they stick up a marina on the Fort Harrison end and make some more dough. What do they care if I ain't got four hundred bucks? Do they worry if Pierre Grass hasn't paid his rent for three years and hasn't got a dime? So they evict us. They take our houses because we built it on their land . . . and they get themselves another tenant. There's always someone around who'd grab a house on an island for four hundred bucks. If they kick me off, I'll burn my house down. No bankers are goin' to get it, by God."

"You should have bought the island, Henry. *Mon Dieu*, Henry's a rich man," Pierre said noisily, attracting more listeners. "He told me that he and Prin had saved fifty thousand dollars! What do you think of that? Just the other day, he was griping to me he could only get a couple of thousands bucks a year interest. Ain't that a shame? *Pauvre homme!*"

Henry shrugged, "I didn't even know that Trotter Island was for sale."

"That's the way it is in this society," Herman Snole said, nosing into the conversation. Herman is about five-foot-three. He compensates for his height by being infallible. His eyes are close together, and his mouth is usually twisted in a cynical smile that he forces over protruding teeth. "Even if you knew it was for sale, Henry, you wouldn't have had the brains to buy it. There's two kinds of people in this world. Those who got the money, and those they take it away from. You're a good example of the last kind. You sweat your balls off. So at fifty-one you've saved fifty thousand dollars. That's about a thousand dollars for every year you lived. Big deal. Best you can do now is stick it in the bank or buy some nice safe stock and get a couple of thousand a year interest. Is the government happy you got it? Like hell it is. It doesn't even want you to be self-supporting. It takes your measly two grand and taxes hell out of it. In a couple of years, Henry, you'll be spending the principal just to live, and then you'll be broke. You know why? Because you're a dumb turd!"

"Don't call me a dumb turd!" Henry warned him. "I'll pick you up by the balls and twist the crap out of you."

"Okay," Herman said, "You're a smart turd."

Henry nodded happily.

"See what I mean?" Herman sneered at the group. But no one did, except maybe Mendes and me, who grinned at each other.

10

Henry climbed on the wreck and waved his hands for attention. "Let's get going. This meeting is hereby called to order. Every one will please cut out the crap and pay attention. As you all know we got problems to solve before we can relax. The first thing is dues. As of now every family owes his annual dues. Ten dollars per family same as last year. At the last meeting in September you reelected me President of the Trotter Island Association, and Dathra Rose was reelected Secretary and Treasurer. I have held the office of President for four years. In September, when we have election of officers, I want you to know I ain't available any longer. I've retired from wrestling, and I'm retiring from this job. You've gotta find another patsy. I'm not going to shell out for these gassers and then have to chase everyone on the island to get my money back."

"You can chase 'em with Dathra, Henry," someone yelled. "That should be fun."

Henry scowled. "We agreed to pay for what we drink and eat at these meetings. There's two dollars and seventy-five cents left over from last year . . . so when Dathra passes among you to get some dough for your dues some of you just betta cough up." Henry stopped. He glared at Hardon Pine, who was lying on the beach propped lazily on his elbow. When Dathra walked in front of him, Hardon had hooked her skirt with his foot. He had her trapped and was peering appreciatively up her legs.

"Hey, Henry," he yelled, "your treasurer ain't wearing pants. Looks like she's ready for business."

"Cut the clowning," Henry said angrily, "or I'll pick you up and chuck you in the water." He searched the fire-lighted faces a minute. "Knotty Pine stop fiddling around with Pierre Grass and go sit near Hardon until this meetin' is over. As I was saying, we agreed to pay for what we drink and eat. Thirsty's keg of grappa cost us four dollars. We bought ten cans of grapefruit juice at forty-nine cents a can. That's four dollars and ninety cents."

"You mean the juice costs more than the grappa?" Papa Bonnelli interrupted. "From now on, I vote we drink da damn stuff straight."

"We ain't votin' on anything," Henry said. "Let's conduct this meeting accordin' to rules. Stop shootin' off your mouth unless the President recognizes you. Pierre Grass sold us fifty lobsters for a dollar piece. That fifty dollars. There's one lobster for everyone, and, if I catch any pig eatin' more'n his share, I'll pin his ears back. There's all the clams you can eat. King Rose dug 'em, and he wanted to donate them, but to hell with that . . . the Trotter Island Association pays its own way. We'll pay him ten dollars for his time. There were four cases of beer left over from the meetin' last September, so I didn't buy any beer. Tonight's 'meetin' is costing us sixty dollars, and anyone who ain't paid his dues by next Wednesday will receive a personal shakedown from me and Dathra." Henry peered into the crowd sprawled indolently on the beach below him. "Willa, where in hell is your ma?"

I looked around the beach and shrugged. Not only had the Princess not arrived, but King Rose had disappeared. I was pleased with Henry's sudden attention, though, because Bucky, who was sitting beside me, starting on a second glass of grappa, insisted on undoing the zipper on my jeans and was trying to wiggle his fingers against my belly.

"I'll go see what's keeping her," I told Henry. When Bucky tried to follow me, I shoved him toward Penny Otto, who obligingly grabbed him, pushed him flat on the beach, and started kissing him. The party was warming up.

Before walking to our house, I stood on the cliff a moment and watched the fire and the dark water lapping against the shore and the distant lights twinkling across the harbor. Man was in the right perspective on Trotter Island. Balancing the frenzy of his daily activity, he could find here an affinity with the ceaseless flow of life. God, timelessness—call it what you will—that both enveloped him and held him at bay, reminding him that he was mortal and some things were not so valuable as the mores and fashions of a particular moment might lead him to believe.

Approaching the kitchen, I whistled. I didn't feel like interruping any tender love scene. Whatever the multiple relationship of my family and the da Roses might be, they seemed to be happy . . . and *enjoying* each other. Who was I to moralize?

People past forty have a savoir faire that escapes you when you are younger. When I walked in the house, the Princess, dressed in her most abbreviated tassle costume (she has at least twenty different ones . . . tailored to meet the demands of censorship in various cities where she has performed), was leaning over the crib cooing at BoBo. King Rose, standing beside her, smiled easily at me and continued to hold one cheek of my mother's buttocks in his hand. I didn't tell them this scene could well give me a Freudian scar that would last all my life. As a matter of fact, it took King Rose at least a minute to realize that I was somewhat surprised. He slowly removed his hand.

"Your ma has a good firm behind, eh, kid?"

"Hi sugar," the Princes said grinning and unabashed. "I've been waiting for BoBo to conk out. He's just about asleep. I told King Rose that, if I didn't get down to the beach soon,

Henry would be swarming in here like a suspicious lover in an Eyetalian opera."

"Is that all you're wearing?" I asked, admiring her complacency. Except for the two tassles supported by the smallest ribbons across her nipples, she might just as well have been naked. A special G string held one tassle firmly against each buttock. The pièce de résistance was the tassle affixed to a tiny triangle that just managed to cover the front of her. Without any movement at all the tassles combined to give her a wildly sexy look.

She pulled a cotton dress over her head. "I'll probably freeze, but this afternoon I bet Mendes that I could go under the limbo stick and twirl all the tassles at the same time. So, if I decide to try, at least I'm ready." She kissed my cheek. "You know, Willa . . . you mustn't be shocked. Now that I've retired, I've got to keep in shape."

I asked Prin where Grandma Starch was.

"You know that she always goes to bed at nine-thirty sharp. By this procedure," Prin explained to King Rose, "she plans to outlive me and take over Henry again." Prin looked at the clock on the kitchen wall. "Since it is now nine-twenty-five, the old battle axe has just entered the front bedroom closet where she is sliding a nightgown over her head with one hand and removing her corset with the other. In exactly four minutes she will be in bed, thank God!"

We walked to the beach, King Rose in the middle, one arm around each of us, squeezing us happily. He was jubilant. "By God," he sighed ecstatically, "I sure like women. Nothing better than woman in the whole world!"

"If you had a whole harem full, you'd get fed up," the Princess said, giggling. "I tell you . . . isn't a man alive can manage two women at once."

"Oh, King Rose ain't doing too bad." King Rose chuckled. He gave my mother a challenging expression, but she ignored him.

Looking down on the beach I was surprised to see that Henry had abdicated his position on the wreck to Herman Snole, whose flickering mouse eyes immediately picked out the three of us trying to slip into the crowd unnoticed. Herman was explaining to his interested audience that the whole project of building a marina on Trotter Island was a case of wheels within wheels. He stopped his declamation long enough to draw attention to us.

"Glad to see you finally got here, Mrs. Starch," Herman said, giving us the evil eye. "While you have missed some of the discussion . . . no doubt because of more important occupations . . ." vast laughter from everyone on the beach ". . . I think you'll understand the gist of what is going on if you pay attention. As a matter of fact, Mrs. Starch, I have a place for you in Operation Buzz-Off, which is the name I have modestly contributed to our plan to dispose of the Billings & Cabot Development Corporation. . . ."

"Where in hell have you been?" Henry interrupted, edging through the crowd toward us.

"Kissin' and a hugging Kingsley da Rosa," my mother responded promptly and loudly. She bowed to the enthusiastic chorus of laughter. "You can now officially hold hands with Dathra Rose."

"Please," Herman snarled "Let's keep this meeting off the subject of extracurricular sports. We have a problem concerning our fair island that temporarily makes sexual concerns insignificant—a problem that should arouse the fighting spirit in each and every one of us."

"Cut out da horse sheet, Herman, and get to the point," Pierre Grass yelled . . . and then, triumphantly, to the crowd, "I ask you let's taka a vote. I say Herman Snole talks horse sheet through his hat most da time."

Everyone agreed, with enthusiastic catcalls and whistles, but Herman was not phased. "It's to save French peasants like Pierre Grass who can't distinguish his ass from a hole in the ground . . . or how to save enough money to pay his annual rent . . . or how to deal with our slippery friends who own the wealth of this world . . . it's to save people like you from your own follies that the Lord gave you an intelligence like mine."

Herman sneered nastily at everyone. "I suppose that most of you have heard of the ABC Electronic Corporation out on Route 128."

"Sure we know," Hardon Pine yelled "You organized the place. That's all we've heard about for two years. You got two thousand women workin for you. They're all members of the International Brotherhood of Electronic Workers. I hear every one of those babes gives you a dollar a week. Whatch' doin with the dough, Herman? Where are you hiding your Cadillac?"

"I account for every cent of dues," Herman snapped. "I make one hundred and thirty-five dollars a week, and I earn every damned penny of it listening to two thousand women who got everything from the clap to falling arches and change of life . . . and blame it all on the union. I'm cheaper than hiring a head-shrinker . . . all for a buck a week."

"See!" The Princess nudged King Rose. "I told you . . . more than one woman at a time is a pain in the behind."

Herman took a long swallow of grappa. "If I get interrupted again, you can all sink up to your ears in Pierre Grass's sheet. I kid you not!" He stared balefully at the crowd. Except for the crackling of the fire, there was dead silence. "Okay," he said, finally continuing. "What you don't know about the A B C Electronic Corporation is that it isn't just the first three letters of the alphabet. A B means Abigail Billings, who inherited ten million dollars from her granddaddy. She owns the controlling interest. C means Cabot . . . namely Reliance Cabot, of Hingham and Cohasset, who ain't exactly poor but wasn't rich enough after he invented the special transistors that they make to keep the company out of the shark's hands."

"You mean that Abigail Billings is a shark?" Knotty Pine asked.

"No, mam." Herman said. "Abigail Billings is a nice plump lady of about forty-five years. When she was a girl, her family sent her to Wellesley, where she learned to direct dramatic shows and run fashion bridges and country-club luncheons. She wasn't too bright . . . but she was smart enough to marry a young man from New York City who didn't mind having a big dimply wife. Maybe sharks and whales like to play together, I don't know. Anyhow, Abigail gave this young man a few playthings, such as the majority of stock of the A B C Electronic Corp. A nice wedding present. Her name ain't Billings now, of course. Hasn't been for ten or twelve years. It's Priestly. Abigail Priestly."

I gasped. "You mean her husband is Sawyer Priestly?"

"You're durn tooting right . . . Willa! Sawyer Priestly is one of the smoothest financial operators in this part of the country" . . . (and a nonpareil with women, I thought) . . . "Your pa was telling me tonight that you work for him, and that is a stroke of luck. You are gonna be our Trojan Horse inside the enemy walls." Everyone applauded, and I nodded dumbly, still not able to believe that Sawyer Priestly, who wanted to go to bed with me, was that smart.

"So now I'm going to tell you about our opponent's Achille's heel," Herman said, going whole-hog on his classical allusions. "I presume that you all know what I mean by the reference to Achille's heel."

"Sure, I know Achilles," Thirsty said. He was snuggling against Jessica Otto, who was hemmed in on the other side by Grandpa Starch—both of them competing for her attention. "Achilles Pamphilos! He runs a Greek restaurant down near Faneuil Hall. What's a matter with his heel?"

"He's got a boil on it!" Mendes East laughed uproariously. "He got it pushing over round heels with his pointed toes. You know what they say about Greeks that own restaurants, don't you?" That made Penny Otto laugh so hard she banged her head against one of the steel drum pans which responded to the thump with a perfect C sharp. Mendes, gasping with laughter, tumbled against her in a heap.

Angrily, Herman started to leave the platform.

"Shut up, all of you!" Henry glowered at the crowd. "The next one that opens his trap, I'll heave in the ocean." He grabbed Herman, who yelped with pain. "You ain't goin' nowhere until you tell us your idea." He held Herman in an armlock while the crowd cheered.

Reluctantly, Herman explained his plan. "Monday, I'm going to call all the girls who work for A B C Electronics out on strike. I'm gonna make it so hot for A B C that Cabot and Priestly won't be able to give Trotter Island a second thought. Most of the girls need a vacation. Our local has never tapped the headquarters strike fund. . . . Be kind of like a holiday for everybody . . . except for Reliance Cabot and Sawyer Priestly. Don't think they like vacations, somehow. Except for themselves, of course."

"What makes you so sure they'll go out? Just because you tell them to?" Mendes asked curiously. "Why in hell should they pay any attention to you?"

"What are you?" Herman demanded. "A rich, capitalistic scab?"

"Seems silly," Mendes said. "If I were earning two bucks an hour just sitting over there listening to music all day and putting wires in tubes or some damned thing or another, I wouldn't pay attention to a little fart like you."

"Oh, you wouldn't?" Herman said darkly. "Well, I'll tell you, you half-assed Gaugin, you go around preaching about freedom and individual rights, but you haven't got sense enough to recognize invasion of privacy when you hear about it. Two months ago the A B C Electronics Corporation decided that they weren't gettin' enough production outa my girls. So what do they do? They go to one of those busy little management consultant companies all run by stinking little characters who think they are God Almighty ever since they got an M.B.A. degree from Harvard. What happens? A month later from every damned column in the building is hanging a loudspeaker. My girls come to work in the morning, half asleep, groggy, and the speakers are blaring away

66

cheery little marches and Spanish polkas that make their blood crawl. Pretty soon they get workin like nuts in the insane asylum just to keep up with the music. Then, before they drive my girls completely off their rockers, they turn it off a little while, until some superintendent spots the pace slowin' down. Bang . . . crash . . . on goes something like Stars and Stripes Forever or the William Tell Overture! Once in a while they figure the girls might be gettin' indigestion or something, so they play some waltzes. Big deal. I tell you, Mendes East," Herman snarled, "artists like you don't know what time is. These birds got all kinds of charts in their offices. I saw them. Tells them exactly the time each day a worker goes into a slump, shows how and when to play the right music. Follow the chart, and the girls are working like hell and can't help themselves. So you know what I'm gonna tell my girls? I'm gonna tell them that damn music is worse than havin' Reliance Cabot look at them in the bathtub without any clothes on. He's tryin to steal the thoughts right out of their brains. Instead of letting them think about their house cleanin' or what they're gonna buy with the green stamps or what was the matter with the old man last night and maybe he doesn't love 'em any more—this monster is fillin their heads full of music and making morons out of them." Herman beamed proudly. "And my girls know I tell them the truth!"

Mendes was reduced to amazed silence. Everyone on the beach cheered. "We got 'em licked already," Papa Bonnelli exulted. "We'll get your ma on the picket line. Everyone will perk up then, by God. Route 128 will be jammed from here to hell and back when they know Princess Tassle is out there fighting for her land."

"Not without clothes!" Henry yelled excitedly.

11

All during Herman Snole's extended peroration, while I was trying to digest the amazing discovery that Sawyer Priestly was a far more devious character than I had ever guessed, I was attempting at the same time to stay out of Bucky's clutches. His gently massaging of my back and his inquisitive fingers running over my jeans were pleasant enough, but I began to fear that I was going to have a hard time keeping my jeans on if I let him continue. I had finished a second glass of Thirsty's grappa, and I am afraid that I was slowly deciding that I might just as well let Bucky initiate me, as the saying goes, into the mysteries of sex. But the decision was not certain yet . . . the Starch side of the family was still in control of Willa's morals.

"Let's go for a walk up to the Fort," Bucky whispered. "They've got everything decided for the time being. Now all they'll do is get blotto and feel each other up for the rest of the evening."

"What makes you so proper?" I asked. "When I came back just a few minutes ago you were feeling up Penny Otto."

"Well, she ain't so old," Bucky said practically. "I'll bet she isn't more than twenty-nine."

"She's thirty-two," I informed him, "and you better watch out. She'd just as soon rob the cradle. She's a desperate woman."

Henry had climbed back on the wreck and was waving and shouting for attention. "It looks as if the formal meetin' of the Trotter Island Association is over," he said. "But in view of the serious situation I think we better at least have a pow next Saturday and get a progress report from Herman Snole."

"Wait a minute," Thirsty said, suddenly leaping to his feet. Jumping up and down, he looked like a tattered skeleton. He weaved excitedly toward the wreck. "I told you, Henry Starch, I had some business to bring before this meeting." Thirsty climbed up on the stage, stumbling tipsily against Henry. "Forgot my durn bag," he hiccoughed. "Hey, Grandpa Starch, stop feelin up Jessie Otto and bring my old Boston Bag up here." Nearly as tight as Thirsty, Grandpa staggered up to the old hull. Henry hauled him and Thirsty's old Boston Bag aboard.

Clutching the handles of the worn bag, Thirsty peered at his audience. "I been savin this for a rainy day . . . and now the day has come." He patted the bag softly. "There's enough money in this bag to buy a couple of Trotter Islands and then some. What's more, I'm gonna give all this money to a Committee to Save Trotter Island. Nomy . . . nomy . . . nomynations are in order," he sputtered, "to elect a committee."

As he said the words, Thirsty excitedly twisted out of Henry's grasp and sailed gracefully over the edge of the deck into the arms of King Rose. King Rose gently sat him back on the platform. "I ain't kiddin," Thirsty said and passed out, snoring noisily.

"Open the bag!" Everyone shouted at once and crowded in around King Rose, who undid the straps and slowly placed twenty solid packs of money on the edge of the wreck.

"I'll be damned!" Henry said unable to believe his eyes. "They're packs of ten-dollar bills! There must be five hundred of them in each pack!"

Every one of the fifty or more people on the beach crammed toward the wreck to get a look at Thirsty's horde, and then someone yelled in dismay. "I'll be a suck-egged mule. The damn things are stuck together in a solid block. You can't get them apart!"

"Get back . . . give us air," Henry yelled. "Pierre, take it easy with that money. Jesus . . . you might tear it. Be careful!"

"You can't tear this stuff," the Princess said, examining a stack. "I think it's a fake. Thirsty stuck one ten dollar bill on top and one on the bottom with a solid piece of wood in between."

"It ain't a fake!" Thirsty came to life and looked around, indignantly. "That's real honest-to-Jesus money. Only trouble is, I can't get it apart. Not one piece at a time, leastways." He pulled a ten-dollar bill out of his pocket and displayed it to the crowd. "Look's good, don't it. Only one trouble." Chuckling, Thirsty turned it over. "It's got Hamilton's picture on both sides. The be-damned stuff can't be peeled apart! Least I ain't figgered any way."

Herman Snole and Mendes East were both studying the packets of money carefully. "How long you had this stuff, Thirsty?" Herman demanded.

Thirsty shrugged. "I found it couple of years ago last September. The day after that big hurrycane. There was thirty packets of it. All soaked together in a beat-up old suitcase. Must have been in the water a year or more. I dried it out. Couldn't get it apart. Then I cooked it. No dice. Tried to slice it with a cheese slicer. Nothin. Even finagled Bill Dooley out of his market one day and tried to slice it on his meat slicer. Joker. Every piece I ever got apart so far either had two fronts or two backs."

"Where's the other ten packs?" Mendes asked.

Thirsty grinned craftily. "You think I'm stupid? I ruined two packs in the last two years fiddling with it. I got eight packs left. If one of you brains figger out how to get 'em apart, you'll have enough money to buy Trotter Island, and I'll have enough to get me a real distillery—instead of all that junk I'm using. I might even go legitimate and pay taxes." Thirsty grinned happily. "I can see the sign now, *Abner Thurston, Distilled Spirits since 1887.*"

"Since 1887," I asked.

"Sure, I was eighty-two last week, and I've been drinkin' since I was ten. How in hell do you think I lived so long anyway?"

After Thirsty's surprise, the gasser slowed down a little. A hundred thousand dollars, even if it is cemented together, has a sobering effect on most people. Everyone managed to finger a bundle of it reverently and offer inane suggestions as to how it might be separated. Every suggestion that was proffered, from freezing it to peeing on it, had been regretfully tried by Thirsty and found unworkable.

The Princess' remark that the money was probably stolen in the Brink's robbery and that even if they did separate it would do them no good was politely ignored.

"We could sell it in South America," Henry said. "Even fifty cents on a dollar wouldn't be bad."

"That's the same as stealing," the Princess said.

"Well, it's no damned worse than showing your pussy to all the bald heads in Christendom," Henry replied.

Mendes East, whom I noticed was enjoying the rapacity of the Islanders, evidently decided to goad them into action. "I hope you won't think it's sacrilegious of me to mention it . . . but I heard that scholars working on the Dead Sea Scrolls had found a way to peel the Scrolls apart."

"Zowie," Hardon Pine said enthusiastically. "You're appointed to go see them tomorrow."

"I think they are in Israel," Mendes said sadly.

"Let's send Morris Shapiro," Pierre Grass said. "Morry, you always said you'd like to go and see what's happening over there."

"I'll go if you'll pay for the plane trip," Morry said, certain that no one on the island, including Henry, would part with the fare.

Bucky was gently edging me out of the crowd. "Come on," he whispered, "the party is getting dull. They are going to spend the rest of the evening hashing over that money. Let's go for a walk."

Tipsily, I let myself be led, still trying to make up my mind. "I'm pretty tight," I said, "I think I should wait a while and have something to eat. They'll be serving the lobsters in a few minutes."

I caught the leer in Bucky's eye when I said I was pretty tight. He urged me along a little faster, pretasting his conquest of Willa Starch. Away from the beach, walking up the road to the abandoned fort, the island seemed to take on a forest life. Bucky had borrowed a lantern. Flashing along the dirt road, and occasionally into the trees, it created a strange night life that hung over us in grotesque threatening shadows.

"It's kind of scary," I said. "I get a feeling that someone may be standing in the woods watching us."

"Everyone's at the gasser," Bucky said.

"I don't know. There are a lot of strangers come to the island in the summer. Maybe some nuts or Peeping Toms. I wouldn't want to end up just a torso."

"You got me, haven't you?" Bucky demanded. "I won't let you come to any harm."

I wasn't so sure about that. "Where are we going?"

"Just up to the old parade ground."

The parade ground is the highest point on Trotter Island. Unused since the Second World War, when a few soldiers were stationed on the island as part of a bomber alert group, the grass grows waist high. It whipped against my legs, and I shivered. On the top of the hill we were without protection from the cool easterly wind. Around the harbor we could see the lights of Hull and Quincy and Boston separated from us by black star-lighted night and blacker water. The Fort has the kind of loneliness that both attracts me and frightens me. I wanted to huddle against Bucky for his warmth and his maleness and then, in the protection of his arms, exult with him at the joy of being together and alive. But how could I convey my emotion to Bucky?

He was leading me to the Civil War administration building, now deserted for years, which had once housed the Post Commander of Fort Harrison. Most of the windows in the old brick building were broken. The glass that remained reflected eerily the starlight with a dull forbidding look that reminded me of a painting by Charles Burchfield. The sky was clear of clouds, and the salt-ocean smell of the east wind was invigorating. My alcohol-befogged brain suddenly cleared, and I realized that I was cold.

"I'm freezing. Let's go back."

Bucky urged me along faster. "Once we get in the shelter of the Post Building you'll be all right. It's really warm tonight. . . . Just the wind makes it seem cool."

"I'm not going inside. The place is full of rats."

We sat on the steps of the half-rotted front porch, and it was warmer. Bucky started to kiss me and tell me that I was the only girl for him. Any other girls that he had made love to just didn't count compared with good old Willa. He con-

71

fessed that he had lived practically a monastic life during the winter, waiting for me to finish college. "Let's get married, Willa," he breathed at me in a husky voice. "No one else knows you as well as me. Gosh, I can remember way back fifteen years ago. You were seven. We came up here and I took off your pants so I could look at you . . . and you looked at me and touched it!"

"All kids do that," I said, embarrassed. I tried to pull away from him, but he had backed me against one of the Ionic columns that supported the roof of the porch. With amazing adeptness he had unhooked my bra and was fumbling with my breasts. He was gentle. I couldn't help it. For a few minutes I relaxed. He kissed my nipples, touching first one breast then the other. Then he undid the zipper on my jeans—and my brain took control.

"No," I protested. "Let's go back."

"Aw, Willa. For God's sakes, what's the matter with me? Don't give me that stuff about never having done it. You had time for plenty of other things at Radcliffe besides studying. Stop being a female teaser who never puts out."

"I'm *not* a female teaser," I said indignantly. But I suppose that I was. After all I *had* walked up to the Fort with him. "Besides, I don't like the words *puts out*. I'm not some tramp you picked up." I always make the mistake of arguing. If I had just maintained an affronted silence it would have precluded discussion.

Whenever I argue with a man I always seem to get into deeper problems.

"Look, Willa, I'm sorry," Bucky said contritely. "I believe you. But you are going to do it some time. . . . Why not now? How about going back to your house and sneaking into your bedroom. The gasser will go on all night."

"No," I said, and then, grasping at straws, I lied. "Anyway, I couldn't. I got my period." By this time I had refastened my bra and was hurrying back to the beach, followed by a reluctant Bucky.

"Aw, Willa . . . cut the crap," Bucky said angrily. "You don't have to lie to me."

"What do you mean—lie to you?"

"You haven't got the curse."

I looked at him astonished. "How do you know, Bucky Bonnelli, what's going on inside of me?"

"I saw you this afternoon in your panties. Remember? And I felt around enough tonight to know you're not wearing anything."

How do you like that? It just goes to show that I *had*

known Bucky too long. A girl needs some privacy. "Listen, stupid," I said, "don't you read the magazines? There's more than one way to stop a flood!"

That got through to him. Although I couldn't see him in the dark, I hope that he blushed. We walked back to the gasser in silence. As we got nearer the beach, I could tell by the noise and the shouting that the party had shifted into full gear. The sound of a guitar and an alcoholic chorus dominated the other noises. They were singing Mendes's favorite calypso, "Nobody's Business But My Own."

Standing on the cliff, we could see Pierre Grass pulling lobsters out of the boiling water and tossing them on a plank. His wife, Jenny, was handing out nutcrackers. A crowd sprawled near the fire was cracking open the succulent lobsters and eating them greedily, dripping shells, lobsters, and water all over themselves.

King Rose, Mendes East, and Mama Bonnelli—shaking the maracas—were in the center of a group. Like skilled Calypsonians, Mendes and King Rose were improvising their own local verses.

King Rose was leading a chorus. He sang in a deep baritone and played his guitar. "Nobody's business. Business. Nobody's business. Business. Nobody's business but his own. Mad Man Starch with men he wrastle. Do it better in bed with Princess Tassle."

The hilarious singers joined in. "Nobody's business. Business. Nobody's business. Business. Nobody's business but his own."

Mendes picked up the next round. "Mad Man Starch say move over, maybe. Gotta get King Rose a blue-eyed baby."

Wild laughter from the chorus: "Nobody's business. Business. Nobody's business. Business. Nobody's business but his own."

Looking up, King Rose saw Bucky and me. "Willa Starch been huggin' that Bucky Bonnelli. Make him feel just like apple jelly."

"Nobody's business. Business. Nobody's business. Business. Nobody's business but her own."

"You can sing that again," Bucky said morosely. He slid down the cliff without waiting for me. "Stay there and watch, if you like," he yelled back. "This kid is having some fun before the night's over."

I watched him stride angrily in the direction of Penny Otto. She embraced him with enthusiasm. It made me mad and proved what I already was pretty sure of. Just so long as she has the usual female appurtenances and tells him that he is wonderful, a man doesn't really give a tinker's damn to whom he makes love. It was especially exasperating to me because at least ten times in the past hour I had said to myself . . . what the heck . . . and in my mind not only had let Bucky made passionate love to me but had vigorously helped him.

Watching the gasser from the cliff and feeling sorry for myself, I decided that I was a pretty sad case . . . not really any more sexually moral than my mother, but educated so darned much that I had lost the female ability to protest a little and then relax and enjoy the inevitable. I, Willa Starch, couldn't make love until I had moralized, argued, and examined every ramification of the emotion. I wasn't satisfied until I finally forced the frightened bird to take wing.

Penny Otto knew the score, by gosh. The next time I dared to look and see what was going on with her and Bucky, I saw them walking arm in arm along the beach away from the crowd. My dark thoughts were interrupted by Mendes East, who scrambled up the cliff and dropped a whole lobster in my hands, followed by one of Jessie's nutcrackers. The lobster was hot and messy and dripped all over me, but excavating the warm flesh and savoring its clean flavor kept my mind off sexual things at least.

Mendes watched me silently for a while. "What's the matter, Willa . . . lose your boy friend?"

I shrugged. "Guess the trouble is that I'm in love with love. Bucky is more practical. He wants the solid substance."

"Most men do . . . but they miss a lot."

"I know . . . but you are even more generalized than Bucky. You told me once that you love everybody."

Mendes chuckled. "I do . . . even my wife. All you have to do is revise your point of view. Instead of trying to achieve perfection, simply relax and enjoy human imperfectability. With that perspective you achieve the ultimate godhead. You see man as infinite possibility always in the process of becoming. You see finally that man, in emulating the creative process, is nothing less than God." Mendes grinned at my bewilderment. "The only God worthwhile in the world, Willa, is the expression of wonder on your face."

"Don't you get lonely for your wife?" I asked, trying to make the conversation more substantive. "Where is she now? Living in Boston?"

Mendes smiled with a quizzical look on his face. "I get a kick out of you, Willa. You and your ma are the only undevious women I ever met. Do you like calypsos?" he asked apparently irrelevantly.

74

I shrugged and sucked at a lobster claw.

"Calypso is direct music. I think, somehow, it will enjoy a great revival in this country. Youngsters like Simon and Garfunkel understand. . . . They are writing a new music and poetry for man that sings and laughs at the daily problems—love, politics—what have you. They attack life from a simple, straightforward point of view that is captivating in this tortuous world. That's what I like about the residents of Trotter Island. They have reduced the business of living to its essence. If Trotter Island has a theme, a musical motif, it should be the calypso we were singing a little while ago."

"That's a devious and roundabout way to tell me to mind my own business." I grinned at him. "Nobody's business but your own . . . honestly Mendes that's not worthy of you. I don't really give a darn about your married life." I watched the gasser for a minute or two and then let him have it. "On the other hand, any man who assumes a name like Mendes should expect a certain female interest."

"For an unmarried female, Miss Starch, you certainly have a wealth of curious knowledge," Mendes looked at me mockingly. "So you read somewhere that Mendes was the phallic god of the Egyptians. . . ."

"Worshipped in the form of a goat," I interrupted. "Are you so virile? The Princess would be interested!"

Mendes shrugged. "My wife graduated from Bryn Mawr. She researched phallic symbolism for a senior thesis. Very daring, you know. She even collected phallic statues and carvings . . . used to show them to our friends. We had friends like the Priestlys and Cabots. You know, people who, in their cocktail moods, flirt with tittering sexual ideas and the rest of the time are frigid as hell. My wife nicknamed me Mendes . . . sarcastically. The nickname stuck . . . I was good old limp Mendes. My wife finally convinced herself that it was so." Mendes patted my head. "This is pretty ripe conversation to be having with a twenty-two-year-old. Have you lost the gist?"

"No," I giggled, "I'm ripe and in the full flower of my youth. From now on it's all downhill. What does Daisy Mae say? 'I'm past my prime.'" Having put the bit in his teeth, I thought Mendes might determine the direction of the evening, but he didn't respond. We watched the gasser in silence. Maybe his wife was right.

12

Below us on the beach, Frank Otto and Henry Able had just trundled in another barrel of Thirsty's grappa. As Frank bent over to maneuver the heavy barrel onto the rocks, Knotty Pine leaped piggyback on his shoulders urging him to get on the ball and open the spigot. From our vantage point, with all the noise, it was difficult to hear what Frank yelled at her, but we could see him rise slowly, and, with Knotty Pine sitting on his shoulders, combining them into a weaving ten-foot monstrosity, Frank calmly walked into the ocean up to his waist and dumped the screaming Knotty Pine, who must have yanked out a whole fistful of hair, into the water.

The firelight reflected on the water, and we could see her rise to the surface, sputtering. As she plodded toward shore, yelling for Hardon to come and beat Frank Otto's brains out, a man whom I couldn't recognize floated by in front of her, stark naked, spouting water out of his mouth like a trained whale. When he saw Knotty Pine he submerged and evidently grabbed at her legs, because she tumbled in over her head again and arose, a side-swiping demon with murder in her eyes. She finally reached shore, threatening in a cracked voice to slice off Frank Otto's balls when she caught up with him.

Like a painting by Hieronymus Bosch the beach had turned into a maelstrom of unrelated activities. Earlier in the evening, Henry had connected a three-hundred-foot electric cord from the house to the beach, and the speakers in the Princess' tape recorder, plugged into an amplifier, were bursting with rock and roll. Hardon, who wasn't aware of what had happened to his wife, was dancing with Susan Otto. Susan, to the delight of the group watching her, had removed her blouse and brassiere and, naked to her waist, was undulating in suggestive riposte, matching every insinuating gesture of Hardon's intricate dance.

About three feet away, completely unperturbed by this display of female mammae, Herman Snole and a half dozen other men had focused a searchlight on the packets of Thirsty's money, and were intently watching as one of the men carefully poked at a packet of it with a pocketknife. After each jab he passed the bundle around for inspection and approval.

A few yards away, on top of the wreck, King Rose was singing a lilting song in Portuguese, joined by Pierre Grass, who was hugging Jessica Otto.

Grandpa Starch and Thirsty had run down to the beach to help Knotty Pine, who was calmly removing every piece of her dripping clothing. While she undressed, she supervised both of them, watching while they solicitously hung up her bra and panties to dry on sticks they had perched near the fire. Knotty Pine was scarcely a gawky, naked six-foot female when a speedboat thundered out of the night, its searchlight cutting a wide swath of light on the beach. For a moment, I thought it was a police boat and the gasser was going to come to a precipitous end. But then I noticed that the boat had a lone driver. He cut the engine and jumped to the deck of the boat. It was Doctor Daniels, wearing bathing trunks. With a whoop of delight he threw out his anchor and dove into the water.

Henry, who had been dancing barefoot with Dathra Rose, left her unceremoniously and ran into the water to greet him. He evidently grabbed the Doctor's hand in a wrestler's grip, because Doctor Daniels suddenly caved in at his knees and slowly sank up to his waist in the water. Then, unexpectedly, he rose to his feet and, with his shoulder, caught Henry under the armpit. With a jiujitsu movement, he rolled Henry over his shoulder and tumbled him headfirst into the water. The enthusiastic crowd cheered Doctor Daniels—extolling his merits, yelling hurrahs, and calling him the Hough's Neck Hoodlum. Happily he flexed his muscles at them. A few minutes later he and Henry were wrestling in earnest, surrounded by a crowd who watched them grunting and groaning on an old double-bed mattress that had washed up on the beach last winter and had long since dried out.

Like a kaleidoscope twisted by a madman, the scene changed, and Knotty Pine, entirely naked, was dancing rock and roll with Grandpa Starch. The Princess was singing with King Rose. Jessica Otto and Pierre Grass had disappeared. Susan Otto was the center of a new group who, despite the insistent throb of music from the tape recorder, were mournfully singing "Sweetheart of Sigma Chi." Papa Bonnelli, his pants rolled up, was surf casting, and Thirsty was snoring with his head in Mama Bonelli's lap. Bucky and Penny were still among the missing, and I was both angry and glad that it wasn't I who was being made love to.

I looked at Mendes, who was still sitting beside me, watching the gasser, bemused. "If you are lonesome," I said, speaking my thoughts aloud, "you can kiss me."

He stared at me with a puzzled expression. Darn you anyway, I thought, you don't have to make me appear more stupid than I am. Just kiss me and leave. And he did! He took me in his arms gently, pushed me back into the grass, and gave me a strong, firm kiss.

"Willa," he sighed, as he jumped to his feet. "I wish I had a daughter like you." He skidded down the embankment, shouting back, "Come on kid. It's time for the limbo."

I stuck out my tongue, hating him for a minute. But, of course, he didn't see me.

Mendes no sooner reached the beach than a rocket shooshed by within inches of my head. It climbed into the sky, trailing lacy blue-and-red fire and exploded with three booms that shook the whole island. Two other rockets followed. In the pale blue glare that illuminated the beach and half the harbor, I could see Bucky and Penny Otto setting fire to a fourth one. Laughing hilariously, they beckoned at me to come and help.

Mendes and Mama Bonnelli had climbed on the wreck, had hung the steel pans that Mendes had made around their necks, and, with King Rose playing his guitar and Papa Bonnelli shaking the maracas, were pounding out the pulsing music of the limbo dance. Frank Otto and Pierre Grass had quickly erected two poles about six feet apart with a crossbar between. The bar was about five feet off the deck. Knotty Pine, still unabashedly naked, and Susan Otto had already shimmied themselves underneath it.

When the crossbar is five feet high, it is simply a starting place for the dance. As the limbo progresses, this limbo stick is lowered six inches at a time. While negotiating each trip under the crossbar, the limbo dancer is accompanied by the frenetic singing of his admirers who keep repeating the chrous "Limbo, limbo, limbo like me," together with various verses chanted to the throbbing beat of the drums. As he goes under the bar the dancer must not touch it with any part of his body or clothing. Legs and calves go under first in a spread-eagle shuffling dance, followed by the pelvis, chest, neck, and finally, triumphantly, the dancer's head, as he slowly glides off his ankles and stands erect.

Mendes told me that the dance was originally a primitive sexual invitation. Any woman who dares venture under the

78

cross stick in this posture is certainly offering herself. The trouble is I can never judge, when Mendes is telling me something like that, whether he is concealing a twinkle in his eye. He told me that in some parts of the Carribbean, steel drumming is outlawed because both the participants and the audience get so aroused that they often end up in a sexual orgy. This, Mendes says, was somewhat irritating to their more stolid British caretakers, who had to worry about taxes and government and tourists and other mundane things and so got no fun out of life. That's probably true. Whenever Mendes and Mama Bonnelli play the drums, I can't help myself. My body begins to weave and live a strange uncontrollable life of its own.

First thing I knew, I was on the wreck too. The limbo stick was now only four-and-a-half feet from the deck. It was still possible to get under without losing too much dignity or revealing really private female places to the row of grinning, cheering males who were peering up at us.

Knotty Pine and Susan Otto, evidently realizing that the next time under would require an ultimate female exposure, gaily refused to go under again, despite the prodding and kidding of the men. Since I was wearing jeans, I was only feebly encouraged. I could hear Bucky yelling at me to take off my pants and stop being a coward. At four feet high, I knew that, pants or not, I wasn't about to go under the crossbar; I'd fall on my back for certain.

Suddenly, everyone was yelling for Princess Tassle.

"Come on Princess . . . put up or shut up," Mendes East teased her. He pounded his drum with new abandon.

My mother cooly took King Roses' hand and jumped to the deck. She flicked off her dress so gracefully, it seemed as if she had never been wearing it. With a sinuous movement of her torso, slowly, one by one, she started each of her tassles whirling. While they were spinning, she lithely leaned back, her legs spread in an inverted V, and danced under the bar. She did it so quickly that the men groaned in disappointment and yelled for the limbo stick to be lowered.

She weaved under again at three-and-one-half feet, taking less than a second to pass under the bar. The entire crowd was now singing hoarsely, chanting the limbo, and watching her. The bar was lowered to three feet. For her to get under now without touching would require a slow careful, undulation, plus a tortuous forward movement on her ankles. She would have to both keep her body moving forward, and, at the same time, keep her buttocks and symphysis in a rotary motion—otherwise the tassles would fall limp. Worse, she

79

would also—though it probably would never occur to my mother—present the grinning male populace of Trotter Island with a very unalluring view of herself. At least I thought the view was unalluring. But I guess females don't appreciate the female anatomy the way males do. The men were cheering her on, and the air was charged with a tense, sexual watchfulness. Even I, with tightened throat as I watched her dance, could feel the sexual impact. And yet, now that she was in front of the limbo stick weaving and gyrating, ready to inch under, she was still moving with such feminine grace and ease that she seemed like a swaying flower instead of a woman. .

Suddenly Henry could stand it no longer. "Prin, you cut it out or I'll tan your behind," he yelled hoarsely. The words were no sooner out of his mouth, than the sound of a shotgun blasted over the crowd. There was almost instantaneous silence. Everyone on the beach stared up, amazed at the bobbing angry incarnation of Grandma Starch. Fiercely she waved Henry's gun at the crowd, threatening to fire the next shot directly at all of us.

"You're indaicent," she screamed. "You dirty hussies. . . . Get on your clothes and get out of sight of the Lord afore I bring his judgment upon you. Hurry up, before I shoot every last one of you dead. The Good Lord would thank me for wiping this Sodom and Gomorrah off the earth."

It was two-fifteen in the morning. In less than five minutes the beach was deserted. My Grandma Starch, five-feet-two inches tall, weighing about one-hundred-and-ten pounds had terminated the first gasser of the season.

13

At six-thirty the next morning my Big Ben, which I had wisely set the night before, rang insanely. Sleepily, I punched all the protuberances, finally reducing it to silence. But it had done its job. I remembered it was Friday, and, although it might be embarrassing to face Sawyer, nevertheless he did owe me one hundred dollars for the week. What's more I was now officially Mata Hari for Trotter Island. I was looking forward to finding out what would happen when Herman's Operation Buzz-Off began at the A B C Electronic Corporation. It would be interesting to watch the imperturbable Sawyer Priestly when he was under attack.

I put on a modest cotton dress that flared nicely at my hips. Before I went downstairs I peeked in my parent's bedroom. The Princess was stretched across the bed, a sheet covering her legs. Her behind and back were bare and golden in the sunlight pouring into the room. Her head and one arm dangled over the side of the bed. I wished her a cheery good-morning. She groaned and opened one eye.

"Good morning . . . good night," she muttered. "Do me a favor, Sugar, and close those damned venetian blinds. Your father opened them an hour ago and has been jabbering at me ever since about some hairbrained idea that he and Pierre Grass have cooked up." I pulled the blinds tight, and she sighed sleepily. "That's my honey. You tell your father that he and Pierre Grass will end up in the jug if they're not careful. And I won't use our money to bail them out." She was asleep again when I tiptoed out.

Henry was in the kitchen with Grandma Starch, who was making breakfast for him and taking care of BoBo. Grandma looked none the worse for her Carrie Nation attack on the gasser. She was angrily recounting the horrendous details of the blasphemous dance that Prin had been doing, and her utter disgust at seeing that harlot Knotty Pine, stark naked, dancing with poor helpless Grandpa Starch.

"She was down there, too . . . your only daughter," Grandma Starch said sternly to Henry, who looked at me helplessly. "Your daughter . . . seeing sights that even I, who have been married fifty years, never saw before in my life. Henry Starch, you have let that immoral wife of yours besmirch this innocent child's mind." She poured coffee for me. "I tell you, girl, it was a sinful day that your ma brought you into this world . . . and that dirty old man Abner Thurston beholdin' the whole thing . . . instead of your ma being where she should have been with daicent relatives attending her. I've tried, and you know it, Willa Starch, to make you a God-fearing woman, but now I see it did no good. You've been tempted by the Devil hisself into evil ways."

Henry had been listening glumly to his mother, but, now that I was under attack, he nodded in sage agreement. "Your Grandma is right, Willa. She brought you up to be a lady. There ain't no real ladies on Trotter Island. Mostly just pigs who have knocked around all their lives . . . and don't much give a crap what they say or do. You should forget everything you saw."

Taking my part in the morality play, I opened my eyes in wide, virgin innocence and said to Grandma, "You know, Gram, that I would never behave that way . . . not after living with you and Grampy so long. You know how modest I am."

Grandma shook her head. "You don't fool me, Willa Starch! When that heathen music is playing your blood starts to boil. I've watched you. You take after your ma. Only way to save yourself now is to marry some God-fearin' boy . . . and not that Bucky Bonnelli either. I watched him last summer slouching around and eyeing you as if you were in heat. You need a man who respects woman . . . not the kind that's always trying to undress them."

I'm afraid I blushed. For a minute I wondered if Grandma had followed Bucky and me up to the parade ground. It was a good thing that I hadn't heeded Bucky's suggestion and tried to sneak into my bedroom. I had a sudden vision of Bucky and me in my bed and Grandma pulling the covers off us, shrieking in dismay.

"Are you going to take me to Boston?" I asked Henry, trying to erase the painful picture from my mind. "If I'm supposed to be Trotter Island's Trojan Horse, I can't sit around here neighing."

Henry bought a small trawler last fall just like Pierre Grass's and the Bonnelli's. With his only experience in navigation and seamanship acquired summers at Trotter Island, Henry is a fearless captain. Tides, wind, and weather do not inhibit my father. He has run aground at least three times that I know of, and been nearly swamped in a northeaster when prudent skippers were safe in harbor; but worse than all else is when Henry attempts to bring his boat alongside a pier or wharf. He either charges like a bull and crashes the boat with an ear-splitting thud, or he misses his target completely and, swearing at all and sundry, shifts the engine from forward to reverse with mad abandon. When he has churned up a sea of foam and waves, he still misses the dock by yards. All other mariners run for cover when they see my father coming in his fishing boat.

I was considerably relieved when Henry said that this morning Pierre Grass was taking us to Boston. Henry looked at his watch. "Come on, Pierre will be waitin' for us. We're going to meet a couple of fellows, and I've gotta go to the bank."

We left Grandma changing BoBo's diaper. She was raving that she was going to wake my mother and give the Princess something to think about. Enticing men out of their senses and not taking care of her child . . . why if she weren't here this morning poor little BoBo would have starved to death. The Lord knew what would happen when she went home. She was thinking of reporting the Princess to the Society for the Prevention of Cruelty to Children, and while she was at it she was going to call her good friend Captain Tim Rafferty and have him alert the whole Harbor police department to the antics on Trotter Island.

Henry and I walked along the water's edge to the western end of the island. The morning sun in a clean blue sky toasted the stones on the beach. In the distance we could see Pierre standing on the dock waiting for us. No one else was in sight. Except for the three of us and Grandma, I guessed that the remaining residents of Trotter Island were still asleep. Today there would be no work. The day after a gasser was recovery day. The only activity on the island was provided by the children who could do anything they wished—except make noise—in complete uninhibited freedom.

A lot of people would be nursing big heads. I hoped in particular that Bucky Bonnelli, who had probably drunk more than his share of Thirsty's grappa, was really suffering. Better . . . maybe he was miserably sick . . . throwing up or something. I hoped so. It would serve him right.

"What are you and Pierre Grass up to?" I asked Henry. "How come you are both eager beavers? I thought I'd probably have to shake you out of bed this morning." That reminded me of the Princess's remark. "What does Prin mean that you and Pierre will end up in the jug?"

"She's crazy," Henry snorted. "She's the one who'll end up in jail . . . for indecent exposure. I don't know what I'm gonna do about your ma."

"You're up to something," I persisted. "Who are you meeting? Why are you going to the bank?"

"Pierre and I got a little business deal, that's all," Henry said shiftily. "I ain't free to reveal any details yet."

"You mean it's nobody's business but your own?"

"Well, sort of . . . at the moment," Henry agreed, smiling.

We were aboard Pierre's boat, ready to shove off, when we saw Herman Snole running down the pier, shouting at us to wait for him. Puffing, he jumped aboard. "Don't know why I live on this damned island anyway," he said testily. "Without a boat I'm always begging rides. Who appreciates what I'm doing to save Trotter Island, anyway?"

"You need a wife," Pierre Grass said. "You got a woman . . . she give you big love one minute lotsa what you call it appre-she-ay-shun . . . tells you what a fine fella you are. Then you look at another woman, one second . . . man . . . you a dirty-no-good-son-a-beach."

"Jennie was probably right," Herman said primly. "I saw you slobbering all over Jessica Otto. All of you got so stinking drunk last night that now you don't care what happens to Trotter Island." Herman shook his head sadly and then recalled Grandma Starch. "She was as funny as a broken crutch with that shotgun. If she had caught you humping Jessie she would have peppered your ass, Pierre." Herman grinned nastily. He shouted at Henry so that he could be heard over the noise of the engine. "That wife of yours can sure shake her snatch, Henry. Gets an old bachelor like me having some unusual ideas."

Henry nodded glumly.

As we thundered across the harbor, Herman, ignoring the fact that we could only hear half of what he was saying, reemphasized how valuable his contribution was going to be to the defense of Trotter Island. Right now he was on his way to A B C Electronics on Route 128.

"At lunch time I'll give my girls the first treatment. Then I'll call an emergency meeting at four o'clock, and that's when I really will give them the business. By the time they go home tonight, they'll be mad as hornets. Monday morning, A B C will be closed down."

Herman insisted that Henry and Pierre should come with him. "I'm doing this for Trotter Island. It'll be an interesting experience for you."

Henry looked at Pierre questioningly. "We've got some things we gotta do . . . couple of fellows to meet. It's up to Pierre."

"I don't have to be out to 128 until eleven o'clock," Herman insisted. "I'll wait for you."

I could see that neither Henry nor Pierre were too enthusiastic, but Herman had them trapped.

"Okay," Pierre said finally. He grinned at Herman. "I lak to see Herman give two tousan' women da business."

Henry waved the keys to Prin's yellow Cadillac. "I borrowed the keys to Prin's car. Needs an airing. It's been in the Motor Mart Garage for two weeks."

I could see that this was going to be a day for the Rover Boys. "Don't forget me. I'll be waiting at quarter past five. I'm not planning to swim home." Henry and Pierre assured

84

me that my fears of hanging around Commerical Wharf until midnight would not come to pass.

"Pierre and I are going to be very damned busy tonight. We'll be back here at five o'clock, don't you worry, Willa."

I refused their invitation for coffee and doughnuts, and promised them I would give them a full report on Sawyer's activities.

Pierre guided his boat in between Commercial Wharf and Long Wharf. I guess I must be provincial. I like Boston. Even though the city planners are trying, I don't think Boston can ever become a big city like New York or Chicago or Los Angeles. No Bostonian—not even the Irish, with their newer heritage—can escape the long Puritan arm reaching out of ancient buildings, crooked streets that never can be straightened, cobblestones that break through the tarred surfaces, and weathered burying grounds where the former population —even with their dust—create an atmosphere that reminds one: A penny saved is a penny earned, a stitch in time saves nine, and haste makes waste.

Commercial Wharf was somnolent and ramshackle in the warm sun, heedless of passing time. This morning, after I waved good-bye, I threaded a path to Atlantic Avenue through hip-booted fishermen, truck drivers, ancient boat skippers, and a couple of Bohemian artists who had crawled out of their sail-loft apartments and were joyously trying to capture the mélange on canvas with unyielding modern line and hectic color.

The Custom House Tower, once a lonely sentinel on the skyline, pointed disdainfully into the clear blue sky, defying the new square boxes and cubes of the Government Center and the State Street Bank to equal its poise and character. It watched me, benign and disdainful, as I darted between trucks, crossed Atlantic Avenue, and finally achieved the haven of State Street. Passing under the stanchions of the Central Artery, I made believe for a second that I was in New York City. But even this huge structure of steel and cement, with commuter automobiles roaring north and south, curves in obedience to the vagaries of the harbor and ancient buildings that thrifty Bostonians wouldn't tear down just to make a speedway straight.

Walking by the dusty offices of the coffee brokers and food provisioners, I could see the Old State House, an imperturbable and proper Bostonian, at the far end of the street, quietly observing the early morning traffic and hurrying bustle of a world it never made.

A block to my right the market area and Salem Street were

coming weekend alive with trucks backing into cellar markets, blocking streets, and sidewalks, while their drivers and the market owners, dressed in white aprons and straw hats, supervised the unloading of meat, eggs, poultry, and vegetables with frantic but good-natured determination.

The confusion of the market delights me. I like to walk along the narrow sidewalks ducking boxes and truck tailgates, peering at the stalls, fingering vegetables, listening to the cheerful exhortations to buy, enjoying the earthy smell of curing meat, fresh vegetables, and sawdust, and cool mouldy odors that blow damply out of the open cellar doors. I guess that I have become a familiar sight-seer. The market men—and the truckers and their helpers unloading or dispatching produce from the narrow sidewalks—don't whistle at me as much as they once did. Now they grin, and some of them say "Hi." Someday I'm gonna tell them that my name is Willa Starch and it's a happy moment for me, smiling at them, joyous that they are alive too and are smiling back.

I unlocked Sawyer's office, and it was no different than I had left it last night. I tried to erase the picture of Converse standing by my desk, but instead spent most of the morning thinking about him and Stephanie. I couldn't help it. I just knew that I would be a lot more fun and loving with Converse than that platinum covered birdbrain, Stephanie Billings.

I had seduced Converse for the fifth time when the telephone went into its firealarm routine and scared me right out of a particularly enjoyable embrace. It was Abigail Priestly. Last night Herman Snole had painted a new picture of Abigail for me. I saw her now as a victim of the smooth Sawyer Priestly, more to be pitied than scorned. So I was more cordial to her. Poor thing, she seemed to be anxious to have some one to talk to. Sawyer is so busy, you know, Miss Starch. Working on one committee or another. Ha, I thought, some committees! Anyway it was going to be better, now. They were launching their new forty-foot Chris Craft this weekend. Before the summer was over she was going to make sure that Sawyer invited me out for a Saturday cruise. Cruising with Sawyer reminded me of a joke about getting torpedoed, but I held my tongue and listened unbelievingly. By being cordial I had released the genie from her bottle. Plump Abigail obviously needed a secretary and confidant more than Sawyer. It occurred to me that if all else failed I might be able to enlist Abigail's aid in Operation Buzz-Off. She finally got to the point of the call. Not to worry. Sawyer would arrive in the office before three o'clock with my pay.

"And, my dear," Abigail finally concluded, "it's been so nice talking with you. We must have another real chat one of these days."

I had scarcely put the phone down when it rang again and Miss Smoky purred at me. When I told her that Sawyer wasn't in, the purring changed to a slight snarl. "You tell Sawyer to call me," she said. She sounded peeved.

"Shall I say who called?" I asked in my smoothest ice-cream voice.

"He'll know," she said emphatically.

"I hope so," I answered silkily. "It's so confusing. Some woman called a few minutes ago and wouldn't leave her name, either. It wasn't you was it?"

Miss Smoky didn't reply, but her phone went down with a bang. Sawyer would certainly catch it, now. I chuckled. It was going to be fun messing up his love life.

Since Sawyer wouldn't arrive until three o'clock, I decided to use the time to poke into his files and see if I could find anything that would aid Operation Buzz-Off. The files in the outer office, where my desk is, were filled with a dull collection of letters, real-estate transactions, correspondence with investment companies, and detailed financial statements of hundreds of small companies that I had never heard of. There was nothing pertaining to the A B C Electronic Corporation and only one letter to the Billings & Cabot Development Corporation. This letter was a year old and stated that Sawyer would be in New York to discuss the future marina location. There was another file in Sawyer's office, but it was locked. His desk was unlocked. The only thing I found of interest was in a bottom drawer. It was a book called "Sexual Freedom." In a feminine handwriting inside the cover was written "For Lambie, who knows more about it than this author!" It was signed: "Pussy." I assumed that Sawyer was "Lambie." It made quite a sylvan picture. I could see Pussy and Lambie gamboling together in a sun-flecked forest like two Walt Disney characters.

The book, written by a man named Rene Guyon, looked as if it might contribute to my education. I decided to relax on the old leather couch in Sawyer's office and see what illumination Mr. Guyon might throw on Sawyer's unrestrained id and libido.

I was so sound asleep when Sawyer arrived that I didn't even hear him open the door. He was considerate, too. He let me sleep, enjoying the view, no doubt, of me with my skirt hiked nearly up to my waist and his sex book folded open on my stomach. I awoke, dazed, to Sawyer's voice on the telephone and wished that there was some yogi incantation I could have said that would let an insubstantiate me vanish right out of the office.

There was no way out. I couldn't crawl to the door and run, because I could see through my eyelashes that although Sawyer was talking on the telephone he was watching me with considerable interest.

"I know all about it, Reliance," Sawyer was saying. "If the women walk out we can't make deliveries on that Air Force contract. Snole knows that, too." Pause, while Sawyer listened, evidently to Reliance Cabot. "Of course I don't know what they want. That's your job. You should have had your ear to the ground. Nipped it in the bud." Pause, and then: "Stop fretting, Reliance. It isn't wages. We settled that two months ago. I told you that you should have had a written contract. It would have prevented this kind of thing." Sawyer's voice had a barbed quality to it.

"I told you that you could only have a gentlemen's agreement with *gentlemen*. Snole is a rabble rouser. All right, I'll meet you out there at five-thirty. See that Converse stays. I'll be interested to know what he may have learned at Harvard. Maybe we can get the National Labor Relations Board to put an injunction on Snole." Sawyer put the telephone down and looked quizzically at me. I guess my eyelids were squeezed too tightly together, because after a second he said, "Good afternoon, Miss Starch, did you have a nice rest?"

I sat up quickly, forgetting the book. It slammed to the floor. Trying to collect my wits, I picked it up and, blushing, handed it to him.

"Interesting reading?" he asked.

"Sort of," I admitted. "I'm sorry I fell asleep. I was up late last night."

"You were a sleeping beauty, Miss Starch, I hated to disturb you! The fact is that, if I weren't busy tonight, I would ask you to stay in town. We could have . . . er . . . relaxed a bit together. It's been a strenuous week." He smiled invitingly at me.

I decided to confront him with Trotter Island. "The truth is, Mr. Priestly, when I left here last night, I didn't think that I would come back."

"You mean that my giving you the key to my apartment disturbed you?"

I looked at him blankly. I had forgotten all about the key! What is more I suddenly realized that I had left his darned key in my other pocketbook. Now . . . at the exact moment that I should have handed it back to him, all I could do was mumble that I was shocked about what was happening to the residents of Trotter Island.

"I guess you may not know, Mr. Priestly . . . but my family has lived on Trotter Island every summer, as long as I can remember." My thoughts were in a mad race to figure out a plausible reason for not returning his key. How could I be angry about his giving the key to me and then tell him that I would give it to him Monday? That would sound real crazy.

"Miss Starch, yesterday I didn't know who did or didn't live on Trotter Island." He shrugged. "Last night I was looking over a list of the lessees. Do you happen to be acquainted with a man named Herman Snole?"

I nodded.

"A particularly disagreeable man," Sawyer said. "Frankly, Miss Starch, I was interested to learn about your mother. It explains your magnetism, somewhat. I understand she has retired. An era has passed. Too bad. But then we have to grow up. Maybe American men are learning to appreciate their beautiful women as something more than an interlude between smutty jokes."

"I'm not ashamed of my parents," I said angrily. "But I am shocked at the high-handed way that your Billings & Cabot Development Corporation is evicting people from their homes." I decided that by this time there was no point in resurrecting the key. I would put it on his desk Monday, and that would be that.

"We are not evicting anyone," Sawyer said coolly. "We simply increased their rent as an economic necessity. You are a woman, Miss Starch . . . and young. Possibly you don't fully grasp these things. To be perfectly honest with you, I would scarcely call Trotter Island the kind of environment that a well-educated young woman would enjoy. I should guess that your mother and father have accumulated sufficient money so that they could retire to a modest home in the suburbs. Trotter Island is really not much better than a Boston Tobacco Road."

It irked me to hear Sawyer moralize about my environment when, probably in his next breath, he would try to seduce me. I answered him in a very arch voice. "I prefer Trotter Island, Mr. Priestly, to living in a prim little house next door to prim little people whose house looks just like mine and whose sole occupation in the summer is mowing lawns and having back yard barbecues, and maybe one ginger ale highball. After which they goose each other, tell a few dirty jokes, and wish they dared do what the residents of Trotter

Island just do naturally!" There you are. That proves I never know when to keep my mouth shut!

Sawyer simply looked at me approvingly. "I agree with you, Miss Starch. Such a life would be a living death. On a somewhat more expensive scale, my wife pursues such ends. Oh, we don't mow our own lawn, and I employ an excellent cook who can be persuaded occasionally to barbecue for us outdoors, but essentially it adds up to the same thing. But, you take the people living on Trotter Island. Really they contribute nothing to the world one way or the other. If the rent increase forces them to move, they will shift their debris and clutter to some other island in the harbor. Or end up living on the city's charity."

"I know," I said bitterly. "I've read about philosophers like you. Your theories were tried by royalty. 'Let 'em eat cake,' Rousseau's Princess said to the peasants starving for bread. It made the Herman Snole of those days pretty mad, too. You better watch out, Mr. Priestly. The people on Trotter Island may not be very smart, but they can be very belligerent."

Sawyer chuckled. I didn't like his intense look. "You should be careful, Miss Starch," he said thoughtfully. "With your fiery eyes and your hair a little mussed from sleeping, you are quite provocative."

I gasped and belatedly tried to capture a more maidenly dignity.

"You are quite delightfully feminine, Miss Starch. But purely in the realm of logic, if you will check some of the files in the front office, you will find careful studies of Newport, California, and Chesapeake Bay. Marinas in these areas have not only recaptured valueless land, but tripled property values for surrounding communities. What we plan for Trotter Island will benefit many more people than it will hurt and, as a by-product of our efforts, those of your Trotter Island friends who are industrious will have increased opportunities for employment."

"What about the residents of Trotter Island who are just plain lazy?" I asked.

Sawyer looked at me puzzled.

"Some people *have* to be lazy, Mr. Priestly. There isn't enough money in the world for everybody to be millionaires."

"Water and human beings always seek their own level, Miss Starch."

Sawyer ignored my "ugh" at his platitude. He looked at his watch and handed me an envelope. "Here's your salary, Miss

90

Starch. I really think we have a great deal in common. I would enjoy pursuing this discussion with you. Unfortunately, I must be out at the A B C Electronic Corporation in less than an hour."

When he had gone, I couldn't help smiling. Water wasn't seeking its own level at A B C. It was getting ready to boil over. Locking the office door I cautioned myself to be very careful not to pursue any arguments with Sawyer. I might still be trying to win as I unwittingly climbed into bed with him.

14

Since it was only quarter-to-five, I decided that Henry and Pierre could wait for me instead of me waiting for them. I took my time and walked around through the market. With my hundred dollars I felt bounteous and rich as any Cabot or Priestly. I bought two huge honeydew melons and, at one of the meat markets, a steak two inches thick. I knew that Henry would be delighted.

The Princess doesn't care much about eating. She is a nibbler. If planning for the weekend meals were left in her hands, by Sunday afternoon we would be lucky to find a jar of peanut butter in the house. Grandma belongs to another era and the ritual of a big Sunday dinner. While she might not get to Mass this Sunday, neither she nor Grandpa would feel that the week had properly culminated unless Sunday at approximately one o'clock a table groaning with a huge pork or ham or pot roast, surrounded by boiled onions, steamed carrots, and heaps of mashed potatoes and gravy, were personally served by Grandpa from the head of the table. The steak would be wildly extravagant in Grandma's eyes, on a par with roast beef or turkey. And when she finished cooking it would be a half inch piece of tough leather. But at least I would have made my propitiation to the gods for a peaceful weekend.

When I finally got to Commercial Wharf, staggering with

two big bags of groceries, it was almost six o'clock. I expected that Henry and Pierre might be exasperated, but at least would be waiting. Not only weren't they waiting, but Pierre's boat was gone. I walked slowly to the end of the wharf examining all the boats, wondering if they might have moved Pierre's to another berth.

Unbelievingly, as I passed the wharf apartments, I saw Bucky Bonnelli calmly staring in one of the eye-level windows. A century ago, the buildings on Commercial Wharf were used for mending sails and fishnets, but now they are divided into tiny apartments occupied by writers, artists, doctors, and a few middle-aged suburbanites who, daring all by moving into a less trammeled environment, hoped to revive the halcyon days of Greenwich Village.

At the end of the wharf I stared out into Boston Harbor, but Pierre's boat was nowhere in sight. Dismaying as the prospect was, it was evident that I was going to have to interrupt Bucky's voyeur session. When I walked back on the wharf he was still staring in the window, oblivious to the world, a six-foot, handsome male with wide shoulders, snugly clothed in a T-shirt, and small buttocks in skin-tight, faded blue jeans. He was wearing rubber fisherman boots. This time a second sense must have alerted him because he turned and waved excitedly at me.

"Hey, Willa, come here and take a look at this!"

"No, thanks," I said. "I'm not a Peeping Tom. I just want to know if you've seen my father and Pierre."

Reluctantly, Bucky left the window. "I can't figure it out," he said bemused.

"Okay, I'm nibbling. What can't you figure out?" If I humored him, I thought I might find out what had become of Henry and Pierre.

"It's like this, see," Bucky said. "Your old man and Pierre have gone back to Trotter. They left me here to wait for you. So it got boring . . . goofing up and down the pier. I started looking in windows to see how these rich slobs live. I looked in three windows. Nothing. Then . . . what do you know? Jackpot! A dame! Sound asleep on a couch, facing the wall. Naked as a bird. Her ass looked like a soft round pear ready to be bitten." Bucky shrugged. "Who could help staring?"

"I could," I said. "I'm not interested in any woman's behind."

Bucky grinned. "Well, to tell you the truth, after looking at it for fifteen minutes I lost a little interest. Curious, though."

"What's curious?" I said, finally shoving my grocery bags

in his arms. It was obvious that he wasn't going to offer to hold them if I listened for an hour.

"A few minutes ago I got impatient. I wondered if maybe she was dead. Was about time she turned over, I figured . . . so I knocked on the window."

I'm afraid I looked at Bucky astonished. Somehow, his complete self-confidence needed puncturing.

"You didn't ask what happened," he asked leering at me.

"I wasn't interested." Bucky looked chagrined. He expected me to continue playing end man. "Okay, what happened?"

"She turned over. A few minutes before you walked up here, this babe turned over. Without a damned thing on she just lay there and stared back at me. She's probably still there. Come on and take a look."

"No, thanks," I said. "When she saw you ogling her she thought it was a maniac. She was probably petrified. Afraid that if she moved you'd come shattering through the window, panting at her with your tongue hanging out like a mad dog."

"Aw, Willa," Bucky groaned, "I'm not that bad."

"That's your opinion. Where is my father?"

Bucky chuckled. "It's a long story. Come on, Henry and Pierre are going to meet us in the Blue Ship Tearoom. I'll treat you to a beer while we are waiting and tell you about the cruise you and I are going on."

Reluctantly, I followed Bucky up the wooden stairs that led to the tearoom. The low-ceiling restaurant commands an excellent view of the harbor. Sitting near a window, I watched a flock of sea gulls following a returning fishing boat and tried to shake the heavy feeling from my eyelids. I was so sleepy that I could scarcely follow Bucky's incoherent babbling. Tonight, I promised myself I would go to bed early and prove to Grandma Starch that I really was a good girl.

"So I told your old man, all right, if Willa comes along to keep me company, I'd go. Otherwise to hell with it."

"Go? Go where?" I slowly became aware that I was involved in whatever Bucky was chattering about.

Bucky looked at me patiently. "I told you. Pierre and your old man are picking up some cargo tonight off a freighter bound for Canada."

"What's that got to do with me? I'm not taking any harbor cruise. What do you want me to do? Give you all a bon voyage party?" I lifted my beer glass and toasted him. "All you men . . . go! Go and have men fun! I am going to bed early."

Bucky sighed. "Look, Henry and Pierre have gone to Trotter to pick up some clothes for you."

"Some clothes for me?"

"You know . . . your jeans, a sweater. You can't go forty miles out to sea in high heels, stockings, and a panty girdle."

"I don't care what Penny Otto wears," I said disgreeably. I could feel the sudden lift of the beer. "I don't want to wear a girdle. And I'm not going forty miles to sea in a fishing boat with you or anyone else. You all must be crazy. What is this cargo, anyway? Gold?" I guess I must have raised my voice. There was only one other couple in the tearoom, but Bucky warned me to be quiet.

"For God's sake, Willa. Keep your voice down. Do you want your old man to spend his declining years in the jug?"

"If my mother can't stop Henry from whatever he is doing, I certainly can't. You've got a nerve to involve me. Especially after last night. I wouldn't be caught dead with you."

"Aw, Willa, I thought it might be like a honeymoon," Bucky said wistfully. "There are two bunks in Pierre's boat. While your old man and Pierre are piloting, we could snuggle down in one of them. They won't need me until they get there. Pierre's boat only makes a few knots an hour so it will take most of the night. It'll be real cozy."

"Bucky Bonnelli . . . you must be insane. I'm not going to let myself get confined with you . . . anywhere!"

"I know. You got your period. But we could at least neck a little."

"You can neck with Penny Otto," I grimaced. "Or do anything else with her that you feel like!"

Bucky pounded the table delightedly. "You're jealous! I'll be damned. I awoke the woman in you at last. Willa Starch is jealous."

I glared at him. What an egomaniac! I wasn't jealous, but it was obvious that no amount of argument would convince him. "Get it through your head, Bucky, I'm not going anywhere with you."

Henry and Pierre were walking toward our table with a waitress in tow. "Bring us all fried clams," Henry told her. He plunked a bottle down on the table. "And bring us four glasses with ice, and don't give me any of that guff that I can't bring my own liquor." The waitress left shaking her head dubiously. "There it is, Willa, my girl, Old Robbie. The finest twelve-year-old Scotch that money can buy. Old Robbie Burns Scotch is gonna solve some of our problems." Henry was speaking with a Scottish burr. I could tell by his exuberance that several jiggers of Old Robbie were already coursing in his blood stream.

"Will someone please explain to me what this is all about?" I demanded. "Daddy, have you gone off your rocker? What kind of promise have you made Bucky? Does Prin know that you are throwing your only daughter at this wolf? What would she think?"

"She thinks you better come with us," Henry mumbled, embarrassed for a moment. The waitress brought glasses with ice, and Henry filled four of them half full. "Taste it," he urged me. "This stuff is so smooth you can drink it straight."

"You'd even stoop to getting me drunk," I accused him, as I took a surreptitious swallow. I gasped and tears came to my eyes. "You call that smooth?"

"You gotta pave the road," Pierre grinned. "Try another. No bumps now."

I did, and it didn't taste so horrible this time.

"Da Princess say: Henry . . . Pierre you big damn fools. If you go, take ma petite. She got da brains for all of you. She tell your father, Henry . . . if your dot-ter say, okay. Okay, then it ain't stealin'." Pierre patted my arm happily. "Bon Dieu. You come. We gotta mask-got."

"He means mascot," Bucky advised.

Slowly I extracted the story. Somewhere forty miles at sea, at one or two a.m. tomorrow morning, a freighter of South American registry travelling from Glasgow and destined for Montreal would rendezvous with Pierre's boat. In addition to its regular cargo were two hundred cases of Old Robbie Scotch which were not listed on the manifest. Twenty-four hundred bottles available for a daring mariner at a price of one dollar a bottle. Still better, this would be a regular monthly occurrence, with absolutely no risk. A good friend of Pierre's personally knew the Captain of the freighter, and this good friend of Pierre's would buy the Scotch, at a considerable profit to Henry and Pierre, tomorrow night at Trotter Island. It was the perfect solution to Pierre's economic problems as well as those of the other impecunious residents of Trotter Island.

"It ain't as if we are stealing," Henry assured me, as he munched on his fried clams. "We just gonna be the middleman. The Billings & Cabot Development Corporation have forced us to do it so we can pay the hijacking price they want for their leases."

"You've got enough money to pay for your own lease," I said.

"Sure," Henry agreed, "but I ain't got enough money to pay *all* the leases. I might have once, but now I ain't got a regular source of income. When I was young I gave the sweat off my. . . ." Henry looked at me apologetically. "Well, you know what I mean. I paid Uncle Sam plenty of dough. All we're gonna do now is take a little back. Whatever is left over from selling the booze we'll put into a war chest for Operation Buzz-Off. Why, right now Herman Snole needs some money to pay pickets. His girls are willing to walk out, but they are bashful about walking up and down in front of A B C Electronics." Henry chuckled. "It won't matter, there's always some characters hanging around Trotter Island be damned glad to picket A B C so long as we can pay 'em a few bucks."

"You'll be smuggling and cheating. The Internal Revenue men won't like it. Who's putting up the money to buy this liquor, anyway?" I knew darn well that it was Henry, and I knew, in my place, the Princess would make him confess.

Henry looked sheepish. "No one's got any money except me. I'm advancing twenty-four hundred dollars. Don't you worry. I'll get it back."

"Don't fret, ma petite," Pierre reassured me. "Imagine. Only one dollar a bottle for this leeker magnifique. And tomorrow night, mon ami, he buy da whole damn ting for six thousand dollars. Two-feefty a bottle. You know how much dis Old Robbie cost wholesale with da taxes? Five seventy-five!"

"If you get caught you'll all go to jail."

But nothing I could say would shake their resolve. Sip by sip of Old Robbie they were gaining new confidence. I was determined not to get mixed up with them. "Why do I have to go? I won't be any help. You can drop me off at Trotter Island."

"You can drop me off, too," Bucky said ignoring the startled expressions of Henry and Pierre. "Papa's got enough money saved to pay the lease on our house for the next couple of years. If Willa isn't going with you, to hell with it—neither am I."

Pierre groaned. "We need Bucky to help move the stuff."

"A case of Old Robbie weighs nearly fifty pounds," Henry explained. "We gotta get it off the freighter fast and get back to Trotter Island before the Coast Guard spots us."

Bucky grinned at me expectantly. I knew that he was just pig-headed enough not to go with them unless I agreed to come. I gave him a nasty look. He was too happy at how easily I had been trapped.

"All right. I'll go. But not to please you, Bucky Bonnelli. Only to help save Trotter Island."

15

On the way out of Boston Harbor past the Boston Lighthouse and the Brewster Islands, I sat on the stern and listened while Henry, Pierre, and Bucky argued about a correct compass course that would assure our meeting with the freighter. As the land slowly disappeared from sight, the waves turned blacker. Pierre's boat started to roll and lurch. The western sky was a rosy glow. Ahead of us was dark cold night and the first twinkling stars. I shivered both from the cold and slight nausea. Stepping on imaginary eggs, my stomach full of undigested clams, I slowly worked my way forward hanging onto the rail.

Pierre had not turned on his port and starboard running lights. The three men had become ominous black shadows clustered around the wheel. They talked in whispered monotones; feeling small and alone, perhaps, and lost in the vast impenetrable night. I wondered if Pierre really knew where he was going. Maybe we were a lost boat that any moment now would plunge over the edge of the world.

I opened the cabin door and peered into the gloom. Henry told me that the Princess had put my jeans and a heavy sweater in a paper bag.

"Will some one light the lantern for me?" I asked. "I think I better change."

"No lights," Pierre said. "Bettah in the dark. Coast Guard not see us, eh? Ask where we go. What we do."

That sounded sensible. I poked around in the dark cabin trying to locate my jeans. Bucky followed me in.

"I don't need your help, thanks. You can just go back outside."

"I'm not bothering you," Bucky said. "Go ahead and change. It's so dark, I can't see you anyway."

He waited until I got my dress off, and then he grabbed me.

"You said that you would leave me alone," I gasped angrily.

"No, I didn't," he chuckled, and tried to pull the shoulder strap on my bra down. "I just told you that I couldn't see you."

I felt his hand on my belly, and then on my fanny. "I still can't see you, Willa . . . but you sure feel good!"

The boat suddenly lurched. I caught the edge of the bunk, and at the same time gave Bucky a good shove. He lost his balance and crashed against the table in the center of the tiny cabin. Henry opened the door and searched the cabin with his flashlight.

"What's going on?" he muttered, looking at Bucky in a heap on the floor.

"Your daughter knocked me down, Henry," Bucky said disgruntled. "She ain't no lady. You brought her up to be a female wrestler."

Henry thought that was very funny.

I asked Henry what time it was. "It's only nine-thirty. We're making about six knots against headwinds. Pierre says we ought to be there about one o'clock. We may have to hang around."

"If no one minds, and Bucky Bonnelli will get out of here, I think I will lie down. I'm really tired and I feel a little uckish."

Reluctantly Bucky picked himself up and went out with the men. I slid into my jeans and pulled on a heavy white turtleneck sweater that I had knitted during psych lectures last winter. I lay limply on the bunk. The boat was rocking violently. In the trough of the waves it wallowed for a second and then crested on the next wave and repeated the performance. I had to concentrate in earnest to keep the fried clams down and travelling in the right direction.

I awoke suddenly with the realization that I had not only fallen asleep but was babbling some nonsense about Converse Cabot.

I opened my eyes and looked into Bucky's. He grinned at me. "You've been snoring like an old sow," he whispered. "You were mumbling something like 'Please, Converse, please not now.' Were you having an erotic dream?" Bucky patted my cheek solicitously. "You know, Willa, with your mouth wide open and your jaw sagging, I don't think Converse would appreciate you."

Sitting up in the bunk I tried to get my bearings. I pushed Bucky's hands away from my middle and discovered that he had unzipped the zipper on my jeans. Henry and Pierre, oblivious to Bucky and me, were sitting in the cabin playing gin rummy by the light of a wheezing gasoline lantern that rocked back and forth over their heads.

The dream I had been having about Converse suddenly being sorry that he had deserted me for Stephanie had probably been caused by Bucky calmly fooling around with me within a few feet of my father.

"You're no better than a necrophiliac, Bucky Bonnelli!" I hissed at him. I hastily zipped the jeans over my exposed belly, caught a hair, yelped, and finally succeeded in refastening myself.

"I was just looking over the situation," Bucky said imperturbably. "You really look kind of pretty down there, Willa."

I wanted to bite him or shove a dagger in his chest. What nerve!

"Have a good sleep, Willa?" Henry asked. If my father had been paying any attention to what had been going on he gave absolutely no sign. "You've been out like a light for nearly three hours."

I shoved Bucky aside and looked at Henry's wristwatch. It was true. It was one fifteen. "Where's the freighter we are supposed to meet?" I asked.

Henry shrugged. "Anytime, now. We're where it's supposed to be. Pierre's tied the wheel. We are travelling very slowly in a huge circle."

Pierre slammed down his cards with a triumphant "Gin! Come on," he said. "We signal again."

Outside he took a long-barrelled instrument that looked like a rifle. He sighted over the stern of the boat and flicked the trigger. It was an Army signalling flashlight that blinked with a red light. The subdued throb of the idling engine and the slap of the prow against the rolling waves was the only sound. We strained to locate some response in the felt black night. There was nothing.

"A wild-goose chase," I said nervously. "Let's go home."

I had scarcely said the words when we heard the pounding beat of huge Diesel engines and saw over our starboard bow, not five hundred feet away, the ominous black outline of a freighter bearing down on us.

Yelling, Pierre grabbed the wheel of his boat and pushed his throttle up to full speed. Bucky blew on a fog horn. Henry frantically flicked the signalling light at the ship. Whoever was at the helm of the freighter seemed to be completely unaware of us. The little speed that we could muster, instead of getting us out of the way, seemed to be bringing us directly into the course of the ship. I could see, and then actually hear, the white froth of the water slapping against the prow of the freighter. We were going to be hit! I screamed, and the silly thought crossed my mind that now, after twenty-two years, I was going to die futilely . . . a virgin.

Then, suddenly, the freighter changed course and gave a weak toot of its whistles. Its engines quieted to a slow chug and finally stopped completely.

Bucky continued to blow his fog horn until Henry grabbed him by the shoulder and said, "I think they've seen us."

We inched alongside the freighter and Henry threw our bumpers over the side. Only a few lights were visible on the ship, but those revealed a dirty hull covered with orange rust spots. A few of the crew leaned over the side and watched us silently. When we were close enough they tossed ropes, which Henry and Bucky caught and fastened to our bow and stern.

About fifteen feet above us a bearded man wearing a braided Captain's hat leaned over the rail of the freighter and demanded to know what we were doing in the middle of the ocean.

"You nearly ran us down, you hambone!" Bucky yelled at him. "Where did you get your papers?"

"Ah, ye must be the noisy lad blowing that damned fog horn." The bearded one spoke with a thick Scottish accent. "Ye want to alert all the shipping for miles around, hey?"

We could hear him giving orders to the crew. A thick rope net was lowered. "Climb in all of ye. We'll tug you aboard."

"I'll wait here," I said to Henry. But when Pierre, Bucky, and Henry stood in the middle of the rope netting waiting to be hauled aboard the freighter, the bearded one yelled, "Come noo, I want all of ye! Let's take a good look at that lassie wearin' pants. Haven't seen a woman with pants or without pants in nearly a month."

I could hear the crew chuckle. "You did this to me." I said to Henry. "My own father using his daughter for bait."

As we swung through the air I felt more like a hooked fish than bait. Clinging to the sides of the rope netting we were pulled up slowly until we were about ten feet above the deck of the freighter. The bearded Captain left us dangling for several minutes while he inspected us, a happy grin on his round face. When he finally gave the order to have us lowered we dropped to the deck in a confused heap. We finally extricated ourselves. Henry, red with anger, told the bearded Captain that for two cents he'd toss him over the side of the freighter, and his crew after him. Then, Henry suddenly stopped blustering. The Captain, from hip level, was calmly pointing a forty-five revolver in our direction. Two more of his crew ambled out of the shadows. One of them held a machine gun aimed casually at us.

"My name is McTare. Captain Harry McTare," the bearded one said, staring at me with unconstrained interest. "Ye will excuse the precautions, but when ye pick strangers out of the sea at this time of night it pays to be careful. Where are ye bound?"

I was beginning to wonder if this was the freighter we were supposed to meet. Henry and Pierre looked doubtful, too.

"We heard there's fish runnin' out here," Henry said.

McTare looked at him carefully for a moment. "What are ye using for bait?"

"Green clams," Bucky said, staring insolently at McTare.

"How many green clams ye got?"

"Twenty-four hundred," Henry said catching the drift of the conversation.

McTare asked who was the Captain of our boat.

"Moi, je suis le capitaine. But he gave us da bait," Pierre said pointing at Henry.

"Ye two will come to my cabin," McTare said gesturing at Henry and me. He grinned at me. "I heard ye call him father. Maybe your daddy will sign ye aboard. We lost our cook in Trinidad. Harry McTare wouldna' make a lass like ye work too hard, and the wages are good."

"She's my girl, McTare," Bucky Bonnelli said cooly. "Keep your greedy eyes off her. She isn't going anywhere with you. She stays right here."

I smiled at Bucky gratefully. At the moment he seemed to be the lesser evil.

"If that young man gives ye any trouble, Blister, fill him full of shot and toss his carcass over the stern," McTare said to the crewman who was carrying the machine gun. Blister, a long scar on his unshaven face, nodded agreeably.

Bucky angrily shouted at McTare that he wouldn't get away with this. McTare ignored him. He told Henry and me to follow another member of the crew, who led us forward and up steel ladders to McTare's cabin. As we climbed to the upper deck I made the mistake of looking back and caught McTare's glance. He grinned. I knew that he had been carefully watching my rear as I climbed the ladder. I don't remember whether it was the beard or his red-rimmed eyes, but McTare's gaze was hypnotic. He gave me the shivery feeling that he owned me.

Compared to the outside of the rusty old freighter, McTare's quarters were luxurious. Panelled in dark mahogany, with heavy leather chairs and a mahogany desk that was littered with maps and books, the cabin was steeped with the heady male odor of tobacco and liquor.

McTare wasted no time. He told the crewman called Birdie to wait outside, and then he turned to Henry, the revolver still in his hand. "Okay, Mister, let's see the color of your clams!"

Uneasily, Henry took out his billfold. He slowly counted out twenty-four one-hundred-dollar bills, placing them in a neat pile on the desk. McTare watched him, picking up each bill, scrutinizing it carefully and then placing it back in the pile.

"Clams is a very good name for them. They keep their mouths shut." McTare said reflectively. He opened the cabin door and said to Birdie, who was standing outside, "Take this man back to his friends. Tell Blister to release the cargo to them. The lass will stay here with me while they load it."

Henry eagerly started for the door.

"Daddy," I wailed, suddenly really frightened. "You aren't going to leave me here *alone* with him?"

"He has no choice," McTare said chuckling. He pushed Henry out the door into Birdie's custody. "Now don't ye worry, lass. No harm will come to ye. It'll take yer Daddy and his friends more'n an hour to load their boat. No need for ye to be setting out there in the damp night air when ye can be in here nice and comfortable with Harry McTare."

He edged me toward a leather couch. His hand strayed slowly across my behind. I didn't know whether to flip in girlish dismay or ignore him. I could hear Henry and Birdie as they clanged across the metal floor plates of the bridge. Finally, the echo of their footsteps stopped and they were gone. The distant sound of voices at the far end of the ship made the sudden silence in McTare's cabin even more intense.

I stood awkardly, the backs of my knees against the edge of the couch, unable to move further away from McTare without sitting down.

"Ye have a bonnie behind, my girl," McTare said, grinning at me. "I canna keep my eyes off it. Nothing I like better in this world than a good strong ass on a woman. Noo, I don't usually care verra much for pants on a female, but those pants ye are wearin' really help gie a man a verra good idea of what he may be gettin'."

McTare's round cheerful face came close to mine as he talked. I finally had no choice to avoid him but to slump down on the leather couch. He immediately sat down beside me. I wondered how I might get him off the subject of my fanny into more prosaic avenues of discussion.

"This is a nice cabin you have," I said. "Have you been at sea many years?"

"Too many years," McTare sighed. "It's no life for a man. Here I am near onto thirty-five years, and no woman anywhere cares whether Harry McTare be alive or dead." He stood up and from a decanter on his desk poured two half glasses of whiskey. Without asking whether I wanted it or not he put one of the glasses in my hand. "Drink it, lass. It will ease your fears."

I took a sip. I remembered the flavor. It was Old Robbie. At least, now I was reasonably sure that Henry and Pierre were on the right boat. Quietly, I put my glass down on a table. I wasn't drinking Old Robbie within a half mile of Harry McTare.

He looked a little disappointed. I told him that I wasn't used to drinking strong liquor, which was true enough.

"To return to the subject of your fair behind, girl. I hope ye won't be thinking me discourteous for discussing it. In ancient times ye know, contests were often held, with nary a bit of shame, to determine which maid might have the fairest posterior." He paused and looked at me speculatively. "I suppose ye might be disconcerted if I asked ye to drop ye pants and let Harry McTare take a look at your ass and enjoy its pristine splendour for a moment."

I agreed with him. I would be disconcerted.

He picked up one of Henry's hundred-dollar bills and waved it at me. "Would be worth one of these fair green papers to me, girl. What do you say to that?"

I would say that Harry McTare had a behind fetish. Maybe even steatopygic desires. But I had sense enough not to say it . . . just think it. McTare had now finished one glass of Old Robbie and was starting on another. He looked at me with shining eyes. I wondered if I ran for it . . . if I could make the door.

"Lass," he whispered excitedly. "Those big round eyes of yours looking at me so sweet and innocent is raising my blood pressure. I think I need to let the steam out of my petcock."

Not with my help, I thought. I wiggled away from him, but he kept moving closer until he had me cornered against the arm of the couch. "Come, my bonnie girl, if ye'll roll in the sack with me for an hour, I'll give ye the whole twenty-four hundred dollars!"

"You mean that you'd give me twenty-four hundred dollars just to make love to me?" My ego just couldn't help responding. I had heard about hundred dollar a night girls. Harry McTare evidently thought I was twenty-four times better. It seemed like easy money. Certainly a better offer than Sawyer Priestly had made me. For a demure, modest-appearing girl, I was beginning to think I must have a fatal attraction for older men.

"Ay, girl, I'd gie ye more than twenty-four hundred dollars. Let your Daddy and boyfriend take their whiskey and ye come with me to Canada. Money means nothing to Harry McTare when it comes to enjoying a woman with a good behind." He grabbed me and kissed me smackingly, his bristling whiskers a forest against my face. "Come on, girl . . . take the money," he whispered huskily. "Let's get to it . . . time's a wastin."

"I've got to pee-pee!" I said pulling away from him. I did have to, too. The thought of jumping in bed with Harry McTare was giving my bladder goose pimples.

"By God, I like that!" McTare guffawed. "A real honest-to-God normal woman with normal functions!" He opened the door to a tiny bathroom. "There's the head, my lass. Sit ye doone on it and Harry McTare will watch ye while ye take a piss!"

"Thanks just the same. I can't go when anyone is looking." I slammed the door in his face. Luckily there was an inside lock. I twisted it with a huge sigh of relief. I wasn't going to leave Harry McTare's bathroom until Henry or Bucky came to rescue me.

I pulled my jeans down and was contentedly enjoying my privacy when I heard a chuckle. I turned my head and looked into the shining eyes of Harry McTare staring at me through the grille of a ventilator just above my head.

"I saw it, my lass!" he exulted. "And she's a beauty!"

16

Bucky and Henry rescued me. It wasn't really a dashing rescue. By the time they had finished loading Pierre's boat I had been cornered in the tiny bathroom for nearly an hour with Harry McTare sighing gustily at me through the ventilator about the salubrious results of bedding down with him. It must have been frustrating for him, because every few minutes he would stop talking, and I could hear him pour some more Old Robbie into his glass. While I refused to engage in a discussion with him, proving at least that I was learning a little from experience, I couldn't help wondering what it would be like to have that bushy face tickling me. Like making love to a gorilla. But the old maid who lives with me helped keep my curiosity in strict control.

When Bucky and Henry finally burst indignantly into the cabin and demanded to know where I was, Harry McTare, quite inebriated, slumped on his leather couch, stared at them with a stricken look. "Take your virgin daughter and get to hell out of here," I heard him say to Henry.

I emerged from the bathroom, looking a little sheepish. Bucky scowled like a cuckolded husband.

McTare's parting words were: "And buy the lass some decent pants. That behind of hers be tempting enough to drive a God-fearin man to ruin."

As we were lowered back into Pierre's boat Henry agreed vociferously. "That man was right, Willa, You're getting more like your ma every day, showing every damn thing you own. I don't want to see you wearin those jeans anymore."

I didn't have time to protest. We no sooner found footing on Pierre's boat amidst cases of Old Robbie piled five and six high than there was a tremendous commotion on the freighter, and Harry McTare was leaning over the side shouting for us to come back.

Luckily, McTare's crew had cast us off. Pierre started the engine and we pulled rapidly away, the shouts receding behind us. A couple of machine-gun bullets whizzed over our heads, and then we were out of range.

"What did you do to that man, Willa?" Henry marvelled. "I never saw anyone so aroused."

"I didn't do a darn thing," I said indignantly. "And I'll thank you to forget the whole matter. It's all your fault anyway for leaving me to a wolf like that."

It was several hours later before I found out what had made Harry McTare so angry. The sky had slowly turned grey in the west and the sun had arisen, a blazing red ball in the east. The freighter was nowhere in sight. Pierre's boat was wallowing horribly. I sprawled across four or five cases of Scotch, hoping either to throw up once and for all, or else on the next crest of a wave just to slide miserably into the dull grey sea and vanish forever. The boat, under the weight of ten thousand pounds of Old Robbie, was riding only a few inches above the water, and I was leaving a trail of fried clams in our wake.

Bucky took me by the shoulders and tried to pull me to a sitting position. He shoved something under my nose that smelled sickeningly of garlic. It was one of Mama Bonnelli's salami sandwiches! "Come on, Willa, even if it kills you eat something. Best cure in the world for seasickness."

"You're a monster," I gasped. "Go away, or I'll puke right on you." The boat was pitching wildly. Lying on the Old Robbie, I was hypnotized by the following sea, made rough and choppy by a damp easterly wind that was blowing behind us. It seemed to me that Pierre's boat was riding lower than it had been. We were slowly settling into the sea. One wave washing over the stern would send us and two hundred cases of Scotch down to Davy Jones. The way I felt, I didn't give a damn.

Bucky put his arm around me. I buried my face in his heavy woolen sweater. "What did that guy, McTare, try to do to you?" he demanded into my ear.

How's that for consideration? I was dying of seasickness and Bucky starts probing my morals. "He tried to do just what you are always trying to do," I managed to say without retching. "He tried to get into my pants."

Bucky looked at me, shocked. "That's vulgar for a girl to say," he said emphatically.

Men are funny. They reserve earthy appraisals for themselves. "Anyway," I said, "at least he didn't try to get it for nothing, like you do. He offered me twenty-four hundred dollars. How do you like that?" I hoped that would really shock Bucky. Surprisingly, it didn't. He looked at me craftily and took his billfold out of his pocket. "I'll give you twenty-four hundred dollars for that privilege!" He fanned across a pile of one hundred dollar bills neatly folded in his wallet.

So it was I who was shocked, and it wasn't from having the same offer twice in the same day. "Bucky, you stole Mc-Tare's money! That's why he was shooting at us!"

"I didn't *steal* it. I just took it off the stupid jerk's desk. He was so crocked he didn't even see me."

Oh, brother. This was something. From my short acquaintance with Harry McTare I didn't believe that he would let Henry get away with two hundred cases of Old Robbie for nothing. "He'll come after you," I said, forgetting that I was seasick. I had a vision of Harry McTare landing on Trotter Island, running after me, demanding "my bonnie behind" in exchange for the money Bucky had stolen. "You better tell Henry and Pierre that after Harry McTare arrives in Canada he's going to come gunning for them. Just you wait," I warned Bucky. "As far as I'm concerned, Billings and Cabot can have Trotter Island. I'm leaving. You are all going to be up to your ears in trouble."

But it was too late to tell Henry and Pierre. They were both quite drunk. As soon as they were safely away from the freighter, they had opened one of the cases of Scotch. The first bottle of Old Robbie had long since disappeared and they were on their second. I guessed that Bucky also had had more than one swallow. My warning about Harry McTare didn't seem to faze him at all. I could smell his ripe-apple breath and suddenly felt his hands probing under my sweater, fumbling at my breasts.

"Christopher Joe," I said angrily, trying not to swear. "I'm fed up with men. You're worse than Harry McTare. Here I am one foot away from death, practically inside-out from throwing up, and you're trying to feel me up."

"Cheer up, Willa. We're almost home." Bucky grinned and let me go. He pointed over the bow. On the western horizon I could see the outer Brewster Islands a few miles away. We might make it yet, and Willa Starch unaccountably still had her stomach inside her body.

But Pierre, who was at the wheel of the boat, instead of holding a straight course started to spin the wheel with happy abandon. The boat wobbled through the water like a snake with arthritis. Henry, laughing uproariously, encouraged him.

"For heaven's sakes, Bucky," I screamed, "they've gone crazy!" I ran forward and grabbed Pierre. "You've got to stop it! If you keep it up the Coast Guard will wonder what is going on, and if they find out . . . kaputt for all of us."

"To hell weeth da Coast Guard," Pierre chuckled happily. He clutched the wheel tightly for a second, gave it another quick turn. We sliced another half circle in the water and then he let go of it completely. For a moment he squeezed his eyes together, apparently trying to focus me better. "Okay, *ma petite*," he said, his voice thick, "you drive *mon bateau*. She go anywhere . . . straight like a fart!" With that Pierre's face became glazed. He slumped to the floor, blocking the narrow passageway between the cases of Old Robbie, and started to snore.

By this time, the boat had turned through two complete circles and our wake of churned water was intertwined in two large parabolas extending nearly out of sight.

We were parallel with the Outer Brewster Islands, and the early morning traffic of weekend pleasure boats was passing us in an easterly direction, or toward Cape Cod Canal. A forty-foot Chris Craft finally got by us on our port side. The skipper, standing on his bridge, yelled at us through a megaphone and demanded to know what in hell we were doing.

Bucky, who had grabbed the wheel and was straddling the recumbent Pierre, shouted back at him. "We're trying to look up our own bung hole!" Bucky waved good-naturedly at the red-faced skipper of the Chris Craft, who cursed at us until we were out of hearing distance.

Henry cackled happily at Bucky's quick retort. He took another slug of scotch and demanded the wheel. "Nevah mine, old Pierre, ol' Mad Man Starch'll get us home. Just give the helm to a master, son."

Bucky shrugged dubiously, and let him take over. I wanted to tell Bucky that he was in better condition to operate the boat, but Henry, singing joyfully, held the wheel in a wrestler's grip.

For the moment, at least, we were on a straight course. I knew that, from passing boats, we must look as if we were sinking or at least a ship in distress. The ocean occasionally spilled into our cockpit. The wind had freshened considerably, creating waves that threatened to submerge us. We weren't more than three miles from Trotter Island, but I was beginning to wonder whether the overloaded boat would make it. If the Coast Guard didn't spot us before long, some conscientious skipper with a radio would surely report our top-heavy condition.

For a few minutes Henry doggedly kept a steady course and we actually passed the channel markers on the correct side. George's Island was on our starboard. If we stayed afloat twenty minutes more we would make Trotter Island.

We passed Hull Gut, and I noticed to my horror that Henry was steering the boat directly into the middle of a sailboat race. A fleet of about fifteen sailboats with their mainsails and jibs close hauled were bearing down on us, running for some marker on the other side of Hull Gut. I don't know much about sailboat racing, but I do know that a sailboat has the right of way over any power boat, and I knew that an enthusiastic sailor on a starboard tack will hold his course and not give an inch to another sailboat. Especially, a sailor will not give way to a power boat which can much more easily shift its course, or reduce its speed to let a sailboat pass.

Henry knew this too. But Henry has an unnatural aversion to sailboats. "Damned useless things," I have often heard him call them. "Made for fancy-pants who have got nothin' else to do but clutter up the ocean." The conflict between the motor boat enthusiasts and the sailors who abhor the stinkpots will go on forever. I was certain that this was not the time to seek a victory.

Henry wouldn't alter his course an inch. A thirty-foot sloop, heeling precariously, its sails a fifteen-degree angle with the horizon, was cutting through the water at a furious clip heading directly toward us. Bucky, leaning over cases of Old Robbie, was studying the boat with Pierre's binoculars. I could vaguely see four people sitting far out on the rail of the boat, clinging to sail ropes, using their weight to keep the boat upright. The wind had stiffened and was blowing about fifteen to twenty miles an hour. As we approached land it felt warmer and the water was not so choppy.

Nervously, I watched the gap between the sailboat and our boat narrow. "Daddy," I screamed. "Give way! Let that sailboat pass in front of us. With all this weight we haven't got enough speed to beat him. We'll hit him. If you squeak by, *he'll* hit *us!*"

"Give way?" Henry asked unbelievingly. This was traitorous. "The hell I will. Let *him* give way. His damned boat is on my course. I've got business to attend to. I ain't giving an inch to a bunch of rich kids who got nothin' else to do but futsy around in sailboats all day."

Bucky guffawed. "Right you are Henry!" He handed me Pierre's binoculars. "Take a look, Willa. Unless I'm seeing things, the pilot of that craft and one of his crew are old friends of yours!"

Looking through the binoculars I was reminded of one of those old time movies, with two puffing locomotives hurtling down the track toward each other. In less than two minutes, unless Henry changed his course, we were going to plough right into the middle of that sailboat. Trying desperately to think of a way to divert Henry and bring him back to sanity, I finally got the binoculars into focus, and found myself looking into the grim face of Converse Cabot!

He was waving furiously, indicating that we should change course and let him pass. Two other men were sitting next to Converse on the high side of the boat. They looked equally perturbed, but I didn't pay any attention to them because my binoculars came to rest on the thirty-dollar, windblown hairdo of Stephanie Billings, who was gracefully hanging onto the sailboat's jib rope.

Grinning, Bucky watched the expression on my face.

"Okay, let Henry crash into them!" I said grimly. I didn't really mean it. If Pierre Grass's lobster tub ever hit the side of Converse's boat it would certainly sink it. Converse might even get hurt or drown. I didn't worry about Stephanie. Maybe she would drown, but I doubted it. Even the fish wouldn't bother with anything as synthetic as she.

We were converging rapidly. I could see the prow of Converse's sloop slicing the water, flipping a spray against the hull and sails as it pounded toward us. Henry opened our throttle to full speed. The noise was deafening. Cases of Scotch slid into the middle of the boat. There was no room to move. Bucky and I were separated by cardboard cases, piled waist-high, that had tumbled into the passageway. The boats were now less than two hundred yards apart. Neither Henry nor Converse were giving an inch.

"Get out of my way, you crazy ass!" I heard Converse yell. "We're in a race! Give way you blasted idiot!"

"Ah, shove it," Henry yelled back. I could see that he was measuring the distance that separated us. With luck he might squeak across Converse's bow. It wasn't cricket. Even if Henry made it, the waves we would leave crossing in front of the sailboat would set it bobbing on the sea.

I could see Converse's face clearly now, angry and contorted. I heard him yell, "You crazy son-of-a-bitch," and saw his mouth sag in a wide "O" as he recognized me. For a second, with about three hundred feet separating us, it looked as if we might actually thunder by in front of his boat.

We might have. But, out of nowhere, a souped-up outboard motorist towing a water skier swooped down on us, and, with a whoop of sheer joy, roared through the space that separated Pierre's boat from Converse's.

Incredibly, I caught a glimpse of King Rose driving the boat, a huge grin on his face. And then my mother, stark naked except for her tassels, zoomed by us on water skis.

Prin held the tow rope with the aplomb of an experienced circus aerialist.

I heard her yell, "Hi, Sugar!" and caught a glimpse of her behind, wet and sparkling in the sun, as she zigged and zagged back toward Trotter Island. As the prow of Converse's sloop ripped into the side of Pierre's boat with a hollow thud, I was certain that any second now I would awake from this nightmare.

"You goddamned fool, you stove a hole in us," I heard Bucky yell. Sure enough the collision with Converse's boat had not only tumbled the cases of scotch into wild disarray, practically burying Pierre, but water was pouring ominously into the boat through a gaping hole in the hull planking.

"I'd have made it," Henry said furiously, "except for your damned mother and her stinking Portguee boy friend. Of all the ham-headed things to do. I'll break every bone in her body when I get hold of her. She must be plastered. Naked as a jaybird, too. I'll kill her, by God!"

"What happened to Converse?" I asked Bucky, who was bailing water with a floor pail he had unearthed.

"Not a damned thing," Bucky said angrily. "When your ma and that foul ball King Rose shot between us your friend, Converse, just headed his boat up and whammed us head on. The prow of that sailboat is probably a piece of curved steel." Bucky pointed over the stern. "There goes your rich boy friend."

I could see Converse's sailboat a half mile away no longer leading, but catching up on three others just like it. "That's what I call Boston aplomb," Bucky said distastefully. "He doesn't even give a damn if we sink."

"Do you mean to tell me that you know who that maniac is?" Henry demanded. "I'm gonna sue the bastard."

"That's a Cabot," Bucky said. "They aren't satisfied taking Trotter Island away from us, now they're trying to drown us."

"Oh," I moaned. "He saw me! Converse recognized me!" Any remote possibility that I had been entertaining in my subconscious of usurping Stephanie's place in his affection was gone forever.

"So what, he saw you? Converse saw me . . . oooh-de-ay, ain't life sad?" Bucky mocked. "If Willa Starch doesn't bend her ass and start bailing, and your old man don't stop arguing, we aren't going to get this tub to shore."

I was suddenly aware that I was ankle deep in water.

"Pierre," I screamed. "Pierre will drown!"

Bucky started pulling cases of Old Robbie off the floor. He finally unwedged Pierre and pulled him to his feet. We were within fifty yards of our mooring when the engine spluttered and conked out. The hole in the side of the boat was no longer visible. The water was up to my knees.

The confusion shocked Pierre into sobriety. "Whoo seenk my boat?" he demanded. He grabbed Henry who was still trying to guide us to the mooring. "You theek bastard . . . you did eet. I keel you."

With a swing of his arm Henry brushed Pierre away, knocked him back into the water. I peeled off my sweater and sneakers. We were about two hundred yards from the beach in front of our house.

"You can all drown," I yelled. "I'm going to swim for it!" I jumped and slowly swam for shore. There was no hope for Pierre's lobster boat. A few yards away I trod water and watched it slowly settling straight down into the ocean, while the three men sank up to their waist, each blaming the other for the situation they were in.

As I swam shoreward I heard the throb of a runabout again vibrating the water. It thundered toward me, described an abrupt arc, and skidded to a halt a few feet away. King Rose leaned over, a happy smile on his face, and asked me how the water was. Prin was sitting beside him still dressed in nothing but her tassles.

King Rose pulled me aboard. Prin chuckled. "Baby, you sure look funny . . . like a drowned rat in those wet jeans."

"No funnier than you," I said sourly. "Wait until Daddy gets his hands on you."

King Rose edged his boat alongside Pierre's, which had nearly disappeared. "Who in hell torpedoed you?" he demanded. Bucky and Pierre, standing on the roof of the cabin scowled at him. Henry stared at him with a Killer Starch look on his face. He seemed to have completely lost the power of speech.

If Prin couldn't recognize an approaching cyclone, I could. "Don't you do anything rash, Daddy," I yelled.

Henry said nothing. He stepped into King Rose's boat. Before King Rose could react to save himself, Henry lifted him right out of his seat and heaved him in the water.

"Not me! I didn't do anything!" was all the Princess had time to scream, and Henry picked her up and sent her sailing through the air after King Rose.

Henry took the wheel of King Rose's runabout, waiting until Pierre and Bucky climbed aboard. Nothing I could say would make Henry go back and rescue them. He motored calmly away leaving Prin and King Rose sputtering and cursing and finally forced to swim to shore after us.

17

By Sunday morning at low tide Henry's and Pierre's anger was concentrated entirely on Converse Cabot. Prin and King Rose had admitted to partial responsibility. But, when the discussion shifted from whether Prin and King Rose had actually caused the crash to the shameful business of a mother with a grown daughter dashing around the harbor on water skis, nude, Prin reminded Henry that Grandma Starch wouldn't be a mite happier to know that her only son was smuggling liquor and cheating the United States government. The argument continued most of the night with both Prin and Henry convinced that the other's moral lapse was far the worse.

Prin and King Rose must have felt some guilt, because next day they joined the gang of Trotter Islanders that Henry and Pierre had rounded up to help salvage the Old Robbie. Dressed in a bathing suit, Prin waded hip-deep in soft mud helping about twenty other eager Islanders lug the bottles to shore. After eight hours in water, the cardboard cases and the individual gold boxes, emblazoned with a picture of Robert Burns, had turned to mush. Pierre looked at the mess in horror.

"She no damned good now," he said sadly examining a wet brown bottle.

"What do you mean it's no good?" Henry demanded. "Those bottles are perfectly tight. Didn't hurt the Old Robbie none. Don't forget I got twenty-four hundred dollars tied up in that stuff!"

"No labels . . ." Pierre said, trying to glue a curly sticky label back on one of the bottles. "They all come off. Who in hell will buy eet without labels? No one know she Old Robbie."

Henry sat down in the mud, a mournful expression on his face. He looked about ready to cry. I almost told him that Bucky had his twenty-four hundred dollars, but decided not to. The ethics of the thing were confusing. Of course, I had no doubt of Harry McTare's claim to the money, but I wasn't meddling further. If they were put on the spot, both Bucky and Pierre might agree that Willa's bonnie behind was a reasonable exchange for twenty-four hundred dollars. I wasn't anxious to test them.

The salvage team, plodding through the mud with basketloads of Old Robbie, soon discovered that a few swigs helped immensely in the arduous work of lugging twenty-four hundred bottles through two-foot deep mud to the beach in front of our house.

All afternoon, Grandma Starch tried to dissuade them from their evil business, advising them to leave the accursed stuff where it had sunk and not to be touching it on a Sunday or they would assuredly go to the hot place for this day's work. But no one heeded her exhortations. When the tide finally changed, most of the liquor had been beached, and even Grandpa Starch was singing merrily. He put his arm around Thirsty, who recounted happy bygone days when a rumrunner had gone aground off Race Point in Provincetown. The town's natives and old salts had recovered the liquor, Thirsty recalled, and went on a spree that lasted for weeks.

While the tide was flat, Herman Snole plodded out in the mud to help Henry and Pierre patch the hole in Pierre's boat and bail it out so that it would float again. After Herman sampled the Old Robbie, he told Henry that he was proud of him. Henry had been really trying to help Operation Buzz-Off, and Herman Snole wasn't going to let him down. Before Operation Buzz-Off came to a successful conclusion, Herman wouldn't be at all surprised if the Cabots themselves ended up paying for the Old Robbie.

Converse telephoned me Monday morning. At first I thought that the ill wind that had put him on a tangent with Henry's odd piloting was going to be a wind that blew me some good. It took me a few days to find out differently.

Without preliminaries, Converse demanded to know what insane, stupid, maniacal idiot had been at the helm of the lobster boat.

"Stephanie thought that it was probably that greasy looking character who met you on Commercial Wharf."

How's that for male tact? Converse didn't even ask if I was

114

all right but greeted me with words of wisdom spoken by his female mentor.

"Doesn't he know," Converse demanded, "that a sailboat always has the right of way over a power boat? What's more, I was on a starboard tack and in the most important race of the season. Those sloops and yawls come up and down the coast to meet for this ocean race. I had it in the bag, before that half-wit. . . ."

I interrupted his raving. "Bucky Bonnelli is not a greasy character, and that half-wit who was at the wheel happens to be my father!"

"Your father!" There was a long silence on the other end of the phone.

"My father had a few drinks, but even if he had been sober he probably would have tried to run you down. He has an obsession. He thinks that the idle rich who have time to waste in sailboats, demanding 'right of way' from poor fishermen, ought to be run out of the harbor or permitted to sail only on Sundays, when honest laborers are resting from their toils." I knew it was melodramatic and flamboyant, but I liked the sad picture I was painting. For a moment I was about to portray Henry as an honest, bearded sea captain being harassed by rich playboys in flannel pants.

Anyway, Converse was melodramatic enough. What did I care about his darned race? He had sunk Pierre's boat and nearly drowned me, and after five minutes of conversation he hadn't shown the slightest interest in my health.

"Well, it probably wasn't completely your father's fault," Converse said making an attempt at tact. "If that jackass with the speedboat and the naked woman on water skis hadn't buzzed right between us, your father might have made it." Converse chuckled. "My God I've never seen anything like that in my life."

"You mean you never saw a woman naked?"

"I didn't say that, Willa. I never saw a woman naked on water skis! Do you know who she was?"

So he had probably seen Stephanie naked. I felt the green monster jump on my shoulder.

"The woman on water skis was my mother, and she was being towed by her boyfriend!"

Converse laughed heartily at that. "I know you're kidding, Willa. I detect a sarcastic tone in your voice. You're angry because I'm not concerned about hitting your boat. Tell you what. To show you that my heart is in the right place, I'll pick you up at noon and take you to lunch at Pier Four."

"Are you going to ask Stephanie's permission . . . or is she coming along to chaperone you?" I asked, but I didn't let my faint anger at Converse stop me from accepting the invitation.

I met him at noon on State Street in front of the Custom House Tower. Sitting lean and tan behind the wheel of his red Jaguar, he looked very correct and sure of himself. His was the kind of smooth suavity that needed puncturing, but I already had that plip-plop shivery feeling I get whenever I see Converse, and I was in no position to attack the Cabot equanimity. Why couldn't I be light and flippant with him instead of sighing like a country milkmaid? He had Stephanie. It wasn't fair to have more than one woman contributing to the ego development of Converse Cabot.

Between the Boston businessmen on expense accounts and the tourists gaping through the picture windows that overlook the harbor, it isn't always easy to get a table at Pier Four. But Converse seemed well acquainted. He had evidently made a reservation for a waterfront table. I tried to be casual, while enjoying the luxury of eating lobster and watching the boats passing in the harbor.

I accepted a Manhattan . . . drank it too quickly . . . and found a second one in front of me. I knew my tongue was beginning to say things my brain hadn't properly censored. I wondered if Converse was trying to get me drunk. I was sure of it when he said:

"Sawyer was telling me that Herman Snole lives on a Trotter Island. Do you know him?"

"Sort of," I admitted. "He's self-appointed head of Operation Buzz-Off."

"Operation Buzz-Off?"

"Herman's name for our plan to save Trotter Island for Trotter Islanders." I took another sip of my drink. "After all, Converse, we poor people have to live, too. Turning Trotter Island into a marina and depriving people of their homes . . . well, it may be good business, but I personally don't think it's very ethical or moral."

"Willa," Converse said, "you are confused. No one is shoving your friends around. They can always live on the West Head of Trotter Island. There's no deep water anchorage there. The marina may even give some of them an opportunity to earn an honest living."

"That's what you say now. But the Billings & Cabot Development Corporation has already increased the rents. When the marina is built the land will increase in value. So, Herman Snole's advice is strike them where it will hurt most . . . in their pocketbooks."

116

I noticed the sudden gleam in Converse's eye. "You mean that the walkout at A B C this morning has something to do with the marina being built on Trotter Island?"

I refused to answer, but I was pleased to hear that Operation Buzz-off had started.

Converse sipped a scotch and soda. "Wait until Sawyer hears this!"

"What are you going to tell him?" I asked, alarmed. I knew that I had said too much.

"We guessed that the problem of music being played in the plant was a smoke screen. When the employees realize that Snole has irresponsibly made them go on strike for his personal benefit, they'll tar and feather him. Sawyer is meeting with Snole this afternoon." Converse stood up. "I better telephone him."

"Converse Cabot," I sobbed, and suddenly I was really and truly crying. "If you tell Sawyer I'll never speak to you again." I knew that this wasn't much of a threat. After all, in a few months he would marry Stephanie. Then he wouldn't care if Willa Starch were even alive. He probably didn't much care right now. I was furious with him and aghast at myself for what I had let slip. Being Mata Hari required a savoir faire like Stephanie's, I thought bitterly. Something I would never acquire.

At least Converse was momentarily stopped by my tears. He reached across the table and patted my hand. "Come, come, Willa, you and I will have a long talk. You really aren't seeing things clearly, you know. I think close association with residents of Trotter Island has confused your moral outlook."

Astonished, I stopped crying. "My morals are as good as yours, Converse Cabot! For your information, I'm still a virgin. I'll bet that's more than you can say."

Converse looked at me protectively. I had touched a responsive chord in his heart. I suddenly wondered if my virginity was too direct a challenge. A condition that Converse, perhaps, felt impelled to correct.

"I don't know what special quality you have, Willa. It is one of your peculiar charms that you make me feel as if I should put my arms around you, dry your eyes, and say: 'There, there, Willa . . . don't you worry. Everything will come out all right.' "

My mood brightened. I didn't even ask him sarcastically how Stephanie would feel about such chivalry. Any man that could say that to a girl could just as easily say I love you to her. Maybe, at last, I had found the right formula. All I had to do was apply it.

Converse continued to fondle my hand. "I'm not questioning your sexual morals, Willa. I mean morality in a wider sense. For instance, the morality of deliberately throwing people out of work, as Herman Snole is doing, for his private gain."

"Or the morality of taking people's homes away from them by prohibitive rents," I interjected.

"Or the morality of a drunken father endangering his daughter's life while he tries to run down a harmless sailboat," Converse continued smoothly, hitting below the belt. He ignored my shocked expression. "Or the morality of being towed, naked, around on water skis, like that floosie. . . ."

"That floosie, Converse Cabot, is my mother!"

This time Converse was startled. "You said that on the telephone. I don't believe you."

"I suppose in your little protected cocoon of Harvard College, State Street, Beacon Street, and Cohasset you think everyone's father and mother are pillars of the community," I stormed, heedless of who might be listening at adjoining tables. "Well, it's about time you learned the story of my life. If you want to understand me and my family, you are going to have to get some elastic stitched into your Puritan morals."

While I finished my lobster and drank a third Manhattan, I gave him a brief sketch of life with Prin and Henry and our Trotter Island friends.

"What is more," I finished, "my baby brother is probably the son of King Rose and my mother. And you know something, it doesn't shock me at all. In fact I don't think it is one bit worse than Sawyer Priestly trying to go to bed with me." I smiled idiotically at the waiter, who was lapping up the conversation as he slowly cleared the table. The Manhattans had convinced me that all was well with the world. I really loved everybody. "You know Converse, my father and mother are not really bad. Prin loves Henry. She loves me. To love people, that's really the important thing."

I waited for Converse to say something. While I was talking, he listened, toying with a muddler, horribly self-possessed. He made no comment.

I couldn't hold back my tears any longer. "All right," I said, sobbing and feeling sorry for myself. "Be smug and superior. I know I shouldn't try to breathe the same air as a Cabot. I'm just white trash that went to Radcliffe through the back door." I got up hastily and walked dizzily out of the dining room, tears running down my cheeks. Somehow I

118

made the door, Converse after me, guiding me through the maze of tables and preventing me from stumbling into the curious diners who watched my exit.

Converse led me to his car. I had passed from a happy-with-the-world feeling to a really good crying jag. "Leave me on Commercial Wharf," I told Converse. "I can't go back to Sawyer's office like this."

"Sawyer won't be in town today. He has a union meeting with Snole at four o'clock. Look, Willa, you've got the wrong idea. I'm sorry that I called your mother a floosie. There's no doubt that you've had a rather odd life, but that's not your fault. I'm not criticizing your parents. At least they had the good sense to let your Grandmother bring you up and not drag you around the country. And they did give you a fine education. What you should probably do now is get married and use your background to pursue a more sedate life." While he was talking, Converse had driven me back to State Street. He located a parking place across from Sawyer's office.

I grabbed his head in my two hands and pulled his big, very clean ear close to my lips. After listening to Converse pontificate on my future I experienced a return to hilarity. "Converse," I whispered seductively, "thank you for the proposal. I'd marry you, but I don't think we would be happy. In words I learned at my mother's knee . . . you are an old, dried-up fart!"

I got out of the Jag, slammed the door, waved a merry good-bye to Converse, staggered across State Street, smiled sweetly at a driver who jammed on his brakes to avoid hitting me, pushed the automatic elevator, unlocked Sawyer's office, and flopped once again on Sawyer's leather couch, crying hysterically.

Converse had followed me. He pulled me into his arms and looked at me strangely. "Willa, you are in love with me . . . aren't you?"

I pushed him away. "I hate you, Converse Cabot. You got me drunk so that you could find out what was going on at Trotter Island. I'm going to marry a man called Harry Mc-Tare who loves my behind. But right now I'm going to up-chuck that expensive lunch and those three Manhattans you bought me right into Sawyer's private toilet . . . which should be proof enough to you that I'm no lady like your Stephanie!"

And I did. And I was miserably sick, and Converse held my head, and washed my face, and went down to his car and got a blanket, and wrapped me in it, because I was shivering

—although it was warm. And I was a sobbing female mush . . . unable to take care of herself, and if I had been Converse I would have walked out, disgusted with me. But he didn't. He found aspirins in Sawyer's desk and fed them to me and steadied me while I sat on the toilet, because I was so dizzy I nearly fell off. And he helped me take off my dress so that it wouldn't get any more mussed than it was and made me lie down on Sawyer's couch and covered me with his white navy blanket and told me to stop crying and close my eyes. His hand felt cool on my forehead.

When I awoke it was eight o'clock. Converse was sitting at Sawyer's desk, his feet perched comfortably in a desk drawer, reading that darned book, *Sexual Freedom*, that Sawyer kept in the bottom drawer.

"Oh," I moaned, sitting up slowly, not daring to shake my head. "I'm so sorry Converse. I'm so ashamed."

He sat beside me. "You had a good sleep, Willa. You poor kid. You were really knocked out."

"Did I snore?"

Converse shook his head. Darn that Bucky Bonnelli anyway. I knew that I didn't snore.

"When it got to be quarter-of-five and you were sighing as if you were breathing your last, I knew you couldn't go home. I met your father and a Frenchman on Commercial Wharf and told them you were with friends of mine. I told them I would borrow a boat at Squantum Yacht Club and get you home early."

I looked at Converse terrified. "What did Henry say when he saw you?"

"He didn't recognize me at first, and then he had a moment of doubt and asked if my name was Cabot. After looking at the size of his arm muscles I decided that it was the better part of valor to deny it emphatically. I left him mumbling that when he caught up with young Cabot he was going to wring twenty-four-hundred dollars out of him on the spot. You better tell me the whole story, Willa. But wait. . . ." Converse gently pulled the blanket away from me. He unfastened my bra and took it off.

"Now stand up and take off your panties," he commanded.

I obeyed him. I couldn't help myself. "What are you going to do?" I asked in a shy quaking voice. I was standing in front of him—naked, awkward, not knowing whether I should crouch like September Morn or just stand up straight with my palms back and say simply, "Here I am Converse . . . take me. I love you."

I didn't quite say that, but I implied it.

"Willa, you are a lovely person," Convere said quickly. He took me in his arms.

"Will it hurt?" I asked.

He undressed, and I giggled when I saw his penis pointing eagerly at me. He grinned, and we tumbled together on the floor.

"What about Stephanie?" I asked, but he was too occupied to answer.

It didn't hurt . . . but afterwards there was a spot of blood on his white navy blanket. Converse got a big kick out of that and said that the blanket would always be precious to him. He told me that in some European countries, after the wedding night the bridegroom hung the first-night sheet out the window as testimony to his bride's virginity.

Which brought to mind the question of Stephanie, but all I said was, "But we aren't married are we, Converse . . . so you'll have to hide the blanket?"

And I knew that I was in love with Converse, but I really didn't know whether Converse cared for me or had just risen to the challenge I had given him about my superior moral stature.

When I got in bed that night, after a quiet Chris Craft ride across Quincy Bay, I knew that the truth was I had asked for it. Converse kissed me good night at the pier. He was concerned about my walk so late at night to the east end of the Island, but he didn't say that he would see me again.

In my bed I sobbed to myself. I had asked for it. What did boys say about girls like me: "Oh, Willa . . . she's got hot pants." I guess I did, too. It had been fun on the floor of Sawyer's office. After the first shock, I had warmed to the encounter. At least I had proved to Converse that Willa Starch wasn't just a mental Phi Beta Kappa.

18

Tuesday, I was certain that Converse would call me. Before Sawyer arrived I sat on his leather couch and dreamily tried to recall every minute of yesterday afternoon (well, not every minute, not how sick-drunk I had been) and picked up warmly the languid feeling of lying unashamedly naked on Converse's blanket. I remembered apologizing to him for the violence of my emotion. And the echo of my terror and wonder as I moaned, "Oh . . . Converse . . . Converse . . ." came back to me. He had been ever so gentle, kissing my breasts, laughing at my embarrassment when I finally reluctantly opened my legs and blushed to admit that his tongue on my labia was an electric shock. He would surely drive me insanely delirious if he didn't come inside with all of him I arched to meet his slow thrust. I loved him so much!

I loved him Wednesday, too . . . even when he hadn't telephoned me. Thursday, I wondered if he were sick. When Friday and the whole next week had passed and there was no phone call, I cried so much that I was afraid to look Henry and Prin in the face, and I took to wearing dark glasses to work. Converse's memory of me was not the wonder of our love, but Sawyer's toilet in my deathly embrace while I threw up nauseatingly.

I had reached for a man outside my environment, and I was paying for it. To Converse I was just a tramp from South Boston. A man-seeking female, anxious to get pregnant and raise a brood of children, while my hair became stringy and my stomach relaxed in a permanent protuberance from mashed-potato suppers and neglect. When Converse had said he didn't have a contraceptive I just murmured that I didn't care. Converse's reaction had no doubt been: "Ha! She wants to get pregnant. The old female trick to hook a man."

And so I wondered and cried and tried to justify and reproached myself and tried to hate Converse . . . but I couldn't hate him, because I could remember him lying in my arms and the strong angles of his face softened by his delight and his whisper in my ear: "I could love you very much, Willa."

With "could" goes "but." I know now that the "but" would appear in the form of Stephanie. . . . "But I've been promised to Stephanie . . . you understand, Willa, a family marriage, arranged since our childhood." Or what would hurt worse, "But I love Stephanie more."

Fortunately, Sawyer Priestly was so occupied with the problems of A B C Electronics that he didn't notice that I had changed from effervescent youth to stale, aged sufferance, nor did he notice my eyes red and swollen from continual crying.

But Sawyer was involved with his middle-aged problems. Had he known, I'm sure that he would have given me some sage and non-sequitur advice, such as there were other pebbles on the beach—not omitting Sawyer, himself, of course. He was interested in impressing me that Herman Snole must be out of his mind to involve A B C Electronics with the problems of Trotter Island.

"All this is stupidity, Miss Starch. Piped-in music is certainly not an invasion of an individual's privacy. The best psychologists tell us that for work such as the fine detailed assembling being done at A B C, music is an excellent nerve relaxant." Sawyer shrugged. "But of course, if the women at A B C don't want it, we can discontinue it at a moment's notice."

When A B C Electronics officially announced that the music would be eliminated, Herman Snole had anticipated them. The fourth day of the walkout he announced an Electronic Union Workers' outing to be held Saturday on Trotter Island.

With the cooperation of the local fishermen's union practically all of the female workers and their families were ferried across the harbor. Herman arranged with Henry to purchase half the supply of Old Robbie with union funds at two dollars a bottle, which liquidated Henry's investment and assured supplies for future "gassers."

Saturday evening, Trotter Island was ablaze with bonfires. The outing continued all night and was still going strong Sunday morning. Early in the evening, before the Old Robbie and Thirsty's grappa was flowing beyond control, Herman addressed the happy picnickers and announced that the successful outing would henceforth become an annual affair for all employees of A B C Electronics. Since the Cabots now owned Trotter Island, Herman told "his girls" that he would incorporate into the current negotiations and a new contract a clause stating that the expenses of the outing not only be borne by the Corporation in the future, but also retroactively. This idea was greeted with wild acclaim. I couldn't help but grin. Crafty Herman Snole had figured a way to make the Cabots pay for the Old Robbie.

Then Herman suggested that the real purpose of the walkout was not against the piped-in music. Although he knew that "his girls" would be pleased to have peace and quiet restored so they could chat and gossip normally, nevertheless, even more important was their take home pay. The difficult type of assembly work that they were doing warranted at least a twenty-cent-an-hour increase. This suggestion was adopted enthusiastically by the ladies who started to chant: "We love Herman. . . . Reach your goal with Herman

123

Snole!" Several buxom ladies excitedly scaled the platform and bussed Herman. Flashbulbs popped while the invited press happily recorded the event. Fireworks were lighted, and the accolade to Herman went on undiminished for more than twenty minutes. Later, informal entertainment was provided by some baggy-pants characters who the Princess said were former burlesque comedians. Their repertoire consisted of pouring things down each other's pants, holding their pants out, and peering down at the results with happy astonishment. They were cheered, as was the Princess, who did a modest tassle dance. Mendes East and Mama Bonnelli closed the program with some exotic steel drumming.

Four-column pictures of Herman Snole being kissed by the female workers of A B C Electronics appeared Sunday in all the Boston newspapers, with captions such as. "We love Herman Snole" or "Our protector Herman Snole. . . . To hell with Reliance Cabot!"

Henry and Prin couldn't understand why I was downhearted. Single-handed, Herman Snole was saving Trotter Island. They didn't know that, single-handed, I had lost Converse Cabot, and all there was for me now was a black future playing hide-and-go-seek with Bucky Bonnelli and Sawyer Priestly.

Sawyer characterized the whole business as malicious tampering with the welfare of the employees of A B C and indirectly playing into the hands of the Russians, who would benefit by the work stoppage on important government contracts. He absolved me from any blame.

"Willa, you are too fine a girl to develop a Trotter Island mentality. I've been thinking that you would make a wonderful companion for Abigail. You could come and live with us in a background that would enhance your basic loveliness."

This was a new approach. I wondered if I would be assigned a bedroom in the Priestly home so located that I could, without Abigail being aware, entertain a meandering Sawyer on occasional evenings.

But the strange, wonderful, crazy thing was that Willa Starch, no longer actually a virgin, didn't feel less virginal. In fact the only qualms she had about surrendering herself to Converse Cabot was that she might never have the opportunity again.

I tried to worry about this attitude and wondered if I were really a loose woman, but the tears were not for what I had done. I was in love. I wouldn't have been me—good or bad —unless I loved with all of me.

June, having progressed like a weary snail into its third

week, and still no word from Converse, I decided the Saturday following the Electronic Workers Outing to go in Boston, buy a dress, see a movie, and then wander around the Boston Arts Festival. Later in the evening I would watch the Andre Eglevsky Ballet Company. I knew that somehow I must keep my mind off Converse. Maybe I would accidentally bump into a handsome stranger who would take me by the hand and tell me that he had waited for me all his life. The trouble was that whenever I dreamed this dream the stranger would always look like Converse.

Bucky ferried me into the wharf on his boat, because Henry and Pierre were fishing and lobstering together until Pierre's engine could be overhauled.

I couldn't let Bucky know my mood, so I tried to banter with him. With his natural flair for rubbing salt into wounds, he picked the subject of Stephanie Billings for discussion. He wanted to know if I had seen her since our first meeting.

"She's really quite a dish, with those almond-shaped eyes. What a pair of knockers! I wonder if they are real or rubber." Bucky grinned at me, looking away from the course he was steering. "There's no doubt about yours, Willa. They are the real McCoy. The trouble is that Stephanie knows what tits are for and you don't."

"You mean, like King Rose says, boobies are to nurse babies?" I asked sweetly. "I'd like to see Stephanie with a drooling kid tugging on hers."

Bucky scowled. "Willa . . . you are not only a tease. You are unromantic."

"Listen, Bucky Bonnelli, if I have teased you, I'm sorry. I didn't do it on purpose. I've known you so long that I think of you like a brother. I can't help it if you persist in trying to make out all the time or are spying on me like some shady character. Just last Sunday I tried to find a secluded place to sunbathe, and just when I thought I was alone I got an uneasy sensation that someone was watching me. Good Lord," I sighed, "you'd think that you never saw a naked woman before. You don't even have to spy. You can see the Princess anytime. Last week some sunbathing association made her an honorary member. Now Prin is planning to go to the annual nudist convention. Just drop in the house any time. Henry is raving his head off. Grandma gave up. She pretends that Prin doesn't even exist. Only Grandpa Starch and I don't mind. Prin says she has to practice being bare so she won't be nervous when they crown her Queen-Of-Them-All."

"I heard all about it," Bucky said. "She's trying to convince my old lady that it's good for tits to air them out a lit-

125

tle. Jesus, if Ma ever lets hers out of their harness, they'll bounce on her knees." Bucky turned the boat into Long Wharf and nosed into a vacant berth. "You see, Willa, watching your old lady bare-assed isn't like watching you. I can't help it if I go for you. It's just tough luck that some of the fire burning in your Ma hasn't ignited on you. I saw her in action before she retired. Boy, she had them panting in the back row of the balcony."

I climbed the ladder onto the wharf, Bucky following me. I could feel his hand lingering on my behind, but I wasn't in a good position to protest.

"Couldn't I come with you?" he pleaded. "I haven't got a thing to do today. Where are you going, anyway? Boston is dead on a Saturday afternoon."

"I'm going to look at clothes—girl stuff, you wouldn't like it—and maybe go to a movie. I've spent the last two week-ends on Trotter Island. I need a change." I didn't tell Bucky, but I had a premonition that Harry McTare might show up. Bucky had turned McTare's money over to Herman Snole, President in charge of Operation Buzz-Off. He congratulated Bucky when he heard about the coup and offered to put the money in the Trotter Island treasury. With Herman Snole in possession of Harry McTare's money, I was afraid that Willa Starch might prove to be the ransom.

Knowing that we would have conflicting ideas as to how to spend a Saturday afternoon, I told Bucky that I wanted to be alone.

"Aw, come on, Willa. I'd just as soon look at clothes with you. Later on I'll take you to dinner."

"Where?" I asked. "To some dive in the Combat Zone? Look at you. You can't go anywhere dressed like that."

"What's the matter with the way I'm dressed?

I shrugged. When I looked in his direction I felt like blush-ing. His faded blue jeans were so tight that the hard bunch of his "thing" was clearly outlined. Bucky caught my gaze and chuckled.

"Maybe I didn't go to Harvard like your friend Converse. But I did go to Boston University. How people dress is all relative. I remember reading somewhere that women use to go around with their tits out. It was about the same time men took to wearing codpieces. In those days a man was proud of his size. Men wore gadgets to show what they had. Some of them even stuffed the codpieces to make them look better . . . just like gals today wear falsies." Bucky grinned. "Any-time you want, I can prove to you I don't wear falsies."

I guess I have too strong an imagination. No matter how

126

hard I try I can't develop a superior disdainful air. A girl like Stephanie would have known how to parry with Bucky. I blushed.

Bucky pressed his advantage. "Come on, Willa. I'll go up to Jordan's basement and buy a suit. I need one anyway. Then you won't be embarrassed."

19

So there I was in Jordan's basement watching Bucky paw over shopworn suits which would probably be given to the Salvation Army in a few days. I discovered that Bucky actually had over two hundred dollars in his pocket, which he had earned working for some Boston contractor. When I suggested that he could find a more attractive suit in the Men's Store upstairs he ignored me and insisted on squeezing himself into a nineteen-ninety-five bargain which was nearly as tight as his jeans.

Bucky has wide shoulders and tapering hips. The perfect male, who looks best in a jockstrap, flexing his muscles. I didn't tell him this. He was already egotistic enough parading in front of a mirror. He looked like a sharpie out of the gay nineties. All he needed was a straw hat—and darned if he didn't want to buy one. Since he had forced himself on me, I decided that I might as well make him miserable. I convinced him that the suit was too tight and got the clerk to find a looser one. Then he looked like a helpless ape that had just got dressed for a party. Nothing seemed to hang right over those bulging shoulders and arms.

At least in this suit he didn't look so conspicuous. While he was convincing, the clerk—who I think was afraid to tell him it was impossible—to shorten the cuffs, I fished in my pocketbook for a stale cigarette. I don't smoke except to be sophisticated. Knowing that I was saddled with Bucky all day I needed something to calm my nerves. As I was fumbling with the junk in my pocketbook, which never seems to get organized, I saw something glittery, picked it up, and dropped it

127

back again. I felt a sinking sensation in my stomach. It was the key to Sawyer's apartment! In all the confusion of the past few weeks I had forgotten it. I had meant to return it. I wondered what Sawyer had been thinking all this time. No doubt he was certain that I wasn't so moral as I pretended . . . that given time I would use his key.

The strange thing is that I'm never at all sure what goes on in the dark corners and convolutions of my brain. Maybe I was a little curious to see what sort of lair Sawyer was secretly maintaining in Boston. Without evoking it consciously I knew that if it were possible to sneak into the apartment and take a quick look around without Sawyer being aware I would have done it. I had an idea that the venture might contribute a little to my limited knowledge of men.

Outside on Summer Street, Bucky carrying his jeans in a paper bag, we walked toward the Common. I don't know what possessed me . . . probably the loss of Converse, hanging like a specter in the back of my mind. Anyway, I blurted the whole story about Sawyer's key to Bucky. It was an act of bravado . . . like saying to Converse, "Okay, if you don't want me, someone else does. Just look how Bucky Bonnelli is lapping up what I am saying. He already has a different impression of Willa Starch."

When I finished, Bucky stared at me with an okay-that-isn't-all look on his face.

"And what else . . . ?" he asked with a nasty leer.

"Nothing else," I said, "and you can push those evil thoughts through the hole in your head. I can't help it if I appeal to older men. Just because I have the key to Sawyer's apartment doesn't mean I ever intended to go there or to meet him. I really meant to give it back to him."

We walked slowly toward Tremont Street, while Bucky tried to correlate this new aspect of Willa.

"I happen to know that Sawyer won't be in town today. He is taking some friends on his new boat down to Chatham."

Bucky didn't spark the idea that suddenly jumped in my brain. He just shrugged.

"It occurred to me," I continued lightly, "that it might be fun to see what the place looks like. It's just across the Common on Beacon Street."

Bucky seized my arm like a private detective. "If you've never been there, just how do you know it's just across the Common. Beacon Street is a pretty long street."

Angrily I pulled out of his grasp. "I told you, Bucky Bonnelli, that I never had anything to do with Sawyer Priestly, and I have never been to his apartment. It so happens that the low numbers on Beacon Street are on this end . . . and Sawyer did tell me the number. Why don't you go home? I didn't ask you to come anyway."

"So," Bucky was triumphant. "That's what you were really going to do all along. Shopping and going to the movie . . . brother, I swallowed that gluck hook, line, and sinker! You were really going to have a gander at this guy's apartment. Maybe you even hoped to meet him there . . . an assignation."

"Assignation is old fashioned . . . you mean rendezvous."

Bucky grabbed my elbow. "Never mind what I mean. It is a good thing I tagged along. Sometimes I don't know how anyone so dumb as you could have saved her virginity this long."

I started to cry. Luckily men seldom know what women are crying about. I guess Bucky thought that he had insulted me. The truth was that he was right. I *was* too dumb to be a virgin, anyway. All the right man had to do was to be just a little nice to me, and I would say, "Hurry here I am."

With my melancholy thoughts about Converse I began to suspect that it wasn't a very good idea to have Bucky along on this excursion. If we did get in Sawyer's apartment, I would probably get involved with Bucky in more complicated games than post office, and I might even think I was spiting Converse to surrender to Bucky. I really am a bad little girl, I guess. The only way to keep myself good is to stay out of bedrooms with eager little boys who pick me out for kissing games.

But we were on Beacon Street and not far from the number that Sawyer had given me. I felt a tingling sensation compounded of suspense and fear. It really was a crazy idea. Suppose Sawyer were there after all? Supposing he was in bed with Miss Smoky, and we walked in on him? I giggled, picturing him jumping out of bed and Miss Smoky pulling the sheets over her head. But why was I there? That was a question to confuse Hamlet. Alone, I could have put on an angry I-suspected-as-much approach at finding him with Miss Smoky. After all, he *had* given me the key. Did he think I was going to be a member of a harem? But with Bucky . . . what could I possibly say?

There was no way out now. Bucky was showing a remarkable interest in the project, speculating on how it must be nice to be wealthy and shack up with different dames. We stopped under a sedate street awning numbered with the correct Beacon Street address and walked inside the air-conditioned building. It was shadowy and quiet in contrast to the hot, bright sidewalk. For a second I was blinded, while my eyes were refocusing and adjusting to the cool interior. The lobby of the apartment was deserted.

"Where do we go from here?" Bucky asked and implied with his look that he would bet I knew my way thoroughly.

"How do I know?" I demanded crossly. I remembered that Sawyer had said to take the elevator. Bucky located it. A tiny, self-operated box that would be crowded with three people in it. On the wall were ten buttons. Sawyers' name was beside number eight. I pressed it. Nothing happened.

"Don't tell me that you don't know your key fits there," Bucky said grimly, pointing to a small lock beside the button. I inserted the key, and the elevator door closed. We slowly moved upward.

"What if he is there?" asked Bucky. I was trembling at the thought.

"You can stop worrying," Bucky said. "If he were there when you first pushed the button, we would have gone up. You just unlocked the joint with your key."

Boston elevators aren't fast . . . but this one crept. At the eighth floor the elevator door slowly opened, and Bucky and I walked into Sawyer's apartment like Alice and Aladdin, awe-stricken by the first glimpse of luxury neither of us had ever seen at first hand. We were standing in a living room carpeted with a green and gold Chinese oriental with a pile so high we sank softly into it as we moved timidly about the room. Pale green wall lights that toned the walls had gone on automatically when the elevator door opened. Jade and ivory table lamps created soft shadows in the room. In one wall was a fireplace, and above, it a recess with a slim Kwan Yin statue about three feet tall, carved in jade and ivory. Silhouette nudes drawn in white-on-black paper, obviously of a man and woman having sexual intercourse, hung in a bamboo frame over a long, grey, curved courch.

"Quite a launching pad," Bucky said admiringly. He grinned suggestively and flopped on the couch. "Man you could climb right into outer space from here."

I was still staring at everything, like a country cousin, when I realized that Bucky had taken the elevator key out of my hand. "We'll lock it," he said, pushing the button for the elevator. He locked it and sent it back to the lobby. "The only one who can get it now is Sawyer Priestly—or some other dame with a key." He chuckled. "If I were giving out keys to a joint like this, I'd make darned sure that I made strict appointments for my visiting hours . . . no early or late arrivals permitted."

130

Bucky found decanters filled with liquor on a mahogany sideboard. "When you see this kind of a place on television or in the movies there's always a bucket of ice that never melts." He poured scotch into a glass and tasted it critically. "There must be a kitchen." He opened a door off the living room, revealing a completely equipped railroad type kitchen. "This Sawyer Priestly knows how to live."

I could hear him opening the refrigerator door and snapping ice out of a tray. He returned to the living room jiggling a cocktail shaker.

"Let's live it up, Willa. What's a real snobby drink?"

"Rob Roys," I said, without thinking, and then gasped. I had opened a door on the far side of the room, stared inside for a couple of seconds, and then closed it quickly. I was glad that Bucky was occupied making drinks. I warned myself that I would be just as well off if Bucky didn't see the bedroom. We would drink one drink and leave in a hurry. The bedroom looked as if some French interior decorator enthusiastic about l'amour had designed it as the ultimate background for soft dalliance. The room had lighted with a feathery glow when I opened the door, revealing walls that were black mirrors . . . not just the walls, either, but the ceilings, too. The thought crossed my mind that if you walked around this room naked, you could see yourself coming and going, as well as walking on the ceiling.

And the bed! It wasn't just a bed. It was an altar. To get in it you mounted a dais two feet higher than the rest of the floor. On the dais was a low modern bed in which eight people could have slept comfortably.

I had seen enough in that minute to gain a new perspective on Sawyer . . . and I knew that Monday morning, just as soon as he arrived, he was going to get his key back—fast. Willa Starch wasn't going to be led naked and trembling to that sacrificial altar. Who would have ever thought, seeing Sawyer walk sedately along State Street, that he could have such a Mr. Hyde aspect?

While I was thinking these thoughts, Bucky, working from a cocktail recipe book he had found, had made a shaker full of Rob Roys and handed me a double one in a tall-stemmed cocktail glass. Like the amateur I am, I thirstily gulped it and then remembered the debacle with Converse. It was obvious that unless I was planning a repeat performance I had better drink the Rob Roys very carefully. Already I could feel my toes tingle, and I felt light-headed.

Bucky was prowling around the living room again, and when I saw him push the bedroom door open I knew it

131

wasn't a sane thing to do, but I poured myself another Roy Roy and slugged that one off, too!

What the heck, I thought suddenly. I'm twenty-two and I've only really made love with one man. I don't really know what sex is all about. It would serve Converse right if some other man made love to me. I giggled. What silly thoughts I think! Converse didn't care whether a whole army . . . what did men say? . . . *screwed* me. I wondered what Bucky was doing in the bedroom. I poured a third Rob Roy. The plain truth is that, beneath all the other thoughts racing on the surface of my mind, was a sad longing for Converse, and I knew that while I was smiling and trying to be flippant I was on the verge of tears.

Bucky returned. He sat down beside me and looked at me strangely.

"Where have you been?" I asked.

"I had to use the crapper," Bucky said vulgarly and then apologized. "Okay, I mean bathroom. The faucets and fixtures look as if they were solid gold. Makes you self-conscious when you take a piss . . . as if such common functions only happen to the poor." He chuckled. "Maybe that's true. Maybe when you get rich as this Priestly character you don't shit any more."

I scowled at him.

"Don't *defecate* any more." He poured himself a Rob Roy. "You know, it has always bothered me: What do girls call it? Number Two?"

I didn't answer.

"Have you seen the bedroom?" Bucky asked thoughtfully.

I nodded weakly.

"Boy, this guy must be a rabbit," Bucky said. "He's got this erotic business down to a science." He grinned. "Sorry I was gone so long, but I was reading. Priestly's got a whole collection of erotic books. I think I'll snitch these. Never saw anything like them." Bucky took a couple of paperbound books from his pocket. "Did you ever hear of these *My Secret Life* or *One-Hundred-and-Twenty Days of Sodom?*"

"Why do men like that stuff?" I asked, giving him back the books. "They bore me. Those writers hate women. Making love to them is just a piston-and-suction-pump arrangement! The *Hundred-and-Twenty Days of Sodom*' . . . ugh . . . that was written by the Marquis de Sade. . . . He was so insane that his characters prefer to eat excrement than make love. Authors like that have mental diarrhea." I knew I should have shut up. Bucky was looking at me astonished.

132

"You mean that you've read books like these?" Bucky asked dubiously. There was a tone in his voice that clearly said that this wasn't a nice thing for a girl to have done. "Who gave them to you?" he demanded, vastly suspicious again.

"I heard about them. One of the girls at school had a couple she stole from her father. Then one day, I was walking through the Combat Zone," I grinned at Bucky. "The book store was full of men, reading and not buying. I asked the manager, a very nice Italian boy, what was good to read. He was so shocked to find a live female in his store, he gave them to me to get rid of me. I was disrupting his customers' daydreams."

"Willa, sometimes I think you have done a lot more that you admit," Bucky said suspiciously. "Why did you want to read dirty books?"

"I was curious. I read in Kinsey that women weren't affected by pornography."

"Were you . . . affected?" Bucky asked hopefully.

"Nope," I said. And seeing the disappointment in his eyes I couldn't help laughing. "Honestly, Bucky, men are silly. Sawyer is a good example. Look at this place . . . a seduction chamber. And after he seduces a woman, he'll probably wonder why he went to all the trouble."

I knew the liquor was making me conversational, but then, I seldom had anyone I could talk with. I thought, so what, Bucky might as well know how I feel. "The kind of man I could be excited about is the man who makes love with laughter on his lips . . . a man alive, with the joy of finding me . . . another human being . . . who is alive and joyful . . . a never-ceasing circle. The Princess told me that most men don't make love that way. They go at it like wild men in search of a moment of ecstasy that vanishes before their eyes, and then all there is is an object called a woman who has been a means of relief . . . but now becomes an embarrassing presence at the moment of satisfaction. The Princess says that most men—or women—don't know how to savor love." By this time I realized that I had gone too far. Bucky was looking at me with a sick-calf expression.

"I'm not like that, Willa. At least, I wouldn't be with you."

I slid down on the couch, kicked off my shoes, and put my feet on the cocktail table. "How many girls have you had, Bucky?"

"No so many." He poured another drink. "I'm twenty-four. Maybe I've made love to four . . . five, I guess. But I didn't have any fun. It's no fun in a car or on a blanket with the girl half scared to death." Bucky sighed. "Maybe it could be fun, but girls don't do it for fun. They want to know right away when you are going to marry them, and they are sure that in a few weeks they'll be pregnant."

That's the way Converse thought, too. I brushed a tear from my eye. "Poor Bucky," I said, "Twenty-four years old and never had any fun." I looked at him dizzily and patted his hard jaw. Bucky is quite handsome.

"Let's try Sawyer's bed," he said enthusiastically. He pulled me to my feet.

"No, I don't think that's a good idea, Bucky," I said, knowing that something perverse in me was toying with the idea.

"Aw, come on Willa. You sure aren't like your Ma. I'll bet she wouldn't leave here without trying that bed. She'd be a match for little ol' Sawyer, anytime."

"Bucky, you are making mockery of all the word 'mother' stands for. Remember Whistler's mother." I let myself be led into the bedroom.

"Your Ma would be insulted to be compared with that old hag," Bucky said. "Let me show you the hi-fi rig this guy has got . . . just look at the records." Bucky pulled a switch and caressing music seemed to flow from all four walls and embrace us with fluttering hands of love.

Bucky gave a low whistle. "Wham-bam, I never heard any music like that. I'll bet your ma could do a dance to that that would set you on your ears."

"You have an inflated idea of my mother's abilities," I said. I held onto the edge of the phonograph cabinet to steady myself. "I'll bet I know more about sexual dances than the Princess. All *she* does is *do* them. I made a *study* of them. I took a course in the dance at Radcliffe. This music is derived from Hindu sources. In its insistent repetition it is trying to create an aphrodisiac mood . . . a dance of life itself."

Bucky listened to me dumfounded. While I knew it was silly, I couldn't help leading him on.

"Did you ever hear of the dance done by the nautch girls for the Oriental sultans?" I whispered.

Bucky shook his head limply.

"Neither did the Princess," I said solemnly. "It is a dance so provocative that, when the dancers have finished, the men are in such a state of distress they beg for relief."

Now, you can understand the danger of reading too much.

134

I had never seen a nautch dance, but I had read about them in some book or other devoted to the orient. Under the influence of three Rob Roys I was convinced, moreover, that I should try to do one.

20

It must have been those mirrors and the fetching idea of seeing myself as others saw me. Something in the primitive areas of my brain, something in the insistent beat of the music, something in the expression on Bucky's face—and I was undulating to the rhythm . . . and then I was transformed. I was no longer Willa Starch. I *was* a nautch dancer. Not Willa any longer—a third person, a stranger who was slowly unbuttoning her blouse while she swayed easily. She was air itself blowing lightly through some Japanese willow tree.

The girl in the mirror was naked to the waist. Her arms were a graceful arch above her head, her breasts uplifted. Her fingers were moving in a kind of tantalizing conversation, and now her breasts were smiling at the multiple reflection of the identical man in every corner of the room who was watching her with a lascivious expression on his face. Silently, teasingly, the girl danced, and the music reached out and enveloped her, and she was sex and love incarnate and graceful to look at. And then, somehow, the girl had stepped out of her skirt, and she was naked and barefoot, with the strong legs of a girl dancer, and the arc her hips made as she danced grew wider and wider. Slowly . . . weaving . . . thrusting her belly . . . arching her mound, flexing her knees, she sinuously caressed her own body. When the music stopped, she sank with bent head to the carpet, exhausted.

I looked up in horror! The girl was me! I was sitting in the middle of Sawyer Priestly's bedroom, naked. Bucky Bonnelli was lifting me to my feet, and I was aware for the first time that he, too, was naked and very much ready to write a new chapter in the short history of Willa Starch.

"God! . . . you were wonderful," Bucky breathed huskily. "I never thought you had it in you, Willa. Your old lady can't hold a candle to you." I was aware that Bucky's hands were, one minute, teasing my breasts, the next, touching my belly, then caressing my behind. It was very nice . . . and very confusing . . . because I wanted it to be Converse and not Bucky . . . and I was saying, "No . . . no . . . I don't think so . . . I don't think we should, Bucky . . . no . . . no . . . oh. . . ." when suddenly we heard the elevator door open.

We stared at each other in near shock for a second.

"Jesus," Bucky groaned. "It must be Priestly!"

In a split second I gathered my clothes.

I heard Bucky mutter. "There's no way out! It's either in the closet . . . or brazen it out!"

Rob Roys no longer had me in their possession. I was cold sober.

In the living room we could hear Sawyer's voice and a female voice that I instantly recognized as Miss Smoky's.

"Fire escape," I gasped, feeling as if I might wet the panties I wasn't wearing.

"It's off the living room window," Bucky said hopelessly. He was holding his seersucker suit in a roll in his hands. He looked so silly that, if I hadn't been scared half to death, I would have died laughing on the spot.

He ran on tiptoes around the room looking for a possible hiding place. "We're cornered," he groaned.

"No, we're not. The bed! Under the bed!" I felt as if I were in a Laurel and Hardy movie.

Bucky bounced onto the dais and lifted the purple satin skirt. The bed was low, but there was at least a foot or more between the box springs and the broadloomed floor. It was do or die. Clutching my clothes and pocketbook, I slithered under. It was pitch black. I felt Bucky slide in beside me. In the confusion, he was facing toward the head of the bed, and I was facing south to his north. It made conversation difficult. When I finally grew accustomed to the dim light, darned if I wasn't staring at Buck's still erect jigger. I was not only embarrassing, it was impossible! How could he still be interested when we were both on the brink of catastrophe? We were under the bed less than a minute when Sawyer and Smoky came into the bedroom.

"Stop worrying," I heard Sawyer say. "It's that damned cleaning woman, I'm sure of it. She made herself a pitcher of drinks with my best Scotch and then got herself pie-eyed. This isn't the first time . . . but it's going to be the last!"

I could hear the bathroom door being opened and then the closet door being slid back. "There's no one here. Stop fretting, Pussy. The elevator door was locked when we came in, and I locked it again when we got off."

He must have goosed Pussy—God, what a name—because she tittered and said: "Not yet, Sawyer. I want to take a bath. It's been such a sticky day. But, first, make me a drink, will you, Lambie."

We heard them walk back into the living room.

"Lambie and Pussy! Isn't that cute?" Bucky chuckled and I felt him kissing my belly!

I tried to edge away from him. "Bucky Bonnelli . . . you cut it out! How can you be so playful? If Sawyer catches us under here, he'll have us both arrested for breaking and entering." Then I gasped. I had a sudden vision of Lambie and Pussy in bed together on top of us, making love. If the spring came down, we would be crushed to death under their weight. I told Bucky, but it didn't seem to bother him. He kept right on kissing me, and in the dim light that filtered under the bed I could see that his penis had grown larger than I ever had believed possible.

"If you don't stop this minute, Bucky Bonnelli," I hissed at him. "I'll take a bite out of you that you'll remember as long as you live."

That sobered him up. "What do you want me to do?" he whispered. Raising his head to try and see my face he hit it against a slat in the bed. He stifled a yell of pain. "Darn you, Willa . . . I was having fun for the first time in my life."

"Shhh . . . just let me alone and CONCENTRATE! How are we going to get out of here? They may stay all night."

As I said it, the bedroom door opened again.

"It's beyond me, Pussy." Sawyer's voice had the same endearing quality he had used on me. "Maybe the levis belong to the cleaning woman's son. Maybe she was going to wash them. I tossed them down the waste chute. Stop worrying, my Pussy-Kitty."

"Damn it all," I heard Bucky whisper. "Keep your cotton-pickin' hands off my jeans." I shoved my big toe in Bucky's mouth.

"Did you hear something, Sawyer?" Pussy sounded quite nervous. She was obviously frightened by the condition of the apartment. Maybe she had a husband who was looking for her.

"Pussy . . . it's nothing. It's the heat and your nerves. Drink your drink and then come lie in Lambie's arms for a few minutes All your little worries will vanish."

Oh, brother. They were going to get in bed. My mind raced for some solution. Did I dare crawl out from under the bed and say nonchalantly, "I was waiting for you, Sawyer. When I heard the elevator I got frightened and hid under the bed." Boy, that would throw a clinker in Sawyer Priestly's love life! I almost burst out laughing as I imagined the grim look on Smoky's face as she examined naked me. I really should do it, I thought. If Buck would only stay put, he could clear out later after the dust settled down.

I should have. But I'm a thinker, not a doer, and I just didn't have that kind of aplomb. I kept thinking there must be some other way Bucky and I could get out of the apartment unnoticed. It was bad enough invading Sawyer's love life and listening while he and Pussy made love, but the thought of what effect this might have on Bucky Bonnelli, already frustrated beyond endurance, was scary to contemplate. I regretted ever getting so involved with him.

But Pussy wasn't jumping into bed. "I'm so sticky," she said, playing for time. "It's been such a hot day. I think I'll just dawdle in your big cool bathtub for a while, Lambie."

"I'll dawdle with you," Sawyer said enthusiastically. "There's plenty of room."

I couldn't help grinning. Pussy wasn't going to escape that easily. Evidently she didn't care, because there was a long silence, and then I heard a zipper being pulled.

"Unhook my bra, Lambie," Pussy said. "Ooooh . . . you bad boy." She giggled, "Lambie . . . you are so eager. All right . . . you can take a bath with your little Pussy."

We heard them go into the bathroom and heard water running in the tub, and then the bathroom door was closed.

Squealing with joy, Bucky slid out from under the bed. By the time I had squirmed out after him, he was standing in front of the closed bathroom door carefully inserting a huge gold key into the lock. He turned it and yelled, "Hot damn! It works!" He grabbed me and danced me around insanely.

In the bathroom, Sawyer heard us. The doorknob wiggled furiously and he shouted, "Who's out there? Unlock this door at once!" He pounded on the door.

The sinister evil look of a television desperado spread over Bucky's face. Except that he was naked and still amazingly rampant, he looked like a fast-gun artist about to outdraw the local hero.

"You in there . . ." Bucky snarled. "This is Joe Fluger . . . one of the Fluger gang. I'm holding a machine gun a foot away from this door. If you and your lady friend don't stop squawking, I'm going to tap out a little tune on this typewriter." Buck roared with insane laughter, enjoying his inspirational role to the hilt. "You climb back in that tub with your lady friend. You never had it so good, Chum. Me and my gang are hiding out here for a few days, Priestly . . so take your time. . . . Conserve your energy."

There was absolute silence from the bathroom.

Bucky swaggered toward me. "How's that, kid? Guess that will shut them up."

"Okay," I whispered, trying to sort out my clothes. "I'm not your moll. Forget the Joe Fluger bit. Get dressed and let's get out of here . . . fast."

"Get dressed?" Bucky said pushing me in the direction of the bed. "Why get dressed? God, you're cute, Willa. You've got the biggest eyes and longest lashes I ever saw on a girl, and pretty tits and a damned fine behind."

I shoved him away.

"What the trouble?" he demanded angrily. "You don't have to worry about Priestly and that broad. They can't get out of there. There's no window, only a fan and an air duct. We've got it made! We can use the place all weekend."

Dressing as fast as I could, considering that Bucky was first at my bra and then at my panties, I got free of him.

"You must be absolutely crazy, Bucky Bonnelli. I've completely lost my enthusiasm. From now on, I'm staying on Trotter Island every weekend. I'm through with men. I'm going to be a spinster."

"Well, I'll be a crock. . . ." Bucky said disgustedly. "You brought me here didn't you? I got you out of this mess, didn't I? Did I ask you to dance for me like a dame in heat? Aw, come on Willa . . . you owe it to me."

"I'll charge it," I said, quite convinced that there was going to be no payment. "Look, I'm full of admiration for you. You did some fast thinking. Where did you ever find the key?"

"I saw it when I was in the crapper. I snitched it for Papa. He collects keys. He's got more than two thousand." Bucky chuckled. "Just shows you can get *too* rich. Never could have happened in a poor man's crapper with a built-in lock."

Bucky watched me, still making no attempt to get dressed himself. When I told him to hurry up, he shrugged and said, "What's your sweat? I'm not going anywhere." He held up Pussy's dress from a heap of clothes piled on a bedroom chair. "Hey, smell the perfume this babe is wearing." He examined her bra, holding it in front of him. "Bigger than yours, Willa!" A diabolical grin suddenly broke out on his

139

face. Before I realized what he was doing he had gathered all of Pussy's and Sawyer's clothes in a huge heap.

"Oh, no . . you can't do that," I said, anticipating him.

"The hell I can't." Bucky pushed me away and strode into the kitchen. "I haven't had any fun today, yet!" He opened the waste chute and Pussy's and Lambie's clothes disappeared with a swishing sigh.

Still paying no attention to me, he walked back to listen at the bathroom door. It was very quiet on the other side.

"Priestly," Bucky said in his Joe Fluger voice.

A hollow-sounding "yes" came from the bathroom.

"I just want you to know that no matter how quiet it gets in here . . . one of us Fluger boys is sitting right here on your bed with this little ol' machine gun aimed at the bathroom door. If you and your tomato don't keep your traps shut, you'll come out of there on slabs looking like pin cushions."

Bucky walked back in the living room. "Come on, Willa," he said sprawling naked on the couch. "Let's have a few more drinks and get you back in the mood."

"I'm going," I said. "You can stay here . . get yourself another woman!" I pushed the elevator button.

Bucky watched me with an amused expression on his face. "Who's going to let your friend out? It's Saturday afternoon . . . four-fifteen. I wonder if anyone else knows about this place . . . ? Not his wife, I'll bet you. The cleaning woman would probably find them in a week or two . . . starved to death."

The elevator arrived—and departed without me.

Bucky was right. Somehow we had to make sure that Lambie and Pussy got out of their bathroom prison.

"Herman Snole would sure like to know about this," Bucky said thoughtfully. "Priestly would probably give up Trotter Island—and then some—to get out of this mess. I can see the headlines, now: PROMINENT BOSTON BUSINESSMAN TRAPPED IN LOVE NEST." Bucky jumped up excitedly. "I got it, Willa. Where's the telephone?" He poked around the room and found it under an end table. "You call that Cabot character. It's the Billings and Cabot Development Corporation that actually owns Trotter Island, isn't it? You tell Cabot that you got something very important to tell him . . . something that will affect his whole future . . . you can lay it on thick. Then you tell him that you'll meet him at the Statler-Hilton in an hour."

I listened to Bucky, astonished by his ego, which was now bordering on simple insanity. "Then what do we do? Give him the key to the bathroom and tell him to open it up for a big surprise?"

Bucky shook his head disgustedly. "Don't be cute, Willa. I'll go with you. We'll tell him point blank that we got Sawyer Priestly and some broad who isn't his wife trapped naked in a bathroom. We won't tell him where . . . but if he wants to save Sawyers's reputation he'll get us a written assignment of the deed to Trotter Island. If not, we'll call the Boston newspapers and give one of the reporters the key, and at the same time we'll notify Sawyer's wife."

"That's blackmail!" I said, startled and frightened by Bucky's audacity. "You wouldn't do that! They won't believe you, anyway. Converse is smarter than that. Anyway, you're counting on him not knowing where Sawyer's apartment is."

"That's a sure thing." Bucky said gleefully. "If this were just an ordinary apartment, the Cabots or Billings might know about it. But this is a seduction chamber . . . and I'll bet the only people who have ever been here besides Priestly are dames."

"Well, I'm not telephoning Converse," I said. If I telephoned Converse after what happened in Sawyer's office, that would be the payoff. Willa Starch's morals were low enough in Converse's mind. If he ever knew that I was involved in such a sordid business, he'd try to get me committed to a home for wayward girls. Of all the screwball ideas! But the more I tried to convince Bucky that this way was madness . . . that he was losing his grip on reality . . . the more enthusiastic he became. It was hopeless. He had begun to see himself as the saviour of Trotter Island.

It's the revolution of the depressed masses," Bucky said grimly. "All is fair in love and war. Whose side are you on, anyway, Willa? I think you have gone soft for that Priestly character."

"Please, Bucky," I pleaded. "Stop daydreaming . . . the whole idea is absolutely batty. If you weren't pretty tight from those Rob Roys, you'd admit it. Besides, if it were a good idea, I couldn't do that to Sawyer. He may be a Casanova and all that, but making a scandal and ruining his life, ugh . . . that's a dirty trick."

Bucky shook his head. "I don't agree with you. When Priestly gave you the key to this place, he wasn't inviting you just to play house and patty-cake. When he got tired of you, that would be *your* tough luck! You're a softy, Willa, but I like you. If you want to save this cruddy character, okay . . . go to bed with me right now, and I'll sacrifice Trotter Island for you."

Bucky had a smoochy look on his face. I hastily pulled out of his grasp. "You are completely insane. Let's get out of here first and then discuss it. Maybe when we get out of this atmosphere we can come up with a sensible solution."

"Never mind, Goodie Starch. I've got a better idea." Bucky started to paw through the telephone book. "I'll call Stephanie Billings. I'll bet she'll crawl into the sack with me to save Priestly's reputation."

It was obvious that sexual frustration—or the vision of Sawyer's luxurious trap for unsuspecting females—had caused a complete mental breakdown. Bucky was unhinged, cut loose from his moorings. He refused to leave. When he finally realized that I wasn't going to get in Sawyer's bed with him, he reluctantly got dressed, a moody, sullen expression on his face. He made another pitcher of Rob Roys and sat on the couch drinking them and staring coldly at the statue of Kwan Yin. When I begged him to leave, he ignored me.

I tiptoed into the bedroom and listened at the bathroom door. I could hear Pussy crying and Sawyer trying to soothe her, promising that he would find some way out of their predicament. I felt like a heel. I wondered what I would do if I were trapped naked in a bathroom with Sawyer. I felt sorry for Sawyer Priestly and the amorous necessities that had brought him to such a sorry state. If he had sense enough to leave women alone he would never have got mixed up with Miss Smoky—or worse—hired a girl named Willa Starch with whom he had planned, evidently, to two-time both his wife, Abigail, as well as Miss Smoky. Right now he should be with Abigail, where he told me that he was going to be in the first place—safe, and a Proper Bostonian aboard their cruiser.

Although I could hear Smoky crying I couldn't work up any concern for her . . . which goes to show you that no woman really likes another and all their sorrow goes to the louse who gets them in trouble.

But when I got back into the living room, I *wasn't* sorry for a louse named Bucky Bonnelli.

"Is this the residence of Miss Stephanie Billings?" He grinned at me. "Wait until you hear this, Kid." Then, into the telephone, "Well, you go get her off the pot, sister, I don't care if she *is* busy. Tell her an old friend wants to shoot the breeze with her. . . ." Pause—and then, to me. "Some maid trying to give me the who-shall-I-tell-her-is-calling routine."

"What are you going to say to her?" I asked, aghast, still not believing that he would go through with such a mad idea.

"You're playing out of your league, Bucky Bonnelli. You'll end up in her male curio collection."

Bucky just smirked. "Stephanie, is that you?" he said warmly into the telephone, and his voice was a deep, cultured imitation of a Harvard accent. "You probably won't remember me. I met you last year at the uwontbelieveits affair." He garbled the words so that they were unintelligible. Stephanie evidently clued him in by repeating a name. "Yes . . . that's right . . . the Tom Everts . . . a nice couple. You were with young Converse Cabot. Yes, oh yes, I've known Con for years. Nice chap . . . a little on the dull side. No? Really . . . I never would have thought it possible. Well they do say opposites attract. But I would have imagined that you would have wanted someone with a little more, what do the French call it . . . savvy . . . oh, yes . . . savoir fairy. Well, Converse may not have the savoir . . but he does have the fairy."

Bucky covered the phone and guffawed. "She's agreeing that Converse is a little fruity. He's been in California for two weeks and hasn't even called her. Baby, I'm in like Flynn."

I'm afraid that I squealed my happiness. Converse hadn't called me because he was in California! I didn't care *what* happened now. Maybe Converse loved me after all! Fortunately, Bucky was too occupied to notice that I was a girl again and not a middle-aged spinster.

"Stephanie," Bucky was saying with his horrid accent, "I know that it is presumptuous to ask you and all that, but a very dear friend of mine and your family is in a rather serious jam. Do you know Sawyer Priestly? Yes, I knew that he was a close friend and business associate of your father's. No, honestly Stephanie . . . it isn't something that I can discuss over the telephone. No, Sawyer is not in Marblehead. You can confirm this by checking his home . . . but please, Stephanie, if you do call . . . please be discreet. We've got to keep his wife out of it. Well, you're pretty close to the truth . . . Stephanie, I hope you will keep this between the two of us for the moment. Sawyer asked me to call you particularly. . . ."

I was astounded by the magnitude of Bucky's lie. I tried to wrestle the phone out of his grasp. "The truth is . . . " Bucky was saying, as he fended me off. He covered the phone. "Willa, if you don't get the hell out of here, I'll open the bathroom door and shove you in with Sawyer and his girl friend. . . . Yes, it's a noisy connection, Stephanie. As I was saying, the truth is that Sawyer would prefer that your father or any of the Cabots would not know about this at the moment. I hate to bother you on Saturday night, Stephanie . . . but, really, Priestly is in quite a mess. If you and I don't do something, I'm afraid it'll be a scandal that will rock Boston. Yes . . . it's another woman. Did you know that Sawyer has an in-town apartment? I thought not. It seems that our friend Sawyer Priestly is quite a gay blade. Stephanie, I'm counting on you. We can't let the Cabots, the Priestlys, and the Billings become the laughingstock of Boston. Stephanie, I can't. My car is in Marblehead. Besides there's really no time to lose. You can be in from Cohasset on the expressway in twenty-five minutes. All right. At five-thirty in the Persian Lounge at the Sheraton. Don't worry, I'll recognize you."

Bucky put the phone down with a yelp. "I did it! I did it! She's coming. Oh, Susannah . . . what a night *this* is going to be!" He grabbed me and whirled me around and then put me down in front of the elevator door. "Good-bye, Willa," he said merrily. "I'll be seeing you around."

"Just what are you planning to do with Stephanie?" I demanded.

"You must be a little dense. I'm going to do what I couldn't do with you, Goodie Starch. When little Stephanie finds out what a jam her friend is in, she's going to say . . . all right . . . take me . . . take me . . . but leave my friend go." Bucky was delighted with himself. He laughed at my horrified expression. "The details are really none of your business. The fact is that from five-thirty on I'm playing it by ear. Maybe I'll save Trotter Island . . . maybe I'll get in the sack with Stephanie Billings, the blonde missile, . . . I wonder if she has a silver blonde pussy to match the rest of her?" Bucky's confidence was nauseating. I wanted to sock him. "Stop worrying, Willa . . . just go your way . . . I'll promise you that sometime before morning I'll hand Stephanie the key, and your friend Priestly and his sexpot will get out of their prison."

"I won't let you do it!" I said. "Give me back the key to this apartment this minute. It's mine! Sawyer gave it to me."

Bucky clasped me in a vise-like grip. "Can you move, Willa Starch?"

"No, you big ape. I can scream, though!"

"If you scream, and if you don't get on that elevator now, I'll open the bathroom and toss you in with them. I'll have the door locked on all three of you before you can say Miss Muffet sat on a tuffet." Bucky pushed the elevator button. "Now you get out of here. I'm going to see if I can fit into one of Sawyer's suits."

"You'll never make it. You'll burst the seams. . . . Bucky,"

I wailed, "Let me go. You've got to take me home. How will I get back to Trotter Island?"

Bucky pushed me in the elevator. "You can wait in my boat. There's a nice cozy bunk. Just undress and crawl in. I'll be back sometime and take care of you, too!"

21

By the time the elevator had crept to the lobby I was so angry with Bucky that I decided to go back and show him who was boss. I pushed the button to Sawyer's apartment, but the elevator didn't respond. Sawyer had relocked it when he came in with Miss Smoky, and Bucky had my key. The only thing I could do was to wait until Bucky came down. He had promised to meet Stephanie at five-thirty. He had to come down eventually.

Sitting uneasily in the dimly lighted lobby I tried to ignore a bald-headed houseman who walked by several times staring at me. He finally asked if he could help me, and—after a few minutes, dissatisfied with my no, and evidently thinking I was on the make or something—asked me if I were waiting for a particular tenant. When finally I told him that I was waiting for Mr. Sawyer Priestly, he said:

"Oh, Mr. Priestly won't be in today. It's Saturday. Mr. Priestly rarely comes in on Saturdays."

I couldn't help smiling. Sawyer was sorry now that he had tossed this busybody a red herring. Baldy was examining me so carefully I figured that he must be planning to identify me in court should the need arise.

Fortunately the elevator door opened, and Bucky got off wearing a pinstripe suit, a shirt, and a tie. With his hair carefully combed he looked almost too neat to be Bucky Bonnelli—a transmogrification from Trotter Island to Beacon Street caused by a change of clothing.

Bucky looked at me reproachfully and walked out of the building without a word. I tagged at his heels, knowing that I was adding fuel to the suspicions already burning in the houseman's mind.

On closer inspection, Bucky didn't look quite so sharp. The shirt was much too small at the neck, and the cuffs on Sawyer's coat hung two inches above his wrist. His blue-black beard had grown since morning.

"You need a shave and a new tailor," I said. "Brooks Brothers is where the Ivy Leaguers go."

"I couldn't shave! There's friends of yours in the bathroom, remember?" Bucky crossed Beacon Street and headed toward the Public Gardens. He was walking so fast that I was dogtrotting to keep up with him. "Go away, Willa. Beat it. Don't bother me," he said sharply.

"What about Sawyer and that woman?" I demanded. "Bucky, you can't do this! I won't permit it! There must be some other way to get Sawyer out of that bathroom without ruining his reputation or getting caught ourselves."

"You had your chance. Stop worrying about Priestly. He's as snug as a bug. Probably curled up in the bathtub right now with that babe. Leave me alone, Goodie Starch," Bucky said nastily. "I'm after bigger game."

That made me so mad that I took a swipe at him with my pocketbook, but I only hit air and had to run after him to catch him. He stopped near the statue of Edward Everett Hale, who, oblivious to the pigeons roosting on his head, stared benignly at us. "Now, look here, Willa. If you want to save your precious Sawyer Priestly and that Pussy of his . . . okay, you can do it. Here's the key to the apartment. Here's the key to the bathroom. You're on your own. Go back and let Sawyer out. Plead insanity. See how much Sawyer loves you when you open that door."

I backed away from the keys. One thing I couldn't do, if I had any hope of ever seeing Converse again, was to personally open that door or be anywhere in the vicinity when it was opened. Sawyer might eventually suspect I was involved. At the moment, however, he couldn't prove it.

"Okay, you don't want the keys. You've got one other choice. You've been teasing me all summer. We can go back to Sawyer's apartment and you put up or shut up." Bucky chuckled, enjoying my unhappy expression. "Remember, it's only on the basis of long friendship that I give you the preference. After all, it means I'd have to sacrifice Stephanie!"

I tried to pummel him with both fists, but he caught my arms. "Goodie Starch," he sneered. "Go back to my boat and wait for me. Right now it's you who is batting in the wrong league. And don't try to follow me, or I'll get you involved in this mess right up to your pretty little eyelashes."

146

I watched him heading toward Boylston Street and the Prudential Center. He was an insufferable egomaniac with an inflated idea of his allure for females. I sighed. There was nothing I could do for Sawyer now. His fate was out of my hands.

If there is any moral to his predicament (Bostonians always like to have a moral) it's a Periclean one: To maintain authority the leader must not fraternize with his subjects; or, don't hand out apartment keys to your hired help, regardless of their sexual qualifications; or, if you sow the wind, you'll reap the whirlwind.

With a detached feeling—the residual effect of three Rob Roys, combined with an escape from a fate worse than death (being caught under Sawyer's bed)—I ambled through the vivid tents of the Public Gardens Arts Festival. The local artists had expressed their revenge on the bourgeoisie by squeezing any semblance of reality out of their pictures and creating a carnage of color in tortured blobs and linear wracks. Each painting was thumbing its nose at the curious beholder who no longer knew what a thumb-to-nose meant.

A crowd of thirty or more people was gathered around one canvas. I would have edged my way by and not bothered to look further at this desecration of wonder if someone hadn't said: "The short stocky fellow is the husband of the model."

I stood on tiptoes to see what was going on, but there were too many people in front of me. "What's the matter?" I asked a six-foot-six man standing beside me.

"An outraged husband. The guy looks like a wrestler. Says he's gonna beat the artist to a pulp. The artist is up there arguing with him. Sounds like a ball."

Still not entirely sure, I squeezed forward through the crowd. By elbowing a bulbous woman in a green-and-yellow-print dress (she complained bitterly about pushers and shovers), I reached the rope that formed one side of the aisle through the tent.

It was Henry all right. He was shaking his fist at Mendes East telling him in a stentorian voice that he would not permit his wife to be displayed bare-assed in front of all these snickering idiots. Mendes was trying unsuccessfully to ignore him and, at the same time to prevent Henry from removing a nearly life-size painting from the wall.

At least I now knew that the Princess had actually been posing for a painting. And what a painting! The Princess was standing in a pale green spotlight. She was clinging lightly to a faded velvet theatre curtain, waving her G string over the footlights at an audience of middle-aged men and youngsters who were grinning and cheering her enthusiastically. Mendes had painted more than a resemblance of my mother. He had captured something of her blithe good spirits. While the painting was no doubt provocative, it was the only painting I had seen so far in the show that sang with a lusty exuberance and a love of life. Mendes was offering Rabelaisian good humor and a belly laugh, in contrast to the sterile, hollow, preachers of doom who dominated the show with their paintings. I hastily looked at my program. The painting was captioned "Last Bump . . . End of an Era. *Price $2500.*"

"Henry, you're all shook . . . calm down and look at the thing rationally," Mendes was saying uneasily. "This is the way thousands of people knew Prin. It's a monument to her career. Prin is not just a face to the world. She's an exquisite, vibrant body. If you wanted a woman just for the privacy of your own bedroom, you should never have married a stripper."

"I don't give a damn what Prin used to do," Henry yelled. "She's retired now, and she's forty-two years old. She ain't got brains enough to be modest . . . so I got to be modest for her!"

Henry shoved Mendes away from the painting and lifted it from its hangings. Several hundred people now jammed the tent, and I had a difficult time keeping Henry and Mendes in view. The crowd was good-humored, some encouraging Henry, some Mendes. They had the painting balanced between them, each with a group of unsolicited cohorts tugging on either side of the frame.

"It's not my picture any longer," Mendes shouted hoarsely. "Let go, Henry! I told you, Reliance Cabot bought the picture yesterday!"

Mendes might just as well have thrown a match in a gasoline can. The tent suddenly erupted. I caught a glimpse of Pierre Grass leaping out of the crowd. The rope holding back the excited onlookers gave way. A police siren whined on Boylston Street, but the enthusiastic crowd paid no attention, surging around Henry and Mendes until I couldn't see what was happening. I tried to fight my way into the tug of war to see who was going to win the painting of the Princess. People were yelling and laughing hysterically, inciting the contestants on. Then the police broke through the crowd. A path opened before them. I saw Henry and some men who were arrayed on his side of the painting give a furious tug. The canvas tipped, and Henry and Pierre Grass tumbled with their half of the painting into the arms of the hilarious crowd.

The police pulled Henry and Pierre to their feet, corralled Mendes, and marched all of them past the cheering spectators out of the tent. As he passed, Henry bowed and waved his hands in a triumphant victor's grin. His face was flushed. It wasn't difficult to tell that he and Pierre were incandescent with Old Robbie. Mendes, jacked up under each shoulder by a burly policemen, recognized me. He shrugged fatalistically and said, "It's better the world end with a bang than a whimper!"

I followed the crowd to Arlington Street and watched the police usher Henry, Pierre, and Mendes into a paddy wagon. It didn't look as if I could contribute anything to the altercation, so I let them be taken away without declaring myself.

When I had first recognized Henry, I thought for a moment that I had discovered a way to get back to Trotter Island without Bucky Bonnelli's assistance. But now it seemed likely that the Princess had been right about Henry and Pierre ending up in the jug. I was sure that I wouldn't be able to count on them for transportation tonight. And no one would be more tickled at the reason for their arrest than the Princess herself.

I bought a bag of peanuts. Sitting on the grass near the Swan Boats, I ate hungrily, not even sharing with the insistent pigeons.

I needed a moment to sift the continuing confusion of my life. Why had Reliance bought a painting of my mother and paid twenty-five hundred dollars for it? Was the painting that good? The tense was wrong. *Had* the painting *been* that good? Unless Mendes could repaint it, he would have to return Reliance Cabot's money. If the Princess ever posed for Mendes again, it would be over Henry's dead body. Mendes would blame Henry for destroying Reliance Cabot's property. I could picture Henry spending the rest of his natural life in jail rather than pay anyone twenty-five hundred dollars for a nude painting of his wife—a painting that no longer existed, moreover.

I didn't even want to guess what Converse would think about the whole episode, which would no doubt be reported in high glee by the Boston newspapers. Being linked on the front page of the newspapers with the low morals of the Starch family would be anathema to the Cabots. It occurred to me that, even if I succeeded in prying Converse loose from Stephanie, I would be involved in a Montague-Capulet controversy that would probably finish with me eating the sleeping pills and waking up to find Bucky Bonnelli in the family crypt . . . and the way I felt about Bucky at the moment that would be enough of a reason for me to stab myself.

It was obvious that my problems weren't amenable to reason. I tried Descartes' "I think, therefore I am—" for a minute, but, instead of proving to me that I existed, it reminded me of Sawyer and Miss Smoky, and I wasn't sure that I wanted to prove the reality of the whole thing anyway.

So I sat under the elm trees in the Public Gardens and waited for the Festival Ballet. And, when Andre Eglevsky danced with Maria Tallchief, he didn't know it, but it was me, Willa Starch, sitting under the trees in spellbound admiration, who did a *pas de poisson* into his arms, not Coppelia.

22

When the ballet ended, I pulled my head from the sand and decided to face the inevitable. I took a taxi back to Commercial Wharf. The driver left me with a suspicious question that implied that I would come to no good hanging around the wharves at this time of night. I told him I had a date with a sea monster and to please mind his own business. He backed off the wharf in a huff. I lowered myself into Bucky's boat wondering whether he or something worse would emerge out of the dark shadows. I was prepared to let out an earsplitting scream, but neither Bucky nor any other sinister occupant accosted me. Bucky was either making out with Stephanie or he was in a cell—next to Mendes, Henry, and Pierre. I hoped the latter, and then I didn't, because the shadows of the boat were eery, and I had the feeling that I was being watched. I tried to lock myself in the cabin, but there was no latch on the door, and the chair I pushed against it looked ineffectual and puny. I sat rigidly on the bunk, not daring to light a lamp for fear I would attract unwanted attention, and I listened to the water lapping against the boat, rats scampering among the pilings, and occasional footsteps above me on the wharf that seemed to hesitate, as if the owner of the shoes were contemplating whether to come down the ladder and grab me—shivering and docile with fright.

Fright finally gave way to exhaustion. I awoke with a yell of fear to find Bucky standing over me dressed in his seersucker suit, and the cabin lighted with a dull orange bulb that gave little illumination.

"Shut up," he said disgustedly. "I haven't touched you yet."

I noticed four deep fingernail scratches still wet with blood running from the side of his nose to his left ear. "Been playing in the wrong league?" I asked him and looked at my watch. It was ten minutes past one. "Looks as if you can pitch but can't catch!"

"Shut up," he growled. "Move over in the bunk. We are going to sleep here tonight. It's too dark, and I'm too damned tired to try and find the way back to Trotter. Besides the tide is out."

"I'm not sleeping on this scow with you," I said angrily. "I've got my reputation to think of."

Bucky had taken off his suit and was now in his shorts. He looked at me disgustedly, fished in his billfold, and tossed two ten dollar bills at me. "Go sleep in a hotel, then . . . or sleep on the dock. But you don't have to worry. . . . Tomorrow, I'm going to get myself castrated."

"What happened?" I asked timidly.

Bucky snapped off the light and laid down on the bunk beside me. Pushing me hard against the side of the boat he burrowed out a place for himself. He was silent for a while. "I suppose you'd like to hear all the gory details," he said at last.

I was practically bursting, but I didn't want to appear too eager. "It's up to you."

"She kept me waiting until six o'clock. Then I saw her standing at the entrance of the cocktail lounge with that cool I-am-a-queen look of hers. She recognized me instantly. 'I might have guessed it was some low trick,' she said in a sneery voice. 'Order me a gin and tonic!' She looked at her watch. 'You've got fifteen minutes, Buster. Make it good.' "

"I was wondering how you were going to convince her," I said. "Which did you try first? 'Tell your Daddy to give up Trotter Island, and I'll let Sawyer go!' . . . or, 'Sacrifice your honor and your pink white body to save your family friend!' "

Bucky snorted. "Willa, you have a crude way of expressing yourself and a very poor opinion of me. With a girl like Stephanie, you don't lay it on the line. You've got to be subtle. Of course, I do have an advantage. Stephanie can't help herself. She goes for me."

I tittered. What an ego. With me he could lay it on the line, with Stephanie he had to be subtle . . . and he had the nerve to tell me!

"It took three more drinks in the cocktail lounge and dinner in the Falstaff Room." Bucky chuckled. "She forgot all about the time limit she had set. She even stood Converse up."

"Converse? I thought he was in California."

"He was. He got home last night."

That familiar feeling of loss inundated me. Converse could have called me yesterday. Instead he called Stephanie for a Saturday date. Excuses that I had made for him vanished along with my high hopes. The truth was plain enough: I was not to confuse an afternoon of dalliance in Sawyer's office with the idea of a more lasting relationship. I should have known better, I thought angrily. When I whispered in his ear, "I love you so much, Converse," he hadn't been conjuring pictures of a rose covered cottage with Willa standing in the doorway . . . he had probably been thinking "How in hell do I get out of this mess." So he hadn't telephoned me . . . so I hated him . . . so. . . he, darn it, why kid myself?

"All the time we were eating," Bucky was saying, "she kept telling me that she didn't believe it. Sawyer Priestly would never get himself in such a predicament. Even the *idea* of sturdy reliable Priestly having a mistress and an apartment in Boston was ridiculous. 'If it is true,' she said, 'just where is the apartment? Why all the secrecy?' I could see that she was trying to con me out of the address.

"We weren't getting anywhere. She didn't believe me. It was fast getting down to the level of trading wisecracks, so I decided to hell with Trotter Island. Look, Stephanie, I said, You're a good-looking doll. I don't really give a damn what happens to Priestly and that dame he's locked up with . . . but it would be better if a friend of his opened that bathroom door and not the police.

" 'So what are you proposing?' she asks me. I told her. This time not so subtly. It was nine-thirty, and the tab was already twenty-three dollars and sixty cents. This Stephanie can practically inhale dollar-and-a-quarter drinks. She looks at me with her pencil-line eyebrows raised to the top of her head. 'You must be absolutely mad. Why should I go to bed with you—a complete stranger—in this apartment that sounds like a dream from Kublai Khan . . . to save the reputation of a man who may be in business with my father but, after all, is no close friend of mine. What would probably happen is that I would end up getting raped by you. Sorry, Buster,' she said, 'you just crapped out. Try another roll of the dice!'

This gal was getting me a little burned," Bucky continued. He lighted a cigarette. In the dim glow of the cabin light that was slowly burning out, I leaned on my elbow and watched him smoke. If I could stay awake long enough and used considerable patience, I guessed I would find out eventually what happened to Sawyer and Miss Smoky.

"I stood up," Bucky continued. " 'Good-bye, Stephanie,' I said. 'I'll be seeing you around.'

" What are you going to do about Sawyer?' she demanded.

"I'll leave the key to the bathroom on his coffee table,' I said. Then I'll call the police. I got a friend who reports for the *Record*. I'll call him, too.

" 'Sit down, Bucky,' she said, and she drops the haughty air. 'You're right about one thing. There's something about you I like. And you are the nerviest character I've ever known. I'll tell you what I'll do. I'll make a bargain with you. Show me this apartment. Tell me exactly how you managed to get Sawyer locked inside and prove to me that he is still there. Then I'll consider it. But I'll tell you right now, if I finally agree, you won't have any fun. I think everything about sex is nice except the wrestling in bed . . . and that's just tiring and messy!' "

"So I suppose that you told her about *me*," I said despondently. Once Converse knew that Willa Starch was involved in this business, his opinion of me would scrape to new depths. I could imagine Stephanie telling him the whole shabby story while he listened in puritanical shock.

"The hell I did!" Bucky said. "Accounting for myself was problem enough. I told her that I had been trailing Priestly and persuaded the maid to let me in his apartment. Don't worry, kiddo, I know women better than to let one know that I was mixed up with another all in the same day. I figured this way: Stephanie has listened to my story for nearly four hours. She doesn't believe it, but she's in the mood for adventure, else why has she stayed with me so long, making me go over the details . . . mostly, because she wouldn't be too unwilling to get into the sack with me, Sawyer to the contrary, notwithstanding."

"But you didn't figure right?" I asked.

"Oh, I figured right," Bucky said airily. "Stephanie is really nuts about me, only she doesn't know it yet. Anyway, I got a taxi and we went back. . . ."

"You weren't scared that Sawyer might have gotten out?" I asked. I would never have gone back. The thought of Sawyer possibly sitting there in his living room staring at me—the cause of his ignominy—with a cold malevolent expression gave me the shudders.

"Willa, you have too much imagination," Bucky said patiently. "Sawyer and that dame were in there naked. The building is made of cement and steel griders. The door is good solid pine. And the air shaft wouldn't accommodate a midget. Priestly and the dame wouldn't dare yell for help. Maybe he could dig his way out with a fingernail file in a hundred years of so. If *you* were in the same spot you'd spent the time praying that whoever finally opened the door was deaf, dumb, and blind.

"Anyway, Stephanie and I got back to the apartment. I led her into the bedroom and established contact. Priestly started to plead with me and offered a deal if I'd unlock the door. It was the ideal time to negotiate on Trotter Island, but I knew that I couldn't have my cake and eat it . . . and Stephanie, listening to our conversation bug-eyed, no longer self-possessed and superior, looked like a pretty tasty piece of cake. . . .

"I pushed her back in the living room, and I said, 'Okay, Steph, how about it!'

"She was pretty shocked. But this gal is a cool actor. 'Make me a drink and we'll talk about it,' she said.

"She followed me into the kitchen, opening cabinets and looking inside while I made some more Rob Roys. When I finished she was back on the couch waiting for me with a little grin and a sort of come-on look on her face. I sat down beside her. 'Who killed Cock Robin?' she asked, giggling, and before I had time to finish the poem for her, she shoved a kitchen knife at my groin, and said, 'Don't move, or I'll kill you.'

"The point had nearly punctured me, and I was thinking in another second Bucky Bonnelli isn't going to have any wild oats left to sow, and that I'd probably have to go to Sweden and find some doctor to finish the job. I tried to move, but she sticks the point of the knife in a little deeper. I look at her sorrowfully. 'What kind of dirty trick is this?' I asked. 'Are you trying to destroy my manhood?'

" 'Dirty trick!' she yells. 'Bucky Bonnelli, are you insane?

What kind of a girl do you think I am, that I would go to bed with you—a perfect stranger? Just hand over the key to that bathroom now, or I'll stab you beyond repair.' "

Bucky turned on his side and looked at me. "Are you listening, Willa? You're kind of quiet."

"I'm listening . . . breathless," I said.

"I guess I don't understand women," Bucky sighed. "What harm is a little loving?"

"The only difference between you and Sawyer is financial," I said. "Go on, I'm popeyed with admiration for Stephanie. Did she cut it off for you?"

"Aw, Willa . . . you're silly. I just stared at her for a second. Finally, she couldn't stand it. Her eyes faltered. I reached down and took the knife out of her hand. 'You see, Sparrow,' I told her,' you couldn't do it A man might cut off another man's balls, but a woman could never do that. It goes against nature. You aimed at the wrong place. If you had been serious about killing me you would have stuck the knife in my heart.'

"You know what she did then? She started to cry." Bucky grinned. "From now on, I thought, it's going to be clear sailing. I kissed her and slowly got her undressed. And believe me, she was *dressed*. Peeling that skin tight girdle off her in a delicate sort of way was like trying to skin a fish without a fish knife. She had a couple of more drinks and was half-heartedly kissing me back. Except for stocking ravelling on her legs, I finally had her in her birthday suit. I guided her gently toward the bedroom. . . ."

"You don't have to go on," I said, "I can guess the rest."

"No you can't," Bucky said. "I got her on Priestly's bed, and she was looking at me in a very seductive way, acting kind of shy, and yet hungry-like . . . you know the way girls are."

"Yes, I know," I admitted.

"Well, I thought, up to now it's been a nonproductive day, Bucky Bonnelli, but, at last, you are going to have some fun . . . and the pay-off is going to be better than you ever expected.

"If you're trying to get my goat . . . don't," I said.

"So, I kissed her a second or two, and then, all of a sudden, she jumps up and says in a very shy and beguiling voice, 'Honey, I need my pocketbook. Give me a minute to get ready will you, Hon.' I guess this 'honey' business must have unhinged my brain. Still, I'm a very trusting guy. We had passed the hurdle of the knife routine safely, so what else could happen? So I let her go in the living room. I even

155

heard the dial of the telephone whirr twice before I suspected the worst. I got to the living room just in time to put my finger on the phone as Stephanie whispered, 'Police!'

"How do you like that? She was going to try and get me tossed in the jug. When I put the phone back in the cradle and told her I was very disappointed—her welching on a deal and all that—she became a snarling wildcat. She tried to gouge my eyes out with her long silver fingernails, tried to knee me in the balls, and, when I attempted to calm her down, she sunk her teeth into my shoulder." Bucky sighed. He was quiet for a moment.

"Maybe at last you have found out that you are not God's gift to the female sex," I said sarcastically. "What did you do then?"

"What else *could* I do?" Bucky said. "I pinned her arms behind her back so that I wouldn't get clawed to pieces, flung her in a fireman's carry over my shoulders, got the gold key to Sawyer's bathroom out of my pants, and, before Stephanie Billings could say 'Jack be nimble,' I opened the door and flipped her into Sawyer's arms. Boy was he shocked."

"Oh, no!" I said, horrified. "Now you have done it! You mean that all three of them are in the bathroom?"

Bucky chuckled. "Naked as jaybirds, too! Well, what else could I do? This dame had it made. I would have been her slave. So she crosses me up. I wasn't having any fun. In a few minutes she would have ripped me to shreds. Anyway, I fouled up Priestly good. Alone with one naked dame could be a ball. When I handed him another, he went out of business!"

"Bucky," I said, and tried to shove his feet on the floor. "You didn't solve a thing! You were supposed to get Sawyer and that woman out of the bathroom; instead you've made it worse. We can't leave them there!"

"Stop blowing your stack, Willa." Bucky said grinning. "Listening to Stephanie banging on that door, I figured out . . . what do the French call it? . . . the pièce de résistance. First, I was going to drop Stephanie's clothes down the waste chute, then I got a better idea. I picked up her clothes, folded them neatly, and put them near Sawyer's bed. Then I telephoned Converse Cabot!"

"Oh, my God!" I pounded Bucky's arm. "No . . . no . . . no! You didn't! You couldn't have!" It wasn't going to take any great detective when Converse, Stephanie, and Sawyer compared notes to know that Willa Starch was mixed up in this business. "Please, Bucky, tell me you couldn't get him."

"Oh, I got him all right. Out of bed. This guy Cabot is a

suspicious character. Acted as if I were trying to sell him the Central Artery 'Listen stupid,' I told him. 'You'd better take down this address, and I'm telling you once and for all that you and Priestly better forget this whole bit about a marina on Trotter Island. So far you've got all the employes of A B C Electronics on strike, and if you don't personally unlock Priestly's bathroom door, you'll be reading seventy-two-point headlines in tomorrow's newspapers, such as PROMINENT BOSTON BUSINESSMAN DALLIES IN THE BATHROOM WITH TWO NAKED DILLIES!'

"I'd make a good headline writer, don't you think?" Bucky chuckled.

"Behind bars," I groaned. "That's where you should be. Behind bars with Henry, Mendes, and Pierre—and just about everybody else on Trotter Island."

I told Bucky about the fiasco at the Festival.

"Well, you don't have to worry about me. I'm clean," Bucky said. "Who's going to have me arrested? Priestly or that dame of his? Not on your life. They are praying that I'll keep my mouth shut. Converse or Stephanie? They'd like to, but they aren't going to either. . . ."

"There's *me!*" I wailed. "I should have you locked up. You've ruined my life."

"You mean Converse?" Bucky snorted. "Don't be silly. I saved him for you. When Stephanie tells him that she was nearly raped by that Italian maniac from Trotter Island . . . and I'll bet she lays it on good and thick . . . Converse at first is going to be mad as hell . . . but then the nasty little thought is going to creep into his mind that it's peculiar how easily Stephanie let herself get undressed. No bruises . . . no torn clothes . . . just a neat pile near Sawyer's bed. . . . If it were me, I'd think: There's more here than meets the eye. . . ." Bucky yawned. "I've had a tough day, Willa. How about a little hugging?"

"I'll sleep in this bunk with you, Bucky Bonnelli, not because I think it's a good idea, but because I'm not walking into a hotel at this time of the morning. Just forget that I'm here! And remember your little 'sparrow.' When she catches up with you, she'll make sure. Next time she'll use a bow and arrow, and that will be the end of Cock Robin."

23

I spent the remainder of the night either pinching Bucky's nose to stop him from snoring or foggily pushing his one hundred and eighty pounds off me so that I wouldn't be crushed to death every time he turned over. It was my first experience sleeping with a man. I decided that if I ever married one as restless as Bucky Bonnelli I would insist upon twin beds.

Luckily, I awoke before Bucky and was pulling up the zipper on my dress when he became fully conscious.

"Don't tell me that I slept with a broad all night who wasn't wearing a dress and I didn't even know it," he said sleepily, watching me trying to straighten my hair in the cracked mirror in the cabin. "When did you take it off?"

"Not until you were sound asleep, you can bet," I said. "The way you snored, it sounded as if you were practicing to be a fog horn. Come on. Get dressed. I'm starved. My bones are bent from having you lean against me, and my mouth tastes like Rob Roy died in it."

The wharf was deserted on Sunday morning. Our footsteps rattled on the worn wooden planks. Across the water I noticed that Henry's boat was tied up against Long Wharf. We yelled but there was no answer. Bucky climbed down and looked in the cabin, but there was no one there.

"After I've bought a toothbrush and brushed my teeth for an hour or so," I told Bucky, "we'll go to Police Headquarters and see what happened to them."

Bucky shook his head emphatically. "I'm not going to any police station, thanks. Your old man is a big boy. He doesn't need me to fight his battles."

"You act as if there might be an all-points alarm out for you."

Bucky shrugged. "You can never tell what insane idea Stephanie Billings might dream up. I'm not taking any chances. The police might be too overjoyed to see me."

Atlantic Avenue was lonely, with only an occasional car scurrying along its wide expanse. Unable to locate a taxi, we started to walk toward the Common. Bucky griped that it would be simpler to go back to Trotter. Determined to wash up and take a shower, I announced that I was going to the Y.W.C.A. Besides, the weather didn't look too good. There was a cool east smell of fog in the air.

"It'll be soup out in the harbor by afternoon. What are we going to do in Boston on a Sunday? Go to a museum?" he sneered. "Not me. I'm pooped. Yesterday, I had it."

I walked in silence while he continued to complain. He said that the Princess would probably be worried about me. She'd think I'd been murdered or kidnapped or raped. "Your ma isn't going to appreciate you staying out all night with me. She'll think we shacked up together, and all I'll hear everytime I see her is yuk about her daughter being a nice girl."

"I'm not a nice girl." I said. "I did shack up with you."

"Big shacking," Bucky said sourly. "Goodie Starch . . . one hand across her tits, and one covering her crotch, all curled up in a knot. I might as well have slept with a caterpillar larva. How about making up for it today? It's going to be rainy and cold, anyway. Let's get a nice air-conditioned hotel room. We can soak around in a bathtub together and have a ball."

Bucky waxed enthusiastic, picturing the joys of love and sex for me right up to the toiletries counter in Liggett's Drug Store. I bought two toothbrushes and two small tubes of toothpaste.

"Here," I said, handing him a set, "You may not need to shower, but you better wash your mouth out. Meet me in an hour in the lobby of the Y. . . . You can buy me breakfast."

In the ladies' room I rented a shower stall and toilet. A look in the mirror revealed that my dress wasn't too raunchy looking. I brushed my teeth three times before my mouth felt normal, and then I stayed under the hot shower until I turned light red. I followed that for ten wonderful minutes with a cold needle spray. I decided to hell with my hair. It was cut pretty short, anyhow. If I looked like an African bushman after this soaking, maybe it would dampen Bucky's enthusiasm. When I finally turned the shower off I felt clean and virginal and wished that Converse could see me. I tried staring lasciviously at myself in the full-length mirror, the approved way that women in novels written by men do . . . stroking myself and all that stuff. But I knew it was a fake. I couldn't conjure up any erotic ideas, even about Converse. I just struck myself funny. I examined myself carefully, trying to decide if I were going to be the Unwed Mother of the Year. Everything seemed to be in order, but, just in case, next time I saw Doctor Daniels I was determined to get a prescription for pills . . . or stop playing games with improvident males. "To hell with you, Converse Cabot," I said, wiping the steam off the mirror for the third time so that I could gawk better at my naked self. "My female attachments are as good as Stephanie Billings' anytime."

Since I was sure that the Princess wasn't really in a tizzy over my whereabouts, although Grandma Starch was no doubt giving her a bad time, I didn't hurry. Boston on a Sunday might be ghastly, but it couldn't be as bad as playing hide and seek with Bucky Bonnelli on Trotter Island on a rainy day.

I found Bucky talking with a girl at the reception desk. He had a sour look. I tried to smile him out of it.

"You'll wait longer than forty-five minutes if you get yourself hooked up to Stephanie Billings. Come on, cheer up! You'll feel better when you've eaten breakfast."

In Waldorf's I ordered a pot of coffee, cantaloupe, orange juice, eggs, toast, and doughnuts, and proceeded to make up for the meals I had missed yesterday. Bucky bought a *Sunday Globe* and sat beside me in the booth. He peeled off the funnies and he exploded with laughter. On the front page was a three-column picture of Henry waving a torn canvas and shaking his fist at Mendes East. With open mouth, unable to swallow the piece of cantaloupe I had carved, I read the story:

MAD MAN STARCH PUTS HAMMERLOCK ON ART FESTIVAL

IRATE HUSBAND DENIES PRINCESS TASSLE
HER LAST BUMP!
LOCAL GAUGUIN OF TROTTER ISLAND
PAINTS NATIVES IN UNDRESS!

Last night, in its final week, the Boston Arts Festival was rocked off its staid underpinnings by a near riot. It all started when the well-known local wrestler Henry "Mad Man" Starch, who retired several months ago to a life of sequestered peace and quiet on Trotter Island, discovered that his wife was being displayed fetchingly naked on a five-by-eight-foot canvas at the Festival in what was probably the most awe-inspiring bump of the Princess's long career.

The name Princess Tassle will stir fond memories in the hearts of male Bostonians past forty and all lovers of the ecdysiast art, who will remember her controversial and exciting career. A career that caused local longnoses to rise in prim protest and twice slam shut the doors of the former Old Howard Theatre.

Such are the memories of man and the vicissitudes of fame that most of us have short memories for the "roses of yesterday," and only local oldsters can remember the days when the Old Howard and the environs of Scollay Square were a young man's fond introduction to sin. But former investment banker, Charles North, of Wellesley and Eastham, did not forget. Five years ago, emulating the career of the famous Paul Gauguin, North gave up the sordid business of chasing dollars. Forsaking wife and friends he disappeared into the bohemian world of art, perhaps to prove to doubting Thomases that a Sunday painter's painting need not necessarily hang in family rooms or attics.

Until last night only a few people (certainly not the Festival Committee, who are maintaining a studied silence and disclaim all knowledge of even why the painting was chosen for exhibition) knew that Charles North and Mendes East are one and the same.

Investigation of the shadowy career of Charles Mendes East North reveals that for the past three years he has been living in a shack on Trotter Island avidly painting character studies of the polyglot denizens of that rocky coast line. He has had two showings of his work in the past year and has been extolled by several critics as one of the few moderns with a sense of humor.

The paths of North-East, Princess Tassle, and Henry Starch converged a few months ago, when the Princess obligingly agreed to pose for a painting to commemorate her spectacular career as a tassle-twister. Busy lobstering and living the quiet life of a Boston Harbor fisherman, Mad Man Starch was aware that his wife was posing for North-East. But not until last night, when friends apprised him that the star attraction at the Festival and cynosure of all eyes was a painting called "Last Bump . . . End of an era," was Henry Starch cognizant of the state of his wife's undress.

"She promised when she retired she'd quit showing

161

herself around," Mad Man said last night to reporters. "I ain't mad at Prin. She can't help it, I guess. But that Mendes East didn't have to go and paint her bare. There was nothing else I could do. I tried to get Mendes to take the painting down in a peaceable way. I told him it was downright embarrassing for me, listening to the boys crackin' wise remarks, and Ma Starch having a fit. We got kids and we gotta act more respectable, else they'll get the wrong idea."

The painting, torn in half during the tug of war that ensued between North-East and Henry Starch, is in custody of the Boston Police along with Henry Starch and Pierre Grass, a resident of Trotter Island who joined in the fracas to help his friend Mad Man Starch.

Contacted by reporters at her home on Trotter Island, Princess Tassle said the whole affair was ridiculous, that Henry was acting like a just-married husband, that she had been a stripper for twenty years and didn't give a damn who knew it. "The world is in a hell of a state. They used to have nice clean burlesque shows. Now men have to go to book stores 'for adults only' and buy pictures of women instead of watching the real thing. It's getting so bad two men just as soon kill each other over the painting of a nude pussy."

Asked if she would bail her volatile husband out of the clink, the Princess was adamant. "He destroyed a great work of art," was her comment. "He was actually performing a voodoo ceremony. The very minute that the painting was ripped—at eighteen minutes past seven last night—I fainted dead away. My daughter is so disgusted with her father that she didn't come home last night. I'm distraught. I'll never bail him out. He needs a few weeks in the jug to cool off. Monday I'm withdrawing all of our money from our joint account so he can't get his hands on it."

To read the whole story, Bucky had turned to the inside pages where some enterprising reporter had written a story of the Princess's career, together with photographic highlights of her in various stages of undress. I ate breakfast with a diminished appetite and a leaden feeling in my stomach. A feature box on the inside pages stated that the painting had been purchased by Reliance Cabot of Cohasset who in recent years had acquired a substantial collection of modern art. Reliance Cabot could not be reached for comment.

I tried to imagine what Converse must be thinking about me. No doubt he suspected that I was involved with the business in Sawyer's apartment . . . and now all this publicity. Being associated in any way with the mad doings on Trotter Island would be disgusting to the Cabots. But fate seemed to be against them. One of the sidelight stories speculated that there was probably more to the destruction of North's painting than met the eye and advanced the supposition that Henry had deliberately caused the ruckus to discomfort Reliance Cabot, who was one of the promoters of the marina to be built on Trotter Island. The story of the strike, now in its third week at A B C Electronics, was reviewed, and Henry Snole reiterated that Operation Buzz-Off was only beginning. The citizens of Trotter Island would not be disenfranchised from their land to abet money-mad speculators.

I was certain that I would never see Converse Cabot again. The whole idea had been a mad schoolgirl fancy. My horizons were closing in. The bright lexicon of youth no longer held untold possibilities. I would eventually end up Mrs. Charles "Bucky" Bonnelli, serving ravioli and pizzas to nine little Bonnellis. Either that, or certain spinsterhood.

Eating my way around the hole in a doughnut while Bucky read the paper, I thought about Mendes East and his little rebellion that had got him no further than Trotter Island. I wondered what kind of woman he had married. I even decided to tell him that I would pose in the nude for him. Maybe then he would realize that I was no longer a schoolgirl.

As I ate the hole in the doughnut, deciding that for five cents I'd become a call girl, Bucky asked if I was going to sit and mope all day. I told him that maybe I would leave town. Maybe I'd go to California or Miami and walk around in a bikini and see what happened. I was in no hurry to return to Trotter Island. By this time, Grandma Starch and my mother, without Henry to intervene, would be pulling out each other's hair or Indian wrestling. I tried to persuade Bucky that it would be fun to walk around the deserted streets of Boston and maybe commune with the early Bostonians like Adams and Hancock in the Old Granary Burying Ground. Maybe later in the evening we could sit on the grass and listen to a concert on the Esplanade. In essence I felt like wooing melancholy. But Bucky wasn't interested in being an olden knight to a tearful Goodie Starch.

"You can droop around and moan your fate if you want, but I'm not hanging around you all day with my tongue

163

hanging out. Don't you know that that kind of teasing isn't good for a man? After yesterday, it's a wonder that I haven't got aching balls."

I wisely decided not to inquire what he meant.

24

We took a taxi back to Commercial Wharf. Bucky had been right about the weather. The wind had shifted to northeast, and the lonely wharf, with only a few boats bumping against it in the churning water, and the salt-and-sun-bleached buildings crouched on their pilings, all seemed to be huddling together ominously. The sun was still shining in a small patch of blue sky, but far out in the harbor the cool wind was sweeping across the water, and the thin fingers of fog that hung over the distant islands made them seem remote and inaccessible.

"It's a good thing we're starting back now," Bucky said. "In a couple of hours it'll take a navigator to find Trotter Island."

I shivered. I have conflicting emotions about fog. Sometimes, snug in our house on Trotter Island, I listen to the probing unearthly sound of foghorns or walk across the island to the West Head through the swirling grey nothingness, and the hair crawls on the back of my neck, and goose pimples march up my legs and back. I am lost and alone on this island and the sad *orr-uhh—orr-uhh* in the night spells out the hopelessness of my ever being found. Other times, the fog is a soft cocoon wiping out the confusion and hurry of the world, mysteriously inviting me forward through its mists to something strange and wonderful waiting . . . waiting just for me.

I guess these were old maid thoughts. What I really wanted was to slide down in my fog-damp sheets and shiver against a man who would understand . . . and by his touch on my back and his fingers intertwined with mine . . . reach across the ineffable loneliness that separates one human being from

164

another. I guess that is what fog is . . . the misty curtain through which one person reaches out to another person—but never quite penetrates the whirling murkiness of this dream.

I was so lost in my thoughts that I hadn't noticed that we had reached the berth where Bucky's boat was tied. I was about to climb down the ladder when a bearded face appeared level with the wharf, and then the whole of Harry McTare sprung up the ladder and greeted us with a huge grin! He held an army revolver in his hand, and he chuckled like a man who had just had a steak put in front if him after a long starvation diet. I sucked my breath and yelled for Bucky to run—and, if he had, I would have run after him. I had the feeling that I had walked through the fog into a clearing occupied by a monstrous hairy cannibal.

But Bucky stood his ground and tried to bluff. "Damned if ain't Captain McTare. What brings you to this part of the world?"

"I be slummin' laddie," McTare said, hugely delighted with himself. "I figgered that I wouldn't have to look too far to find a lobster boat of this size and dimension. Here I be, takin' a little Sunday walk . . . feeling nostalgic for the sea, and I find with a little inquiring that I be in double luck . . . not one boat," he gestured toward Henry's boat on Long Wharf, "but two. Supposing ye and the lass just amble down that ladder, and we'll all have a little nip of Old Robbie. There's nothing like Old Robbie to loosen tongues."

Bucky shook his head. "Let's talk right here on the wharf, McTare. It's more open and friendly."

"Laddie, never try a patient man too far." McTare's grin had disappeared, and his revolver hand stiffened. "It isn't a Christian thing to do on a Sunday morning, but since there isn't a soul around to witness it, I think ye should know that Harry McTare is mad enough to put a few holes in ye if necessary."

Bucky shrugged and climbed down the ladder. I followed him. Lounging in the cockpit of Bucky's boat were two of McTare's crew. Neither of them stood up. An open violin case with a machine gun propped against it leaned against one of the canvas deck chairs. They were drinking from a bottle of Old Robbie. Both of them were unshaven, with bloodshot eyes. The one with a deep scar on his face took a swig and then offered me the bottle.

"I see the Captain located his quiff with the trim ass," he chuckled and stared insolently at me.

"Here, now, Blister," McTare said, "that be no way to talk

165

to a bonnie lass. If ye speak like that again I'll belt in your ugly face with the butt of this gun." McTare kicked the other sailor in the shin, "Rummage around in the cabin, Birdie, and find some glasses. You, Blister, cast off this wee tub. We're going to have a little party. We don't want to be shouting and talking and bothering everyone on a Sunday morning. It'll be nice and private out in the harbor."

McTare nudged Bucky with his gun and told him to start the engine. Blister untied the boat from the wharf, jumped back in the cockpit and pushed Bucky away from the wheel. Bucky lunged in the direction of the machine gun, but, as he did, Birdie emerged from the cabin with the glasses and shoved his foot into Bucky's rump. Bucky sprawled on the floor, cursing.

Chuckling, McTare helped him to his feet. "Ay, lad, ye be a little nervous, hey? Well should ye be! Well should ye be! Blister take this boat out toward Nantasket Roads. The lad and lassie have some talking to do, and I feel a bit like listening." He gestured toward the cabin door. Reluctantly I went inside, followed by Bucky. Blister had steered the boat clear of the wharves, and we were already tossing in the choppy water. I clung to the edge of the bunk and, finally, unable to keep my balance, sat on it. Birdie, pouring glasses full of Old Robbie, maintained a precarious swaying stance. McTare pushed Bucky down beside me and sat on a chest facing us.

"We're in for a bit of weather I be thinkin'." He took the glasses from Birdie and handed one to Bucky. "Drink it up. It'll oil your tongue." He handed a glass to me. I let it slide through my hands, trying to make it look like an accident. It spilled on the floor but the darned glass didn't break.

"Ye be thinkin' that's funny, noo, don't ye lass? Ye be thinkin' if I break the glass I'll have to drink from the bottle, and I can stuff my tongue in it, and Harry McTare'll never know the difference." He picked up the glass, took the bottle from Birdie, and filled it again. "I'll gie ye five minutes to drink it, and if ye try any more of those delinquent tricks, I'll tell Birdie to pop ye on the chin and pour the whole bottle down your gullet!"

Harry McTare was obviously no man to tamper with. Frightened, I slowly drained the glass. I noticed that Bucky was trying to make his last.

After the initial gagging, the Scotch went down fairly easy, but it felt as if it had scorched a path to my stomach that would take days to stop burning, and my heart pounded furiously. Harry McTare immediately refilled my glass. "I can't drink any more," I pleaded. "I'd just pass out."

166

McTare grinned. "Ye dinna have to drink at all, if ye'll answer me one question."

I looked at him puzzled and tried to brush the dizziness from my eyes. He took me by the shoulders and shook me gently, but it was enough to scramble my vision.

"Don't ye know better than to steal money from a Scotchman?" Two bearded McTares stared at me. "Who's got the money?"

I tried to look at Bucky, but he was sitting too close, and I couldn't focus on him well. What could I do? Point at Bucky and say he took it? I knew that Bucky didn't even have it. The fat was in the fire now. At least for the moment, Harry McTare was more interested in his money than my anatomy.

"Well, I see that neither one of ye is talkin'," McTare said grimly. "One thing to be sure—those little green clams didn't fly away." He refilled Bucky's glass. "Drink up, lass. Another round and we'll all be one happy family."

I wondered if I dared slurp the second drink, but one look at the stern expression on McTare's face convinced me it would do no good. The only thing that could save me now was Bucky confessing, and, even if he did, it still seemed hopeless.

I drank the second drink slowly. "If I finish this drink," I said, trying to avoid his hypnotic eyes, "I'll get good and sick and toss a mess of bacon and eggs and doughnuts and cantaloupe all over you." The way the words came out, I knew that alcoholic asphyxia was slowly settling in, and I knew that Harry McTare's plan wasn't going to work. I was so scared that I had to pee-pee, so I started to cry, and I found it surprisingly easy to sob a little and squeeze out a steady stream of tears.

From what I could discern of Harry McTare, he looked as if he had uncorked a monster. "Noo, noo, lassie, dry your eyes. Never let it be said that Harry McTare forced an innocent child to drunkenness. Money dinna mean that much to me. If ye would just be willin to agree to the little proposition that I made you a few weeks ago, I'd ask no more about the whereabouts of the money."

"You mean if I let you look at my behind, you'll let us go?" For a moment I had the mad idea of hiking up my skirt and letting him look.

"Well . . . a little more than that lass," McTare said genially. "To fondle it a bit, too."

I couldn't help grinning at Bucky, who had turned dull red with anger. McTare was poaching on his territory.

"You keep your filthy mouth shut, McTare. Willa Starch is

an innocent kid. You haven't any right to talk to her that way." Bucky chug-a-lugged his old Robbie. *"I* took your stinking money. If you want it back, tell that damned fool you call Blister to take us to Trotter Island, and I'll get it for you."

I crossed my fingers. What if Herman Snole had spent the money? Expenses in connection with Operation Buzz-Off and the strike at A B C Electronics had probably been heavy. Maybe Bucky figured that if we got McTare to the Island we'd have him outnumbered. Anyway, for the moment my bonnie behind was safe. I slumped dizzily on the bunk.

Bucky shook me. "Are you all right, Willa?"

"Sure y-m-okay . . . jus' a little stinky."

"She drank nearly a pint," I heard someone say from a great distance.

"Puleeze go. Lemme be . . . gotta cis-cis."

"Can I help you, Willa? Are you gonna be sick?" Bucky pulled me to a sitting position.

"Doan need n . . . ee male help . . . gonna die if I doan pee-pee."

McTare shuffled out of the cabin, followed by Bucky and Blister. From another world I heard him say, "That's the pissingest woman I ever knew!" Then the cabin door closed, and I slid and fell and clutched, and finally, laughing hysterically, lowered myself onto the unscreened little toilet in the prow of the boat. Sitting on a boat toilet when a boat is flipping and tossing from side to side is a complicated business. Twice I slipped right off my perch onto the floor. I realized dimly that I was quite drunk. When I finally managed to go, I got to wondering how a man could ever aim in such conditions, and that interesting idea reduced me to a cataclysm of laughter that ended in hiccoughs. The boat had slowed down, and we were wallowing in a lopsided forward motion. Hiccoughing, I rushed from the cabin. "Stop it," I yelled. "Whaddya tryin' . . . hic . . . to do, make me sick?" I stumbled into the arms of Harry McTare.

"Hang on lass. Skidding around a boat like that, you're likely to go sailing right over the rail into the drink." Water was splashing down his face. I was suddenly aware that it was raining. It felt cool on my face. The only trouble was that everything seemed hazy. Either it was awfully foggy, or I wasn't seeing too clearly. I whooshed the air around with my arms, but the mist didn't go away. I wondered if the fog we were plowing through was actually as thick as it seemed, or whether I had developed a Scotch-saturated vision. Twenty or thirty minutes ago the sun had been shining. Now we seemed to be in a sauna. Someone seemed to have been pouring cold water on a hot radiator. I accused McTare, but he just shoved me away. We were surrounded by a soft grey moisture that lay thick around us in all directions. I hung over the side of the boat. Closer to the water, about a foot or two above the rolling sea, the air was clear.

"Someone jump overboard," I yelled happily. "If you float on your back you can see where we are." No one responded. So I climbed on the rail and was about to jump in and offer my services. Birdie grabbed me around the middle and pulled me aboard.

Bucky emerged from the cabin with a long foghorn shaped like a tin ice-cream cone. He blew it once, a deep *orr-uhh*. McTare yanked it out of his hands and tossed it overboard.

"Damn ye, lad cut that out! We ain't advertising. I don't give a tuppence who we hit . . . just tell Blister what direction to steer. I ain't aiming to stay out in this slop all day."

"You horse's ass," Bucky snarled indignantly. "I'm no navigator. Trotter Island is somewhere southeast of us, and so are a half-dozen other islands, shoals, sand bars . . . not to mention boats of all descriptions. You're supposed to be a fuckin' Captain. . . . Let's see you. . . ."

Before he could finish, McTare cuffed him across the face. "That be a turrible word to use in the hearing of an innocent lass. See that ye mind your tongue, lad, or I'll toss ye overboard after your blasted foghorn."

I couldn't help laughing and hiccoughing all at once. "Tol you to wash your mouth out," I said to Bucky, who scowled at me. I could vaguely see that he was pretty mad. "Doan punch him Bucky," I said. "No chin under that hairy beard . . . jus' hair . . . all hair." I gave McTare's beard a tweak. He roared angrily and cuffed me on the fanny.

25

Blister was inching the boat forward, the engine scarcely turning. Birdie had gone up in the bow and was peering into the mist. Except for the occasional blast of a foghorn, which intensified the loneliness, we seemed to be in a hushed world —as if life around us had forever ceased and we were pushing forward in a purgatorial search for an island that didn't exist.

I knew I was getting soaking wet. Drunk as I was, I dimly realized that my dress was clinging tight to my breasts, and my nipples, shivery and erect, were receiving increasingly attentive glances from Bucky and McTare. Bucky suggested that I go back in the cabin and try to dry out, but McTare told him to let the lass stay out in the air, it would sober her up.

Somewhere ahead of us in the thick muck we heard a scream, and then the dark shadow of a Chris Craft cruiser loomed a few yards in front of us. I could see three women in the cockpit of the boat. They were waving and yelling. We were heading directly for the middle of their boat!

Blister evidently expected them to pass in front of us. But we were on top of them before it was apparent that they weren't moving.

"They're anchored!" Bucky shouted, and Blister whipped the wheel in a semicircle. We scraped gently against the side of the long Chris Craft. The engine of our boat, rebelling against Blister's treatment, sputtered, coughed several times and finally conked out. Bucky caught the rail of the Chris Craft with a boat hook, and I found myself grinning cheerily into the face of Stephanie Billings.

"You nearly ploughed right into us," she said angrily, and then a look of astonishment appeared on her face as she recognized Bucky. "You . . . !" she hissed. She picked up a fishing pole and swung widely.

Bucky ducked and it whizzed over his head, lashing McTare across his cheek. He roared like a wounded hippopotamus and grabbed Bucky by his shirt.

"Cast off, ye half-wit," he shouted. He yanked the boat hook out of Bucky's hand. "Ye damned bitch," McTare complained ruefully, rubbing his cheek as we drifted away from the Chris Craft. "Ye need to have yur bottom worked on!"

Blister was trying unsuccessfully to rouse Bucky's engine to life. The self-starter chugged wearily a few times and finally didn't respond at all.

"No power in yur battery, lad. Toss out your anchor afore we drift to sea."

"Toss it over yourself, McTare," Bucky said angrily. "I don't give a damn if we drift to Europe."

McTare snatched the machine gun out of Birdie's hands, released the safety, and aimed at Bucky. I screamed, but it was too late. McTare squeezed the trigger. Rat-a-tat-tat. I expected to see Bucky in a crumpled heap, but miraculously he was still standing.

"That burst was over yur head, lad! Cast over that anchor right noo, or the next round'll be in yur belly."

Pale and shaken, Bucky tossed the anchor overboard and fastened the rope on the front cleat. The Chris Craft had vanished in the veil of fog but we could hear the women yelling at us, demanding to know what was happening.

"Miss Starch," a voice called out of the fog. "This is Converse Cabot's mother, Desire Cabot. Please help us. We are marooned here. My husband and Converse went ashore two hours ago in our dinghy. I'm afraid that something has happened to them. Miss Starch . . . can you or your friends hear me?"

I couldn't answer. I was still hiccoughing, and the slow rolling of Bucky's boat from side to side was making me pretty oopsy. Desire. Holy cow . . . what a name! Almost as bad as Princess. Meet our mothers Desire and Princess. I had only seen the women for a drunken second or two. Not counting Stephanie, one woman was quite plump and beamingly fortyish . . . the other, who was wearing tweed Bermudas, had a strong gothic jaw and a Gibson girl grey-black hairdo. That had to be Desire! Desire . . . wheee!

"We hear you, Mrs. Cabot," Bucky shouted. "How far are we from shore?"

"About two hundred yards," Desire responded with a measured New England accent. "We could see shore easily when we anchored. Have you a dinghy? Would you row us ashore?"

Blister and Birdie had already dropped Bucky's dinghy in the water. McTare looked at it speculatively. "M'am," he yelled into the fog, "if ye want to jump in the water we'll tow ye ashore. Otherwise, I'm sorry to tell ye there ain't room enough."

"One of your men could row back and get them," I said.

"Lass, I'm here on business. This ain't no excursion boat."

"Listen, McTare," Bucky said, "I'll make a deal with you. Get that tomato that tried to swat me and bring her ashore with us. The other biddies can stay on the cruiser. If you do, I'll get your money back without any more fuss."

"Lad, if ye'll assign me proprietary rights to this wee drunken lassie with the bonnie behind, we'll make it a deal!"

My premonition that I would be sold out had been right.

"It's not his behind to trade," I informed McTare. "Go ahead. Get the blond tigress. He'll look good with the other

171

side of his face clawed up. Matching scratches are all the rage this year."

McTare rubbed his face and opined that he owed the blonde a little excitement. He told Blister to row over and get her and not to take any guff from the two old bags. With oarlocks squeaking, and a happy grin on his ugly face, Blister disappeared into the gloom. Then we heard a squabble of voices with Desire Cabot's dominating the conversation. She insisted that being the oldest she should take precedence and be rowed ashore. Finally Blister's patience was exhausted.

"Shut up your trap, you gabby old fart, or I'll do your old man a favor and slice off your stinking tongue. You, Blondie . . . lower your ass into this boat before I come aboard and toss you in like a sack of spuds."

There was no further conversation. We heard the oars squeaking again, and the dinghy reappeared through the fog, with Stephanie Billings sitting on the rear seat, staring at us in queenly rage.

Blister pulled alongside. McTare decided that Bucky would row. Blister secured the oars and moved into the bow seat. Bucky dropped into the middle seat, setting the dinghy rocking violently. Stephanie hung on grimly. Bucky suggested that when we all got into the rowboat it was going to be more crowded than Priestly's bathroom. Stephanie gave him an acid look but held her tongue. Birdie clambered into the rowboat alongside Blister; with his weight added to Blister's, the prow submerged for a second, and water poured into the boat. Stephanie, certain that they would capsize, screamed. Birdie yelled good-naturedly for McTare to get aboard and restore the balance. McTare lumbered into the dinghy, clutching the machine gun against his chest. He gingerly located himself next to Stephanie, leaving about three inches of space for me on the back seat. The boat was riding so low in the water that a good ripple would swamp it. Fortunately, the wind had dropped, and the water was glassy with oily slick and jellyfish floating sedately near the surface. The fog was thicker and more pervasive than ever. I felt as if the last five or six percent of me that wasn't water would soon dissolve into the moisture.

"No room for me," I told McTare. "Jus' as soon stay here. Maybe I'll swim over and talk with Desire." I imagined myself emerging dripping from the ocean and climbing aboard the Chris Craft to chat with Mrs. Cabot. Funny! Between hiccoughs and laughter, I waved goodbye to Bucky and McTare.

"You get aboard fast!" McTare said, squeezing against Stephanie. "Push over and sit on the right cheek of your ass, lassie. It'll gie our wee drunkie room to sit on her left cheek. Between you, you'll have a whole ass on the seat!" As he spoke, he pulled me, an awkward flaying mass, into the boat. Water poured into the stern. We bobbed precariously for a second, while Bucky held onto the side of his boat until we were in balance again.

"Of all the damned-fool business," Stephanie said, reluctantly sitting sideways in a puddle of water. "Why didn't you let her stay? With a shikker like her aboard we'll sink before we get ashore."

"You think I don't know what a shikker is?" I demanded, trying to glare at her but unable to bring her into clear focus. "Push her overboard, McTare! She doan like the way we smell. Look at the way her nose is curled!" I lunged at Stephanie in a vain attempt to shove her into the water, but McTare caught my arm. Again we bobbled uncertainly. There was a half-inch of water on the floor of the rowboat. Bucky was rowing very cautiously, knowing that if he crabbed an oar or got us out of balance we would certainly sink. McTare asked if he was rowing in the right direction. Bucky shrugged. For all he knew we might be on our way back to Boston.

"How were things in Priestly's crapper?" Bucked asked Stephanie, who was maintaining an uncomfortable silence. "A bit crowded for any real fun, wasn't it?"

"Only a moron would gloat over such a cheap trick," Stephanie said bitterly. "My regret is that I didn't stab you!"

"So, now you've got a second chance," Bucky chuckled. "Think of the loss to the world. As the poets say, I'd never be able to fill you with a daughter fair . . . or get you fat with child—what is the poetic way to say it anyway?" He flipped his right oar across the surface of the water and slurped a spray across Stephanie's face. "Oops, excuse me! The thought of having my male glory cut off made me all sixes and sevens."

"You bastard," Stephanie jabbed her free foot into Bucky's shin and he yelled indignantly. The boat rocked violently.

"Hurray, we're going swimming," I screamed.

"What in hell is going on here?" McTare shouted. "Ye damned bitches, stop it afore ye discombobulate us. And you," he said shaking Stephanie violently, "when I get ye ashore I'm going to blister your bottom. Leave the lad alone while he's rowing."

"Tell him to shut his mouth then," Stephanie said. She looked as if she might spit at McTare. The veneer of culture

173

was wearing thin. A few days on Trotter Island, and Stephanie might even become human.

"She really likes me," Bucky said imperturbably. "Just a few hours ago she was romping in bed with me shaking her bare belly most fetchingly. You know women, McTare. They can't help being perverse."

McTare grinned. "And I'll wager it's a fair belly the lass has. I wouldn't mind enjoying a look myself."

"No freighter Captain'll ever get a look at that patrician belly, McTare," I advised. "Bucky nearly lost an eye in *his* attempt."

"At least I don't act like a female cat in heat," Stephanie said cooly. "You can stop yowling at Converse any time now. He's mine!"

My hiccoughs turned to a sob. I couldn't hold back the tears that welled up in my eyes. Bucky came to my rescue.

"You mean that Converse forgave you? When he opened Priestly's bathroom door and found you bollicky bare-ass, what did you tell him? That he was dreaming? That you were really out walking without your Maidenform bra?" Bucky laughed nastily. "When I see him, I'll tell him that you were an eager cat in heat—not yowling, but almost . . . that I had to lock you in the bathroom to protect my virginity."

Stephanie turned an angry purple color.

"Keep calm a second longer lassies," McTare said, "I see a pier over to our right. Pull strong on left oar, lad. Now ease in on your right one."

Deep in a swirling fog, I could see the pilings of the pier on the West Head. Bucky rowed carefully alongside the landing float, which is connected to the pier with a wooden gangway. Before we touched the float, McTare leaped out of the rowboat, followed by Blister and Birdie. Their sudden departure jarred the boat into a bobbing frenzy. The ocean poured in the side and stern. McTare tossed his machine gun to Blister; then he leaned over to pull Stephanie erect and onto the float. Angrily she grabbed his hand and yanked. Off balance, roaring in dismay, McTare plunged into the rowboat against Bucky. The impact of McTare's weight knocked Bucky right out of the boat into the water. He came to the surface sputtering and furiously grabbed the side of the rowboat, deliberately forcing it down until water poured in the side. McTare pounded at his fingers trying to stop him. But it was too late. The rowboat slowly rolled into the water, and I went under . . . Stephanie on top of me, both of us flailing angrily at each other.

Blister and Birdie were rolling on the float, helpless with

174

laughter. McTare, a soaking, bearded monster, hoisted his howling self onto the float.

"Ye bloody asses, if you think it be so funny," he snarled, "try a swim yurself."

Before either of them realized his intention, he swooped down and first grabbed Blister and tossed him in with us—followed by Birdie, who, by this time, was so hysterical with laughter that he was unable to withstand the demoniacal anger of Harry McTare. McTare waited until Stephanie was grasping the side of the float and trying to pull herself aboard, and then, with a devilish grin, he dragged her out of the water. With a deft movement, while she was still gasping for breath, he undid the belt on her shorts and yanked them down to her knees. While Stephanie was screaming and trying to pull the shorts back over her naked behind, McTare picked her up, sat down on an overturned rowboat, and forced her across his knees. He gave her five resounding smacks that sounded wet and stinging on her bare flesh and then dropped her unceremoniously. She lay panting with anger, swearing in Army language at McTare.

Bucky clambered onto the float and slid on hands and knees toward the machine gun that Blister had dropped, but Birdie, treading water, clutched his ankle and dragged him back.

McTare pulled me out and recovered his machine gun. Unable to stand up, I stretched flat, heedless of my clinging wet clothes, and tried to stop the fog-enclosed world from revolving. A messy kaleidoscope composed of McTare and Bucky leaned over me solicitously, and Stephanie, with her shorts refastened and a haughty look on her face, shifted before my eyes. Grinning, I watched faces merge, come apart, and then remerge into new and fascinating groupings. Stephanie wore McTare's beard and Bucky had silver blonde hair. I closed my eyes. Someone inside my head was pounding so hard I thought my skull would burst.

"I'm sick," I moaned. "Oh . . . I'm so sick!"

"She's a sloppy drunk," I heard Stephanie say from a great distance. "Disgusting."

"If you don't shut up," Bucky told her, "McTare will pop you on the chin and pour a bottle of Old Robbie down your gullet. It'll sting worse than your behind does!"

"None of you is going to get away with this!" Stephanie said tersely. "I don't know what you are all up to . . . but the police are going to hear about this! Assault and battery . . . kidnapping. My father is a lawyer. You'll all be behind bars before he gets through with you."

Before she had finished, Stephanie was screaming again. I forced my eyes open in time to see Blister holding her in his arms, kicking and yelling—and then he dropped her back into the water. As she came to the surface he leaned over, wound her blonde hair in his hand, and pulled her head above the surface. Water streaming from her eyes, choking, she stared at him dazedly.

"You gonna be a nice girl and stop all this nasty talk about police?" Blister held her head ready to duck her again. "Say you're sorry!"

"I'm sorry," Stephanie sputtered glumly.

Blister standing over her, she crawled miserably back on the float.

McTare shook me gently. "Can't ye get up, lass? We've got business to do."

"Lemme alone . . . wanta die."

"I guess the wee lass has a drunkie's bonnet," I heard McTare say. He told Bucky to pick me up and carry me. "I've had a bellyfull of this kiddie business. All I want is my rightful money and I'll be leaving ye to yur nonsense."

Despite my soaking dress and almost dead weight, Bucky lifted me easily. I couldn't open my eyes because the Devil himself was hammering on my eyeballs, but I knew that we were walking down the pier and up the dirt road where most of the houses on Trotter Island nestled in the lee of the West Head.

"I'm too heavy. Lemme walk," I sighed in Bucky's ear.

"How? On your knees? If you listened to me, Goodie Starch, we'd be shacked up nice and comfortable in a hotel room. . . . Instead we are kidnapped by Bluebeard himself."

26

We were half way up the hill to Herman Snole's house, when I realized that I must have wandered off into an alcoholic no-man's-land peopled with grinning monsters, sea worms, and jellyfish—that all had a face like McTare's and a thin raspy voice like Thirsty's.

The voice was real enough. It was Thirsty. From Bucky's arms I smiled forlornly into his wizened face.

"What are you doing to my little Willa?" he demanded.

Bucky put me down. My knees buckled, and I swayed against him, but I managed to peer into Thirsty's worried face and assure him that I was just fine.

"The weirdo with the beard got her drunk," Bucky said. "He's teed off because I took his money. Where's Herman Snole?"

"Got my little girl drunk!" Thirsty's eyes were flashing, and his Adam's apple bobbed indignantly. "That's a terrible thing. When her Daddy hears about this, Mister, he'll clobber you."

McTare stared down at Thirsty as if he was about to turn off the gas under a boiling teakettle. "Be this creature really alive? Or did someone dig up a graveyard and reassemble a bag of bones?" McTare roared happily. "I be thinking I'll take ye back to Boston and sell ye to some sawbones to hang by ye shining dome in a closet."

"My name is Abner Thurston," Thirsty said haughtily. "I was born before you, and I'll be living long after you have blown a fuse and the worms are crawling in and out of your eyeballs." Thirsty turned his back on McTare and said to Bucky, "When I heard all the commotion, I hustled down. Thought it might be Willa's Daddy and Grandma and Herman Snole coming back from Boston. Frank Otto took them in early this morning to bail Henry out."

For a moment I felt entirely sober. "Bail Henry out?" I squealed. "Oh, my God . . . what are they using for money?"

Bucky didn't react so quickly, but it finally dawned on him. "You mean Herman is providing the bail money? How much will it cost?"

He gradually picked the story out of the voluble background that Thirsty, not caring that it was foggy and practically raining, seemed determined to supply. Prin had refused bail for Henry. Grandma Starch, furious, said that Henry wouldn't be in jail in the first place if he had married a decent woman who kept her clothes on. Grandma appealed to Herman Snole. Herman guessed that it would cost a boodle, but he did have the twenty-four-hundred dollars that Bucky gave him, and, after all, it really was Henry's money. Moreover, since Henry had wrecked Mendes' painting, which Reliance Cabot had already purchased . . . well, there were no two ways about it, rescuing Henry was a part of Operation Buzz-Off. Herman had tried to convince Grandma to wait

177

until Monday morning, but Grandma insisted that she knew a good Irish policeman wouldn't keep her only son in jail on the Lord's day, particularly if they had the money to pay his ransom.

"Bucky stole the money," Thirsty said, ignoring my attempts to hush him up. And then, pursuing some kind of insane logic: "Old man Cabot paid twenty-five hundred dollars for that painting of Prin. Yesterday, Mendes told Herman Snole that he should give the money to Cabot. Mendes said it was Henry and Pierre's money, anyway, and they had ruined the painting. I told Mendes that I would give old man Cabot his money back, but Mendes didn't think Reliance Cabot would be happy with my money."

McTare listened patiently, while Thirsty cackled his story. "If this old coot be saying that my green clams is mixed up in yur shennannigans, Harry McTare will fast be losing patience with the lot of ye. All right, lad, who has my money noo?"

Bucky shrugged unhappily. "You better shoot me now, McTare and get it over with. Maybe all the bulbs will light up and I'll jangle for you while the jackpot falls out."

"It's no use, McTare," I hiccoughed. "You'll only get three lemons." Then I decided to be a martyr and save Bucky. The Jeanne d'Arc of Trotter Island. "Let him go, McTare, I surrender. You can have my honor and my behind!" It was the least I could do. After all, McTare's money was being used to bail my father out of the jug.

McTare grinned at me. "Lass, I appreciate the offer . . . since, except for the blonde one that I just paddled, I don't know when I've seen a fairer behind. But right noo I be feeling a bit dubious about women. They're so damned switchable. My green clams are more reliable." McTare patted his machine gun. He looked at us all grimly. "Afore this day be over I'll squeeze my money out of someone on this island. After I do, lassie, we'll return to a discussion of your bonnie posterior."

"Must we stand here soaking wet, talking nonsense in the middle of a fog?" Stephanie demanded. "Just have Bonnelli arrested for stealing your money. You'll be doing society a favor. He'll end up in jail eventually, anyway."

McTare chuckled. "Noo, noo, lass this be no problem for the police. Have ye never heard about honor among thieves?" McTare bent down and stared at the bobbing ball in Thirsty's throat. "All right, you scraggy coot, take us where we can dry ourselves out and get some grub."

Muttering dire plans on how he would terminate McTare's

career if he got the chance, Thirsty led us through the fog toward Mendes' shack on the top of the West Head. Thirsty cooled down sufficiently to tell us that the Princess was with Reliance Cabot and Converse Cabot. Stephanie, evidently deciding that he was the lesser evil, walked beside Thirsty and tried to probe him. Bucky and I followed, with Blister, Birdie, and McTare a grumbling rear guard.

Stephanie's wet hair had lost its luster and clung to the back of her head. Her wobbling rump was pink-tight in her wet nylon shorts—so tight that she was wide open to review by the rear flanks. But, damn it, she still managed to exude her glossy I-am-above-all-this manner.

Bucky was so hypnotized by the undulating bobble of her behind that he occasionally forgot that he was guiding me, and I wandered dizzily out of his reach. The safari stopped until Willa was recaptured, and then we went on.

While Bucky was enamoured of Stephanie's rear, Thirsty was evidently enthralled by her breasts pointing in the air through her wet blouse. In a very friendly and cavalier manner he told her that he had seen Reliance and Converse when they anchored their Chris Craft. "About two or three hours ago. They had an outboard motor on their dinghy. They putted into the float and stomped up the pier, demanding to know where Willa Starch lived . . . where they could find Mendes East. King Rose and I figgered they were up to no good. Soon as we got the chance we dumped the gas out of their outboard and stashed away their oars. Both of them went up to Mendes East's shack. When they found that they couldn't get back to their boat . . . there's a couple of old frumps out there waiting for them . . . they were kind of mad, but Prin insisted they have a glass of my grappa with some grapefruit juice, and pretty soon they were feeling better. Next thing you know, Prin is teaching old man Cabot how to do some of those Calypso dances, and he is trying to give your ma a squeeze and a hug, just the way all men do. Tomorrow's the Fourth of July. Tonight's going to be the best gasser of the year. It's gonna be a damned shame if Grandma don't get Henry out of the jug."

All the way up the hill to Mendes' shack, Thirsty, pleased to be the cynosure of Trotter Island knowledge, rattled on, his paper-thin excitable voice growing more quavery as he spoke. He turned and whispered to Bucky not to worry about that goon, McTare. Thirsty would take care of him.

"I'll stick him in my dungeon," he yelped happily, jumping up and down like a reincarnation of Old Ben Gunn. "You just wait and see what else I got in my dungeon, Willa. A

179

pretty big fish. Old Thirsty is gonna save this island yet. You'll see . . . you'll see. . . ."

"What are ye gabbin about?" McTare, his beard sodden-looking and bedraggled, shouted from the rear. "Shut your flapping mouth, spindle bones, and be for gettin' where yur takin' us."

"He's a Bolshevik from Russia," Thirsty muttered under his breath. "Thinks I'm half dead does he? Before this day is over I'll haul down his sails!"

Guided by Bucky, I had staggered dizzily almost to the door of Mendes' shack. But just before we got to the porch my wobbly legs gave out. I flopped face down in a damp growth of wild grass and daisies. I heard the yells of consternation, but I couldn't look up. The grass was wet and cool, and I was gaspingly sick. I didn't really care what happened. The blood in my head was throbbing so wildly that it would have been easier to die on the spot. I couldn't stop crying, and I didn't want to stop, because I had plenty to cry about. When Converse saw me once again, a drunken lush, he would surely be disgusted. I suppose that Stephanie could have stayed in the water for a week or two wrapped in a cement corset and come out cool and sophisticated. I was a soaking, sopping, sloppy, red-eyed hag, with my hair plastered against my head and my breath smelling worse than Thirsty's distillery.

Despite my protests that I wanted to stay where I was and die peacefully, Bucky picked me up. Cursing McTare for getting me so drunk, he carried me inside Mendes' shack. Instantly, I was surrounded by the warm glow of a potbellied stove, cigarette smoke hanging thick in the air, and the pulsing beat of a cha-cha record scratching somewhere in the shadowy recesses of the cottage. I opened my eyes narrowly and peered at Mendes; Grandma Starch; the Princess; King Rose; Dathra; Penny, Jessica, and Susan Otto; and a tall grey-haired man with a strong ruddy face who looked at me coldly. I guessed that he was Reliance Cabot.

Converse was there, too.

Bucky passed me into Converse Cabot's arms. "She's all yours, old man, for drunk or worse, until all the Scotch is gone, do you part."

I squinted up into Converse's surprised face and sobbed, "I'll love you forever." Then I passed into an alcoholic trance. I could hear voices, but I had lost the power of response. I closed my eyes and let an ocean of tears fall on Converse's shoulder.

"Willa, Willa, Honey . . . what has happened to you? You

need a guardian!" Converse said. I tried to convince myself that he was holding me possessively and tenderly all at once. Maybe if he concluded that I was a partial half-wit it would arouse his protective instinct and put me on a more even basis with Stephanie. While everyone was trying to talk at once, I looked into Converse's eyes with my mouth open and the best moronic expression I could muster.

I heard Stephanie, louder than anyone else, acidly recalling the indignities she had suffered, with particular reference to how she had been stripped and assaulted on her bare fanny. She tried to incriminate me, implying that McTare was my friend, but, damp as I was, Converse continued to hold me.

Prin, when she found out that McTare was responsible, called him a stupid gorilla, kicked him in the shin, and conked him twice on the head with a maraca that she was holding. The seeds in it rattled wildly, and McTare's head resounded with a hollow thump. Bellowing like an enraged moose, he pushed Prin against the wall.

"Line up here . . . all of ye!" he yelled angrily. "Ye, lad, set the lassie doon on that couch and get over there with the rest of them."

Converse put me down. Did his lips brush against my cheek? . . . I wasn't sure. As he straightened out from his bent-over position he whipped around and swung his fist at McTare's face. But McTare rolled with the punch, and Converse missed him completely. McTare cracked him across the head and shoved him into Penny Otto's arms. "Stay out of this business, lad. I got nothin against ye, but if ye get in my way again I'll bust yur noggin for ye."

Converse tried to tell him that he was insane and he wouldn't get away with it.

"Aw shut up," Blister said, pointing the machine gun at him. "Stick your hands in the air before I open your arteries up. Right, Captain?"

"Right, Blister," McTare said grimly. "Birdie, search all of them."

Birdie enjoyed his job. He patted the men, feeling for billfolds and then, not to discriminate, patted the women until McTare, annoyed by their screaming, told him to cut it out.

The search yielded nothing. McTare opened the men's billfolds one at a time, and flung them back disdainfully. "I be looking for my twenty-four hundred dollars . . . not chicken feed." He grabbed Mendes. "Ye be the painter fella I read about? Where's the money ye got for that naked painting? Tell me afore I tear this shack down, board by board."

"I returned Mr. Cabot's money an hour ago," Mendes said

nervously. "But that isn't your money, anyway. Your money has gone to Boston with Herman Snole."

McTare's eyes gleamed. "I don't give a tinker's damn whose money it is." He thrust his bearded face into Reliance Cabot's. "All right, mister. Hand it over!"

Reliance Cabot fished a paper out of his pocket and handed it to McTare.

"It be a damned check!" McTare roared disgustedly. He tore it to bits. "Ye think that be verra funny, don't ye? Well, mister, I'm getting my rightful money afore I leave this island. If I don't, me and my lads might just decide to take it out in trade with some of these ladies."

Blister and Birdie guffawed delightedly. I started to shiver uncontrollably, not because I was alarmed at McTare's intentions, but because my nerves must have recovered a little from their alcoholic shock and were trying to remind me that I was soaking wet.

"You dirty man. You should be ashamed of yourself!" Susan Otto walked brazenly up to McTare and gave him a highly-charged sexual stare. "The poor little thing is scared to death. She thinks you mean to harm her. Why don't you pick on someone your size?"

McTare looked at her approvingly. "I might just be doing that, lady, and your size be just about right." McTare tried to dislodge Thirsty, who was tugging on his arm. "Let go, ye old coot. What do ye want?"

"I'll give you your danged money!" Thirsty said, excitedly. "I'm the richest man on Trotter Island. Just you come with me."

"Be you cracked, old man? Where did ye get any money?"

Everyone at once tried to reassure McTare it was true. Thirsty had a secret cache of money he had found on the beach. What was twenty-four hundred dollars? Thirsty had thousands. King Rose described it enthusiastically. Bucky glowingly pictured the piles of it. At least a hundred thousand dollars. No one mentioned that it would take a Houdini to unglue it.

"All right," McTare said, convinced in spite of himself. "We'll take a look at the old greezer's treasure." He lifted Thirsty off the ground and shook him until his teeth were rattling. "It better be true, old man. Because, if it ain't, Harry McTare will toss ye back in the cemetery bone by bone."

"Please!" I moaned. "If you are going to the East Head take me with you. I'm freezing, and I'm sick."

"We'll all go," Prin said happily. "Willa and her girlfriend should get some dry clothes on before they catch their death of cold."

I didn't dispute the status of Stephanie's friendship, but when McTare probed Thirsty and discovered that it was nearly a mile across the island, he shook his head. "All of ye can stay here and continue with yur party. No one else is goin' anywhere in this fog. Me lads and me will go and see if the old man is lying or not." He looked at me—shivering and miserable—and changed his mind. "All right, if yur boyfriend wants to tote ye home, ye can come."

Both Converse and Bucky stooped over to pick me up. They collided and forgot me while they glared at each other.

"Doan need anyone to carry me," I said, unable to control the squeakiness in my voice. I got off the couch and staggered into Converse's arms.

Bucky argued with McTare that Converse couldn't possibly carry me a mile across the beach to East Head. He would go along to help. When Stephanie insisted that she was just as wet and cold as I was, Prin told her that I had plenty of clothes and I could find something dry for her to wear. We were both about the same size, though she did think Stephanie had a little fuller boobies. I thought maybe Prin was going to try to weigh them to make sure, but Stephanie wisely didn't get that close to her.

Then the Princess insisted that she should come, too. "My poor baby needs to be put in a hot tub, and maybe she needs an emetic to get that awful liquor out of her system. You ought to be in jail for this!" she said to McTare.

McTare chuckled and told her not to worry—that he'd take care of the wee lassie. He complimented my mother on my fine behind and suggested that if she thought I needed an enema he'd be pleased to help do the job. "Done it many times for my crew on long sea voyages," he said, patting my behind affectionately.

McTare finally agreed that Bucky, Converse, Stephanie and I could go. He tried to convince Blister that he should stay in Mendes' shack and keep an eye on things, but Blister wasn't having any of that. He grinned sourly and said that he had trusted McTare before and ended up with the short end of the stick. "If the old beach rat really has any dough, the chances are I'd never see you or Birdie again."

Reliance Cabot had listened to all this discussion impassively. Finally, he could stand it no longer. "This is the silliest damned business I've ever heard of," he asserted. "You can all do what you want, I suppose, but this is *my* island, and before anyone goes traipsing around I'm going to insist on a

183

little hospitality. One of you row out to my boat and get my wife and Abigail Priestly."

If I hadn't felt so woozy, I know I would have been astonished. The plump woman with Desire was my telephone companion Cheery Abigail! I wondered where Sawyer was. I made up my mind that if my head would only stop aching I would try and find out what had happened when Converse had opened Sawyer's bathroom door.

McTare informed Reliance that he didn't give a hoot in hell about Desire and Abigail. From what he had seen of them Reliance was better off with the Princess. "This fog is gonna last a couple of days—no kind of weather for navigation. My advice to ye, mister, is leave the old bags sit it out on your boat and have yourself a little fun. After I see whether this old coot be tellin' the truth, I'll be back and join ye to see what makes this little gooseberry pie tick." Grinning, he chucked Susan Otto under the chin.

27

Converse carried me more than halfway across the island. I nuzzled his neck and tried to find some way to ask him if he loved me, but I was really afraid to ask, and all I could say was that I was sorry. I said it over and over again sobbing drunkenly, unable to stop. Converse kept shushing me and saying that it was all right. But the magic words "I love you" didn't come out.

Partly because of the fog and partly because of my bleary condition I had the feeling that I was alone with Converse and we were plodding through the wet and murky afternoon to our own house and bed. My daydream went so far as to have Converse help me out of my wet clothes and, with a big turkish towel, rub a glow of life back into my frozen body. I repeated this part several times, anticipating the rest of the dream and what would happen later when Converse took me in his arms. Just as I was pretasting how wonderful it would be, Converse stumbled and Bucky offered to carry me the
184

rest of the way. As Converse shifted the soggy load called Willa Starch, I heard Thirsty assuring McTare that it wasn't much farther to my house.

Bucky grumbled that I was no feather and he wondered how Converse had managed to carry me so far. He told me that, if I was goofing off and really could walk, to get on my pins, because I wasn't in Converse's arms now and I was a spoke in the wheel of progress. He was sure that he was going to make out with Stephanie.

When I assured him that I was going to die any moment, he struggled on. "Converse is not so dumb as I thought," Bucky whispered. "Last night I helped him get a different perspective on Stephanie. He figured it out just the way I thought . . . that old Steph didn't get so neatly undressed without being a little bit willing. Con told her that maybe they had known each other too long . . . like you and me. I think he is trying to let her down gently. You've got your man, Willa . . . Converse Cabot loves you!"

"Who told you all this?"

Bucky chuckled. "Didn't I tell you? Stephanie goes for me. She hasn't quite forgiven me for last night, but just a few minutes ago she was actually laughing about it. She remembered how dejected Sawyer looked sitting naked on the toilet. Mrs. North was sprawled in the bathtub. The only place left for Steph was balancing on the edge of the tub facing Sawyer. Boy, can you imagine that scene? Both of them naked and mad as hell . . . nagging Priestly to get them out of the bathroom . . . insisting that it was all his fault for having such a seduction chamber in the first place."

"Did you say Mrs. North?" Some of Bucky's conversation filtered through the fog, both literal and figurative, that I was swirling in.

"Yeah, Mrs. Charles North! How about that? The babe that you were calling Miss Smoky is really Mendes East's wife. . . . Only, like it said in the paper, Mendes' real name is Charles North, and he's loaded with dough. Sawyer Priestley has been shacking up with her ever since Mendes pulled out to live on Trotter Island. Real cozy, huh? Don't let Converse Cabot get you shook. These Back Bay Bostonians are only upper-culture Trotter Islanders."

I was too bewildered to absorb everything that Bucky had told me, but I was certain that I never wanted to set eyes on Sawyer Priestly again. After all, I was the one who had set the wheels in motion that resulted in a Cabot-Billings-Bonnelli conclave in his hideaway. If Sawyer ever located me, he might feel a dark compulsion to commit another trunk murder, dismembering Willa Starch and mailing me in pieces to various parts of the country. At the moment I felt I really deserved it.

I could sense Bucky laboring under the load of me and guessed that we were now on the path from the beach to our house. Opening one eye, I was reminded that the fog was external as well as internal. I knew we were only a few hundred feet from the house, but it was a dense swirling mist of a world, and we all seemed to be wearily plodding toward some evanescent goal.

But at last we arrived. As soon as McTare had closed the door and shut out the fog, he reassumed command, issuing rapid-fire orders to Blister and Birdie, telling them to keep a watchful eye on all of us. In the kitchen, McTare opened the refrigerator and surveyed its contents disgustedly. Prin was on her usual weekend starvation diet.

"Ain't enough here to feed a canary." He plunked a jar of peanut butter on the table, along with a bottle of pickled herring and some bacon and eggs. "Birdie, my belly be stuck to my backbone. Make us some grub afore we go up to Fort Harrison and see whether this old skinflint is giving us a cock-and-bull story about being the richest man on Trotter Island."

Bucky sat me on a kitchen chair. With my head sagging on my chest, I watched the proceedings with a feeling of nausea. McTare spread a huge glob of peanut butter on bread and started to chew it with his mouth open. He obviously wasn't too happy because he spit the half-chewed mess into the sink. "This ain't no food for a starving man," he said disgustedly. "You got any grub at your shack, old coot?" he demanded, nudging Thirsty, who sprang to his feet and told him in a quavery voice that he reckoned he had a ham that was three or four days old. It could be a mite dried out.

Thirsty didn't seem to be concerned about McTare's inevitable reaction when he finally discovered that the richest man on Trotter Island was not only insolvent but had assets that were quite frozen together. Not only was Thirsty unruffled, but he actually kept urging McTare to stop worrying about his stomach and hurry with him up to Fort Harrison if he wanted to get his twenty-four hundred dollars. In the meantime, Birdie started to fry bacon and eggs. With the smell hanging heavily and greasily in the room, I thought I would surely up-chuck.

McTare eyed me sympathetically. "Take the lass upstairs and put her in her beddie," he told Bucky. "And let the other lass get her ready."

"Ready for what?" Stephanie demanded. She was smoking one of Prin's cigarettes. The smoke curled disdainfully out of her nostrils.

"For an enema," McTare said calmly. He continued to eat, as if this were the most normal response in the world. "A flushing is the only thing that will put the lass back on her feet. Look at her. She looks about ready to die."

McTare wasn't far wrong. I couldn't hold my head up. Converse had put a wet towel on my forehead and was patting my hand sympathetically, but even that didn't help. I was beyond caring what happened, but McTare's words did strike a faint spark. Maybe he was joking, but, knowing him, I wasn't taking any chances. "No one's giving me an enema!" I moaned. "Converse . . . Bucky, save me from this madman."

"You just be shy," McTare said patting my shoulder. "But don't ye worry, lass. There's nothing like a good purging to stop a man's bonnet from throbbing. As Captain of my ship, many be the times I have stuck a pokey into a man's rear. Just as soon he was uncorked he began to feel as right as rain."

"I'm not a man. I'm a *woman!*" I yelled, as Bucky carried me up the stairs.

"In that area, lass, we all be about the same," I heard McTare chuckle.

Bucky led the way to my bedroom, explaining unnecessarily to Converse that he knew where it was . . . after all he had known me practically all my life. I held my breath, wondering if he was going to tell Converse that we had played Doctor together. But he didn't . . . probably realizing that Stephanie, who was being followed by Blister, carrying the inevitable machine gun, might not react too favorably to this information.

Bucky put me down carefully on my bed. Converse smiled at me and held my hand. I tried to smile back, but it was a feeble effort. I was shivering, and my head was aching beyond the laws of probability. Bucky started to unzip my dress.

"Get your hands off her!" Converse snapped, pushing him away.

"Aw, don't be sappy, Cabot," Bucky said. "You gonna let her lie here in these wet clothes?"

"Both of you can go downstairs!" Stephanie said grimly. "I'll take care of her."

Bucky and Converse looked at Stephanie dubiously. I can't say that I was charmed with the idea, but there didn't seem

187

to be any other choice. They finally departed, grinning a little sheepishly and hoping that I would feel better soon.

"All right," Stephanie said as soon as they were out of hearing, "your male audience has gone. You can turn off the poor, sick-Willa act. Get your own damned clothes off!" She calmly began to unbutton her blouse. "What have you got that I can wear?"

This not only proves that women are bitchy and, in the last analysis, can't stand each other—especially where male competition is involved—but also shows that, given an opportunity to run the world, their first act would be to start a gigantic extermination program of other women until one of them was the last alive. Maybe I don't exactly believe this, but that's the way I felt at the moment. Stephanie was a rat. But if she had been lying on the bed in a state of alcoholic paralysis instead of me, I'd have probably said the same thing.

"Go to hell!" I muttered. I staggered to my feet and, with a bursting head, managed to extricate myself from my wet dress and damp panties. My bra clasp was a different proposition. I fumbled with it dizzily, wondering if I should beg for aid. When I finally managed to unhook the soaking-wet elastic, I realized that Stephanie, who had taken off her own wet clothes, was pawing around naked in my closet, taking her choice of my best shirt-style blouse and my new green Italian silk shorts.

It wasn't a friendly thing to do, and I suppose that she was really my guest, but I was fed up with Stephanie Billings. I yanked the shorts out of her hands and grabbed for my blouse. In a second we were a clawing, screaming Chinese puzzle of naked females, rolling over and over on my bedroom floor . . . determined to see who would be the first to rip the other to shreds.

When McTare opened the door, still chewing a mouthful of food, I had Stephanie in an armlock that Henry had taught me, and she was pulling my hair so hard that it was only a matter of seconds before she would have scalped me.

McTare, blocking the doorway, stared at us dumbfounded for a second. "Well, if this ain't the damndest sight I ever saw," he marvelled. "Leave them be," he said, disappointed when Converse pushed McTare aside and grabbed me and Bucky grabbed Stephanie and undid us. "Ah, lad, ye should have let the lassies fight it out . . . best two falls out of three."

From the doorway Blister, Birdie, and Thirsty had watched us popeyed.

"Best girlie show I ever saw," Blister said approvingly. They all looked disappointed when Converse pulled the blankets off my bed and draped them around us, while Stephanie and I ignoring him, glared at each other, and explained to anyone that was interested that there was no bitch in the world that would equal the other. In the midst of this fervid conversation I suddenly realized that if my head had been aching before so that I could scarcely see, now I was completely sightless.

"Need to throw up," I sighed.

I was quickly rushed into the bathroom, where everyone watched me sorrowfully, and Converse, experienced in the vagaries of Willa Starch, held my head over the sink. But, though I gagged and sounded horribly as if I were making my final gurgles, nothing would come up. Converse tried to encourage me to shove a finger down my throat—and even obligingly proffered his—but he might as well have told me to poke a finger in my eye. I couldn't do it.

McTare was exploring the medicine cabinet and the towel closet. Beaming, he emerged with an enema bag. "It's too far doon," he said. "Ye got to work on the other end." He leaned over the sink and tried to whisper, but, having bellowed all his life, it came out like a roar. "Lass, tell me when did you have a bowel movement?"

For some reason cacophagic subjects seem to amuse men. They were all panicked with laughter; even Converse was grinning.

"Doan know . . . doan care. Go way all you damn fools. Very funny, I don't think!" I said angrily.

But McTare was probably right. In the past forty hours or so I had lived as if I no longer had human processes going on inside. But no man was going to give me an enema. Not even a doctor. McTare might be able to perform medical and ministerial functions in an emergency . . . but not on Willa Starch.

"Lemme die! Go way." I stared blearily at the seven occupants of the bathroom all crowded into the tiny space and staring at me, a wild wreck of a woman wrapped in a cotton blanket. What would Grandma Starch think if she could see me now? The thought struck me so funny that I started to laugh hysterically, and the hiccoughs that had subsided sometime ago returned with a vengeance.

"Hoist the lass onto her beddie," McTare ordered. "We'll gie her a little flushing, and she'll be gud as new!"

I heard Converse shout for McTare to leave me alone. "You've done enough to her already, you damned moron. I'm not going to permit this. This is assault. You'll get life imprisonment."

McTare sighed. "Ye be daft, lad. I luv this lassie like me own daughter. Harry McTare will not let any harm come to her. Blister . . . tell him to help carry the lass to her beddie. Tell him Harry McTare isna' joking."

Blister pointed the machine gun ominously at Converse. Reluctantly, he and Bucky carried me into the bedroom while I yelled for Henry, Prin, and Grandma and called Bucky and Converse utter cowards because they wouldn't knock Blister down and take the machine gun away from him. I had a sure foreknowledge that there was no escape. . . . When McTare got something in his mind he was inflexibly bound to do it—the enema was inevitable, but I *wasn't* going to relax and enjoy it.

In a few seconds, McTare appeared with a bulging enema bag and a big grin on his whiskered face. He held the tube in the air. "Noo, lassie, if ye'll cooperate, I'll clear the room and gie you a little privacy."

"Don't touch me," I screamed and scooted to the far side of the bed.

Birdie grabbed me, rolled me on my stomach, and yanked the blanket up to my hips.

"Please," I yelled. "I've got a very sensitive behind. No man ever touched me there."

By this time, everyone was laughing. "Big joke," I yelled. "It should happen to you." I knew I was lost. If it was going to happen I didn't need such a large audience. I begged McTare. If he would make everyone go downstairs, I would discuss it with him. Maybe I'd even let him do it.

"Everyone leave except Blister and Converse," McTare said happily. "We'll fill the lass with this nice warm water and then we'll all go doon and leave her be."

"Not Converse . . . not Blister. They've got to go, too," I begged when the others had gone. This would be the final ignominy. Even knowing it had happened would be enough, but seeing it . . . oh God . . . that way romance would take wing forever.

But McTare was made of coarser clay. "Blister must stay because he has the 'convincer.' The Cabot lad has been looking at ye with big cow eyes. If he be going to marry ye, he shouldn't mind knowing ye parts and carin' for them all. I'll hold the bag. Come noo, lay over on your left side."

McTare patted my behind. "That be the fairest behind I ever laid eyes on," he said, handing the nozzle to Converse, who suddenly kissed my neck and told me not to worry.

"Spread her cheeks, lad," I heard McTare say. "Ease it in. Gently . . . gently . . . ah, that's right! All right, lass, here come the water. Hold on tight!"

"Oh, Converse . . . Converse," I moaned. "How can you ever love me now?"

28

I awoke slowly . . . aware that I had been sleeping on my stomach, and with the incredulous feeling that someone was kissing my behind . . . not only kissing but nibbling. For a second I wondered if I had been invaded by McTare, and I was afraid to move for fear that the hand that was caressing my back and my calves ever so lightly, making me feel tingly and pleasantly excited, might become more insistent and demanding.

Out of the corner of my eye I noticed that the room was early-morning grey and the fog still leaned heavily against the window. Afraid that if I moved I might be in for worse trouble, I tried to reconnoiter. What time was it? Had I slept around the clock? My head was aching, but in a light, detached way.

Whoever was kissing me suddenly stopped, got off the bed, and pulled a light cotton blanket over me. I heard him moving quietly around the room. Was he going to leave? Who was it? There were only three possibilities . . . Converse . . . Bucky . . . or, God forbid . . . McTare. Where was everybody, anyway? The house was singularly quiet and seemed to be suspended in a fog-isolated world. It was a day to snuggle in bed . . . and not alone. I waited . . . tense . . . certain that any minute whoever was in the room would take me in his arms and I would arise screaming—or hold him tight against me, murmuring my delight.

And then I heard the bolt on my bedroom door being softly slid back, and whoever had been dallying with me was suddenly gone. I heard footsteps going down the stairs and I was so disappointed that I nearly ran to the door and yelled,

"Come back . . . please come back!" It just *had* to be Converse. It had to be! I touched my behind where it had been kissed and tried to recall whether there had been a scratchy feeling but I couldn't remember for sure. If it had been McTare . . . surely he wouldn't have been so quietly gentle. No . . . after a minute or two he would have rolled me on my back and said something like, "Lass, I canna stand it a second more, let me come aboard." Still . . . maybe I had misjudged McTare. . . .

No . . . more likely it was Bucky. I gasped. Suddenly I was sadly certain that it was Bucky. I remember that after Stephanie had left I had gotten out of bed and slid the bolt on the door. Whoever had been importunately kissing my behind and running his hands shiveringly on the inside of my legs, tracing a delicate love message . . . whoever it was . . . had climbed up the porch roof and come in my window. Only Bucky would do that. I was glad now that I hadn't called him back. A great feeling of unhappiness swam into my mind and dislodged the tears I was holding back. If Bucky had been in my room it would mean that Stephanie had gone . . . fog or not . . . and if Stephanie had gone . . . Converse and the whole Cabot family had left, too.

And so I had to remember it . . . whether I wanted to or not, and I didn't really want to. Of course, Converse had gone. After that disgraceful business with him seeing me . . . so disgustingly . . . so intimately revealed . . . so open . . . showing the animalistic functioning that was Willa Starch . . . what else would he do except leave . . . anything to get away from a girl who was so gross and common.

Unwillingly, I recalled that he had been gentle. After I screamed for McTare to stop . . . for God's sake, no more, that I was about to burst . . . Converse had swept me into his arms and rushed me into the bathroom. Crying, sobbing, I begged him to leave me alone. I was horribly, sickeningly not in control of myself. But he had stayed and put cool washclothes on my head and whispered to me to stop worrying. Grinning, he told me that he was getting to be an old hand at taking care of dipsomaniacs. And then he was sorry, because I didn't think it was funny that the only two times that I had been alone with him this summer I had been cock-eyed. Please, please, I begged him, leave me . . . go downstairs. I'll be all right. No man should ever see a woman like this . . . not ever . . . not even if they were married years and years.

Converse laughed at me and tried to reassure me. He wasn't disgusted. He ran warm water in the tub, and while I sat there in an agony of shame he recalled for me equivalent episodes in his life. The time that he had been so sick with a strep infection that the pretty nurse who sat with him around the clock for two nights practically breathed for him. But it wasn't the same, I told him. For a nurse it was a job. She was paid to do it.

And then he unrolled the blanket that I had still wound around me and that wasn't covering much of importance, anyway, and pulled me out of my hunched-over, sobbing position. He held my face in his hands and kissed my salty lips and then lifted me up and put me in the tub.

"Willa Starch," he said, soaping me and washing me in a very thorough and methodical fashion, "will you please stop worrying. This is a wonderful privilege. I never gave a woman a bath before . . . it's a very enjoyable business."

But my head wouldn't stop aching, and I slumped against the side of the tub with Converse's arm holding me from sliding down. I continued to cry, mostly because I wasn't enjoying it when he soaped my breasts ever so carefully and washed the rest of me as if he were on a wonderful voyage of discovery. Why couldn't my head have stopped pounding so that I could have revelled in the serious expression of his face and the wondrous feeling of his searching fingers.

For a moment I lost the thread of recollection. My mind seemed to want to stop forever and recreate this idyll. What had happened next? I vaguely remembered McTare yelling from downstairs telling Converse to hurry up, that he'd give him five minutes more . . . and if Converse didn't come down he'd come up and take charge of any nursing duties. Hurriedly, Converse had helped me out of the tub and toweled the swaying Willa Starch dry, while she hung desperately onto a towel rack lest she collapse.

Then I was in bed, and Converse had gone, and I felt drained and terribly, terribly tired. I heard the front door slam and McTare bellowing as usual and the voices of Thirsty and Blister in a soprano-baritone argument. And then the house was silent. I dozed into a frightening world peopled with murky monsters that swooped down on me as I ran and ran across an endless beach—unable to escape them as they floated against my face, laughing raucously, staring at me with bloodshot eyes. I awoke whimpering, with Stephanie, still wrapped in my pink-and-white cotton blanket, shaking me gently.

"Hey, wake up, you're having a nightmare."

I stared at her. "Where am I? Have I been asleep long?"

"Not more than five minutes."

"It seemed like forever. Why are you here? Didn't you go?"

"No clothes," she grinned. "McTare didn't want me to go, anyway. He's sworn off women."

"That's what he gets for stripping away the illusion and the intrigue. Converse will never be the same," I sighed. "It's probably just as well. You'll look all the better to him."

Stephanie sat in the old Boston rocker that Grandma Starch had given me for my room.

"I'm sorry about the clothes business," I told her, unable to keep my eyes opened and watch her. "You can help yourself, There's a cute orange print in the closet. Slips are in the dresser drawer, and some panties, if you want them. I don't think my bras are big enough to fit you."

Stephanie was silent for a moment, then she said softly, "Have you ever made love with Bucky?"

I told her that I hadn't, but it wasn't from lack of his trying. I wanted to reverse the question and ask about Converse and her, but then I decided I didn't want to know.

"I guess that's the way he is with any woman," Stephanie said. "It's stupid. I've been engaged three times. I never thought any man could make me so unsettled. I could hate him just as easily. . . ."

"What about Converse?" I forced my eyes open.

Stephanie shrugged. "Everyone expects it. But it would be so dull. Really, Converse is *so* predictable. I could reel him back in . . . not because you aren't competition, in a way . . . but because he'll do what's expected of him, and Reliance and Desire expect a Billings-Cabot merger. If he married you, you'd end up like Eliza Doolittle with Converse as Professor Higgins, trying to improve your manners and morals, and the Cabots and half of Boston society wagging their tongues and wondering why he did it."

"So go home now! You've seen how the peasants live," I said wearily. I was too tired to argue with her. She could reel Converse in anytime she wanted to. What an egomaniac! I really wanted to weep, but suddenly I was dozing again, and those drooling monsters were chasing me—just where they had left off before.

Stephanie, dressed in my orange print and looking quite ravishing to demented me, was leaning over me again. "If I were you I'd give up sleeping. You might transmigrate forever into that other world. You sounded as if you were being raped by ten thousand demons."

"Go away," I pleaded. "When you are in my room, my subsconscious mind keeps me awake to the danger. Go home.

194

Take Converse with you . . . marry him . . . only let me die in peace."

"No one is going anywhere in this fog," Stephanie said. "I've made up my mind. Bucky wants me to spend the night on his trawler. It would be kind of romantic in this fog and all. Daddy would die . . . my God, if I should get pregnant and have to marry him . . . what a horrible name . . . Stephanie Bonnelli! Oh well . . . maybe I'll be lucky. Maybe one night of it will be enough to disillusion me. . . ."

I think Stephanie gave me a lot more advice about not getting involved with Converse, but it entered my brain somewhat deliriously, a counterpoint to the pursuing demons, until finally Stephanie actually became one of them and chased me off the edge of the world into an endless void.

Trying to remember what Stephanie had said, wondering why she had changed her mind—because I was certain that she had and that Bucky had just been in my room—I must have drifted off to sleep again. I awoke squealing my indignation. Bucky had come back in the room and was kissing my behind again.

I turned over, yelling, "Buck Bonnelli . . . you cut it out! . . . and my mouth was immediately closed with a kiss and I was looking into the twinkling eyes of Converse Cabot!

"It's not true," I sighed. "I'm dreaming it. You went home last night."

His lips grazed my ear. "Does Bucky Bonnelli kiss your behind, too?"

"Oh, no," I cried, and kissed his chin and lips and nose. "You are the only man who has ever touched it. But after what you saw . . . after that awful business when McTare made you. . . ."

Converse kissed me silent. "McTare convinced me that the only kind of woman for me is one with normal functions." And then he chuckled. "Willa . . . this is a magic island ruled over by a kindly Prospero, and you are Miranda, his daughter."

I looked at him wonderingly. "You are obviously bewitched. But don't leave . . . not ever. If this be a spell cast by some wonderful Ariel . . . let it last fifty more years!"

"Fifty years!" Converse was kissing my breasts. I suddenly realized that he was naked, too. "You'll be seventy-two years old, my fulsome one . . . and probably not so eager."

"And I'll have dried out old dugs, and you won't want to kiss them, anyway."

"Oh, I don't know . . . aged wine is very mellow."

I nibbled his cheek, and felt him warm and searching

against my belly. I touched his penis gently and couldn't help smiling. "The only other one I ever touched was skinny and nowhere near so big!"

"When was that?" He curled a hair on my bush and threatened to yank it out.

"Oh, about fifteen years ago. . . . Bucky wanted to play husband."

He yanked the hair and I yelled. "You can't make me jealous. I have a blanket with a brown spot on it, my innocent one. I think I may frame the spot and hang it over the fireplace in our library. It would make a better conversation piece than a moose head."

For that I bit him and tried to calm the excitement and near panic that seized me. "You said *our* library? What about Stephanie?" The mist vanished for a second. I knew that I must be dreaming the whole thing. Any minute the drooling monsters would return, and this tongue on my breast and the gentle hand touching me—exploring the contours of my knees, my calves, inquisitive at my center, tracing figures on my belly and playful on my nipple and the convolutions of my ear—would be just a dream. And if it weren't a dream, it wouldn't last. Hadn't Stephanie practically told me that Converse wouldn't dare marry me?

Since Converse hadn't answered . . . too busy touching and snuggling on the landscape of me . . . I repeated the question and gave it a nasty hook. "What about Stephanie? I suppose you have done this with her many times?"

"A couple of times," he replied coolly. "But she didn't like it as much as you do. She suffered me out."

"How do you know I like it?"

"If you don't, why do you sigh so happily and arch so eagerly toward me?"

I hastily pulled away. I read somewhere that a girl shouldn't be so eager. Maybe Stephanie had the right idea. I tried to explain this feeling to Converse.

"Don't be silly, Willa. It's your warmth and hungry eagerness that fans the fire higher in me."

"This could be dangerous. We might go up in smoke! Anyway, you haven't answered my question. Not only . . . what about Stephanie, but where is she? And where is Prin and Henry and McTare and Bucky . . . and oh, my gosh . . . Grandma? Grandma certainly would not approve of this."

Converse looked at me a second, a wide grin on his face. "You are an inquisitive one." He transferred his attention to my stomach, buried his face in it, and blew a noisy rat-a-tat-tat that sounded loud enough to be heard on the beach. I

196

tried to shush him, but he did it again and informed me that this was the flourish preceding an important announcement. "You are supposed to ask me what the queen's messenger has to announce."

"Good sire . . . what has the queen's messenger to announce?"

"Queen Stephanie, more familiarly addressed by Bucky Bonnelli as, 'old Steph', has disappeared with that Italian from Milan . . . or was it Naples? Anyway, like the island in the Tempest, there are all kinds of plots and subplots afoot."

I pushed him away. "You better start from the beginning . . . or at least where I left off. What time is it? What day is it?"

"About ten-thirty . . . the day after yesterday. But let's not reminisce . . . the moment is too pleasant. I'd rather make love."

"Can't we do both? We've got all day. Lock the door. If Prin comes home, I'll tell her to go away and not interrupt this dream."

"Shall we make it a test of endurance?" Converse challenged.

"Well, not exactly . . . first I need to get in condition; all athletes do that. But it is delightful. Couldn't we make it a way of life?"

"You mean we wouldn't eat?"

"Oh . . . yes . . . each other . . . and occasionally sandwiches as necessary."

"The world would disown us. Our friends would hate us."

"Why? Oh . . . don't answer. I know already. Stephanie told me. I'd be a liability to you. You'd have to teach me how to speak English and which fork to use, and all your friends would say, 'He didn't want to . . . but he had to marry her. She's just a tramp from South Boston. Poor Converse.' And pretty soon you'd get an apartment on Beacon Street like Sawyer has, or else you'd divorce me and go back to Stephanie and tell her you were sorry." I sighed. "I'd rather you had the apartment."

Converse whistled, "That was a short life. I really think you have a rather dim view of me. First, I was generalizing . . . something I know females don't approve of. I meant that people would despise us if we admitted that all we want to do was spend our lives enjoying each other. Love is an aberration that you are supposed to outgrow. Read the newspapers, the magazines, the novels. Do you find anything about love? Anyone knows that war, politics, and buying and selling things are more important."

"We wouldn't outgrow it, would we, Con? If we would, I'd rather not start." I hugged his face against my breasts and then let him go and looked at him searchingly. "Is is true? Can Stephanie reel you in any time she wants to? Do you have to marry her?" I told him what Stephanie had said about his father and mother. "What about your mother? Desire . . . oh, Converse, that's not really her name is it?"

Chuckling, Converse kissed my eyes and nose and lips and neck . . . and then I grabbed him. "No you don't! I want some answers! Was it you who was kissing me? Why did you leave? I think I'm mad at you. Who do you think you are? You've got a nerve! You made love to me and then you went away for three weeks and pretended I didn't exist."

Converse looked at me helplessly. "I kept count. You asked me six questions in two seconds. You'd probably make a better lawyer than I." He shrugged. "It was me kissing you, and it was very enjoyable, until I remembered that your insides were probably quite empty, so I made you some breakfast."

He pointed at the table beside my bed. I hugged him and ravenously finished the toast and coffee he had brought. Some jam slipped off on my belly, and he smeared it around until I complained that I was an awful mess, and then he happily kissed it away telling me that it was the best strawberry jam he ever ate.

He was nibbling on my breasts again when I reminded him that he had answered only two questions. I squeezed him warningly and told him I wouldn't let go until he answered them all.

"I had to go to California. You can blame it on your Trotter Island maniacs. With the strike at A B C, we had to reschedule some of our production at a subsidiary so that we could meet deliveries. All the time I was gone, I kept thinking, 'I suppose I'll have to get married, eventually. Who shall it be? Margaret? Ruth? Eleanor? Charlotte? Minnie? Stephanie? Willa?' It wasn't an easy decision to make . . . so I tried 'eeny, meeny, miny, moe' . . . and Willa won . . . Ow!" he yelped as I really grabbed him. "I can't help it. With me, you marry history. Desire is really my mother's name. Look up the passengers on the first boat . . . there was a girl named Desire something or other. Please . . . how can you ask questions or talk about the past when *you* are present— and so pulsatingly delectable?"

"Are you kissing me or biting me?" I asked, shivering happily. "What boat?"

I felt his teeth squeezing . . . ever so softly. "The May-flower, silly!"

I scooched my face down to his lips until we were curled nearer to the foot of the bed than the top. "What would De-sire think of us like this . . . and your father, Reliance? See . . . I'm a curious cat and can only concentrate on one thing at a time. You better start from the beginning and tell me what happened."

"It's a long story," Converse grinned at me. "Are you testing my powers of endurance?"

"No. But it does look as if it may stay foggy all day. I wouldn't want you to give out too soon."

"Don't worry," Converse reassured me. "I'm hoping that we'll be here for days."

"I've got eighteen thousand or so until I'm seventy-two. Let's never leave. But first help me find my place. I must have skipped a chapter to get to this blissful part of the book. My female instincts won't let me really enjoy this until I find out how it happened."

Converse leaned back on the pillow, his arm under his head and stared at the ceiling. "I suppose marriage can get prosaic. Look at Sawyer Priestly . . . maybe it all happened because Abigail only wanted to talk, too."

I leaned over him on my elbow, with my breast near his face, and grinned at him. "Gosh, I didn't mean to dampen your enthusiasm. Oh, Converse, I love you so much . . . even if I should talk incessantly. I promise to make your life magical and every moment filled with warm bubbling laugh-ter." I gave him a hundred tender kisses and then bit him to prove it.

He rolled over and held my face in his hands and kissed me gently. "I could talk better if I were inside you. Remem-ber Aristophanes' theory of creation in the Symposium? How Zeus sliced all the men in half—the way you'd slice an egg —and gave each of the halves opposite privy parts?"

I nodded. "And, ever since, men and woman have been trying to heal the wound and make one out of two. I read it! Only one trouble."

"What?"

"I'm so hungry to be rejoined to the other part of me I may never get to hear how all this came about!"

29

"You aren't going to believe it," Converse said. He held me in his arms and whispered the story. "Abner Thurston is the hero of Trotter Island. This morning at an Independence Day breakfast marvelously cooked by Jessica Otto—creating a temporary lull in what your mother assured Reliance was the most fabulous gasser in the history of Trotter Island, a gasser which was beginning to perk up steam again when I left to visit you—Herman Snole proposed that a hundred-foot-high statue of Thirsty be erected on the East Head, holding a bottle of Old Robbie or grappa aloft . . . possibly wired so that the bottle would light up the harbor and become a beacon for mariners for generations to come."

"You sound crazier than any Trotter Islander already," I observed.

Converse laughed. "This place is infectious. I'm discovering facets of my personality that I never knew existed. I don't know whether I was drinking grappa or Old Robbie last night . . . but your father insisted this morning that I volunteered to form a committee to raise the money. Reliance said that I told everyone who would listen that Thirsty in bronze would become a minor Statue of Liberty . . . give éclat and prestige to Boston in the eyes of the world!"

"Did you say my father? Henry got out of jail? For heaven's sakes, bring me up to date . . . you have me breathless." And vastly excited too, I thought. The warmth of Converse's flesh and the pleasant male odor of him was becoming an aphrodisiac. "Hurry . . . tell me what happened . . . before I explode!"

"Bucky must have suspected," Converse said, kissing my ear. "But I had no idea that Thirsty wasn't taking us directly to the money. In fact, I was as much in the dark as McTare and didn't really believe that the money existed. I expected that when the chips were down, McTare would be blustering all over the place . . . and that somehow Bucky and I would have to get the gun away from him and bring him to his senses.

"Thirsty led us up to Fort Harrison and along the top of the grassed-over parapets of the old Civil War fort. I assumed that we were going to his shack. Thirsty was jabbering continually about his money and the liquor he distilled and his theories about longevity based on a substantial daily intake of alcohol to dissolve the poisons and bugs. McTare was following us, with Blister and Birdie the rear guard. Suddenly, Thirsty stopped talking and pointed to a moss-covered cement stairway that led down into the fort.

" 'Down there,' Thirsty said.

" 'What do ye mean down there,' McTare demanded. 'I be fed up with this Cook's tour. Who in hell be down there, ye old rat?' "

"Converse," I interrupted, astonished. "You have a better Scottish accent than McTare's."

"If you don't keep still, you may never hear what amazing business transpired down those stairs." Converse proceeded to kiss me with a great deal of passion.

"Please," I begged. "I'm in an agony of indecision . . . whether to say I can't wait . . . or prolong the ecstasy. Can you last?"

Converse grinned. "If I keep my eyes off your breasts and the lovely curve of your hips, and your belly-button grinning at me . . . all of you flagrantly inviting my touch . . . I might last another twenty minutes or so . . . but they should really give an Olympic Gold Metal for such an accomplishment. I won't promise."

"Let's try," I suggested, snuggling close to him. "I do have to know what happened. If we fail . . . people can't say we didn't try."

Converse looked at me dubiously. "All right. There we were, four male Alices listening skeptically while Thirsty, the Mad Hatter, explained that Wonderland was just below our feet. He wasn't taking any chances. He told us that he had more than one hundred and fifty thousand dollars down there. He never knew who might be prowling around his shack, so he had hidden the money in one of the abandoned dungeons in the fort.

" 'It's pretty dark down here,' Thirsty said, leading the way. 'The only light comes in through those little slits facing out into the harbor.'

" 'Embrasures . . . musket slits,' Bucky explained. 'We used to play war up here when I was a kid. It's damp as hell down there and filled with rats.'

"By this time we were at the bottom of the stairs and feeling our way along a granite-lined tunnel that evidently led deep into the fort. It was so dark outside from the fog that the light coming in the musket slits was negligible. We were slurching along in three or four inches of stagnant rain water. I could hear rats skittering ahead of us.

"McTare was cursing, and it was apparent that Thirsty, slipping along ahead like a frail ghost out of the Civil War, had outfoxed him. We could hear Thirsty laughing madly, but there were so many cross-corridors, pitch black, leading in all directions, that we couldn't tell whether Thirsty and his insane laughter was in front of us or behind us.

" 'Hey, ye damned old gally-bagger, where be ye? Come back here and let me grab ye by yur suspenders?' McTare yelled, and his voice echoed up and down the corridors, sounding like an army of Scots marching in the torpedo chute of Fort Harrison.

"McTare's bellowing was greeted by a long damp silence. Thirsty had disappeared. Then, from somewhere down one of the long dark corridors—from what seemed to be a great distance—we heard a strange voice . . . certainly not Thirsty's.

" 'Help . . . whoever is out there . . . help! We're trapped in this dungeon.'

"McTare lighted a match. It flared a second and then went out, making the black seem more intense. 'Who in hell said that?' he demanded. 'Blister, if that be ye, I don't think it funny.'

"Blister denied it. 'You can hang around in this tomb if you like, McTare. I'm getting my ass out of here. It smells like a damned graveyard. Probably haunted by some creep that's been dead a hundred years.'

"Birdie agreed. 'I expect Dracula to jump on me and start sucking the blood out of me any second.'

" 'Aw shut up, ye old ladies,' McTare said disgustedly. 'Damn ye, ye old geezer?' he bellowed into the impenetrable darkness. 'When Harry McTare gets his hands on ye, he'll squeeze the guts out of both ends of ye. Ye'll look like a broken tube of toothpaste. Where in hell be ye?'

"Just ahead of us a candle flame flickered and then burst into full flame. For a second, while it glittered, Thirsty's head appeared, as if it were floating, unattached to any body.

" 'Cripes, someone cut the old bastard's head off,' Blister muttered.

" 'Over here, McTare' Thirsty said. We could see his face, wrinkled and cadaverous. 'Right over here . . . in this little

202

room. Here's your money.' Thirsty waved a packet of money, and then another.

"McTare plunged after him. The candle blew out—or Thirsty blew it out. An ominous clang of metal dropping on concrete reverberated through the damp corridor. The wet cement floor vibrated under our feet. I wondered for a second if Thirsty had shot off some old Civil War cannon. It felt as if a ton of metal had been dislodged and thundered to the floor. When the echoes stopped, there was dead silence for a second, and then McTare was roaring madly.

" 'What in blazes was that? Where in hell be ye now, ye old fox. Blister . . . Birdie! . . . sound off, so I can locate ye. It's blacker than the bottom of an outhouse!'

"Blister and Birdie started yelling. We could hear McTare shuffling around in the dark somewhere in front of us, complaining that he had lost the location of the door. Then we heard footsteps coming down the stairs from the top of the fort and Thirsty appeared *in back of us* swinging a blazing gasoline lantern that made grotesque shadows of us all. Thirsty was grinning so that his toothless gums back to his uvula shone resplendently.

"For the first time, with the corridor lighted up, we could see that we were in a narrow tunnel lined with small cells.

" 'We're in a damned prison,' Birdie said, and the words were no sooner out of his mouth than we all saw McTare for the first time. He was grasping the bars of a portcullis . . . his eyes bloodshot, a wild, animal look on his face . . . speechless . . .'"

"What's a portcullis?" I interrupted. "What was that noise you heard? What about that other voice calling for help? Was that Thirsty?" And then I couldn't help it—I laughed.

"What's so funny?"

"You! I never knew that a Proper Bostonian could tell a story so dramatically. A minute ago you scowled just like McTare."

Converse's fingers idled across my belly button and began to lightly trace the triangle below it . . . so delicately that I nearly burst from the voluptuous feeling. Ooooh, I thought, I'll never dare tell you how much I love you. I began to wonder if this was where the story was going to stop.

But Converse had more fortitude than I. "Willa, I am a lawyer . . . remember? You are going to spend a good part of your life listening to cases and summations. You are going to be my jury to practice on. . . ."

"Will you always excite your jury like this?"

"Always," he agreed solemnly, continuing his gentle explorations. "To answer your questions in order. A portcullis is a barred metal gate with openings about the size of a garden trellis, and spiked steel at the bottom. The noise we heard was this metal gate slamming into place, confining McTare in one of the dungeons.

" 'I got you! I got you!' Thirsty yelled jubilantly.

"He swung his lantern back and forth in front of the infuriated McTare, careful to stay out of reach of the arm grasping at him through the portcullis.

" 'Call me an old coot . . . call me a half-wit, will you? Get my little girl Willa Starch drunk, will you, and give her an enema for all the world to see? You're a bad man, McTare, but I got you. You're in the Corridor of Dungeons, where they kept prisoners during the Civil War. You can stay here until you rot. It'll take a derrick to raise that gate. By the time you get out you'll be a smaller pile of bones than Abner Thurston.' "

"Oh, my gosh," I said, feeling a little sorry for McTare but admiring Thirsty, my Don Quixote, more. "I'll bet McTare was furious."

"McTare has lost the power of speech. He tugged furiously at the gate, demanding that Birdie and Blister pull at the same time on the other side. But Blister wouldn't put the machine gun down, and Birdie only pulled halfheartedly. The thing weighed too much anyhow. Thirsty must have discovered how it was hung and how to release it, but it was apparent to all of us that some kind of chain hoist would have to be rigged up before McTare would be free.

"Bucky suddenly realized that Thirsty had gone into the granite blocked dungeon first in order to entice McTare after him. He asked Thirsty how he had managed to escape without being guillotined by the gate.

" 'Through the musket slit!' Thirsty cackled joyously and pointed to the dim light coming from the outside into McTare's prison. 'Let me see you try it, McTare! Squeeze your fat belly through that hole, and when you get stuck in the middle, with your head in daylight, I'll be waiting out there to bounce rocks off you!'

" 'Blister! . . . Birdie!' McTare yelled, purple with rage. 'Don't let that bag of bones get away with this. The old geezer knows how to lift this gate. Make him do it!'

"But Blister had other ideas. He pointed the machine gun at Thirsty. 'Who else you got locked up in here? A couple of minutes ago I heard someone yelling for help.'

" 'And where's the stack of money I saw you waving at

McTare?' Birdie demanded. He grabbed Thirsty so tightly by the throat that Thirsty's breath came out in little whistles.

" 'The money is in there with McTare,' Thirsty gasped. He must have realized that he had miscalculated. He should have trapped Blister and Birdie, too, and, like the tailor in the fairy tale, got three at one blow.

"Birdie grabbed the lantern away from Thirsty and held it close to the gate, lighting up the interior of the dungeon. We could see that Thirsty must have used the place for winter headquarters. It was littered with debris that he had rescued from the ocean, as well as hundreds of bottles of Scotch. A table and an old steel innerspring with a mattress on it were in one corner.

"McTare roared to life when he saw the Scotch. He grabbed a bottle, twisted off the seal and took a huge swallow. 'It's my Old Robbie, ye thief! Even if the labels be gone, I'd know Old Robbie anywhere.'

" 'McTare. Search around in there and find the old boy's money,' Birdie said. 'We don't give a damn about the Scotch.'

"McTare tossed the debris around furiously and, finally, with a happy yell, located the money. He brought a packet of it over to the gate and, in the lantern light, examined it in amazement. 'The old stinking rat has glued it together. How do ye get it apart, old man?'

" 'You'll never get it apart, McTare.' Thirsty quavered, rubbing his throat. 'I didn't lie to you. There's thousands there—but it's stuck together forever.'

" 'Let me look at a stack of it, McTare. The old man is off his noggin. We'll get it apart, don't you worry.' Birdie was unable to conceal the cupidity in his voice. He reached through the gate and tried to snatch the money out of McTare's hand, but McTare was too quick for him. He grabbed Birdie's arm and yanked him tight against the iron grille. 'No one's getting his hands on this money until I get out of here.'

"Blister pointed the machine gun at McTare. 'I hate to do this McTare,' he grinned evilly, 'but if I was on the other side of the gate you'd do the same thing thing. Hand over that dough or I'll rip your guts apart.'

"McTare cursed them both and told them that they were worse than vipers. 'Go ahead, ye blasted idiots. Murder me. What in hell good will it do ye? Ye canna lift the gate. How are ye going to get in here and get the money when I'm dead?'

"Blister looked at him blankly and stroked his scarred face thoughtfully. Slowly it dawned on them that—for the moment, at least—McTare held the trump card. Birdie collared

Thirsty again and was shaking him violently when another idea occurred to Blister.

" 'Old man, a few minutes ago I heard someone yelling for help. Who else you got locked up in here?'

"Thirsty refused to answer.

" 'If there's anyone else in this place,' Blister yelled, 'sound off!'

"When the echoes subsided a male voice responded faintly . . . about three hundred yards away down one of the black corridors. 'Who are you? Help us! We're trapped down here!'

"Ignoring McTare, who cursed them for leaving him, Blister urged us along the corridor, forcing Thirsty to lead the way. Groping along after him, we finally stopped in front of a barred metal door with a small grating just above eye level. Taking no chances, Blister pinned Thirsty against the wall, and Birdie waved the lantern in front of the opening.

" 'There's some one in there,' he said, peering in. 'Damned if it ain't a man and a tomato. Who in hell are you? How did you get in there?' "

30

"Who was it?" I demanded excitedly. Converse was taking too much delight in prolonging the story.

He was kissing me again.

"Guess," he said, as his hand teased my legs apart.

"I can't. In a second I won't even be able to think."

"It was a friend of yours."

"Ohhh . . . Converse, I guess I don't really care who it was!"

"Let me come inside, and I'll tell you."

I agreed that this was probably necessary. A few minutes later . . . blended . . . I murmured, "We are belly to belly. Can you last?"

"Can you?"

I was dubious . . . but such a nice feeling should be capable of infinite extension. "I'll try. Who was it?"

"Sawyer Priestly and Shirley North!"

I closed my eyes. I was dreaming. "Oh, my God." I waited for the drooling monsters to return, but nothing happened.

Converse chuckled. "I told you this island was under a spell. This time Caliban was at work. Anyway, when Bucky realized that it was Sawyer trapped again with Mrs. North . . . and this time right on Trotter Island . . . he was beside himself. He clapped Thirsty on the back and hugged him. 'They say that opportunity never knocks twice', he yelled through the grating at Sawyer, 'but it did this time. Priestly, do you recognize the voice. This is Joe Fluger of the Fluger gang. And you know who is standing right beside me . . . your savior from bathrooms, Converse Cabot . . . only this time he hasn't got the key.'

" 'Cabot . . . is that you out there?' I heard Priestly say, as if he were unable to believe it.

"I hated to admit it," Converse said nibbling on my ear. "I knew that Sawyer would naturally assume that there was something mighty peculiar about me finding him . . . locked up with Shirley North twice in twenty-four hours."

" 'Get us out of here.' Sawyer said, and his voice was charged and tense. 'I'm fed up with these schoolboy pranks. First there's a strike at A B C, and then the mad business in my apartment. I have an idea that you and Reliance are more than a little involved. It's damned peculiar to me, Converse, that you are always on the outside looking in.'

" 'Let's stop all this jabbering,' Blister interrupted him. 'Mister . . . how did you get on this island? Have you got a boat? The boat we came on ain't running. We'll get you out of there if you got transportation for us . . . otherwise you and your quiff can slobber around in there for the next century.'

"Echoing down the corridor, we could hear McTare cursing us blasphemously. Blister chuckled and said to Priestly, 'Looks as if you'll have to put up with a noisy cellmate just down the corridor until he runs out of gas.'

"After demanding who Blister was and what right he had to speak to Sawyer Priestly so high-handedly, and insisting that I, Converse Cabot, inform this madman just who Sawyer Priestly was, Priestly finally realized that this approach was getting him nowhere. He cooled down and admitted that he had a cruiser anchored off the East Head.

" 'All right, old man,' Blister said, corralling Thirsty and pointing at a large keyhole in the cell door. 'Let's have the key.'

" 'There ain't no key!' Thirsty grinned at him. 'Leastways, if there is, I've never seen it.'

" 'What do you mean there's no key?' Birdie demanded. 'How did they get in there?'

" 'They fell in from the top,' Thirsty said. 'We were walking along the parapet, and whoom . . . down they went.'

" 'We did not fall, Converse. We were pushed!' It was Shirley North. She put her face up to the grating, and from the light of Thirsty's lantern she looked pretty mussed and bedraggled. 'Please, Converse, help us get out of here. All that we need is a ladder. There's a hole in the roof about fifteen feet above us.'

"Shirley explained that she and Sawyer had come ashore from Sawyer's cruiser about noon. 'It was getting foggy. An old man watched us beach Sawyer's pram. Sawyer asked him if Reliance Cabot had arrived. The old man said that we were on the wrong side of the island . . . that Reliance's boat was moored off the West Head. He said that he would show us the way. Sawyer thought it was strange that we had to cross the fort and climb way up here, but the old man said it was the shortest way. Then, suddenly, the old man was walking behind us. I felt the ground give way and tried to jump back . . . but he shoved us. It's a wonder we didn't break a leg. We landed in a pile of dirty soaking wet army mattresses. Oh Converse . . . it's terrible the place is full of rats. Get us out of here!'

" 'You're a genius, Thirsty,' Bucky whooped. 'Wait until Herman Snole hears about this . . . and wait until we bring Mendes East and Abigail Priestly over here. Priestly . . . you should write a book on new places to shack up. First a bathroom . . . now a dungeon!'

"A whispered conference took place between her and Sawyer, and then Sawyer said in a very subdued voice. 'Converse, is it true? What is Abigail doing on this cursed island?' "

Converse chuckled. "I told him that Abigail had called Desire last Friday and was unhappy because she was going to be alone on the Fourth of July weekend . . . that Sawyer told her that he had to go to New York to the headquarters of the Electronic Workers Union of America to convince them that Herman Snole was irresponsible and should be removed from his job as local representative. Desire invited Abigail to spend the weekend in Cohasset. When Reliance decided early this morning to cruise out to Trotter Island to look over the place for the first time and to talk with Charles North, Abigail and Desire decided to come along."

Converse had paused in his story and was kissing my

breast. "Why did your father want to talk with Mendes? . . . and why did Stephanie have to tag along? Converse . . . if you don't stop it . . . I may skyrocket right out of this room."

"It's hard to resist when it points right at me and says please kiss me."

"My breasts don't talk," I said primly.

Converse laughed. "All right. Old Steph came along to find Bucky Bonnelli. I'm not sure exactly what happened in Sawyer's apartment, but she intimated that castration would be really too good for him. Since they have been missing all night and didn't show up for breakfast at Jessica Otto's, I assume that she changed her mind.

"Reliance wanted to find out what had happened at the Boston Arts Festival—first-hand from Mendes—and see if he could persuade Mendes to paint a duplicate of the picture. It seems that years ago Reliance had seen the very young Princess Tassle at the Old Howard Theatre and had gone backstage and interviewed her for the Harvard Lampoon. Reliance was quite impressed and extolled her virtues both physical and mental in an article that reads almost like a love letter to your mother. Buying Mendes' painting was like buying back his youth. Desire, of course, only tolerates this nonsense. 'Your father is regressing,' she says. 'He'll be fifty next year. At that age a man gets quite desperate. Reliance wishes that he were twenty-five again and knew what he knows now. He would have married a burlesque queen and been the envy of all the men at his club.' "

"So Converse Cabot is going to profit by his father's mistakes," I said.

"What do you mean?"

"Marry the burlesque queen's daughter. Oh, gosh," I sighed, as he paid me back for the sarcasm by kissing me quite wildly. "I'm glad that your father didn't marry the Princess."

"Why?"

"We might have ended up brother and sister, and this would be illegal." I shivered. "I just happened to think . . . what is Sawyer doing on Trotter Island? Was he looking for me? He'd probably be pleased to end the career of Willa Starch permanently. Did you finally get him and Shirley North out of the dungeon?"

"Sawyer isn't looking for you. He isn't even angry with you. When it comes to a pretty woman, Sawyer has a blind spot. He is certain that you are the innocent victim of a gang of cutthroats headed by Bucky Bonnelli, Herman Snole, and your father. Sawyer came out here today because he is convinced that Reliance doesn't care whether a marina is built on Trotter Island or not. He believed that Reliance might actually be playing footsies with Herman Snole to keep the strike going until Sawyer would agree that the whole marina idea was impractical. This morning, on the telephone, Sawyer gave Reliance an ultimatum. The strike is costing A B C nearly a hundred thousand dollars a day. He intimated that unless Reliance settled the strike by Tuesday and stopped all this nonsense about Operation Buzz-Off that he could be replaced as President. Sawyer is fed up with the muddling of the Cabots."

Converse looked at me speculatively for a moment and then evidently decided the only solution was to continue the story. "Anyway," he said, "when Sawyer realized that Abigail was actually on Trotter Island and might find him confined in such damning circumstances with Shirley North, he didn't wait for Bucky's proposition. He told Bucky that the Trotter Islanders had won. If Bucky would help him get out of the dungeon and off Trotter Island, he would make a deal with him."

Converse grinned. "Bucky Bonnelli is a promoter. He agreed to help Priestly, if Sawyer would guarantee that all contracts for the construction of a marina on Trotter Island would be handled by the Bonnelli Construction Company."

I leaped away from Converse's embrace. "It's a sellout! Bucky Bonnelli is a louse. He's supposed to be helping Operation Buzz-Off. Now he's in business with the enemy. Oooh . . . what a faker he is. He hasn't any construction company."

Converse looked at me ruefully. "Willa . . . I think you are paying more attention to this story than to making love. You pulled away so fast that I lost you."

I hugged him and helped him find his way back. "You'll have to admit that making love this way is kind of fun. In all the books I've read it never lasts anywhere near so long . . . and the people who write those books make it so serious, so deadly . . . or so world-shaking. I like it better this way, with laughter and grins. You do feel very good Converse." I kissed him with little kisses and caught his tongue and tasted it. "Gosh, I wonder if people ever get stuck together . . . what would happen if we couldn't get apart and Grandma or Prin found us this way? Jimmy . . . what would we do?"

That made Converse laugh so hard that we had to rejoin all over again.

"Just wait until Henry and Herman hear what Bucky has

done," I said, again picking up the subject of Trotter Island. "He's a Benedict Arnold. How could he ever buy a construction company?"

"Don't worry. If Priestly, Tom Billings and my father can ever agree that the investment will pay off, they would have to spend several million of Abigail's dollars to build the marina. With that kind of contract, Bucky could probably put together a construction company overnight."

Converse was nuzzling at my neck and in the curve of my shoulder and tracing the contours of my behind. "Don't be too harsh on Bucky," he said. "First, I think that he may be trying to impress Stephanie . . . and second, it was a verbal agreement. While I wouldn't want to impugn Sawyer, I'd guess that, considering the circumstances and the predicament that he was in, he would have promised Bucky half-ownership of A B C Electronics if Bucky had asked him. Sawyer could always welsh on the deal should the necessity arise. You see, Abigail has all the money. Just so long as Sawyer is a good boy, she lets him make the decisions. I suppose she doesn't even suspect that Sawyer might be a bad boy. No one else did until yesterday. Sawyer is a pretty smooth operator. He might be able to squirm out of almost any predicament . . . except Shirley North. Shirley belongs to the same Garden Club as Abigail, and Shirley has the reputation of a hot little minx. Abigail would not take kindly to such a predatory female making eyes at her Sawyer."

Converse chuckled. "Bucky had no sooner settled the deal with Sawyer and was persuading Thirsty to help him locate a ladder or a length of rope, than Blister awoke him to the facts of life."

" 'You two ain't goin nowhere! This slob and his quiff stay right where they are. Do you hear me?' Blister yelled into the grating. 'Just cool your ass, bud. Birdie and me will get you and the dame out of there all in good time. When we do, we'll all hightail it to your boat and leave this crummy island. But first things first. We either gotta get McTare out of that cell . . . or talk him into passing that money through the grating.'

"Thirsty tried to tell them that the money wasn't any good. If they persuaded McTare to give it to them, they could never get it apart. But neither Blister nor Birdie paid any attention. Sawyer, listening to this conversation with his head to the only opening in the cell door, was completely bewildered. He finally decided that I was wholly responsible.

" 'Cabot,' he said angrily, as Blister forced us to go back to McTare's cell, 'I'm holding you personally responsible. Your

211

father's job, his stock, and the whole of A B C may go up in smoke if I don't get out of here!'

"As we followed Thirsty down the damp corridor, prodded from the rear by Blister with his machine gun, Bucky whispered to me that we really ought to tackle these two and wrap the damned machine gun around Blister's squat neck. Blister heard him. He warned us that he had been a machine-gunner in World War II. He explained in gory detail how he had wiped out a whole platoon of Mussolini's Eyetalians in North Africa and then had eaten a hearty lunch of C rations. To knock off a few troublemakers, one of whom was an Eyetalian, wouldn't phase him a bit. 'You'd fall over easy as tenpins,' he scowled. 'Don't go getting me hot and bothered. I got an itchy finger on this trigger.'

"We finally got back to McTare, and it occurred to me that he hadn't been bellowing for at least ten minutes. When we crowded in front of his cell we found out why. McTare had found a candle and was sitting at a wooden table piled high with the solid stacks of Thirsty's money. In the flickering light McTare was slowly dribbling Old Robbie over it. He grinned at us and held up a single ten dollar bill . . . and then another.

" 'He got it apart!' Thirsty squealed. 'Danged if he ain't got it unglued! Let me see one, McTare! Has it got Hamilton's head on both sides?'

"In his excitement Thirsty got dangerously close to the bars. McTare snatched at him and caught him by his suspenders, drawing him tight against the portcullis. 'Ye damned old gally-bagger, I should squeeze the piss out of ye!'

"McTare was pulling Thirsty's suspenders so hard that the buttons popped off Thirsty's pants. Thirsty's suspenders snapped themselves around the bars of the cell and twitched across McTare's nose. Cursing, McTare tossed a ten-dollar bill at Thirsty who flipped back into our arms like a coiled spring.

" 'Ye half-brain, I just poured Old Robbie on it, and it comes apart gud as noo. Blister . . . Birdie . . . get me out of here, we'll be rich men!'

"Bucky examined the damp ten-dollar bill, astonished to find that it had opposite sides. 'Good God, we tried everything on that money. Not even grappa would loosen it. Old Robbie must be made with paint softener. I wouldn't drink any more of that stuff if I were you, McTare. It'll dissolve your guts.'

" 'Lad, I be drinking Old Robbie since I grew hair around

my rod . . . and I'll tell ye, Harry McTare be a better man now than then!'

" 'It ain't your money, McTare,' Thirsty said, putting the money in his pocket. 'I found it. I might give you a few thousand, but the rest is mine.'

" 'Old man, ye be balmy. No one gets any of this until I get out of here . . . then maybe I'll gie ye a few dollars for finding it.'

" 'You'll never get out of there, McTare,' Thirsty cackled. 'You'll rot in there, and, when you're dead, I'll squeeze in the musket slit and jump up and down on your stinking corpse, and then I'll take it all!'

"This idea brought Blister to life. 'Birdie, I got it,' he said excitedly. 'Take the old geezer outside and stuff him through the musket slit.'

" 'Then what.'

" 'Then he can hand us the money!'

" 'And what do ye think *I'll* be doing?' McTare roared. 'Blister, ye ain't had a brain that worked for years. If the old man be stickin his bald noggin through that slit, I'll chomp it off.'

" 'Shoot McTare first,' Birdie calmly suggested.

"Quickly McTare picked up the candle and threw it in a heap of rubbish in a corner of the dungeon. Flames leaped up, and, while we watched with our mouths open, McTare tossed a handful of ten-dollar bills in the fire.

" 'Have you gone crazy, McTare?' Blister yelled, coughing and rubbing his eyes.

" 'Shoot me, ye low worm, and before Harry McTare croaks he'll toss the whole stinking pile of money in the fire!'

"By this time the smoke from the burning rags and debris, fanned by the draft that was blowing through the musket slit, was smarting our eyes and choking us. We could scarcely see.

" 'For God's sakes, Harry,' Blister gasped. 'Put out that damned fire and let's talk sensibly. Just pass the money out to Blister and me. You'll get out of there eventually. Birdie and me will meet you in Boston and split it up.'

"Blinded by the smoke, Blister must have come too close to the cell, because suddenly he was grunting, and, as the air cleared a little, we could see that McTare had caught him around the neck in a vise-like grip and was pulling his head inexorably through one of the gratings.

" 'Harry . . . for God's sake, let go . . . you're strangling me.' Blister was hanging desperately onto the machine gun with one hand. He swung wildly through the grating with the other, but McTare ignored his punches. 'Harry . . . we were

213

only kidding . . . you know Birdie and I wouldn't have left you here. Harry . . . we've always been pals . . . Harry . . . I'm suffocating. . . .'

" 'Ye dirty skunk,' McTare hissed. 'Shove that machine gun in here afore I finish ye!'

"The machine gun clattered on McTare's side of the cell. With a roar of triumph, he let go of Blister and picked it up. Stamping out the burning rags and paper, he aimed the machine gun at Blister.

" 'Damn the two of ye. I always knew that I couldn't trust ye.'

"Birdie was paralyzed against the wall. 'Don't shoot me, Harry!' he yelled. 'It's all Blister's fault. You know me, Harry. I'm your pal!'

"McTare stared at them speculatively for a second and then suggested that they get down on their knees and say their last prayers."

Converse paused and looked at me hungrily. "Willa . . . Willa . . . you're listening to me . . . so wide-eyed and innocent . . ." He continued his gentle explorations, but now more insistently. "Willa . . . I love you . . . you win . . . you have more perserverance than I."

I gasped and returned his kisses even more passionately. "Converse . . . wait . . . you can't stop now! I'm cliff-hanging!"

Converse laughed. "Why not? That's really the end of the story."

"You mean McTare shot them!"

"Honey, you underestimate Blister and Birdie. I doubt whether McTare intended to shoot them, but they were taking no chances. McTare had been buffeted too long and was not amenable to reason. What is more, the balance of power had changed. But power has its limitations. McTare couldn't shoot around corners! Instead of dropping to his knees, Blister tried that old gambit:

" 'Look out behind you, McTare!' he yelled, and, as Mc-Tare flinched, both of them ran . . . clattering down the black corridor shouting their delight at having outwitted McTare. They ran and ran . . . and we never saw them again."

"Where could they go? They must be on the island."

"We thought so, until we got a ladder from one of the deserted Army barracks and stuck it through the roof of the dungeon. Naturally, when Sawyer and Shirley climbed out they were anxious to leave . . . fog or no. We followed them to the beach, where Sawyer had left his pram. It was gone

. . . and so was Sawyer's thirty-thousand dollar cruiser. Blister and Birdie had decided that the risks of a foggy voyage on a stolen boat were preferable to the wrath of Harry McTare.

"I think Sawyer felt as if he had been trapped by elves and pixies. If this keeps up, I fear for his reason. Both he and Shirley were covered with mud and filth and smelly from the stagnant water that covered the floor of the dungeon. But Bucky took no pity. He reminded Sawyer of his promise and badgered him with graphic descriptions of Abigail's surprise if she ever discovered them . . . two sorry-looking lovebirds . . . wandering forlornly around Trotter Island.

"Sawyer finally repeated his promise that Bucky would unconditionally be the chosen contractor if a marina were ever built on Trotter Island. In exchange, Bucky would keep his mouth shut and take them to Boston tomorrow on his boat. Bucky would also have to provide a place for them to spend the night.

"Grinning, Bucky offered Thirsty's shack, and Thirsty agreed without protest. He was going to spend the night with McTare and make sure the danged fool didn't burn any more of that money. Thirsty generously offered Shirley his moth-eaten mattress and assured her there were no bugs in it. We left Sawyer and Shirley drinking grappa straight from the bottle and boiling water from Thirsty's well . . . preparing to give each other a bath in Thirsty's old tin tub.

"Bucky had plans for the evening. He hoped I didn't mind, but Stephanie and he had to find out whether they could make beautiful music together. Bucky seemed very anxious to start conducting the orchestra. It was only seven-thirty, but the fog was so thick it was practically dark. Thirsty insisted on joining McTare. He told us that it was no trouble at all to slide back into the dungeon through the musket slit. We told him this looked like certain suicide. We tried to warn him that McTare was very headstrong and dangerous, but Thirsty said that McTare was only a danged old bag of wind.

"Thirsty split up his four-day-old ham and some stale bread, leaving half with Sawyer and Shirley. We found McTare sitting in the dark. The only candle had burned up in the fire he had started. When he discovered that Thirsty was actually willing to spend the night with him and would share his ham . . . the darned old fool looked astonished and started to blubber.

" 'Thirsty, ye be the only friend Harry McTare has in the whole world,' he cried. 'I'll not forget it. Ye can have half of this money right noo!'

"We watched while Thirsty slithered through the musket slit. When he arrived in the cell, Harry enthusiastically bussed him on his bald head. Bucky assured them that we would round up all the male Trotter Islanders and, tomorrow . . . the Fourth of July, rig up a winch, lift the portcullis, and set them free. Before we left, Thirsty and McTare had divided up the money. By the light of Thirsty's gasoline lantern they were playing gin rummy for a dollar a point."

Converse laughed. "They had everything . . . food . . . cards . . . Old Robbie. The only thing they lacked was women. About midnight last night, Susan Otto, when we told her the story, decided to remedy that. She said McTare was really an old dear and she would slide through the musket slit and join him even if she had to strip and grease herself. I have a feeling that McTare may never escape from Trotter Island.

"And neither will I," Converse said, kissing me enthusiastically. "This is a magic tipsy isle . . . and I am Ferdinand from Milan . . . who has found you."

"Ferdinand? He was a bull!" I teased him, and then begged for mercy. "Wait . . . wait . . . please, Converse! What about your father and mother? All this time was Reliance left alone with Prin? With a gasser building up . . . oh, dear. Your father will bear permanent scars. And your mother marooned on your boat. . . ." I was really afraid to ask Converse where his father had spent the night. "Why didn't you come back here and wake me?"

Converse sighed. "When we finally found our way back here through the fog, Stephanie was sitting in the kitchen, gnawing her fingernails. She said that you were conked out. I tried your door, but it was locked. Bucky suggested that I shinny up the porch roof. I did—and climbed in your window and kissed you on each breast before I covered you. You groaned a little but kept right on sleeping. I didn't have the heart to wake you up. You were breathing so heavily and sighing in your sleep. I decided you were too tired for love."

I kicked Converse's ankle. "I'm never too tired for love! Was I snoring?" I asked anxiously. I really couldn't understand how he could love me. Every time he had seen me this summer I was the ultimate wreck of a female.

Converse assured me that, if I was snoring, it was a soft and feminine snore.

"I had to go back to the West Head," he continued, "to see if Reliance was going to try and get the boat back to Cohasset or Boston . . . or whether he was going to stay anchored and spend the night aboard. A bit of a problem, since Abigail was his guest. Knowing my mother, she would probably make him spend the night in the cockpit. It just wouldn't be proper for Reliance Cabot to bunk down with two women. Using one of your father's lanterns to find our way through the fog, Stephanie, Bucky, and I walked across the beach. Half way across, a bonfire flared up on the West Head. We arrived at the beginning of a gasser to end gassers. When I found Reliance, I knew that, fog or not, he was in no condition to navigate to Cohasset. The party had moved into Mendes' front yard . . ." Converse paused. "Willa . . . I guess you know something about gassers?"

I admitted that I did.

"Well, Reliance had launched himself on a sea of Old Robbie. He had his arm around Herman Snole who was telling him to drink up . . . enjoy himself . . . that it really was Reliance's Scotch and A B C Electronics would be paying for it sooner or later. Reliance thought that this was hysterically funny. He even agreed with Herman that the lady workers of the Electronic Workers of America were underpaid. This sudden rapport between Reliance and Herman Snole had me completely bewildered. Last week at a union meeting they spent two vituperative hours politely cursing each other. I finally discovered the reason. Herman is a Republican. Reliance was so elated to discover a Republican labor leader that he decided there was still hope left in the world. Reliance offered to make him Vice-President in charge of Personnel. Reliance's best lines all evening were, 'Wait until Sawyer Priestly hears about this!'

"I was engrossed in the conversation between my father and the amazing Herman Snole, when suddenly I was lifted clear off the ground and twirled like a pinwheel over the heads of the enthusiastic crowd. Looking down, I found myself staring into the happy red face of your father, who assured me that he really should toss me into the fire for smashing into Pierre Grass's boat, but he wasn't going to do it . . . because Prin said that I was in love with you and, to-morrow being Independence Day, I deserved some special kind of understanding and consideration.

" 'Willa Starch is a good girl,' Henry said. 'After all she is my daughter . . . but she has inherited some crazy and ornery ideas from her mother. You'll probably have to tan her behind regularly to keep Willa on the straight and narrow.'

" 'I went to jail to keep Prin respectable,' Henry continued, still holding me over his head, "and what does Prin do? Nothing! If it weren't for Ma and Herman Snole, I'd be over there in Boston rotting until doomsday in the pokey. But I

217

forgave her. It won't do you any good to get mad at a female Starch, son. Let me be a lesson to you.'

"Henry put me down, and, when the world stopped revolving I realized somewhat dizzily that I was standing between Desire and Abigail Priestly, both of whom were having one teensy glass of Old Robbie to celebrate their rescue by Mad Man Starch, who had found them, lonely and neglected, in Reliance's cruiser and brought them ashore.

"Neither of them was lonely now. Abigail was delighted with the adventure of being 'marooned' on Trotter Island. It was just like Swiss Family Robinson. Wait until she told Sawyer about this! And, even better, she had found Charley North's hideout . . . and actually been inside it! Imagine calling himself Mendes East and leaving his wife Shirley. He was a Boston Gauguin . . . all the papers said so.

" 'But don't you worry about Shirley,' Abigail said, snuggling up to Mendes. 'She hasn't been pining away for you. Shirley North knows how to take care of Shirley.' "

Converse grinned. "You don't have to worry about Abigail. When you have ten million dollars, words of wisdom fall from your mouth. Evey male resident of Trotter Island is entranced with her. King Rose told her he preferred plump women. He couldn't wait for his wife, Dathra, to put on some weight. In the meantime, since Dathra was nothing but skin and bones, it was a delight to put his arms around Abigail. He hoped she wouldn't mind a little squeezing. Giggling, Abigail told him to help himself.

"With all the men vying for Abigail's attention, your mother, wearing only her tassels, danced the limbo to a very small male audience. She alternated with Reliance, who took turns with her under the limbo stick. Reliance is a limbo convert. Mendes taught him how to play the steel drums.

" 'It's better than yoga,' Reliance said, ignoring Desire's admonition that tomorrow she'd be rubbing Sloan's liniment on him. 'I'm going to have Prin down to the plant to teach all my executives. We'll make limbo dancing a midmorning revitalizer.'

"Abigail told Reliance that it would be a shame to bring civilization to Trotter Island. Reliance was right. A marina here wouldn't be profitable anyway. She adored Trotter Island . . . just the way it was. It would be terrible to commercialize this last vestige of natural living. She would talk it over with Sawyer when he got back from New York. She wouldn't let him make displaced persons out of all these nice people.

"Later on, Henry told Mendes that he was sorry about the

218

fracas at the Boston Arts Festival and if Reliance wanted a painting of Prin . . . it was all right with him, and. . . ."

"Converse . . ." I interrupted, closing his mouth with a kiss, "I really don't think I can wait any longer. . . ."

"You don't want to hear about Abigail playing leapfrog without her girdle, and Desire and Prin singing 'Queenie . . . Queen of them all,' and Grandma Starch blowing her stack. . . ."

"But it all ended happily, didn't it?" I sighed, running my fingers lightly over his belly. "Everybody is matched up with everybody else . . . and everybody loves everybody. . . ."

"Willa . . . you are magic . . and I love you!"

I couldn't keep the tears of happiness from my eyes. I hugged him. And then I remembered something. I couldn't help it. "Can you wait? . . . just another minute?" I asked him seriously.

Converse looked dismayed but agreed to humor me.

I jumped out of bed and ran to my little bookcase. Furiously, I turned the pages of Shakespeare . . . found it, and read:

FERDINAND: *Wherefore weep you?*
MIRANDA: *At mine unworthiness, that dare not offer*
What I desire to give, much less take
What I shall die to want, but this is trifling;
And all the more it seeks to hide itself,
The bigger bulk it shows. Hence bashful cunning!
And prompt me, plain and holy innocence!
I am your wife, if you will marry me
If not I'll die your maid; to be your fellow
You may deny me; but I'll be your servant
Whether you will or no.

I was going to read Ferdinand's next line . . . which shows what can happen to you if you marry an egghead . . . But Converse sat up in bed and slowly took the book out of my hands. He pulled me gently toward him, until I was kneeling on the bed beside him. He kissed my breasts gently . . . very gently.

"Now, Willa . . . now! Now and always."

"Oh. Oh . . . Converse!"

Epilogue

Most stories of young love end on a happily-ever-after theme, and, as you have seen, my story is no exception. But, maybe like me, you get to wondering what happens after ever-after.

I remember reading a long story about a girl who finally surrendered her virginity (it got boring waiting) and then, after a hectic life of sin in Paris, finally came home, got married, and settled down to a placid and dull connubial bliss in an exurb of New York City . . . or was it Connecticut? Probably. Anyway, by the time she was a matronly forty she recalled her flagrant youth as if it belonged to a world of childhood fantasy and wish fulfillment. She became, in essence, the epitome of the excellent housewife, mother, and club woman. A grown-up!

Now, I do not object to this. But if I were a man I would find this suburban respectability somewhat dull. I have a theory that Converse says is cockeyed, but I believe it anyway. The reason men stray is that their wives are too predictably proper.

So, in the summer, when life becomes too routine and garden parties and barbecues have become a simpering bore—no longer even alleviated by minor flirtations—I put on my tight jeans (they still fit) and Converse and I and the boys, and sometimes Reliance, who believes that Prin is still queen of them all, sail by the expensive marina that Bucky built on the East Head of Trotter Island and join Prin and Henry and all the Trotter Islanders for a gasser. Penny Otto hugs Converse. And Harry McTare, who took over the Otto females when Frank Otto disappeared, still thinks I have "the fairest behind of all." He asks Converse for permission "to have an up-to-date bare view of it."

Occasionally, Mr. and Mrs. Charles Bonnelli motor over in their handsome cruiser that Bucky charges as a tax deduction to the Bonnelli and Billings Construction Company. Stephanie, who a few years ago took lessons in tassle dancing from my mother, dances the limbo. She claims that this is better for one's figure than being shook and vibrated in a reducing salon.

In the winter—in New England at least—it is a little more difficult to combat respectability. Its wooly mantle seems to clutch one tighter in direct proportion to the amount of clothes one wears to combat the weather.

Sitting in Converse's study a few evenings ago, watching him as he burrowed deeper and deeper into some legal problem until the only sounds in the room were the wind moaning around the leaded glass windows and the sputtering of a Valentine log in the fireplace, I told him that I had finally finished the book I had started last fall about our wooing summer.

There was no answer. Converse was with me physically, but mentally he had departed to a world guided by fine rules and regulations designed to save man from himself.

"Did you hear what I said?" I asked, a little peeved that he could receive this momentous announcement so calmly. After all, I was sure Stephanie, for example, couldn't write a book.

"You said that you had written a book about. . . . My God, Willa . . . NO!" Converse dropped his papers on the desk and then, in a typical male way, instead of asking me about the book said, "With two youngsters to take care of how could you find time to write?"

"I've always been a frustrated writer," I said, determined not to get mad. "Ever since I was in the first grade I've been trying to write my autobiography. Somehow, I always seem to get sidetracked. Anyway, last fall, when Bucky started first grade. . . ."

"Do you have to call him Bucky?" Converse interrupted. "His name is Reliance."

I stuck my tongue out at him. "I didn't argue with you when you named Stephen."

Converse grinned. "I deny any connection. I just happened to like the name. We couldn't name him Henry after your father . . . some of the Cabots around here might have considered it an unnecessary duplication."

"Stephanie was dancing pretty close to you last Saturday at the club," I remarked, taking the female prerogative of tackling the subject from another point of view. "She'd hop in the sack with you any time you beckoned."

"She always would have. She's got Trotter Island fever, contracted from too close association with her husband and your mother . . . both of whom appeal to some primitive instinct in Stephanie."

"Don't blame my mother," I said, and, since I had temporarily diverted his attention, I sat on his desk. It's big enough. It would actually be possible to lie down on it, but I compromised and curled up in front of him, happy that he was a little disgruntled. He tried to shuffle his papers and books out from under me. "It's marriage," I continued leaning on my elbow and smiling at him. "It can get dull. Bucky Bonnelli is so busy being the biggest contractor, financially and physically, in New England that he has probably forgotten the joy of making love in front of a roaring fire. But you're lucky. . . ." I switched on my husky come-on voice. "You married me . . . and I won't let you forget."

Converse shook his head. "Not tonight . . . I've got work to do. Anyway, the last time we tried that I singed my behind and you got pregnant."

I snapped off the light on his desk and slid to the floor in front of him. Swiftly, the way I had learned from Prin, I glided out of my dress and stood demurely in front of him.

"My God, Willa, why are you wearing only a dress . . . in the middle of February?"

"Want to see me do a belly dance? I practiced. I can do it better than those Arab girls we saw in Cairo last year." I swayed suggestively in front of him.

"Willa!" Converse said, looking around apprehensively. "It's only eight o'clock. You don't know *who* might drop in unexpectedly. Where's Martha? Has she put the kids to bed? What if she come downstairs looking for you?"

It's easy to see that over the years I've had a bit of a problem trying to make a roué out of Converse . . . but I haven't given up. "Bucky and Stevie were in bed an hour ago. If Martha had come down she would find us frolicking barebottomed. She would leave discreetly, and, tomorrow, all grins and chuckles, she'd say, 'Lord, Miss Willa . . . I sure love that man of yours. He doan care . . . when he decides to do it, he just ups and does it . . . no matter where he is!' "

This kind of flattery never fails.

"Come here," Converse said, grinning as he grabbed at me.

"What about the work that you have to do?"

"I just decided that it would be more fun to douse you with that bottle of fifty-year-old Madeira that we brought back from Spain."

"Huh . . . after eight years of marriage my bare white body isn't enough. You need stimulation."

"You liked it the last time I did it."

"I still do . . . but you got to drink more wine than I did. Besides, there's a spot on the rug from the last time that will never come out. . . . Converse," I wailed as he started to hunt in the liquor cabinet. "It's so sticky!"

"Converse, do you think this will last forever?" I asked later, lying on top of him. The side of me near the fireplace was simmering like a special meat course steeped in wine by an enthusiastic chef. The other side was slowly becoming Baked Alaska. But at least I knew I wasn't respectable.

"What do you mean, last forever?" Converse asked sleepily.

"Well, my book is finished, but I'm not sure about the ending. Is it too soon to say they lived happily ever after?"

"Your book!" Converse rolled me off him onto the rug. "That's what started this. Let me read it!"

"Now? It's ten-thirty." But never ask incipient authors to show off their wares. They have no pride. I bounced upstairs, naked, into Stephen's room, found the manuscript beside a chewed-up Teddy bear where I had left it, and was back in the study, breathless, in less than two minutes. Converse was still lying on the floor staring at the beamed ceiling. I dropped the book on his bare middle and plopped down on the rug beside him.

Happily, I watched him as he read—thrilled when he chuckled a little, dismayed when I saw a frown on his face. Occasionally I tried to stop him, telling him to come up for air and let me know whether he liked it or not, but all he would do was change position, grunt an unintelligible answer, and keep on reading. By one o'clock I had bitten off two fingernails and nervously finished the bottle of Madeira. Finally Converse read the last page.

"Come over here," he said grinning. "Take that blanket off!"

"Oh, no you don't. I'm half frozen waiting. Besides . . . we've already covered that ground. What about the book? Do you like it?"

"It's unquestionably the craziest book I've ever read. It's like going to a Fourth of July celebration and watching the fireworks go off for an hour or two. But," Converse looked at me sadly, "you can't show it to any publishers."

"Why not?"

"Honey . . . it's not respectable! People don't act that way. If they did the world would collapse . . . all our moral standards would vanish."

"People *do* act that way," I said a little miffed. "I wrote it just the way it happened."

Converse chuckled. "That's the trouble, Willa. You've got to stop trying to prove that suburbia should adopt Chaucerian moral standards and give up respectability. Believe me, Reliance would be shocked. Desire would be more convinced than ever that you have inherited a wild strain of blood. Just one tiny example: Whoever heard of a book where the heroine gets an enema?"

I shrugged. "Some of the books I've read . . . all the characters *and* the author would benefit from a good enema. Better an enema than rape, murder, castration, and infidelity-for-the-hell-of-it."

People like to read about murders and violence. The writer's mission is to give his *reader* an enema. Catharsis, Aristotle calls it. Besides, your book is not only too happy, it doesn't follow the rules about proper beginning, middle, and end. Nothing really important happens . . . no climaxes and denouements."

"What do you mean nothing important happens?" I said, peeved. "I *got you* didn't I? What else is there? What's more important to write about than love?"

Converse stared at me. "You know . . . you may be right," he said thoughtfully.

"So what do you think? Should I end it: 'So Converse and Willa lived happily ever after'?"

"You mean, no conflict . . . you'll never be angry with me again as long as we live?"

"Uh . . . huh," I murmured kissing his ear.

"That's good. . . ." Converse said. "I meant to tell you that you were right. Last Saturday Old Steph intimated that it *would* be fun to climb into the sack with me."

I wacked him on the bare behind. "According to the best novelists, that means *no* happy ending. At the best, tears and sad recriminations for life. At the worst, Willa neurotic, trying to 'transfer' to her psychologist. Only one trouble."

"What?"

"My mother told me never to worry. If a girl uses what the good Lord gave her to the best advantage—which includes what's above the neck as well as below it—and if she never gets jealous, and never gets mad when her man admires a stray pussy or even pets it a little, and pats her man gently when he is sick or just weary, and is convinced that he is the best lover and the best provider, and. . . ."

"Good God . . . who ever heard of a woman like that?"

"I did. . . . Me!"

Converse grinned, and then he started to laugh. The laughter turned into a hysterical gale, tears ran down his eyes, and he hugged me and gasped:

"Oh. Oh . . . Willa! Willa!"

Seems to me that's the way I ended the story eight years ago.